Bestselling author **Tess Gerritsen** is also a doctor, and she brings to her novels her first-hand knowledge of emergency and autopsy rooms. But her interests span far more than medical topics. As an anthropology student at Stanford University, she catalogued centuries-old human remains, and she continues to travel the world driven by her fascination with ancient cultures and bizarre natural phenomena.

D1101805

The
BONE
GARDEN

TESS GERRITSEN

BANTAM PRESS

LONDON · TORONTO · SYDNEY · AUCKLAND · JOHANNESBURG

TRANSWORLD PUBLISHERS
61–63 Uxbridge Road, London W5 5SA
A Random House Group Company
www.rbooks.co.uk

First published in Great Britain
in 2007 by Bantam Press
an imprint of Transworld Publishers

A CIP catalogue record for this book
is available from the British Library.

ISBNs 9780593057773 (cased)
9780593057780 (tpb)

Addresses for Random House Group Ltd companies outside the UK
can be found at: www.randomhouse.co.uk
The Random House Group Ltd Reg. No. 954009

The Random House Group Ltd makes every effort to ensure that the papers
used in its books are made from trees that have been legally sourced from
well-managed and credibly certified forests. Our paper procurement policy
can be found at: www.randomhouse.co.uk/paper.htm

Typeset in 11.5/16pt Goudy by
Falcon Oast Graphic Art Ltd.

Printed in Great Britain by
Clays Ltd, St Ives plc

2 4 6 8 10 9 7 5 3 1

Mixed Sources
Product group from well-managed
forests and other controlled sources
www.fsc.org Cert no. TT-COC-2139
© 1996 Forest Stewardship Council
FSC

*In memory of Ernest Brune Tom, who always
taught me to reach for the stars*

ACKNOWLEDGMENTS

It's been a long, hard year for me as I labored to bring *The Bone Garden* to life. More than ever, I'm grateful for the two angels who've stood by me, rooted for me, and always told me the truth—even when I didn't want to hear it. Here's a huge thanks to my agent, Meg Ruley, who knows all about the care and feeding of a writer's soul, and to my editor, Linda Marrow, who has some of the best story instincts in the business. Thanks also to Selina Walker, Dana Isaacson, and Dan Mallory for all the ways they made this book so much better. And to my wonderful husband, Jacob: If they gave out awards for "best writer's spouse," you'd win it, hands down!

THE BONE GARDEN

March 20, 1888

Dearest Margaret,

I thank you for your kind condolences, so sincerely offered, for the loss of my darling Amelia. This has been a most difficult winter for me, as every month seems to bring the passing of yet another old friend to illness and age. Now it is with deepest gloom that I must consider the rapidly evaporating years left to me.

I realize that this is perhaps my last chance to broach a difficult subject which I should have raised long ago. I have been reluctant to speak of this, as I know that your aunt felt it wisest to keep this from you. Believe me, she did it solely out of love, as she wanted to protect you. But I have known you from your earliest years, dear Margaret, and have watched you grow into the fearless woman you have become. I know that you firmly believe in the power of truth. And so I believe that you would want to know this story, however disturbing you may find it.

Fifty-eight years have passed since these events. You were only an in-fant at the time, and would have no memory of them. Indeed, I myself had almost forgotten about them. But this past Wednesday, I discovered an old news clipping that has been tucked all these years in my ancient copy of Wistar's Anatomy, and I realized that unless I speak of it soon, the facts will almost certainly die with me. Since your aunt's passing, I am now the only one left who knows the tale. All others are now gone.

I must warn you that the details are not pleasant. But there is nobility in this story, and heartbreaking courage as well. You may not have considered your aunt endowed with these qualities. No doubt she seemed no more extraordinary than any other gray-haired lady whom one passes on the street. But I assure you, Margaret, she was most worthy of our respect.

Worthier, perhaps, than any woman I have ever met.

Now the hour here grows late, and after nightfall, an old man's eyes can stay open only so long. For now, I enclose the news clipping, which I earlier mentioned. If you have no desire to learn more, please tell me, and I will never again mention this. But if indeed the subject of your parents holds any interest for you, then at my next opportunity, I will once again pick up my pen. And you will learn the story, the true story, of your aunt and the West End Reaper.

With fondest regards,
O.W.H.

One

The present

So this is how a marriage ends, thought Julia Hamill as she rammed the shovel into the soil. Not with sweet whispers goodbye, not with the loving clasp of arthritic hands forty years from now, not with children and grandchildren grieving around her hospital bed. She lifted a scoop of earth and flung it aside, sending rocks clattering onto the growing mound. It was all clay and stones, good for growing nothing except blackberry canes. Barren soil, like her marriage, from which nothing long lasting, nothing worth holding on to, had sprouted.

She stamped down on the shovel and heard a clang, felt the concussion slam up her spine as the blade hit a rock—a big one. She repositioned the blade, but even when she attacked the rock at different angles, she could not pry it loose. Demoralized and sweating in the heat, she stared down at the hole. All morning she had been digging like a woman possessed, and beneath her leather gloves blisters were peeled open. Julia's digging had stirred up a cloud of mosquitoes that whined around her face and infiltrated her hair.

There was no way around it: If she wanted to plant a garden in this spot, if she wanted to transform this weed-choked yard, she had to keep at it. This rock was in her way.

Suddenly the task seemed hopeless, beyond her puny efforts. She dropped the shovel and slumped to the ground, rump landing on the stony pile of dirt. Why had she ever thought she could restore this garden, salvage this house? She looked across the tangle of weeds and stared at the sagging porch, the weathered clapboards. *Julia's Folly*—that's what she should name the place. Bought when she hadn't been thinking straight, when her life was collapsing. Why not add more flotsam to the wreckage? This was to be a consolation prize for surviving her divorce. At thirty-eight years old, Julia would finally have a house in her own name, a house with a past, a soul. When she had first walked through the rooms with the real estate agent, and had gazed at the hand-hewn beams, spied the bit of antique wallpaper peeking through a tear in the many layers that had since covered it, she'd known this house was special. And it had called to her, asking for her help.

"The location's unbeatable," the agent had said. "It comes with nearly an acre of land, something you seldom find anymore this close to Boston."

"Then why is it still for sale?" Julia had asked.

"You can see what bad shape it's in. When we first got the listing, there were boxes and boxes of books and old papers, stacked to the ceiling. It took a month for the heirs to haul it all away. Obviously, it needs bottom-up renovations, right down to the foundation."

"Well, I like the fact that it has an interesting past. It wouldn't put me off buying it."

The agent hesitated. "There's another issue I should tell you about. Full disclosure."

"What issue?"

"The previous owner was a woman in her nineties, and—well, she died here. That makes some buyers a bit squeamish."

"In her nineties? Of natural causes, then?"

"That's the assumption."

Julia had frowned. "They don't know?"

"It was summertime. And it took almost three weeks before one of her relatives discovered . . ." The agent's voice trailed off. Suddenly she brightened. "But hey, the land alone is special. You could tear down this whole place. Get rid of it and start fresh!"

The way the world gets rid of old wives like me, Julia had thought. *This splendid, dilapidated house and I both deserve better.*

That same afternoon, Julia had signed the purchase agreement.

Now, as she slumped on the mound of dirt, slapping at mosquitoes, she thought: *What did I get myself into?* If Richard ever saw this wreck, it would only confirm what he already thought of her. Gullible Julia, putty in a Realtor's hands. Proud owner of a junk heap.

She swiped a hand over her eyes, smearing sweat across her cheek. Then she looked down at the hole again. How could she possibly expect to get her life in order when she couldn't even summon the strength to move one stupid rock?

She picked up a trowel and, leaning into the hole, began to scrape away dirt. More of the rock emerged, like an iceberg's tip whose hidden bulk she could only guess at. Maybe big enough to sink the *Titanic*. She kept digging, deeper and deeper, heedless of the mosquitoes and the sun glaring on her bare head. Suddenly the rock symbolized every obstacle, every challenge that she'd ever wobbled away from.

I will not let you defeat me.

With the trowel, she hacked at the soil beneath the rock, trying to free up enough space to pry the shovel underneath it. Her hair slid into her face, strands clinging to sweaty skin as she reached deeper into the hole, scraping, tunneling. Before Richard saw this place, she'd turn it into a paradise. She had two months before she'd have to face another classroom of third graders. Two months to uproot these weeds, nourish the soil, put in roses. Richard had told her that if she ever planted roses in their Brookline yard, they'd die on her. You need to know what you're doing, he'd said—just a casual remark, but it had stung nevertheless. She knew what he'd really meant.

You need to know what you're doing. And you don't.

She dropped onto her belly and hacked away. Her trowel collided with something solid. Oh, God, not another rock. Shoving back her hair, she stared down at what her tool had just hit. Its metal tip had fractured a surface, and cracks radiated from the impact point. She brushed away dirt and pebbles, exposing an unnaturally smooth dome. Lying belly-down on the ground, she felt her heart thudding against the earth and suddenly found it hard to take a breath. But she kept digging, with both hands now, gloved fingers scraping through stubborn clay. More of the dome emerged, curves knitted together by a jagged seam. Deeper and deeper she clawed, her pulse accelerating as she uncovered a small dirt-filled hollow. She pulled off her glove and prodded the caked earth with a bare finger. Suddenly the dirt fractured and crumbled away.

Julia jerked back onto her knees and stared down at what she had just revealed. The mosquitoes' whine built to a shriek, but she did not wave them away and was too numb to feel their stings. A breeze feathered the grass, stirring the sweet-syrup smell of Queen Anne's lace. Julia's gaze lifted to her weed-ridden property, a place she had hoped to transform into a paradise. She'd imagined a vibrant garden of roses and peonies, an arbor twined with purple clematis. Now when she looked at this yard, she no longer saw a garden.

She saw a graveyard.

"You could have asked for my advice before you bought this shack," said her sister, Vicky, sitting at Julia's kitchen table.

Julia stood at the window, staring out at the multiple mounds of dirt that had sprung up like baby volcanoes in her back garden. For the past three days, a crew from the medical examiner's office had practically camped out in her yard. She was now so accustomed to having them tramp in and out of her house to use the toilet that she'd miss having them around when the excavation was done, and they finally left her alone again, here in this house with its hand-hewn beams and its history. And its ghosts.

Outside, the medical examiner, Dr. Isles, had just arrived and was crossing toward the excavation site. Julia thought her an unsettling sort of woman, neither friendly nor unfriendly, with ghostly pale skin and Goth-black hair. She looks so calm and collected, Julia thought, watching Isles through the window.

"It's not like you to just jump into something," said Vicky. "An offer on the first day you saw it? Did you think anyone else would snatch it up?" She pointed to the crooked cellar door. "That doesn't even shut. Did you check the foundation? This place has got to be a hundred years old."

"It's a hundred and thirty," Julia murmured, her gaze still on the backyard, where Dr. Isles stood at the edge of the excavation hole.

"Oh, honey," Vicky said, her voice softening. "I know it's been a tough year for you. I know what you're going through. I just wish you'd called me before you did something this drastic."

"It's not such a bad property," Julia insisted. "It's got an acre of land. It's close to the city."

"And it's got a dead body in the backyard. That'll really help its resale value."

Julia massaged her neck, which was suddenly knotted with tension. Vicky was right. Vicky was always right. Julia thought: I've poured my bank account into this house, and now I'm the proud owner of a cursed property. Through the window, she saw another newcomer arrive on the scene. It was an older woman with short gray hair, dressed in blue jeans and heavy work boots—not the sort of outfit one expected for such a grandmotherly type. Yet one more queer character wandering through her yard today. Who were these people, converging on the dead? Why did they choose such a profession, confronting every day what most people shuddered to even contemplate?

"Did you talk to Richard before you bought it?"

Julia went still. "No, I didn't talk to him."

"Have you heard from him at all lately?" Vicky asked. The change in her voice—suddenly quiet, almost hesitant—made Julia at last turn to look at her sister.

"Why are you asking?" said Julia.

"You were married to him. Don't you call him every so often, just to ask if he's forwarding your mail or something?"

Julia sank into a chair at the table. "I don't call him. And he doesn't call me."

For a moment Vicky said nothing, just sat in silence as Julia stoically stared down. "I'm sorry," Vicky finally said. "I'm so sorry you're still hurting."

Julia gave a laugh. "Yeah, well. I'm sorry, too."

"It's been six months. I thought you'd be over him by now. You're bright, you're cute, you should be back in circulation."

Vicky *would* say that. Suck-it-up Vicky who, five days after her appendectomy, had charged back into a courtroom to lead her team of attorneys to victory. She wouldn't let a little setback like divorce trip up her week.

Vicky sighed. "To be honest, I didn't drive all the way over here just to see the new house. You're my baby sister, and there's something you should know. Something you have a *right* to know. I'm just not sure how to—" She stopped. Looked at the kitchen door, where someone had just knocked.

Julia opened the door to see Dr. Isles, looking coolly composed despite the heat. "I wanted to let you know that my team will be leaving today," Isles said.

Glancing at the excavation site, Julia saw that people were already packing up their tools. "You're finished here?"

"We've found enough to determine this is not an ME case. I've referred it to Dr. Petrie, from Harvard." Isles pointed to the woman who had just arrived—the granny in the blue jeans.

Vicky joined them in the doorway. "Who's Dr. Petrie?"

"A forensic anthropologist. She'll be completing the excavation, purely for research purposes. If you have no objection, Ms. Hamill."

"So the bones are old?"

"It's clearly not a recent burial. Why don't you come out and take a look?"

Vicky and Julia followed Isles down the sloping yard. After three days of digging, the hole had grown to a gaping pit. Laid out on a tarp were the remains.

Though Dr. Petrie had to be at least sixty, she sprang easily to her feet from a squat and came forward to shake their hands. "You're the homeowner?" she asked Julia.

"I just bought the place. I moved in last week."

"Lucky you," Petrie said, and she actually seemed to mean it.

Dr. Isles said, "We sifted a few items from the soil. Some old buttons and a buckle ornament, clearly antique." She reached into an evidence box sitting beside the bones. "And today, we found this." She pulled out a small ziplock bag. Through the plastic, Julia saw the glint of multicolored gemstones.

"It's a regard ring," said Dr. Petrie. "Acrostic jewelry was quite the rage in the early Victorian era. The names of the stones are meant to spell out a word. A ruby, emerald, and garnet, for instance, would be the first three letters in the word *regard*. This ring is something you'd give as a token of affection."

"Are these actually precious stones?"

"Oh, no. They're probably just colored glass. The ring isn't engraved—it's just a mass-produced piece of jewelry."

"Would there be burial records?"

"I doubt it. This appears to be something of an irregular interment. There's no gravestone, no coffin fragments. She was simply wrapped in a piece of hide and covered up. A rather unceremonious burial, if she was a loved one."

"Maybe she was poor."

"But why choose this particular location? There was never a cemetery here, at least not according to historical maps. Your house is about a hundred thirty years old, am I right?"

"It was built in 1880."

"Regard rings were out of fashion by the 1840s."

"What was here before 1840?" Julia asked.

"I believe this was part of a country estate, owned by a prominent Bostonian family. Most of this would have been open pasture. Farmland."

Julia looked up the slope, where butterflies skimmed across blossoms of Queen Anne's lace and flowering vetch. She tried to picture her yard as it once must have been. An open field, sloping down to the tree-shaded stream, with grazing sheep meandering through the grass. A place where only animals would wander. A place where a grave would quickly be forgotten.

Vicky stared down at the bones with a look of distaste. "Is this—one body?"

"A complete skeleton," Petrie said. "She was buried deep enough to be protected from scavenger damage. On this slope, the soil's quite well drained. Plus, judging by the fragments of leather, it looks like she was wrapped in some kind of animal hide, and the leaching tannins are something of a preservative."

"She?"

"Yes." Petrie looked up, sharp blue eyes narrowed against the sun. "This is a female. Based on dentition and the condition of her vertebrae, she was fairly young, certainly under the age of thirty-five. All in all, she's in remarkably good shape." Petrie looked at Julia. "Except for the crack you made with your trowel."

Julia flushed. "I thought the skull was a rock."

"It's not a problem distinguishing between old and new fractures. Look." Petrie dropped to a squat again and picked up the skull. "The crack you made is right here, and it doesn't show any staining. But see this crack here, on the parietal bone? And there's another one here, on the zygomatic bone, under the cheek. These surfaces are stained brown from long exposure to dirt. That tells us these are pre-morbid fractures, not from excavation damage."

"Pre-morbid?" Julia looked at her. "Are you saying . . . ."

"These blows almost certainly caused her death. I would call this a murder."

In the night, Julia lay awake, listening to the creak of old floors, the rustle of mice in the walls. As old as this house was, the grave was even older. While men were hammering together these beams, laying down the pine floors, only a few dozen paces away the corpse of an unknown woman was already moldering in the earth. Had they known she was here when they built on this spot? Had there been a stone marking the site?

Or did no one know she was here? Did no one remember her?

She kicked aside the sheets and lay sweating atop the mattress. Even with both windows open, the bedroom felt airless, not even a whisper of a breeze to dissipate the heat. A firefly flashed on and off in the darkness above her, its light winking forlornly as it circled the room, seeking escape.

She sat up in bed and turned on the lamp. The magical sparks overhead transformed to an ordinary brown bug flitting about near the ceiling. She wondered how to catch it without killing it. Wondered whether the fate of one lone bug was worth the effort.

The phone rang. At eleven thirty, only one person would be calling.

"I hope I didn't wake you," said Vicky. "I just got home from one of those endless dinners."

"It's too hot to sleep anyway."

"Julia, there was something I wanted to tell you earlier, when I was there. But I couldn't, not with all those people around."

"No more advice about this house, okay?"

"This isn't about the house. It's about Richard. I hate to be the one to tell you this, but if I were you, I'd want to know. You shouldn't have to hear this through the grapevine."

"Hear what?"

"Richard is getting married."

Julia clutched the receiver, gripping so tight her fingers went numb. In the long silence, she heard her own heartbeat pounding in her ear.

"So you didn't know."

Julia whispered: "No."

"What a little shit he is," Vicky muttered with enough bitterness for them both. "It's been planned for over a month, that's what I heard. Someone named Tiffani with an *i*. I mean, how cutesy can you get? I have no respect for any man who marries a Tiffani."

"I don't understand how this happened so quickly."

"Oh, honey, it's obvious, isn't it? He had to be running around with her while you were still married. Did he suddenly start coming home late? And there were all the business trips. I wondered about those. I just didn't have the heart to say anything."

Julia swallowed. "I don't want to talk about it right now."

"I should have guessed. A man doesn't ask for a divorce right out of the blue."

"Good night, Vicky."

"Hey. Hey, are you okay?"

"I just don't want to talk." Julia hung up.

For a long time, she sat motionless. Above her head, the firefly kept circling, desperately searching for a way out of its prison. Eventually it would exhaust itself. Trapped here without food, without water, it would die in this room.

She climbed up onto the mattress. As the firefly darted closer, she caught it in her hands. Palms cupped around the insect, she walked barefoot to the kitchen and opened the back door. There, on the porch, she released the firefly. It fluttered away into the darkness, its light no longer winking, escape its only objective.

Did it know she'd saved its life? One puny thing she was capable of.

She lingered on the porch, breathing in gulps of night air, unable to bear the thought of returning to that hot little bedroom.

Richard was getting married.

Her breath caught in her throat, spilled out in a sob. She gripped the porch railing and felt splinters prick her fingers.

And I'm the last to find out.

Staring into the night, she thought of the bones that had been buried just a few dozen yards away. A forgotten woman, her name lost to the centuries. She thought of cold earth pressing down as winter snows swirled above, of seasons cycling, the decades passing, while flesh rotted and worms feasted. I'm like you, another forgotten woman, she thought.

And I don't even know who you are.

Two

November 1830

DEATH ARRIVED with the sweet tinkling of bells.

Rose Connolly had come to dread the sound, for she'd heard it too many times already as she sat beside her sister's hospital bed, dabbing Aurnia's forehead, holding her hand and offering her sips of water. Every day those cursed bells, rung by the acolyte, heralded the priest's arrival on the ward to deliver the sacrament and administer the ritual of extreme unction. Though only seventeen years old, Rose had seen many lifetimes' worth of tragedy these last five days. On Sunday, Nora had died, three days after her wee babe was born. On Monday, it was the brown-haired lass at the far end of the ward, who'd succumbed so soon after giving birth that there'd been no chance to learn her name, not with the family weeping and the newborn baby howling like a scalded cat and the busy coffin maker hammering in the courtyard. On Tuesday, after four days of feverish agonies following the birth of a son, Rebecca had mercifully succumbed, but only after Rose had been forced to endure the stench of the putrid discharges crusting the sheets and oozing from between the girl's legs. The whole ward smelled of sweat and fevers and puru-lence. Late at night, when the groans of dying souls echoed through the corridors, Rose would startle awake from exhausted slumber to find reality more frightful than her nightmares. Only when she stepped outside into the hospital courtyard, and breathed in deeply of the cold mist, could she escape the foul air of the ward.

But always, she had to return to the horrors. To her sister.

"The bells again," Aurnia whispered, sunken eyelids flickering. "Which poor soul is it this time?"

Rose glanced down the lying-in ward, to where a curtain had been hastily drawn around one of the beds. Moments ago, she had seen Nurse Mary Robinson set out the small table and lay out the candles and crucifix. Although she couldn't see the priest, she heard him murmuring behind that curtain, and could smell the burning candle wax.

"Through the great goodness of His mercy, may God pardon thee whatever sins thou hast committed . . ."

"Who?" Aurnia asked again. In her agitation, she struggled to sit up, to see over the row of beds.

"I fear it's Bernadette," said Rose.

"Oh! Oh, no."

Rose squeezed her sister's hand. "She may yet live. Have a bit of hope."

"The baby? What of her baby?"

"The boy is healthy. Didn't you hear him howling in his crib this morning?"

Aurnia settled back against the pillow with a sigh, and the breath she exhaled carried the fetid odor of death, as if already her body was rotting from within, her organs putrefying. "There's that small blessing, then."

Blessing? That the boy would grow up an orphan? That his mother had spent the last three days whimpering as her belly bloated from childbed fever? Rose had seen far too many such *bless-ings* over the past seven days. If this was an example of His benevolence, then she wanted no part of Him. But she uttered no such blasphemy in her sister's presence. It was faith that had sustained Aurnia these past months, through her husband's abuse, through the nights when Rose had heard her weeping softly through the blanket that hung between their beds. What good had faith done poor Aurnia? Where was God all these days as Aurnia labored in vain to give birth to her first child?

If you hear a good woman's prayers, God, why do you let her suffer?

Rose expected no answer, and none was received. All she heard was the priest's futile murmurings from behind the curtain hiding Bernadette's bed.

"In the name of the Father and the Son and the Holy Ghost, be there quenched in thee all power of the devil, through the laying on of my hands, and through the invocation of the glorious and holy Virgin Mary, Mother of God."

"Rose?" Aurnia whispered.

"Yes, darling?"

"I'm greatly afeard 'tis time for me as well."

"Time for what?"

"The priest. Confession."

"And what small sins could possibly trouble you? God knows your soul, darling. Do you think He doesn't see the goodness there?"

"Oh, Rose, you don't know all the things I'm guilty of! All the things I'm too ashamed to tell you about! I can't die without—"

"Don't talk to me of dying. You can't give up. You have to *fight*."

Aurnia responded with a weak smile and reached up to touch her sister's hair. "My little Rosie. Never one to be afraid."

But Rose was afraid. Terribly afraid that her sister would leave her. Desperately afraid that once Aurnia received the final blessing, she'd stop fighting and give up.

Aurnia closed her eyes and sighed. "Will you stay with me again tonight?"

"Surely I will."

"And Eben? Hasn't he come?"

Rose's hand tensed around Aurnia's. "Do you really want him here?"

"We're bound to each other, himself and me. For better or worse."

Mostly for worse, Rose wanted to say, but held her tongue. Eben and Aurnia might be bound in marriage, but it was better that he stayed away, for Rose could scarcely abide the man's presence. For the past four months, she had lived with Aurnia and Eben in a Broad Street boardinghouse, her cot squeezed into a tiny alcove adjoining their bedroom. She had tried to stay out of Eben's way, but as Aurnia had grown heavy and weary with pregnancy, Rose had taken on more and more of her sister's duties in Eben's tailor shop. In the shop's back room, cramped with bolts of muslin and broadcloth, she had spied her brother-in-law's sly glances, had noticed how often he found excuses to brush against her shoulder, to stand too close, inspecting her stitches as she labored over trousers and waistcoats. She had said nothing of this to Aurnia, as she knew Eben would certainly deny it. And in the end, Aurnia would be the one to suffer.

Rose wrung out a cloth over the basin, and as she pressed it to Aurnia's forehead, she wondered: Where has my pretty sister gone? Not even a year of marriage and already the light had left Aurnia's eyes, the sheen gone from her flame-colored hair. All that remained was this listless shell, hair matted with sweat, face a dull mask of surrender.

Weakly, Aurnia lifted her arm from beneath the sheet. "I want you to have this," she whispered. "Take it now, before Eben does."

"Take what, darling?"

"This." Aurnia touched the heart-shaped locket that hung around her neck. It had the genuine gleam of gold, and Aurnia wore it night and day. A gift from Eben, Rose assumed. Once, he had cared enough about his wife to give her such a fancy trinket. Why was he not here when she needed him most?

"Please. Help me take it off."

"It's not the time for you to be giving it away," said Rose.

But Aurnia managed to slip off the necklace by herself, and she placed it in her sister's hand. "It's yours. For all the comfort you've given me."

"I'll keep it safe for you, 'tis all." Rose placed it into her pocket. "When this is over, darling, when you're holding your own sweet babe, I'll put it back around your neck."

Aurnia smiled. "If only that could be."

"It *will* be."

The receding tinkle of bells told her the priest had finished his ministrations to the dying Bernadette, and Nurse Robinson quickly scurried over to remove the screen in preparation for the next set of visitors, who had just arrived.

Everyone in the room fell silent with expectation as Dr. Chester Crouch walked onto the maternity ward. Today, Dr. Crouch was accompanied by the hospital's head nurse, Miss Agnes Poole, as well as an entourage of four medical students. Dr. Crouch started his rounds at the first bed, occupied by a woman who had been admitted just that morning after two days of fruitless labor at home. The students stood in a semicircle, watching as Dr. Crouch slipped his arm under the sheet to discreetly examine the patient. She gave a cry of pain as he probed deep between her thighs. His hand reemerged, fingers streaked with blood.

"Towel," he requested, and Nurse Poole promptly handed him one. Wiping his hand, he said to the four students: "This patient is not progressing. The infant's head is at the same position, and the cervix has not fully dilated. In this particular case, how should her physician proceed? You, Mr. Kingston! Have you an answer?"

Mr. Kingston, a handsome and dapper young man, answered without hesitation, "I believe that ergot in souchong tea is recommended."

"Good. What else might one do?" He focused on the shortest of the four students, an elf-like fellow with large ears to match. "Mr. Holmes?"

"One could try a cathartic, to stimulate contractions," Mr. Holmes promptly answered.

"Good. And you, Mr. Lackaway?" Dr. Crouch turned to a fair-haired man whose startled face instantly flushed red. "What else might be done?"

"I—that is—"

"This is *your* patient. How will you proceed?"

"I would have to think about it."

"*Think* about it? Your grandfather and father were both physicians! Your uncle's dean of the medical college. You've had more exposure to the medical arts than any of your classmates. Come now, Mr. Lackaway! Have you nothing to contribute?"

Helplessly the young man shook his head. "I'm sorry, sir."

Sighing, Dr. Crouch turned to the fourth student, a tall dark-haired young man. "Your turn, Mr. Marshall. What else might be done in this situation? A patient in labor, who is not progressing?"

The student said, "I would urge her to sit up or stand, sir. And if she is able, she should walk about the ward."

"What else?"

"It's the only additional modality that seems appropriate to me."

"And what of bleeding the patient as a treatment?"

A pause. Then, deliberately: "I am not convinced of its efficacy."

Dr. Crouch gave a startled laugh. "You—*you* are not convinced?"

"On the farm where I grew up, I experimented with bleeding, as well as cupping. I lost just as many calves with it as without it."

"On the *farm*? You are talking about bleeding *cows*?"

"And pigs."

Nurse Agnes Poole snickered.

"We are dealing with human beings here, not beasts, Mr. Marshall," said Dr. Crouch. "A therapeutic bleeding, I've found in my own experience, is quite effective for relieving pain. It relaxes a patient enough so that she may properly dilate. If the ergot and a cathartic don't work, then I will most certainly bleed this patient."

He handed the soiled towel back to Nurse Poole and moved on, to Bernadette's bed. "And this one?" he asked.

"Though her fever has abated," said Nurse Poole, "the discharge has become quite foul. She spent the night in great discomfort."

Again, Dr. Crouch reached under the sheet to palpate the internal organs. Bernadette gave a weak groan. "Yes, her skin is quite cool," he concurred. "But in this case . . ." He paused and looked up. "She has received morphine?"

"Several times, sir. As you ordered."

His hands came out from beneath the sheet, fingers glistening with yellowish slime, and the nurse handed him the same soiled towel. "Continue the morphine," he said quietly. "Keep her comfortable." It was as good as a death pronouncement.

Bed by bed, patient by patient, Dr. Crouch made his way down the ward. By the time he reached Aurnia's bed, the towel he used to wipe his hands was soaked with blood.

Rose stood to greet him. "Dr. Crouch."

He frowned at her. "It's Miss . . ."

"Connolly," said Rose, wondering why this man could not seem to remember her name. She had been the one to summon him to the lodging house where, for a day and a night, Aurnia had labored without success. Rose had been here at her sister's bedside every time Crouch had visited, yet he always seemed flummoxed when they met anew. But then he did not really *look* at Rose; she was just an accessory female, unworthy of a second glance.

He turned his attention to Nurse Poole. "And how is this patient progressing?"

"I believe the daily cathartics you prescribed last night have improved the quality of her contractions. But she has not complied with your orders to rise from bed and walk about the ward."

Staring at Nurse Poole, Rose was scarcely able to hold her tongue. Walk about the ward? Were they mad? For the past five days, Rose had watched Aurnia fall steadily weaker. Surely Nurse Poole could see the obvious, that her sister could scarcely sit up, much less walk. But the nurse was not even looking at Aurnia; her worshipful gaze was fixed on Dr. Crouch. He reached beneath the sheets, and as he probed the birth canal, Aurnia gave a moan of such agony that Rose could scarcely stop herself from wrenching him away.

He straightened and looked at Nurse Poole. "Although the amniotic sac is ruptured, she is not yet fully dilated." He dried his hand on the filthy towel. "How many days has it been?"

"Today is the fifth," said Nurse Poole.

"Then perhaps another dose of ergot is called for." He took Aurnia's wrist and felt the pulse. "Her heart rate is rapid. And she feels a bit feverish today. A bleeding should cool the system."

Nurse Poole nodded. "I'll assemble the—"

"You have bled her enough," cut in Rose.

Everyone fell silent. Dr. Crouch glanced up at her, clearly startled. "What relation are you again?"

"Her sister. I was here when you bled her the first time, Dr. Crouch. And the second time, and the third."

"And you can see how she's benefited," said Nurse Poole.

"I can tell you she has not."

"Because you have no training, girl! You don't know what to look for."

"Do you wish me to treat her or not?" snapped Dr. Crouch.

"Yes, sir, but not to bleed her dry!"

Nurse Poole said, coldly: "Either hold your tongue or leave the ward, Miss Connolly! And allow the doctor to do what's necessary."

"I have no time to bleed her today, anyway." Dr. Crouch pointedly looked at his pocket watch. "I have an appointment in an hour, and then a lecture to prepare. I'll stop in to see the patient first thing in the morning. Perhaps by then, it will be more obvious to Miss, er—"

"Connolly," said Rose.

"—to Miss Connolly that further treatment is indeed necessary." He snapped his watch closed. "Gentlemen, I shall see you at the morning lecture, nine A.M. Good night." He gave a nod, and turned to leave. As he strode away, the four medical students trailed after like obedient ducklings.

Rose ran after them. "Sir? Mr. Marshall, isn't it?"

The tallest of the students turned. It was the dark-haired young man who'd earlier questioned the wisdom of bleeding a laboring mother, the student who'd said he'd grown up on a farm. One look at his ill-fitting suit told her that he indeed came from humbler circumstances than his classmates. She had been a seamstress long enough to recognize good cloth, and his suit was of inferior quality, its woolen fabric dull and shapeless and lacking the sheen of a fine broadcloth. As his classmates continued out of the ward, Mr. Marshall stood looking at her expectantly. He has tired eyes, she thought, and such a weary face for a young man. Unlike the others, he gazed straight at her, as though regarding an equal.

"I couldn't help but hear your words to the doctor," she said. "About bleeding."

The young man shook his head. "I spoke too freely, I'm afraid."

"Is it true, then? What you said?"

"I only described my observations."

"And am I wrong, sir? Should I allow him to bleed my sister?"

He hesitated. Glanced, uneasily, at Nurse Poole, who was watching them with clear disapproval. "I'm not qualified to give advice. I'm only a first-year student. Dr. Crouch is my preceptor, and a fine doctor."

"I've watched him bleed her three times, and each time he and the nurses claim she's improved. But to tell God's truth, I see no improvement. Every day, I see only . . ." She stopped, her voice breaking, her throat thick with tears. She said, softly: "I only want what's best for Aurnia."

Nurse Poole cut in: "You're asking a *medical student*? You think he knows better than Dr. Crouch?" She gave a snort. "You might as well ask a stable boy," she said, and walked out of the ward.

For a moment Mr. Marshall was silent. Only after Nurse Poole was out of the room did he speak again, and his words, though gentle, confirmed Rose's worst fears.

"I would not bleed her," he said quietly. "It would do no good."

"What would you do? If she were your own sister?"

The man gave the sleeping Aurnia a pitying look. "I would help her sit up in bed. Apply cool compresses for the fever, morphine for pain. I would see above all that she receives sufficient nourishment and fluids. And comfort, Miss Connolly. If I had a sister suffering so, that's what I would give her." He looked at Rose. "Comfort," he said sadly, and walked away.

Rose wiped away tears and walked back to Aurnia's bed, past a woman vomiting in a basin, another whose leg was red and swollen with erysipelas. Women in labor, women in pain. Outside, the cold rain of November fell, but in here, with the woodstove burning and the windows shut, the air was close and stifling and foul with disease.

Was I wrong to bring her here? Rose wondered. *Should I have instead kept her at home, where she would not have to listen all night to these terrible groans, these pitiful whimpers?* The room in their boardinghouse was cramped and cold, and Dr. Crouch had recommended Aurnia be moved to the hospital, where he could more easily attend her. "For charity cases such as your sister's," he'd said, "the cost will be only what your family can bear." Warm meals, a staff of nurses and physicians—all this would be waiting for her, Dr. Crouch had assured them.

But not this, thought Rose, looking down the row of suffering women. Her gaze stopped on Bernadette, who now lay silent. Slowly, Rose approached the bed, staring down at the young woman who, only five days ago, had laughed as she'd held her newborn son in her arms.

Bernadette had stopped breathing.

Three

"How LONG CAN this blasted rain keep up?" said Edward Kingston, staring at the steady downpour.

Wendell Holmes blew out a wreath of cigar smoke that drifted from beneath the hospital's covered veranda and fractured into swirls in the rain. "Why the impatience? One would think you have a pressing appointment."

"I do. With a glass of exceptional claret."

"Are we going to the Hurricane?" said Charles Lackaway.

"If my carriage ever shows up." Edward glared at the road, where horses clip-clopped and carriages rolled past, wheels throwing up clots of mud.

Though Norris Marshall also stood on the hospital veranda, the gulf between him and his classmates would have been apparent to anyone who cast even a casual glance at the four young men. Norris was new to Boston, a farm boy from Belmont who had taught himself physics with borrowed textbooks, who'd bartered eggs and milk for lessons with a Latin tutor. He had never been to the Hurricane tavern; he did not even know where it was. His classmates, all graduates from Harvard College, gossiped about people he did not know, and shared inside jokes he did not understand, and although they made no overt efforts to exclude him, they did not need to. It was simply understood that he was not part of their social circle.

Edward sighed, huffing out a cloud of smoke. "Can you believe what that girl said to Dr. Crouch? The gall of her! If any of the Bridgets in our household ever spoke that way, my mother would slap her right out into the street."

"Your mother," said Charles, with a tone of awe, "quite terrifies me."

"Mother says it's important that the Irish know their place. That's the only way to maintain order, with all these new people moving into town, causing trouble."

New people. Norris was one of them.

"The Bridgets are the worst. You can't turn your back on 'em or they'll snatch the shirts right out of your closet. You notice something's missing, and they'll claim it was lost in the wash or that the dog ate it." Edward snorted. "Girl like that one needs to learn her place."

"Her sister may well be dying," said Norris.

The three Harvard men turned, obviously surprised that their usually reticent classmate had spoken up.

"Dying? That's quite a dramatic pronouncement," said Edward.

"Five days in labor, and already she looks like a corpse. Dr. Crouch can bleed her all he wants, but her prospects do not look good. The sister knows it. She speaks from grief."

"Nevertheless, she should remember where charity comes from."

"And be grateful for every crumb?"

"Dr. Crouch is not bound to treat the woman at all. Yet that sister acts as though it's their right." Edward stubbed out his cigar on the newly painted railing. "A little gratitude wouldn't kill them."

Norris felt his face flush. He was about to offer a sharp retort in defense of the girl when Wendell smoothly redirected the conversation.

"I do think there's a poem in this, don't you? 'The Fierce Irish Girl.' "

Edward sighed. "Please don't. Not another one of your awful verses."

"Or how about this title?" said Charles. " 'Ode to a Faithful Sister'?"

"I quite like that!" said Wendell. "Let me try." He paused. "Here stands the fiercest warrior, this true and winsome maid . . ."

"Her sister's life the battlefield," added Charles.

"She—she—" Wendell pondered the next verse in the poem.

"Stands guard, unafraid!" Charles finished.

Wendell laughed. "Poetry triumphs again!"

"While the rest of us suffer," Edward muttered.

All this Norris listened to with the acute discomfort of an outsider. How easily his classmates laughed together. How little it took, just a few improvised lines of verse, to remind him that these three shared a history he was not part of.

Wendell suddenly straightened and peered through the rain. "That's your carriage, isn't it, Edward?"

"About time it showed up." Edward lifted his collar against the wind. "Gentlemen, shall we?"

Norris's three classmates headed down the porch steps. Edward and Charles splashed through the rain and clambered into the carriage. But Wendell paused, glanced over his shoulder at Norris, and came back up the steps.

"Aren't you joining us?" said Wendell.

Startled by the invitation, Norris didn't immediately answer. Though he stood almost a full head taller than Wendell Holmes, there was much about this diminutive man that intimidated him. It was more than Wendell's dapper suits, his famously clever tongue; it was his air of utter self-assurance. That the man should be inviting him to join them had caught Norris off guard.

"Wendell!" Edward called from the carriage. "Let's go!"

"We're going to the Hurricane," said Holmes. "Seems to be where we end up every night." He paused. "Or have you other plans?"

"It's very kind of you." Norris glanced at the two men waiting in the carriage. "But I don't think Mr. Kingston was expecting a fourth."

"Mr. Kingston," said Wendell with a laugh, "could use more of the unexpected in his life. Anyway, he's not the one inviting you. I am. Join us for a round of rum flips?"

Norris looked at the rain, falling in sheets, and longed for the warm fire that would almost certainly be burning in the Hurricane. More than that, he longed for the opening that had just been offered him, the chance to slip in among his classmates, to share their circle, if only for this evening. He could feel Wendell watching him. Those eyes, which usually held the glint of laughter, the promise of a quip, had turned uncomfortably penetrating.

"Wendell!" Now it was Charles calling from the carriage, his voice raised in an exasperated whine. "We're freezing here!"

"I'm sorry," said Norris. "I'm afraid I have another engagement this evening."

"Oh?" Wendell's eyebrow lifted in a mischievous tilt. "I trust she's a charming alternative."

"It's not a lady, I'm afraid. But it's simply something I can't break."

"I see," said Wendell, though clearly he didn't, for his smile had cooled and already he was turning to leave.

"It's not that I don't want—"

"Quite all right. Another time, perhaps."

There won't be another time, thought Norris as he watched Wendell dash into the street and climb in with his two companions. The driver flicked his whip and the carriage rolled away, wheels splashing through puddles. He imagined the conversation that would soon take place in that carriage among the three friends. Disbelief that a mere farm boy from Belmont had dared to decline the invitation. Speculation as to what other engagement, if not with a member of the fair sex, could possibly take precedence. He stood on the porch, gripping the rail in frustration at what he could not change, and what could never be.

Edward Kingston's carriage disappeared around the corner, bearing the three men to a fire and a convivial evening of gossip and spirits. While they sit warm in the Hurricane, thought Norris, I shall be engaged in quite a different activity. One I would avoid, if only I could.

He braced himself for the cold, then stepped into the downpour and splashed resolutely toward his lodgings, there to change into old clothes before heading out, yet again, into the rain.

The establishment he sought was a tavern on Broad Street, near the docks. Here one would not find dapper Harvard graduates sipping rum flips. Should such a gentleman wander accidentally into the Black Spar, he would know, with just a glance around the room, that he'd be wise to watch his pockets. Norris had little of value in his own pockets that night—indeed, on any night—and his shabby coat and mud-spattered trousers offered little enticement to any would-be thieves. He already knew many of these patrons, and they knew his impoverished circumstances; they merely glanced up as he stepped in the door. One look to identify the newcomer, and then their disinterested gazes dropped back to their cups.

Norris moved to the bar, where moonfaced Fanny Burke was filling glasses with ale. She looked up at him with small, mean eyes. "You're late, and he's in a foul mood."

"Fanny!" one of the patrons yelled. "We gettin' those drinks this week or what?"

The woman carried the ale to their table and slammed down the glasses. Pocketing their money, she stalked back behind the bar. "He's around back, with the wagon," she said to Norris. "Waiting for you."

He had not had time for supper, and he glanced hungrily at the loaf of bread she kept behind the counter but didn't bother to beg a slice. Fanny Burke gave nothing away for free, not even a smile. With stomach rumbling, he pushed through a door, walked down a dark hall crammed with crates and trash, and stepped outside.

The rear yard smelled of wet straw and horse dung, and the interminable rain had churned the ground into a sea of mud. Beneath the stable overhang, a horse gave a nicker, and Norris saw that it was already harnessed to the dray.

"Not going to wait for you next time, boy!" Fanny's husband, Jack, emerged from the shadows of the stable. He carried two shovels, which he threw in the back of the wagon. "Want to be paid, get here at the appointed hour." With a grunt, he hoisted himself onto the buckboard and took the reins. "You comin'?"

By the glow of the stable lantern, Norris could see Jack staring down at him, and felt the same confusion he always did, about which eye he should focus on. Left and right skewed in different directions. *Wall-eyed Jack* was what everyone called the man, but never to his face. No one dared.

Norris scrambled up into the dray beside Jack, who didn't even wait for him to settle onto the bench before giving the horse an impatient flick of his whip. They rolled across the muck of the yard and out the rear gate.

The rain beat down on their hats and ran in rivulets down their coats, but Wall-eyed Jack seemed scarcely to notice. He sat hunched like a gargoyle beside Norris, every so often snapping the reins when the pace of the horse flagged.

"How far we going this time?" asked Norris.

"Out of town."

"Where?"

"Does it matter?" Jack hacked up a gob of phlegm and spat into the street.

No, it didn't matter. As far as Norris was concerned, this was a night he simply had to endure, however miserable it might prove to be. He wasn't afraid of hard work on the farm, and he even enjoyed the ache of muscles well used, but *this* sort of work could give a man nightmares. A normal man, anyway. He glanced at his companion and wondered what, if anything, gave Jack Burke nightmares.

The dray rocked over the cobblestones, and in the back of the cart the two shovels rattled, a continuous reminder of the unpleasant task that lay ahead. He thought of his classmates, no doubt sitting that moment in the warmth of the Hurricane, enjoying a last round before heading off to their respective lodgings to study Wistar's *Anatomy*. He'd prefer to be studying, too, but this was the bargain he'd struck with the college, a bargain he'd gratefully agreed to. This is all for a higher purpose, he thought, as they rolled out of Boston, moving west, as the shovels rattled and the dray creaked in rhythm to the words running through his head: *A higher purpose. A higher purpose.*

"Came by this way two days ago," said Jack, and spat again. "Stopped at that tavern there." He pointed, and through the veil of falling rain, Norris saw the glow of firelight in a window. "Had me a nice chat, I did, with the proprietor."

Norris waited, saying nothing. There was a reason Jack had brought this up. The man did not make pointless conversation.

"Said there's a whole family in town, two young ladies and a brother, ailing from the consumption. All of 'em doing quite poorly." He made a sound that might have been a laugh. "Have to check in again tomorrow, see if they're getting ready to pass on. Any luck, we'll have three at once." Jack looked at Norris. "I'll be needing you for that one."

Norris gave a stiff nod, his dislike of this man suddenly so strong he could scarcely abide being seated next to him.

"Oh, you think you're too damn good for this," said Jack. "Don't you?"

Norris didn't answer.

"Too good to be around the likes of me."

"I do this for a greater good."

Jack laughed. "Some high-and-mighty words for a farmer. Think you're going to make a fine living, eh? Live in a grand house."

"That's not the point."

"Then the more fool, you. What's the point if there ain't money in it?"

Norris sighed. "Yes, Mr. Burke, of course you're right. Money is the only thing worth laboring for."

"You think this will make you one of those gentlemen? You think they'll invite you to their fancy oyster parties, let you court their daughters?"

"This is a new age. Today, any man can rise above his station."

"Do you s'pose *they* know that? Those Harvard gentlemen? Do you s'pose they'll welcome you?"

Norris went silent, wondering if perhaps Jack had a point. He thought once again of Wendell Holmes and Kingston and Lack-away, sitting in the Hurricane, sleeve to well-tailored sleeve with others of their kind. A world away from the filthy Black Spar, where Fanny Burke reigned over her foul kingdom of the hopeless. I, too, could have been at the Hurricane tonight, he thought. Wendell had asked, but was it out of courtesy or pity?

Jack snapped the reins, and the dray jolted ahead through mud and ruts. "Still a ways to go," he said and gave a snorting laugh. "I hope the *gentleman* here enjoys the ride."

By the time Jack finally pulled the rig to a stop, Norris's clothes were soaked through. Stiff and shaking from the cold, he could barely make his muscles obey as he climbed out of the cart. His shoes splashed ankle-deep in mud.

Jack thrust the shovels into his hands. "Make quick work of it." He grabbed trowels and a tarp from the cart, then led the way across sodden grass. He did not light the lantern yet, as he did not want to be seen. He seemed to know the way by instinct, weaving among the headstones until he stopped at bare earth. There was no marker, only a mound of dirt turned muddy in the rain.

"Buried just today," said Jack, taking a shovel.

"How did you know about this one?"

"I ask around. I listen." Eyeing the grave, he muttered, "Head should be at this end," and scooped up a shovelful of mud. "Came through here a fortnight ago," he said, flinging the mud aside. "Heard this one was near to giving up the ghost."

Norris set to work as well. Though it was a fresh burial and the dirt had not settled, the soil was soaked and heavy. After shoveling only a few minutes, he no longer felt the cold.

"Someone dies, people talk about it," panted Jack. "Keep your ear to the ground and you'll know who's about to go in. They order coffins, buy flowers." Jack flung aside another scoop and paused, wheezing. "Trick is not to let 'em know you're interested. They get suspicious, you got yourself complications." He resumed digging, but at a slower pace. Norris did the lion's share, his shovel splashing deeper and deeper. Rain continued to fall, puddling in the hole, and Norris's trousers were caked with mud all the way up to his knees. Soon Jack stopped shoveling entirely and climbed out of the hole to squat at the edge, his wheezing now so loud that Norris glanced up, just to be certain the man was not on the verge of collapse. This was the only reason the old miser was willing to share even a penny of his profits, the only reason he ever brought along an assistant: He could no longer do it alone. He knew where the prizes were buried, but he needed a young man's back, a young man's muscles, to dig them up. And so Jack squatted and watched his assistant work, watched the hole deepen.

Norris's shovel hit wood.

"About time," grunted Jack. Beneath the cover of the tarp, he lit the lantern, then grabbed his shovel and slid back into the hole. The men scraped away mud from the coffin, working so close to-gether in the cramped space that Norris gagged on the odor of Jack's breath, foul with the stench of tobacco and rotten teeth. Even this corpse, he thought, could not smell so putrid. Bit by bit, they cleared away the mud, revealing the head end of the coffin.

Jack slipped two iron hooks under the lid and handed one of the ropes to Norris. They climbed out of the hole and together pulled against the lid, both of them grunting and straining as nails squealed and wood groaned. The lid suddenly splintered and the rope went slack, sending Norris sprawling backward.

"That's it! That's good enough!" said Jack. He lowered the lantern into the hole and looked down upon the coffin's occupant.

Through the shattered coffin lid, they could see that the corpse was a woman, her skin pale as tallow. Golden ringlets of hair framed her heart-shaped face, and resting upon her bodice was a nosegay of dried flowers, the petals disintegrating under the falling rain. So beautiful, thought Norris. An angel, too soon called to heaven.

"Fresh as can be," said Jack with a happy cackle. He reached through the broken lid and slipped his hands under the girl's arms. She was light enough that he could drag her, unassisted, out of the coffin. But he was wheezing as he lifted her from the hole and laid her on the tarp. "Let's get her clothes off."

Norris, suddenly feeling nauseated, didn't move.

"What? Don't want to touch a pretty girl?"

Norris shook his head. "She deserves better."

"You didn't have no problem with the last one we dug up."

"That was an old man."

"And this is a girl. What's the difference?"

"You know there's a difference!"

"All I know is that she'll fetch the same price. And she'll be a lot pleasanter to strip." He gave a soft cackle of anticipation and pulled out a knife. He had neither the time nor the patience to undo the buttons and hooks, so he simply slipped the blade under the neckline of the corpse's dress and rent apart the fabric, tearing the gown open down the front to reveal a gossamer-thin chemise beneath it. He went at his task with gusto, methodically ripping open the skirt, pulling off the tiny satin slippers. Norris could only watch, appalled by the violation of this young woman's modesty. And to be violated by a man such as Jack Burke! Yet he knew it must be done, for the law was unforgiving. To be caught with a stolen corpse was serious enough; to be caught in possession of a corpse's stolen property, even a fragment of her dress, was to risk far worse penalties. They must take nothing but the body itself. So Jack ruthlessly stripped away the clothes, removed the rings from her fingers, the satin ribbons from her hair. He tossed them all into the coffin, then glanced at Norris.

"You gonna help carry her back to the wagon or not?" he growled.

Norris stared down at the naked corpse, her skin white as alabaster. She was painfully thin, her body consumed by some long and unforgiving illness. She was beyond help now; perhaps some good could still come of her death.

"Who's out there?" a distant voice shouted. "Who trespasses?"

The challenge sent Norris diving onto the ground. At once Jack doused the lantern and whispered: "Get her out of sight!" Norris dragged the corpse back into the open grave, then both he and Jack scrambled into the hole as well. Pressed close to the corpse, Norris felt his heart pounding against her chilled skin. He did not dare move. He listened for the footsteps of the approaching watchman, but all he could hear was the beating rain, and the thump of his own pulse. The woman lay beneath him like a compliant lover. Had any other man known the touch of her skin, felt the curve of her bare breast? *Or am I the first?*

It was Jack who finally dared to raise his head and peer out of the hole. "I don't see him," he whispered.

"He could still be watching."

"No man in his right mind would be out in this weather any longer than he has to."

"What does that say about us?"

"Tonight the rain's our friend." Jack gave a grunt as he rose, straightening stiff joints. "Best we move her quick."

They did not relight the lantern, but worked in the darkness. While Jack lifted the feet, Norris gripped the nude body beneath the arms, and he felt the corpse's damp hair drape across his arms as he lifted her shoulders from the hole. Whatever sweet fragrance had once blessed those blond ringlets was now masked by the faint odor of decay. Already her body had begun its inevitable journey to putrefaction, which soon would erode her beauty as skin disintegrated, as eyes sank to hollows. But for now the girl was still an angel, and he handled her gently as he lowered her onto the tarp.

The rain slowed to a drizzle as they quickly refilled the hole, shoveling mud back onto the now vacant coffin. To leave the grave open would only advertise that resurrectionists had been at work here, that the body of a beloved had been snatched. They took the time to cover their tracks rather than risk setting off an outraged inquiry. When the last of the earth had been replaced, they smoothed over the ground as best they could with their shovels, working only by the dim glow through the clouds. In time, the grass would grow in, a headstone would be planted, and loved ones would continue to lay flowers on a grave where no one slept.

They wrapped the corpse in the tarp, and Norris carried her in his arms like a groom bearing his new bride across the threshold. She was light, so pitifully light, and it took no effort at all to bring her across the wet grass, past the gravestones of those who had passed on before her. Gently he set her on the cart. Jack carelessly tossed the shovels beside her.

She was treated with no greater care than the tools rattling next to her, her corpse jolted like mean cargo as they rode through an icy drizzle back to town. Norris found no reason to exchange words with Jack, so he kept his silence, longing only for the night to be over so he could part ways with this repellent man. As they neared the city, they shared the road with other carts and carriages, other drivers who would wave and occasionally call out greetings of shared misery. *Not a night to be out, eh? How'd we get so lucky? It'll be sleet by morning!* Jack cheerily returned the greetings, betraying not a hint of anxiety about the forbidden load he was hauling.

By the time they turned onto the cobblestoned street behind the apothecary shop, Jack was whistling. Anticipating, no doubt, the cash that would soon line his pocket. They rumbled to a stop on the paving stones. Jack jumped down from the dray and knocked on the shop's back door. A moment later the door opened, and Norris saw the glow of a lamp shining through the crack.

"We got one," said Jack.

The door opened wider, revealing the bearded, heavyset man holding the lamp. At this hour, he was already dressed in his night-clothes. "Bring it in, then. And be quiet about it."

Jack spat on the stones and turned to Norris. "Well, come on, then. Bring her in."

Norris lifted the tarp-covered body and carried her through the open doorway. The man with the lamp met his gaze with a nod of recognition. "Upstairs, Dr. Sewall?" asked Norris.

"You know the way, Mr. Marshall."

Yes, Norris knew the way, for this was not his first visit to this dark alley, nor was it the first time he had carried a corpse up this narrow stairway. On the last visit, he had struggled with his bur-den, panting and grunting as he'd dragged the corpulent body up the stairs, fat naked legs bumping against the steps. Tonight, his burden was much lighter, little more than the weight of a child. He reached the second floor and paused in the dark. Dr. Sewall squeezed past him and led the way up the hall, his footsteps creak-ing heavily across the floorboards, the flame of his lamp casting dancing shadows on the walls. Norris followed Sewall through the last doorway, into a room where a table waited to receive its pre-cious merchandise. He gently set down the corpse. Jack had fol-lowed them up the stairs and stationed himself at one end of the table, the sound of his wheezing magnified by the stillness of the room.

Sewall approached the table and pulled back the tarp.

In the flickering lamplight, the girl's face seemed to glow with the rosy warmth of life. Wet tendrils of hair released droplets of rain-water that trickled down her cheek like glistening tears.

"Yes, she's in good condition," murmured Dr. Sewall as he peeled away the tarp, exposing the naked torso. Norris had to suppress the urge to stay the man's hand and prevent this violation of a maiden's modesty. He saw, with disgust, the lascivious glint in Jack's eyes, the eagerness with which he leaned in for a closer look. Gazing down at the girl's face, Norris thought: I am sorry that you must suffer this indignity.

Sewall straightened and gave a nod. "She'll do, Mr. Burke."

"And she'll make for some fine entertainment, too," said Jack with a grin.

"Entertainment is not why we do this," Sewall retorted. "She serves a higher purpose. Enlightenment."

"Oh, of course," Jack said. "So where's my money? I'd like to be paid for all this *enlightenment* I'm providing you."

Sewall produced a small cloth bag, which he handed to Jack. "Your fee. There'll be the same when you bring another one."

"There's only fifteen dollars in here. We agreed on twenty."

"You required Mr. Marshall's services tonight. Five dollars is credited toward his tuition. That adds up to twenty."

"I know damn well what it adds up to," said Jack, ramming the money into his pocket. "And for what I provide, it's not nearly enough."

"I'm sure I can find another resurrectionist who'd be quite satisfied with what I pay."

"But no one who'll deliver 'em to you this fresh. All you'll get is rotten meat crawling with worms."

"Twenty dollars per specimen is what I pay. Whether or not you need an assistant is your decision. But I doubt that Mr. Marshall here will work without adequate compensation."

Jack shot a resentful look at Norris. "He's my muscle, that's all. I'm the one who knows where to find 'em."

"Then keep finding them for me."

"Oh, I'll have one for you, all right." Jack turned to leave. In the doorway, he paused and reluctantly looked back at Norris. "The Black Spar, Thursday night. Seven o'clock," he snapped, and walked out. His footsteps thumped heavily down the stairs, and the door slammed shut.

"Is there no one else you can call on?" asked Norris. "He's the worst kind of filth."

"But those are the people we're forced to work with. All resurrectionists are alike. If our laws were more enlightened, then vermin like him would not be in business at all. Until that day, we're forced to deal with the likes of Mr. Burke." Sewall moved back to the table and looked down at the girl. "At least he manages to procure usable cadavers."

"I'd happily choose any employment but this, Dr. Sewall."

"You wish to be a physician, do you not?"

"Yes, but to work with *that* man. Is there no other task I could perform?"

"There's no need more pressing to our college than the procurement of specimens."

Norris gazed down at the girl. And said, softly: "I don't think she ever imagined herself as a *specimen*."

"We are all specimens, Mr. Marshall. Take away the soul, and any body is the same as another. Heart, lungs, kidneys. Beneath the skin, even a young lady as lovely as this one is no different. It's always a tragedy, of course, for one so young to die." Briskly, Dr. Sewall pulled the tarp over the corpse, and it gently billowed down over the girl's slender frame. "But in death, she will serve a nobler purpose."

Four

The sound of moaning awakened Rose. Sometime in the night she had fallen asleep in the chair beside Aurnia's bed. Now she lifted her head, her neck aching, and suddenly saw that her sister's eyes were open, her face contorted in pain.

Rose straightened. "Aurnia?"

"I cannot bear this any longer. If only I could die now."

"Darling, don't say such a thing."

"The morphine—it gives me no relief."

Rose suddenly focused on Aurnia's bedsheet. On the stain of fresh blood. She shot to her feet in alarm. "I'll find a nurse."

"And the priest, Rose. Please."

Rose hurried from the ward. Oil lamps cast their weak glow against the shadows, and the flames wavered as she ran past. By the time she returned to her sister's bed with Nurse Robinson and Nurse Poole, the stain on Aurnia's sheets had spread to a widening swath of bright red. Miss Poole took one startled look at the blood and snapped to the other nurse: "We move her to surgery at once!"

There was no time to send for Dr. Crouch; instead, the young house physician, Dr. Berry, was roused from his room on the hospital grounds. Blond hair in disarray, his eyes bloodshot, Dr. Berry stumbled sleepily into the surgery room where Aurnia had been rushed. Instantly he paled at the sight of so much bleeding.

"We must be quick about it!" he said, and fumbled through his bag of instruments. "Must evacuate the womb. The baby may have to be sacrificed."

Aurnia gave an anguished cry of protest. "No. No, my baby must live!"

"Hold her down," he ordered. "This will be painful."

"Rose," pleaded Aurnia. "Don't let him kill my baby!"

"Miss Connolly, leave the room!" snapped Agnes Poole.

"No, we'll need her," said Dr. Berry.

"There are two of us to hold down the patient."

"Even you and Nurse Robinson may not be strong enough once I begin."

Aurnia writhed as a fresh contraction gripped her, and her moan rose to a scream. "Oh, God, the pain!"

"Tie down her hands, Miss Poole," ordered Dr. Berry. He looked at Rose. "And you, girl! You're her sister?"

"Yes, sir."

"Come here and keep her calm. Help hold her down if need be."

Shaking, Rose moved closer to the bed. The iron smell of blood was overwhelming. The mattress was soaked a brilliant red, and Aurnia's blood-streaked thighs were fully exposed, all attempts at protecting her modesty forgotten in the more pressing concern of saving her life. One glance at young Dr. Berry's ashen face told Rose that the situation was grim. And he was so young, surely too young for such a crisis, his mustache a pale wisp on his upper lip. His surgical instruments were soon scattered across a low table as he frantically rummaged for the right tool. The instrument he picked up was a frightening device, by all appearances designed to maim and crush.

"Don't hurt my baby," Aurnia moaned. "Please."

"I'll try to preserve your child's life," said Dr. Berry. "But I need you to lie perfectly still, madam. Do you understand?"

Aurnia managed a weak nod.

The two nurses tied down Aurnia's hands, then stationed themselves on either side of the bed, each grasping a leg.

"You, girl! Take her shoulders," Nurse Poole ordered Rose. "Keep her pressed to the bed."

Rose moved to the head of the bed and placed her hands on Aurnia's shoulders. Her sister's milk-white face stared up at her, long red hair spilling across the pillow, green eyes wild with panic. Her skin gleamed with sweat and fear. Suddenly her face contorted in pain and she tried to rock forward, her head lifting off the bed.

"Hold her still! Hold her!" ordered Dr. Berry. Grasping his monstrous forceps, he leaned in between Aurnia's thighs, and Rose was grateful that she did not have to witness what he did next. Aurnia shrieked as though her very soul was being wrenched from her body. A burst of red suddenly splattered the young doctor's face and he jerked back, his shirt sprayed with blood.

Aurnia's head flopped back against the pillow and she lay panting, her screams now reduced to whimpers. In the sudden quiet, another sound rose. A strange mewing that steadily crescendoed to a wail.

The child. The child is alive!

The doctor straightened, and in his arms he held the newborn girl, the skin bluish and streaked with blood. He handed the baby to Nurse Robinson, who quickly wrapped the crying infant in a towel.

Rose stared at the doctor's shirt. So much blood. Everywhere she looked—the mattress, the sheets—she saw blood. She looked down into her sister's face and saw that her lips were moving, but through the wails of the newborn she could not hear the words.

Nurse Robinson brought the swaddled infant to Aurnia's bed. "Here's your little girl, Mrs. Tate. See how lovely she is!"

Aurnia struggled to focus on her new daughter. "Margaret," she whispered, and Rose felt the sudden sting of tears. It was their mother's name. *If only she were alive to see her first grandchild.*

"Tell him," Aurnia whispered. "He doesn't know."

"I'll send for him. I'll *make* him come," said Rose.

"You have to tell him where I am."

"He knows where you are." *Eben just never bothers to visit.*

"There's too much bleeding." Dr. Berry thrust his hand between Aurnia's thighs, and she was now so dazed that she scarcely flinched at the pain. "But I can feel no retained placenta." He swept aside his soiled instruments, sending the forceps thudding to the floor. Pressing his hands on Aurnia's belly, he kneaded the flesh, vigorously massaging the abdomen. The blood continued to soak into the sheets, seeping in a wider and wider stain. He glanced up, and his eyes now reflected the first glint of panic. "Cold water," he ordered. "As cold as you can get it! We'll need compresses. And ergot!"

Nurse Robinson set the swaddled infant in the crib and scurried from the room to fetch what he had asked for.

"He doesn't know," Aurnia moaned.

"She *must* lie quiet!" Dr. Berry ordered. "She exacerbates the hemorrhage!"

"Before I die, someone must tell him he has a child . . ."

The door flew open and Nurse Robinson hurried back in, carrying a basin of water. "It's as cold as I could make it, Dr. Berry," she said.

The doctor soaked a towel, wrung it out, and placed the frigid compress on the patient's abdomen. "Give her the ergot!"

In the cradle, the newborn cried harder, her wail more piercing with each breath. Nurse Poole suddenly blurted: "For pity's sake, take that baby out of here!" Nurse Robinson reached for the infant, but Nurse Poole snapped: "Not you! I need you here. Give it to *her.*" She looked at Rose. "Take your niece and quiet her down. We need to attend to your sister."

Rose took the screaming infant and reluctantly crossed toward the door. There she stopped and looked back at her sister. Aurnia's lips were even paler now, the last remnants of color slowly draining from her face as she whispered silent words.

Please be merciful, God. If you hear this prayer, let my sweet sister live.

Rose stepped out of the room. There in the gloomy hallway, she rocked the crying infant, but the baby would not be comforted. She slipped her finger into little Margaret's mouth, and toothless gums clamped down as she began to suck. At last, silence. A cold wind had found its way into the dark passage, and two of the lamps had blown out. Only a single flame glowed. She stared at the closed door, shut off from the one soul whom she held dear.

No, there's another to love now, she thought, looking down at baby Margaret. *You.*

Standing beneath the single flickering lamp, Rose studied the baby's pale and downy hair. The eyelids were still swollen from the travails of birth. She examined five little fingers and marveled at the hand's plump perfection, marred only by a heart-shaped strawberry mark on the wrist. So this is what a brand-new life feels like, she thought, looking down at the sleeping child. So rosy, so warm. She placed her hand on the tiny chest and through the blanket felt the beating of her heart, quick as a bird's. Such a sweet girl, she thought. My little Meggie.

The door suddenly swung open, spilling light into the hall. Nurse Poole came out of the room, closing the door behind her. She halted and stared at Rose, as though surprised to see her still there.

Fearing the worst, Rose asked: "My sister?"

"She still lives."

"And her condition? Will she—"

"The bleeding has stopped, that's all I can tell you," snapped Nurse Poole. "Now take the baby to the ward. It's warmer there. This hall is far too drafty for a newborn." She turned and hurried away down the corridor.

Shivering, Rose looked down at Meggie and thought: Yes, it's far too cold here for you, poor thing. She carried the baby back to the lying-in ward and sat down in her old chair beside Aurnia's empty bed. As the night wore on, the baby fell asleep in her arms. Wind rattled the windows and sleet ticked against the glass, but there was no word of Aurnia's condition.

From outside came the rumble of wheels over cobblestones. Rose crossed to the window. In the courtyard, a horse and phaeton rolled to a stop, the canopy concealing the face of the driver. The horse suddenly gave a panicked snort, its hooves dancing nervously as it threatened to bolt. A second later Rose saw the reason for the beast's alarm: merely a large dog, which trotted across the courtyard, its silhouette moving purposefully across cobblestones that glistened with rain and sleet.

"Miss Connolly."

Startled, Rose turned to see Agnes Poole. The woman had slipped into the ward so quietly Rose had not heard her approach.

"Give me the baby."

"But she sleeps so soundly," said Rose.

"Your sister cannot possibly nurse the baby. She's far too weak. I've taken the liberty of making other arrangements."

"What arrangements?"

"The infant asylum is here to fetch her. They'll provide a wet nurse. And most certainly, a fine home."

Rose stared at the nurse in disbelief. "But she's not an orphan! She has a mother!"

"A mother who most likely will not live." Nurse Poole held out her arms, and her hands looked like unwelcoming claws. "Give her to me. It's for the baby's own good. You certainly cannot care for her."

"She has a father, too. You haven't asked him."

"How can I? He hasn't even bothered to show up."

"Did Aurnia agree to this? Let me speak to her."

"She's unconscious. She can't say anything."

"Then I'll speak *for* her. This is my niece, Miss Poole, my own family." Rose hugged the baby tighter. "I'll give her up to no stranger."

Agnes Poole's face had gone rigid in frustration. For a dangerous moment she appeared ready to wrench the baby from Rose's arms. Instead, she turned and swept out of the ward, her skirt snapping smartly with every stride. A door slammed shut.

Outside, in the courtyard, the horse's hooves clattered nervously on the stones.

Rose went back to the window and watched as Agnes Poole materialized from the shadows of the walkway and crossed to the waiting phaeton to speak to the occupant. A moment later the driver snapped the whip and the horse clopped forward. As the vehicle drove out the gate, Agnes Poole stood alone, her silhouette framed by the glistening stones of the courtyard.

Rose looked down at the baby in her arms and saw, in the sleeping face, a miniature in flesh of her own dear sister. *No one will ever take you from me. Not while I still breathe.*

Five

The present

"THANK YOU for seeing me on such short notice, Dr. Isles." Julia took a seat in the medical examiner's office. She'd come straight from the summer heat into the frigid building, and now she looked across the desk at a woman who seemed perfectly at home in this chilly environment. Except for the framed floral prints on the wall, Maura Isles's office was all business: files and textbooks, a microscope, and a desk that looked ruthlessly organized. Julia shifted uneasily in the chair, feeling as if she were the one now under the microscope lens. "You probably don't get many requests like mine, but I really need to know. For my own peace of mind."

"Dr. Petrie's the one you should be talking to," said Isles. "The skeleton is a forensic anthropology case."

"I'm not here about that skeleton. I've already spoken to Dr. Petrie, and she had nothing new to tell me."

"Then how can I help you?"

"When I bought the house, the real estate agent told me that the previous owner was an elderly woman who'd died on the property.

Everyone assumed it was a natural death. But a few days ago, my next-door neighbor mentioned there'd been several burglaries in the area. And last year, a man was seen driving up and down the road, as if he was casing the houses. Now I'm starting to wonder if . . ."

"If it wasn't a natural death?" said Isles bluntly. "That's what you're asking, isn't it?"

Julia met the medical examiner's gaze. "Yes."

"I'm afraid I didn't perform that particular autopsy."

"But there's a report somewhere, isn't there? It would give a cause of death, wouldn't it?"

"I'd have to know the name of the deceased."

"I have it right here." Julia reached into her purse and took out a bundle of photocopies, which she handed to Isles. "It's her obituary, from the local paper. Her name was Hilda Chamblett. And these are all the news clippings I could find about her."

"So you've already been digging into this."

"It's been on my mind." Julia gave an embarrassed laugh. "Plus, there's that old skeleton in my backyard. I'm feeling a little uneasy that two different women have died there."

"At least a hundred years apart."

"It's the one last year that really bothers me. Especially after what my neighbor said, about the burglaries."

Isles nodded. "I suppose it would bother me, too. Let me find the report." She left the office and returned moments later with the file. "The autopsy was done by Dr. Costas," she said as she sat down at her desk. She opened the file. " 'Chamblett, Hilda, age ninety-two, found in the backyard of her Weston residence. Remains were found by a family member who had been away and had not checked on her for three weeks. Time of death is therefore uncertain.' " Isles flipped to a new page and paused. "The photos aren't particularly pleasant," she said. "You don't need to see these."

Julia swallowed. "No, I don't. Maybe you could just read me the conclusions?"

Isles turned to the summary and glanced up. "You're sure you want to hear this?" At Julia's nod, Isles once again began to read aloud. " 'Body was found in a supine position, surrounded by tall grass and weeds, which concealed it from view beyond only a few feet . . .' "

The same weeds I've been battling, thought Julia. I've been pulling up the same grass that hid Hilda Chamblett's body.

" 'No skin or soft tissue is found intact on any exposed surfaces. Shreds of clothing, consisting of what appears to be a sleeveless cotton dress, still adhere to parts of the torso. In the neck, cervical vertebrae are clearly visible and soft tissues are lacking. Large and small bowel are largely missing, and remaining lungs, liver, and spleen have defects with serrated margins. Of interest are fluffy, shredded strands, presumed to be nerve and muscle fibers, found in all limb joints. Periosteum, including skull, ribs, and limb bones, also have similar fluffy strands. Noted around the corpse are numerous bird droppings.' " Isles looked up. " 'Assumed to be from crows.' "

Julia stared at her. "You're saying *crows* did that?"

"These findings are classical for crow scavenging. Birds in general have been known to cause postmortem damage. Even cute little songbirds will peck and pull at a corpse's skin. Crows are considerably larger and carnivorous, so they can skeletonize a corpse quickly. They devour all soft tissues, but they can't quite pull off nerve fibers or tendons. Those strands remain attached to the joints, where they get frayed by repeated pecking. That's why Dr. Costas described the strands as *fluffy*—because they'd been so thoroughly shredded by the crows' beaks." Isles closed the folder. "That's the report."

"You haven't told me the cause of death."

"Because it was indeterminable. After three weeks, there's too much scavenger damage and decay."

"Then you have no idea?"

"She was ninety-two. It was a hot summer, and she was out alone in her garden. It's reasonable to assume she had a cardiac event."

"But you can't be sure."

"No, we can't."

"So it could have been . . ."

"Murder?" Isles's gaze was direct.

"She lived alone. She was vulnerable."

"There's no mention here of any disturbance in the house. No signs of a burglary."

"Maybe the killer didn't care about robbery. Maybe he was just interested in *her*. In what he could do to *her*."

Isles said quietly: "Believe me, I do understand what you're thinking. What you're afraid of. In my profession, I've seen what people can do to other people. Terrible things that make you question what it is to be human, whether we're any better than animals. But this particular death just doesn't ring any alarm bells for me. Common things are common, and in the case of a ninety-two-year-old woman found dead in her own backyard, murder isn't the first thing that comes to mind." Isles regarded Julia for a moment. "I can see you're not satisfied."

Julia sighed. "I don't know what to think. I'm sorry I ever bought the house. I haven't had a good night's sleep since I moved in."

"You haven't been living there very long. It's stressful, moving into a new place. Give yourself some time to get used to it. There's always an adjustment period."

"I've been having dreams," Julia said.

Isles didn't look impressed, and why would she? This was a woman who routinely sliced open the dead, a woman who'd chosen a career that would give most people nightmares. "What sort of dreams?"

"It's been three weeks now, and I've had them almost every night. I keep hoping they'll go away, that it's just from the shock of finding those bones in my garden."

"That could give anyone nightmares."

"I don't believe in ghosts. Really, I don't. But I feel as if she's trying to talk to me. Asking me to *do* something."

"The deceased owner? Or the skeleton?"

"I don't know. *Someone*."

Isles's expression remained utterly neutral. If she believed Julia was unhinged, her face didn't reveal it. But her words left no doubt where she stood on the matter. "I'm not sure I can help you with that. I'm just a pathologist, and I've told you my professional opinion."

"And in your professional opinion, murder is still a possibility, isn't it?" insisted Julia. "You can't rule it out."

Isles hesitated. "No," she finally conceded. "I can't."

That night, Julia dreamed of crows. Hundreds of them were perched in a dead tree, staring down at her with yellow eyes. Waiting.

She startled awake to the noise of raucous caws and opened her eyes to see the light of early morning through her uncurtained window. A pair of black wings glided past like a scythe wheeling through the sky. Then another. She climbed out of bed and went to the window.

The oak tree they occupied was not dead, as in her dream, but was fully leafed out in the lush growth of summer. At least two dozen crows had gathered there for some sort of corvid convention, and they perched like strange black fruit among the branches, cackling and rattling their glossy feathers. She had seen them in this tree before, and she had no doubt that these were the same birds who had feasted on Hilda Chamblett's corpse last summer, the same birds who had pecked and pulled with sharp beaks, leaving behind leathery shreds of nerve and tendon. Here they were again, looking for another taste of flesh. They knew she was watching them, and they stared back with eerie intelligence, as if they knew it was only a matter of time.

She turned away and thought: I have to hang some curtains on this window.

In the kitchen, she made coffee and spread butter and jam on toast. Outside, the morning mist was starting to lift, and it would be a sunny day. A good day to spread another bag of compost and dig in another bale of peat moss in the flower bed by the stream. Though her back still ached from laying bathroom tiles the night before, she did not want to waste a single day of good weather. You are allotted only a limited number of planting seasons in your lifetime, she thought, and once a summer is gone, you'll never get it back. She'd wasted too many summers already. *This one is for me.*

Outdoors, there was a noisy eruption of cawing and flapping wings. She looked out the window to see the crows suddenly lift simultaneously into the air and fly away, scattering to the four winds. Then she focused on the far corner of her yard, down near the stream, and she understood why the crows had fled so abruptly.

A man stood on the edge of her property. He was staring at her house.

She jerked away so he couldn't see her. Slowly, she eased back toward the window and peeked out. He was lean and dark-haired, dressed against the morning chill in blue jeans and a brown pullover sweater. Mist rose from the grass in feathery wisps, weaving sinuously about his legs. Trespass any farther on my property, she thought, and I'll call the police.

He took two steps toward her house.

She ran across the kitchen and snatched up the cordless phone. Darting back to the window, she looked out to see where he was, but could no longer glimpse him. Then something scratched at the kitchen door, and she was so startled, she almost dropped the phone. *It's locked, right? I locked the door last night, didn't I?* She dialed 911.

"McCoy!" a voice called out. "Come on, boy, get away from there!"

Glancing out the window again, she saw the man suddenly pop up from behind tall weeds. Something tapped across her porch, and then a yellow Labrador trotted into view and crossed the yard toward the man.

"Emergency operator."

Julia looked down at the phone. Oh, God, what an idiot she was. "I'm sorry," she said. "I called you by mistake."

"Is everything all right, ma'am? Are you certain?"

"Yes, I'm perfectly fine. I hit speed dial by accident. Thank you." She disconnected and looked outside again. The man was bending down to clip a leash onto the dog's collar. As he straightened, his gaze met Julia's through the window, and he gave a wave.

She opened the kitchen door and stepped out into the yard.

"Sorry about that!" he called out. "I didn't mean to trespass, but he got away from me. He thinks Hilda still lives there."

"He's been here before?"

"Oh, yeah. She used to keep a box of dog biscuits just for him." He laughed. "McCoy never forgets a free meal."

She walked down the slope toward him. He no longer frightened her. She could not imagine a rapist or murderer owning such a friendly animal. The dog was practically dancing around at the end of the leash as she approached, eager to make her acquaintance.

"You're the new owner, I take it?" he said.

"Julia Hamill."

"Tom Page. I live right down the road." He started to shake her hand, then remembered the plastic bag he was holding and gave an embarrassed laugh. "Oops. Doggy doo. I was trying to pick up after him."

So that's why he'd crouched momentarily in the grass, she thought. He was just cleaning up after his pet.

The dog gave an impatient bark and jumped up on his hind legs, begging for Julia's attention.

"McCoy! Down, boy!" Tom yanked on the leash, and the dog reluctantly obeyed.

"McCoy, as in real McCoy?" she asked.

"Um, no. As in Dr. McCoy."

"Oh. *Star Trek.*"

He regarded her with a sheepish smile. "I guess that dates me. It's scary how many kids these days have never heard of Dr. McCoy. It makes me feel ancient."

But he was certainly not ancient, she thought. Maybe in his early forties. Through her kitchen window, his hair had appeared black; now that she was closer, she could see threads of gray mingled there, and his dark eyes, squinting in the morning sunlight, were framed by well-used laugh lines.

"I'm glad somebody finally bought Hilda's place," he said, glancing toward the house. "It was looking pretty lonely there for a while."

"It's in rather bad shape."

"She really couldn't keep it up. This yard was too much for her, but she was so damn territorial, she'd never let anyone else work in it." He glanced toward the patch of bare earth, where the bones had been exhumed. "If she had, they might've found that skeleton a long time ago."

"You've heard about it."

"The whole neighborhood has. I came by a few weeks ago to watch them digging. You had a whole crew out here."

"I didn't see you."

"I didn't want you to think I was being too nosy. But I was curious." He looked at her, his eyes so direct it made her feel uneasy, as though she could feel his gaze probing the contours of her brain. "How do you like the neighborhood?" he asked. "Aside from the skeletons?"

She hugged herself in the morning chill. "I don't know."

"You haven't decided yet?"

"I mean, I love Weston, but I'm a little spooked by the bones. Knowing she was buried here all those years. It makes me feel . . ." She shrugged. "Lonely, I guess." She stared toward the grave site. "I wish I knew who she was."

"The university couldn't tell you?"

"They think the grave's early nineteenth century. Her skull was fractured in two places, and she was buried without much care. Just wrapped in an animal hide and dumped into the ground, without any ceremony. As if they were in a hurry to dispose of her."

"A fractured skull and a quick burial? That sounds an awful lot like murder to me."

She looked at him. "I think so, too."

They said nothing for a moment. The mist had almost lifted

now, and in the trees, birds chirped. Not crows this time, but song-birds, flitting gracefully from twig to twig. Odd, she thought, how the crows have simply vanished.

"Is that your phone ringing?" he asked.

Suddenly aware of the sound, she glanced toward the house. "I'd better get that."

"It was nice meeting you!" he called out as she ran up the steps to her porch. By the time she made it into her kitchen, he was moving on, dragging the reluctant McCoy after him. Already she'd forgotten his last name. Had he or had he not been wearing a wedding band?

It was Vicky on the phone. "So what's the latest installment of *Home Improvement?*" she asked.

"I tiled the bathroom floor last night." Julia's gaze was still on her garden, where Tom's brown sweater was now fading into the shadows beneath the trees. That old sweater must be a favorite of his, she thought. You didn't go out in public wearing something that ratty unless you had a sentimental attachment to it. Which somehow made him even more appealing. That and his dog.

". . . and I really think you should start dating again."

Julia's attention snapped back to Vicky. "What?"

"I know how you feel about blind dates, but this guy's really nice."

"No more lawyers, Vicky."

"They're not all like Richard. Some of them do prefer a real woman to a blow-dried Tiffani. Who, I just found out, has a daddy who's a big wheel at Morgan Stanley. No wonder she's getting a big splashy wedding."

"Vicky, I really don't need to hear the details."

"I think someone should whisper in her daddy's ear and tell him just what kind of loser his baby girl's getting married to."

"I have to go. I've been in the garden and my hands are all dirty. I'll call you later." She hung up and immediately felt guilty for that little white lie. But just the mention of Richard had thrown a shadow over her day, and she didn't want to think about him. She'd rather shovel manure.

She grabbed a garden hat and gloves, went back out into the yard, and looked toward the streambed. Tom-in-the-brown-sweater was nowhere in sight, and she felt a twinge of disappointment. *You just got dumped by one man. Are you so anxious to get your heart broken again?* She collected the shovel and wheelbarrow and moved down the slope, toward the ancient flower bed she'd been rejuvenating. Rattling through the grass, she wondered how many times old Hilda Chamblett had made her way down this overgrown path. Whether she'd worn a hat like Julia's, whether she'd paused and looked up at the sound of songbirds, whether she'd noticed that crooked branch in the oak tree.

Did she know, on that July day, that it would be her last on earth?

That night, she was too exhausted to cook anything more elaborate than a grilled cheese sandwich and tomato soup. She ate at the kitchen table with the photocopied news clippings about Hilda Chamblett spread out in front of her. The articles were brief, reporting only that the elderly woman had been found dead in her backyard and that foul play was not suspected. *At ninety-two, you are already living on borrowed time. What better way to die,* a neighbor was quoted as saying, *than on a summer's day in your garden?*

She read the obituary:

Hilda Chamblett, lifelong resident of Weston, Massachusetts, was found dead in her backyard on July 25. Her death has been ruled by the medical examiner's office as "most likely of natural causes." Widowed for the past twenty years, she was a familiar figure in gardening circles, and was known as an enthusiastic plantswoman who favored irises and roses. She is survived by her cousin Henry Page of Islesboro, Maine, and her niece Rachel Surrey of Roanoke, Virginia, as well as two grandnieces and a grandnephew.

The ringing telephone made her splash tomato soup on the page. Vicky, no doubt, she thought, probably wondering why I haven't called her back yet. She didn't want to talk to Vicky; she didn't want to hear about the lavish plans for Richard's wedding. But if she didn't answer it now, Vicky would just call again later.

Julia picked up the phone. "Hello?"

A man's voice, gravelly with age, said: "Is this Julia Hamill?"

"Yes, it is."

"So you're the woman who bought Hilda's house."

Julia frowned. "Who is this?"

"Henry Page. I'm Hilda's cousin. I hear you found some old bones in her garden."

Julia turned back to the kitchen table and quickly scanned the obituary. A splash of soup had landed right on the paragraph listing Hilda's survivors. She dabbed it away and spotted the name.

. . . her cousin Henry Page of Islesboro, Maine . . .

"I'm quite interested in those bones," he said. "I'm considered the family historian, you see." He added, with a snort, "Because no one else gives a bloody damn."

"What can you tell me about the bones?" she asked.

"Not a thing."

Then why are you calling me?

"I've been looking into it," he said. "When Hilda died, she left about thirty boxes of old papers and books. No one else wanted them, so they came to me. I admit, I just shoved them aside and haven't looked at them for the past year. But then I heard about your mysterious bones, and I wondered if there might be something about them in these boxes." He paused. "Is this at all interesting to you, or should I just shut up and say goodbye?"

"I'm listening."

"That's more than most of my family does. No one cares about history anymore. It's always *hurry, hurry, hurry* on to the hot new thing."

"About those boxes, Mr. Page."

"Oh, yes. I've come across some interesting documents with historical significance. I'm wondering if I've found the clue to who those bones belong to."

"What's in these documents?"

"There are letters and newspapers. I have them all right here in my house. You can look at them, anytime you want to come up to Maine."

"That's an awfully long drive, isn't it?"

"Not if you're really interested. It doesn't matter to me one way or the other whether you are. But since this is about your house, about people who once lived there, I thought you might find the history fascinating. Certainly I do. The tale sounds bizarre, but there's a news article here to substantiate it."

"What news article?"

"About the brutal murder of a woman."

"Where? When?"

"In Boston. It happened in the autumn of 1830. If you come up to Maine, Miss Hamill, you can read the documents for yourself. About the strange affair of Oliver Wendell Holmes and the West End Reaper."

Six

1830

ROSE DRAPED HER SHAWL over her head, wrapped it tight against the November chill, and stepped outside. She had left baby Meggie nursing greedily at the breast of another new mother in the lying-in ward, and tonight was the first time in two days she'd left the hospital. Though the night air was damp with mist, she inhaled it with a sense of relief, grateful to be away, if only for a short time, from the odors of the sickroom, the whimpers of pain. She paused outside on the street, breathing in deeply to wash the miasma of illness from her lungs, and smelled the river and the sea, heard the rumble of a carriage passing in the fog. I've been locked away so long among the dying, she thought, I've forgotten what it is to walk among the living.

Walk she did, moving swiftly through the bone-chilling mist, her footfalls echoing off brick and mortar as she navigated the warren of streets, toward the wharves. On this inhospitable night, she passed few others, and she hugged her shawl tighter, as though it offered a cloak of invisibility against unseen eyes that might regard her with hostile intent. She picked up her pace, and her breath seemed un-naturally loud, magnified by the thickening fog that grew ever denser as she moved toward the harbor. Then, through the rush of her own breathing, she heard footsteps behind her.

She stopped and turned.

The footsteps moved closer.

She backed away, her heart hammering. In the swirling mist, a dark form slowly congealed into something solid, something that was coming straight at her.

A voice called out: "Miss Rose! Miss Rose! Is that you?"

All the tension drained from her muscles. She released a deep breath as she watched the gangly teenager emerge from the fog. "Dash it all, Billy. I should box your ears!"

"For what, Miss Rose?"

"For scarin' me half to death."

From the pathetic look he gave her, you'd think she *had* boxed his ears. "I didn't mean to," he whimpered. And of course it was true; the boy couldn't be blamed for half of what he did. Everyone knew Dim Billy, but no one wanted to claim him. He was a constant and annoying presence on Boston's West End, wandering from barn to stable in search of a place to bed down, begging a meal here and there from scraps handed out by pitying housewives and fishmon-gers. Billy wiped a filthy hand across his face and whined, "Now you're all wrathy at me, ain't you?"

"What're you doing out and about at this hour?"

"Lookin' for my pup. He's lost."

More likely ran away, if the pup had any sense. "Well then, I hope you find him," she said, and turned to continue on her way.

He trailed after her. "Where're *you* going?"

"To fetch Eben. He needs to come to the hospital."

"Why?"

"Because my sister is very ill."

"How ill?"

"She has a fever, Billy." And after a week in the lying-in ward,

Rose understood what lay ahead. Within a day of giving birth to baby Meggie, Aurnia's belly had begun to bloat, her womb to drain the foul discharge that Rose knew was almost invariably the beginning of the end. She had seen so many of the other new mothers on the ward die of childbed fever. She had seen the look of pity in Nurse Robinson's eyes, a look that said: *There is nothing to be done*.

"Is she going to die?"

"I don't know," she said softly. "I don't know."

"I'm afraid of dead people. When I was little, I saw my own da dead. They wanted me to kiss him, even though his skin was all burned off, but I wouldn't do it. Was I a bad boy not to do it?"

"No, Billy. I've never known you to be a bad boy."

"I didn't want to touch him. But he was my da, and they said I had to."

"Can you tell me about it later? I'm in a hurry."

"I know. Because you want to fetch Mr. Tate."

"Go look for your pup now, why don't you?" She quickened her pace, hoping that this time the boy would not follow her.

"He's not at the lodging house."

It took her a few paces to register what Billy had just said. She stopped. "What?"

"Mr. Tate, he's not at Mrs. O'Keefe's."

"How do you know? Where is he?"

"I seen him over at the Mermaid. Mr. Sitterley gave me a spot of lamb pie, but he said I had to eat it outside in the alley. Then I saw Mr. Tate go in, and he didn't even say hello."

"Are you sure, Billy? Is he still there?"

"If you pay me a quarter, I'll take you."

She waved him away. "I don't have a quarter. I know the way."

"A ninepence?"

She walked away. "Or a ninepence, either."

"A large cent? A half cent?"

Rose kept walking and was relieved when at last she was able to shake off the pest. Her mind was on Eben, on what she would say to him. All the anger that she'd been holding in against her brother-in-law was now rising to a boil, and by the time she reached the Mermaid, she was ready to spring on him like a cat with claws bared. She paused outside the doorway and took a few deep breaths. Through the window, she saw the warm glow of firelight and heard the rumble of laughter. She was tempted to simply walk away and leave him to his cups. Aurnia would never know the difference.

It's his last chance to say goodbye. You have to do this.

Rose pushed through the door, into the tavern.

The heat from the fireplace brought prickles to her cold-numbed cheeks. She paused near the entrance, gazing around the room at patrons gathered at tables, huddled at the bar. At a corner table, a woman with wild dark hair and a green dress was laughing loudly. Several men turned to stare at Rose, and the looks they gave her made her pull her shawl tighter, even in that overheated room.

"You want to be served?" a man called out to her from behind the bar. This must be Mr. Sitterley, she thought, the barkeep who'd given Dim Billy a taste of lamb pie, no doubt to shoo the boy out of his establishment. "Miss?" the man asked.

She said. "It's a man I'm looking for." Her gaze came to a stop on the woman in the green dress. Sitting beside her was a man who now turned and shot Rose a resentful look.

She crossed to his table. On closer inspection, the woman seated beside him looked thoroughly unappealing, the bodice of her dress soiled with spilled drink and food. Her mouth gaped open, revealing rotting teeth. "You need to come to the hospital, Eben," said Rose.

Aurnia's husband shrugged. "Can't you see I'm busy grieving?"

"Go to her now, while you can. While she still lives."

"Who's she talking about, darlin'?" the woman said, tugging on Eben's sleeve, and Rose caught a nauseating whiff of those rotting teeth.

Eben grunted. "My wife."

"You didn't tell me you had a wife."

"So I'm tellin' you now." He took a sip of rum.

"How can you be so heartless?" said Rose. "It's been seven days since you've been to see her. You haven't even come to see your own daughter!"

"Already signed over my rights to her. Let the ladies at the infant asylum have her."

She stared at him, appalled. "You can't be serious."

"How'm I supposed to care for the brat? She's the only reason I married your sister. Baby on the way, I did my duty. But she was no cherry, that one." He gave a shrug. "They'll find a good home for her."

"She belongs with her family. I'll raise her myself, if I have to."

"You?" He laughed. "You're just months off the boat, and all you know is a needle and thread."

"I know enough to look after my own flesh and blood." Rose grabbed his arm. "Get up. You *will* come with me."

He shook her off. "Leave me alone."

"Get up, you bastard." With both hands, she hauled on his arm, and he stumbled to his feet. "She has but a few hours left. Even if you have to lie to her, even if she can't hear you, you *will* tell her you love her!"

He shoved her away and stood swaying, drunk and unsteady. The tavern had fallen silent, save for the crackle of flames in the fire-place. Eben glanced around at all the eyes watching him in disapproval. They'd all heard the conversation, and clearly there was no sympathy for him here.

He drew himself up straight and managed a civil tone. "No need to rail at me like a harpy. I'll come." He gave his jacket a tug, neatened his collar. "I was only finishing up my drink."

With head held high, he walked out of the Mermaid, stumbling over the threshold as he stepped out the door. She followed him outside, into a mist so penetrating, the dampness seemed to seep straight into her bones. They'd walked only a dozen paces when Eben abruptly turned around to face her.

His blow sent her reeling backward. She staggered against a

building, her cheek throbbing, the pain so terrible that for a few seconds the world went black. She did not even see the second blow coming. It whipped her sideways and she fell to her knees, felt icy water soaking into her skirt.

"That's for talking back to me in public," he snarled. He grabbed her by the arm and dragged her across the cobblestones, into the mud of a narrow alley.

Another blow slammed into her mouth and she tasted blood.

"And that's for the four months I've had to put up with you. Always taking her side, always lined up against me, the two of you. My prospects ruined, all because she got herself knocked up. You think she didn't beg me for it? You think I had to seduce her? Oh, no, your *saintly* sister wanted it. She wasn't afraid to show me what she had. But it was spoiled goods."

He wrenched her to her feet and shoved her up against a wall.

"So don't play the innocent with me. I know what kind of trash runs in your family. I know what you want. The same thing your sister wanted."

He rammed up against her, pinning her against the bricks. His mouth closed over hers, his breath sour with rum. The blows had left her so dazed she could not summon the strength to push him away. She felt the hardening against her pelvis, felt his hand groping at her breasts. He yanked up her skirt and clawed at her petticoat, her stockings, tearing through fabric to reach naked flesh. At the touch of his hand on her bare thigh, her spine snapped taut.

How dare you!

Her fist caught him beneath the chin, and she felt his jaw slam shut, heard teeth smack together. He screamed and staggered backward, his hand clapped to his mouth.

"My tongue! I've bit my tongue!" He looked down at his hand. "Oh, God, I'm bleeding!"

She ran. She darted out of the alley, but he lunged after her and grabbed a handful of her hair, scattering pins across the stones. She twisted away and stumbled over her torn petticoat. The thought of his hand on her thigh, his breath on her face, sent her scrambling back to her feet. Hiking her skirt above her knees, she bolted head-long into the disorienting mist. She did not know which street she was on, or in which direction she was headed. The river? The harbor? All she knew was that the fog was her cloak, her friend, and the deeper she plunged into it, the safer she would be. He was too drunk to keep up, much less navigate the maze of narrow streets. Already his footsteps seemed more distant, his curses fading, until all she could hear was the pounding of her own feet, her own pulse.

She rounded a corner and came to a halt. Through the rush of her own breathing, she heard the clattering wheels of a passing carriage, but no footsteps. She realized she was on the Cambridge road, and that she'd have to double back to return to the hospital.

Eben would expect her to go there. He'd be waiting for her.

She leaned down and ripped away the entangling strip of petticoat. Then she started walking north, staying to the side streets and alleys, pausing every few paces to listen for footsteps. The fog was so thick, she could see only the outline of a wagon passing on the road; the clop of horse's hooves seemed to come from all directions at once, the echoes fractured and scattered in the mist. She fell in step behind the wagon, trotting after it as it moved up Blossom Street, in the direction of the hospital. If Eben attacked, she would scream her lungs out. Surely the wagon's driver would stop and come to her aid.

Suddenly the wagon turned right, away from the hospital, and Rose was left standing alone. She knew the hospital was straight ahead of her, on North Allen, but she could not yet see it through the fog. Eben was almost certainly waiting to pounce. Staring up the street, she could sense the threat that loomed ahead, could picture Eben hulking in the shadows, anticipating her arrival.

She turned. There was another way into the building, but she would have to trudge across the damp grass of the hospital common to the rear entrance. She paused at the edge of the lawn. Her route was obscured by fog, but she could just make out, through fingers of mist, the glow of hospital windows. He would not expect her to hike across this dark field. Certainly he himself would not go to such an effort if it meant soiling his shoes in the mud.

She waded into the grass. The field was saturated with rain, and icy water soaked through her shoes. The lights from the hospital intermittently faded out in the mist and she had to stop to regain her bearings. There they were again—off to the left. In the darkness, she had veered away from her goal, and now she corrected course. The lights glowed brighter now, the fog thinning as she climbed the gentle slope toward the building. Her sodden skirts clung to her legs, slowing her down, making every stride an effort. By the time she stumbled out of the grass, onto cobblestones, she was clumsy on cold-numbed feet.

Chilled and shivering now, she started up the back stairway.

Suddenly her shoe slid across a step slick with something black. She stared up at what looked like a dark waterfall that had cascaded down the stairs. Only as her gaze lifted to the source of that waterfall did she see the woman's body draped across the stairs above, her skirts splayed, one arm flung out, as though to welcome Death.

At first Rose heard only the drumming of her own heart, the rush of her own breath. Then she heard the footstep, and a shadow moved above her like an ominous cloud blotting out the moon. The blood seemed to freeze in Rose's veins. She looked at the looming creature.

What she saw was the Grim Reaper himself.

Her voice mute and choked with terror, she stumbled backward and almost fell as she hit the bottom step. Suddenly the creature swooped toward her, black cape billowing like monstrous wings. She whirled to flee, and saw empty lawn ahead, roiling with mist. A place of execution. *If I run there, I will surely die.*

She pivoted to the right and sprinted alongside the building. She could hear the monster in pursuit, its footsteps closing in behind her.

She darted into a passage and found herself in a courtyard. She ran to the nearest door, but it was locked. Pounding on it, she shrieked for help, but no one opened it.

I am trapped.

Behind her, gravel clattered across the stones. She spun around to face her attacker. In the darkness she could make out only the movement of black on black. She backed up against the door, her breaths coming out in sobs. She thought of the dead woman, and the waterfall of blood on the stairs, and she crossed her arms over her chest in a feeble shield to protect her heart.

The shadow closed in.

Cringing, she turned her face in anticipation of the first slash. Instead she heard a voice, asking a question that she did not immediately register.

"Miss? Miss, are you all right?"

She opened her eyes to see the silhouette of a man. Behind him, through the darkness, a light winked and slowly became brighter. It was a lantern, swaying in the grasp of a second man, now approaching. The man with the lantern called: "Who's out here? Hello?"

"Wendell! Over here!"

"Norris? What's all the commotion?"

"There's a young woman here. She seems to be hurt."

"What's the matter with her?"

The lantern swung closer, and the light dazzled Rose's eyes. She blinked and focused on the faces of the two young men who were now staring at her. She recognized them both, just as they recognized her.

"It—it's Miss Connolly, is it not?" said Norris Marshall.

She gave a sob. Her legs suddenly went out from under her and she slid down the wall, to land on her rump against the cobblestones.

Seven

THOUGH NORRIS had never before met Mr. Pratt of Boston's Night Watch, he had known other men just like him, men too puffed up on authority to ever acknowledge the undeniable fact, recognized by everyone else, that they are stupid. It was Pratt's arrogance that Norris found most annoying, right down to the man's walk, his chest thrust out, arms swinging in a martial beat as he strutted into the hospital dissection room. Though not a large man, Mr. Pratt gave the impression that he thought he was. His only impressive feature was his mustache, the bushiest Norris had ever seen. It looked like a brown squirrel that had sunk its claws into his upper lip and refused to let go. As Norris watched the man taking notes with a pencil, he could not help staring at that mustache, picturing that imaginary squirrel suddenly leaping away and Mr. Pratt giving chase after his fugitive facial hair.

Pratt finally looked up from his pad of paper and regarded Norris and Wendell, who stood beside the draped body. Pratt's gaze moved on to Dr. Crouch, who was clearly the medical authority in the room.

"You say you have examined the body, Dr. Crouch?" asked Pratt.

"Only superficially. We took the liberty of bringing her into the building. It did not seem right to leave her lying there on the cold steps, where anyone might trip over her. Even if she were a stranger, which she is not, we owe her at least that small modicum of respect."

"Then you are all acquainted with the deceased?"

"Yes, sir. Only when we brought out the lantern did we recognize her. The victim, Miss Agnes Poole, is the head nurse of this institution."

Wendell interjected: "Miss Connolly must have told you this. Didn't you already question her?"

"Yes, but I find it necessary to confirm everything she's told me. You know how it is with these flighty girls. Irish girls in particular. They're likely to change their story depending on which way the wind blows."

Norris said, "I'd hardly call Miss Connolly a flighty girl."

Watchman Pratt fixed his narrowed gaze on Norris. "You know her?"

"Her sister is a patient here, in the lying-in ward."

"But do you *know* her, Mr. Marshall?"

He didn't like the way Pratt was studying him. "We've spoken. In regard to her sister's care."

Pratt's pencil was scribbling on the pad again. "You are studying medicine, is that correct?"

"Yes."

Pratt eyed Norris's clothing. "You have blood on your shirt. Are you aware of that?"

"I helped move the body from the steps. And I assisted Dr. Crouch earlier in the evening."

Pratt glanced at Crouch. "Is this true, Doctor?"

Norris felt his face redden. "You think I would lie about it? In Dr. Crouch's presence?"

"My only duty is to uncover the truth."

You're too stupid to recognize the truth when you hear it.

Dr. Crouch said, "Mr. Holmes and Mr. Marshall are my apprentices. They assisted me earlier this evening on Broad Street, at a difficult delivery."

"What were you delivering?"

Dr. Crouch stared at Pratt, clearly thunderstruck by the man's question. "What do you think we were delivering? A cart of bricks?"

Pratt slapped his pencil down on the pad. "There is no need for sarcasm. I simply wish to know everyone's whereabouts tonight."

"I find this outrageous. I am a physician, sir, and I have no need to account for my activities."

"And your two apprentices here? Were you with them the entire evening?"

"No, we were not," said Wendell, rather too casually.

Norris looked at his fellow student in surprise. Why offer this man any unnecessary information? It would only feed his suspicions. Indeed, Watchman Pratt now looked like a mustachioed cat at the mouse hole, ready to pounce.

"When were you not in each other's company?" asked Pratt.

"Would you like an account of my visits to the pisspot? Oh, and I do believe I took a crap as well. How about you, Norris?"

"Mr. Holmes, I do not appreciate your foul brand of humor."

"Humor is the only way to deal with questions as absurd as these. We're the ones who *summoned* the Night Watch, for God's sake."

The mustache twitched. The squirrel was now getting agitated. "I see no need for blasphemy," he said coldly, and slipped his pencil into his pocket. "Now then. Show me the body."

Dr. Crouch said, "Shouldn't Constable Lyons be present?"

Pratt shot him an irritated look. "He will get my report in the morning."

"But he should be here. This is serious business."

"At this moment, I am in authority. Constable Lyons will be advised of the facts at a more reasonable hour. I see no reason to rouse him from his bed." Pratt pointed to the draped body. "Uncover her," he ordered.

Pratt had assumed a nonchalant pose, jaw thrust out in the attitude of a man too cocky to be rattled by anything so minor as the sight of a corpse. But when Dr. Crouch pulled off the sheet, Pratt could not suppress a gasp, and he suddenly flinched away from the table. Although Norris had already viewed the corpse and had, in fact, helped carry it into the building, he, too, was shocked yet again by the mutilations performed on Agnes Poole. They had not undressed her; they scarcely needed to. The blade had slashed open the front of her dress, laying bare her injuries, injuries so grotesque that Watchman Pratt remained frozen and unable to utter a sound, his face as pale as curdled milk.

"As you can see," said Dr. Crouch, "the trauma is horrific. I have waited to complete the examination until an official could be present. But all it takes is a cursory glance to see that the killer has not merely sliced open the torso. He has done far, far more." Crouch rolled up his sleeves, then glanced at Pratt. "If you wish to see the damage, you'll have to step up to the table."

Pratt swallowed. "I can . . . see it well enough from here."

"I doubt that. But if your stomach is too weak to handle it, there's no sense in your getting sick all over the corpse." He pulled on an apron and tied the strings behind his back. "Mr. Holmes, Mr. Marshall, I'll need your assistance. It's a good opportunity for you both to get your hands dirty. Not every student is so fortunate this early in his education."

Fortunate was not the word that came to Norris's mind as he stared into the gaping torso. Growing up on his father's farm, he was no stranger to the smell of blood or the butchering of pigs and cows. He had gotten his hands dirty, all right, helping the farmhands as they scooped out offal and stripped away the hides. He knew what death looked like and smelled like, for he had labored in its presence.

But this was a different view of death, a view that was too intimate and familiar. This was not a pig's heart or a cow's lungs that he stared at. And the slack-jawed face was one that, only hours ago, had been suffused with life. To see Nurse Poole now, to look into her glazed eyes, was to catch a glimpse of his own future. Reluctantly, he took an apron from the wall hooks, tied it on, and took his place at Dr. Crouch's side. Wendell stood on the other side of the table. Despite the bloody corpse that lay between them, Wendell's face revealed no revulsion, only a look of intent curiosity. *Am I the only one who remembers who this woman was?* Norris wondered. Not a pleasant human being, to be sure, but she was more than a mere carcass, more than an anonymous corpse to be dissected.

Dr. Crouch soaked a cloth in a basin of water and gently sponged blood away from the incised skin. "As you can see here, gentlemen, the blade must have been quite sharp. These are clean cuts, very deep. And the pattern—the pattern is most intriguing."

"What do you mean? What pattern?" asked Pratt in a strangely muffled and nasal voice.

"If you would approach the table, I could show you."

"I'm busy taking notes, can't you see? Just describe it for me."

"Description alone will not do it justice. Perhaps we should send for Constable Lyons? Surely *someone* in the Watch has the stomach to do his duty?"

Pratt flushed an angry red. Only then did he finally approach the table, to stand beside Wendell. He took one glimpse into the gaping abdomen and quickly averted his gaze. "All right. I've seen it."

"But do you see the pattern, how bizarre it is? A slice straight across the abdomen, from flank to flank. And then a perpendicular slice, straight up the midline, toward the breastbone, lacerating the liver. They are so deep, either one of these cuts would have caused death." He reached into the wound with bare hands and lifted out the intestines, painstakingly examining the glistening loops before he let them slide into a bucket at the side of the table. "The blade had to be quite long. It has sliced all the way to the backbone and nicked the top of the left kidney." He glanced up. "Do you see, Mr. Pratt?"

"Yes. Yes, of course." Pratt was not even looking at the body; his gaze seemed to be fixed, almost desperately, on Norris's blood-streaked apron.

"And then there is this vertical slice. It, too, is savagely deep." He lifted up the rest of the small bowel in one mass, and Wendell quickly positioned the bucket to catch it as it came tumbling over the side of the table. Next came other abdominal organs, resected one by one. The liver, the spleen, the pancreas. "The blade incised the descending aorta here, which accounts for the great volume of blood on the steps." Crouch looked up. "She would have died quickly, from exsanguination."

"Ex—what?" asked Pratt.

"Quite simply, sir, she bled to death."

Pratt swallowed hard and finally forced himself to gaze down at the abdomen, now little more than a hollowed-out cavity. "You said it had to be a long blade. How long?"

"To penetrate this deep? Seven, eight inches at the least."

"A butcher's knife, perhaps."

"I would certainly classify this as an act of butchery."

"He could also have used a sword," said Wendell.

"Rather conspicuous, I would think," said Dr. Crouch. "To be clattering around town with a bloody sword."

"What makes you think of a sword?" asked Pratt.

"It's the nature of the wounds. The two perpendicular slashes. In my father's library, there is a book on strange customs of the Far East. I've read of wounds just like these, inflicted in the Japanese act of seppuku. A ritualistic suicide."

"This is hardly a suicide."

"I realize that. But the pattern is identical."

"It is indeed a most curious pattern," said Dr. Crouch. "Two separate slashes, perpendicular to each other. Almost as if the killer were trying to carve the sign of . . ."

"The cross?" Pratt looked up with sudden interest. "The victim wasn't Irish, was she?"

"No," Crouch said. "Most definitely not."

"But many of the patients in this hospital are?"

"It is the hospital's mission to serve the unfortunate. Many of our patients, if not most, are charity cases."

"Meaning Irish. Like Miss Connolly."

"Now, look here," said Wendell, speaking far more forthrightly than he should have. "Surely you're reading too much into these wounds. Just because it resembles a cross doesn't mean the killer is a papist."

"You defend them?"

"I'm merely pointing out the defects in your reasoning. One can't possibly draw such a conclusion as you're doing, merely because of the peculiarity of these wounds. I've offered you just as likely an interpretation."

"That some fellow from Japan has jumped ship with his sword?" Pratt laughed. "There's hardly such a man in Boston. But there are plenty of papists."

"One could just as likely conclude the killer *wants* you to blame the papists!"

"Mr. Holmes," said Crouch, "perhaps you should refrain from telling the Night Watch how to do its job."

"Its *job* is to learn the truth, not make unfounded assumptions based on religious bigotry."

Pratt's eyes suddenly narrowed. "Mr. Holmes, you are related, are you not, to the Reverend Abiel Holmes? Of Cambridge?"

There was a pause, during which Norris glimpsed a shadow of discomfort pass across Wendell's face.

"Yes," Wendell finally answered. "He is my father."

"A fine, upstanding Calvinist. Yet his son—"

Wendell retorted: "His son can think for himself, thank you."

"Mr. Holmes," cautioned Dr. Crouch. "Your attitude is not particularly helpful."

"But it is certainly noted," said Pratt. *And not forgotten*, his gaze clearly added. He turned to Dr. Crouch. "How well acquainted were you with Miss Poole, Doctor?"

"She administered to many of my patients."

"And your opinion of her?"

"She was competent and efficient. And most respectful."

"Had she any enemies that you're aware of?"

"Absolutely not. She was a nurse. Her role here was to ease pain and suffering."

"But surely there was the occasional dissatisfied patient or family member? Someone who might turn his anger on the hospital and its staff?"

"It's possible. But I can think of no one who—"

"What about Rose Connolly?"

"The young lady who found the body?"

"Yes. Had she any disagreements with Nurse Poole?"

"There may have been. The girl is headstrong. Nurse Poole did complain to me that she was demanding."

"She was concerned about her sister's care," said Norris.

"But that is no excuse for disrespect, Mr. Marshall," said Dr. Crouch. "On *anyone's* part."

Pratt looked at Norris. "You defend the girl."

"She and her sister appear to be quite close, and Miss Connolly has reason to be upset. That's all I'm saying."

"Upset enough to commit violence?"

"I didn't say that."

"How, exactly, did you happen to find her tonight? She was outside, in the courtyard, was she not?"

"Dr. Crouch asked us to meet him in the lying-in ward, for a fresh crisis. I was on my way here, from my lodgings."

"Where are your lodgings?"

"I rent an attic room, sir, at the end of Bridge Street. It's on the far side of the hospital common."

"So to reach the hospital, you cross the common?"

"Yes. And that's the way I came tonight, across the lawn. I was almost to the hospital when I heard screams."

"Miss Connolly's? Or the victim's?"

"It was a woman. That's all I know. I followed the sound, and discovered Miss Connolly in the courtyard."

"Did you see this creature she so imaginatively describes?" Pratt glanced at his notes. " 'A caped monster like the Grim Reaper, with a black cape that flapped like the wings of a giant bird.' " He looked up.

Norris shook his head. "I saw no such creature. I found only the girl."

Pratt looked at Wendell. "And where were you?"

"I was inside, assisting Dr. Crouch. I heard the screams as well, and ventured outside with a lantern. I found Mr. Marshall in the courtyard, along with Miss Connolly, who was cowering there."

"Cowering?"

"She was clearly frightened. I'm sure she thought one of us was the killer."

"Did you notice anything unusual about her? Other than the fact she appeared frightened?"

"She *was* frightened," said Norris.

"Her clothing, for instance. The condition of her dress. Did you not notice it was badly ripped?"

"She'd just fled a killer, Mr. Pratt," said Norris. "She had every right to be disheveled."

"Her dress was *torn*, as though she'd been viciously grappling with someone. Not one of you?"

"No," said Wendell.

"Why don't you just ask her how it happened?" suggested Norris.

"I have."

"And what did she say?"

"She claimed it happened earlier in the evening. When her sister's husband attempted to molest her." He shook his head in disgust. "These people are like animals, breeding in the tenements."

Norris heard the ugly note of prejudice in the man's voice. *Ani-*

mals. Oh, yes, he'd heard that name used for the Irish, those immoral beasts who were always whoring, always procreating. To Pratt, Rose was just another Bridget, a filthy immigrant like the thousands who crammed the tenements of South Boston and Charlestown, whose unclean habits and snot-nosed offspring had touched off citywide epidemics of smallpox and cholera.

Norris said, "Miss Connolly is hardly an animal."

"You know her well enough to say that?"

"I don't believe that *any* human being deserves such an insult."

"For a man who scarcely knows her, you rise quickly to her defense."

"I feel sorry for her. Sorry that her sister is dying."

"Oh, that. *That* is over with."

"What do you mean?"

"It happened earlier this evening," said Pratt, and he closed his notebook. "Rose Connolly's sister is dead."

Eight

WE HAD NO CHANCE *to say goodbye.*

Rose washed Aurnia's body with a damp cloth, gently wiping away the smudges of dirt and dried sweat and tears from a face that was now strangely smooth of all worry lines. If there was a heaven, she thought, surely Aurnia was already there, and could see the trouble Rose was in. *I am afraid, Aurnia. And Meggie and I have nowhere to go.*

Aurnia's neatly brushed hair gleamed in the lamplight, like coppery silk draped across the pillow. Though she was now bathed, the stench remained, a fetid odor clinging to the body that had once embraced Rose, once had shared a girlhood bed with her.

You are still beautiful to me. You will always be beautiful.

In a little basket beside the bed, baby Meggie slept soundly, unaware of her mother's passing, of her own precarious future. How clear it is that she is Aurnia's child, thought Rose. The same red hair, the same sweetly curving mouth. For two days, Meggie had been nursed on the ward by three new mothers, who had willingly passed the child among them. They had all witnessed Aurnia's agonies, and they knew that but for the whims of providence any one of them might also be a client for the coffin maker.

Rose glanced up as a nurse approached. It was Miss Cabot, who had assumed authority since Nurse Poole's death.

"I'm sorry, Miss Connolly, but it's time to transfer the deceased."

"She's only just passed on."

"It's been two hours now, and we have need of the bed." The nurse handed a small bundle to Rose. "Your sister's belongings."

Here were the pitifully few possessions that Aurnia had brought with her to the hospital: her soiled night frock and a hair ribbon and the cheap little ring of tin and colored glass that had been Aurnia's good-luck charm since her girlhood. A charm that had, in the end, failed her.

"Those go to the husband," Nurse Cabot said. "Now she must be moved."

Rose heard the squeaking of wheels, and she saw the hospital groundsman pushing in a wheeled cart. "I've not had enough time with her."

"There can be no further delay. The coffin is ready in the court-yard. Have arrangements been made for burial?"

Rose shook her head. Bitterly, she said, "Her husband has arranged for nothing."

"If the family is unable to pay, there are options for a respectful interment."

A *pauper's burial* was what she meant. Crammed into a common grave with nameless peddlers and beggars and thieves.

"How much time do I have to make arrangements?" asked Rose.

Nurse Cabot impatiently glanced up the row of beds, as though considering all the other work she had to do. "By tomorrow noon," she said, "the wagon will come to pick up the coffin."

"So little time?"

"Decay does not wait." The nurse turned and gestured to the man who had stood quietly waiting, and he pushed the cart to the bedside.

"Not yet. *Please.*" Rose pulled at the man's sleeve, trying to tug him away from Aurnia. "You can't put her out in the cold!"

"Please don't make this difficult," said the nurse. "If you wish to arrange a private burial, then you'd best see to the arrangements before tomorrow noon, or the city will take her to the South Burying Ground." She looked at the groundsman. "Remove the deceased."

He slid burly arms beneath Aurnia's body and lifted her from the bed. As he placed the corpse into the handcart, a sob escaped Rose's throat and she plucked at her sister's gown, at the skirt, now crusted brown with dried blood. But no cries, no pleading, could alter the course of what would happen next. Aurnia, clothed only in linen and gauze, would be wheeled out into the frigid courtyard, fragile skin bumping against splintery wood as the cart rolled across the cobblestones. Would he be gentle as he placed her into the coffin? Or would he merely roll her in, dropping her like a carcass of meat, letting her head thump against bare pine boards?

"Let me stay with her," she pleaded, and reached for the man's arm. "Let me watch."

"Ain't nothin' to see, miss."

"I want to be sure. I want to know she's treated right."

He gave a shrug. "I treat 'em all right. But you can watch if you want, I don't care."

"There's another issue," said Nurse Cabot. "The child. You can't possibly take adequate care of it, Miss Connolly."

The woman in the next bed said: "They came by when you were out, Rose. Someone from the infant asylum, wantin' to take her. But we wouldn't allow it. The nerve of those people, tryin' to make off with your niece when you weren't even here!"

"Mr. Tate has signed away his parental rights," said Nurse Cabot. "He, at least, understands what's best for his baby."

"He doesn't care about the baby," said Rose.

"You're far too young to raise it yourself. Be sensible, girl! Give it to someone who can."

In answer, Rose snatched up Meggie from her basket and held

her tightly against her breast. "Give her to a stranger? I'd have to be on my deathbed first."

Nurse Cabot, faced with Rose's clearly insurmountable resistance, at last gave a sigh of exasperation. "Suit yourself. It'll be on your conscience when the child comes to grief. I have no time for this, not tonight, with poor Agnes . . ." She swallowed hard, then looked at the groundsman, who still waited with Aurnia's body on his cart. "Remove her."

Still holding tightly to Meggie, Rose followed the man out of the ward, into the courtyard. There, by the yellow glow of his lamp, she stood vigil as Aurnia was laid into the pine box. She watched him pound in the nails, hammer echoing like pistol shots, and with every blow she felt a nail being driven into her own heart. The coffin now sealed, he picked up a lump of charcoal and scrawled on the lid: A. TATE.

"Just so there's no mix-up," he said, and straightened to look at her. "She'll be here till noon. Make your arrangements by then."

Rose laid her hand on the lid. *I'll find a way, darling. I'll see you properly buried.* She wrapped her shawl around both herself and Meggie, then walked out of the hospital courtyard.

She did not know where to go. Certainly not back to the lodging house room that she'd shared with her sister and Eben. Eben was probably there now, sleeping off the rum, and she had no wish to confront him. She'd deal with him in the morning, when he was sober. Her brother-in-law might be heartless, but he was also coldly sensible. He had a business to maintain, and a reputation to uphold. If even a hint of malicious gossip got out, the bell over his tailor shop might fall silent. *In the morning,* she thought, *Eben and I will come to a truce, and he'll take us both in. She is his daughter, after all.*

But tonight they had no bed to sleep in.

Her footsteps slowed, stopped. She stood exhausted on the corner. Force of habit had sent her in a familiar direction, and now she gazed up the same street that she had walked earlier that evening. A Dearborn carriage clattered past, pulled by a swaybacked horse with a drooping head. Even so poor a carriage, with its rickety wheels and patched canopy, was an unattainable luxury. She imagined sitting with her weary feet propped up on a little stool, protected from the wind and rain while that carriage bore her like royalty. As it rolled past, she suddenly saw the familiar figure that had been standing right across the street from her.

"Did y'hear the news, Miss Rose?" said Dim Billy. "Nurse Poole's been killed, over at the hospital!"

"Yes, Billy. I know."

"They said she was slit right up her belly, like this." He slashed a finger up his abdomen. "Cut off her head with a sword. And her hands, too. Three people saw him do it, and he flew away like a great black bird."

"Who told you that?"

"Mrs. Durkin did, over at the stable. She heard it from Crab."

"There's a fool of a boy, Crab is. You're repeating nonsense, and you should stop it."

He fell silent, and she realized she had hurt his feelings. His feet were dragging like giant anchors across the cobblestones. Beneath his shoved-down cap, enormous ears protruded like drooping saucers. Poor Billy so seldom took offense, it was easy to forget that even he could be wounded.

"I'm sorry," she said.

"For what, Miss Rose?"

"You were only telling me what you heard. But not everything you hear is the God's truth. Some people lie. Some are the devil's own. You can't trust them all, Billy."

"How do *you* know it's a lie? What Crab said?"

She'd never heard such a note of petulance in his voice before, and she was tempted to tell him the truth: that she had been the one who'd found Nurse Poole. No, better to stay silent. Whisper a word in Billy's ear, and by tomorrow who knew how the tale would have changed, and what far-fetched role she would have in it?

Let there be no whisper of my name.

She began to walk again, heading for familiar territory, the baby still sleeping soundly in her arms. Better to bed down in the gutter you know. Perhaps Mrs. Combs down the street would grant her and Meggie a corner in her kitchen, just for tonight. I could repair that old cloak of hers, she thought, the one with the badly mended rip. Surely that was worth a small spot in the kitchen.

"I told the Night Watch everything I saw," said Billy, practically dancing up the street beside her. "I been out, y'know, lookin' for Spot. I been up and down this street ten times, and that's why the Watch says I'm a good one to talk to."

"That you are."

"I'm sorry she's dead, 'cause she won't be sendin' me out on errands anymore. Gave me a penny every time, but last time she didn't. That's not fair, is it? I didn't tell *that* to the Night Watch, 'cause they'll think I killed her for it."

"No one would think such a thing of you, Billy."

"You should always pay a man for his work, but she didn't that time."

They walked together, past darkened windows, past silent houses. It's so late, she thought; everyone is asleep except for us. The boy stayed with her until she came, at last, to a stop.

"Aren't you going in?" said Billy.

She gazed up at Mrs. O'Keefe's lodging house. Her tired feet had automatically brought her to this door, through which she had walked so many times before. Up the stairs would be her narrow bed, tucked into the curtained alcove in the room she'd shared with Aurnia and Eben. The thin curtain had not been barrier enough to muffle the sounds from the other bed. Eben's grunts of lovemaking, his snores, his hacking cough in the morning. She remembered his hands groping at her thighs tonight, and with a shudder she turned and walked away.

"Where are you going?" Billy said.

"I don't know."

"Aren't you going home?"

"No."

He caught up to her. "You're going to stay awake? All night?"

"I need to find someplace to sleep. Someplace warm, where Meggie won't get cold."

"Isn't Mrs. O'Keefe's house warm?"

"I can't go there tonight, Billy. Mr. Tate is angry with me. Very, very angry. And I'm afraid he might . . ." She halted and stared at the mist, which coiled at her feet like grasping hands. "Oh, God, Billy," she whispered. "I'm so tired. What am I going to do with her?"

"I know a place you could take her," he said. "A secret place. But you can't tell anyone about it."

Dawn had not yet lifted the darkness when Wall-eyed Jack harnessed his horse and climbed up onto the buckboard. He guided the dray out of the stable yard and onto icy cobblestones that gleamed like glass under the lamplight. At this hour, his was the only wagon on the street, and the clip-clop of the horse's hooves, the rattle of the wheels, were unnervingly noisy in the otherwise silent street. Those stirring awake in their beds, hearing the rattle of his wagon rolling past, would assume it was just a tradesman passing by. A butcher hauling carcasses to market, perhaps, or the mason with his stones, or the farmer delivering bales of hay to the stableman. It would not occur to those drowsy people in their warm beds what sort of cargo would soon be loaded onto the wagon that now rolled past their windows. The living had no wish to dwell on the dead, and so the dead were invisible, nailed into pine boxes, sewn into shrouds, moved furtively on rattling carts under cover of night. What no one else has the stomach for, here I am, thought Jack with a grim smile. Oh, there was money to be made in the snatching trade. The clop of the horse's hooves pounded out the poetry of those words again and again as his dray rolled northwest, toward the Charles River.

There's money to be made. There's money to be made.

And that's where you'd find Jack Burke.

In the fog ahead, a crouching figure suddenly materialized right in front of the horse. Jack pulled up sharply on the reins and the horse halted with a snort. A teenage boy scampered into view, zigzagging back and forth in the street, long arms waving like octopus tentacles.

"Bad pup! Bad pup, you come to me now!"

The dog gave a yelp as the boy pounced and grabbed him around the neck. Straightening, the struggling dog now firmly in his grip, the boy stared wide-eyed as he suddenly saw Jack glaring at him through the mist.

"You damn half-wit, Billy!" snapped Jack. Oh, he knew this boy well enough, and what a nuisance he was, always underfoot, always searching for a free meal, a place to bed down. More than once, Jack had had to chase Dim Billy out of his own stable yard. "Get outta the road! I could've run right over you."

The boy just gaped at him. He had a mouthful of crooked teeth and a head too small for his gangly teenage body. He grinned stupidly, the mutt struggling in his arms. "He doesn't always come when I call. He needs to behave."

"Can't even look after yourself, and you got a damn dog?"

"He's my friend. His name's Spot."

Jack eyed the black mutt, who as far as he could see had no spots anywhere. "Now, there's a right clever name I've never heard before."

"We're out lookin' for a bit o' milk. Babies need milk, y'know, and she drank up all I got for her last night. She'll be hungry this morning, and when they get hungry, they cry."

What *was* the fool boy babbling about? "Get outta my way," said Jack. "I got business to attend to."

"All right, Mr. Burke!" The boy moved aside to let the horse pass. "I'm gonna get myself some business, too."

Sure ya will, Billy. Sure ya will. Jack snapped the reins, and the wagon lurched forward. The horse took only a few paces before Jack abruptly pulled him to a stop. He turned to look back at Billy's spindly figure, half hidden in the mist. Though the boy had to be sixteen or seventeen, he was only bones and sinew, about as sturdy as some clackety wooden puppet. Still, he'd be an extra pair of hands.

And he'd be cheap.

"Hey, Billy!" Jack called. "You want to earn a ninepence?"

The boy hurried up to him, arms still in a stranglehold around his unfortunate pet. "What for, Mr. Burke?"

"Leave the dog and climb in."

"But we need to find milk."

"You want your ninepence or what? You can buy milk with it."

Billy dropped the dog, who immediately trotted away. "You go home now!" Billy ordered it. "That's right, Spot!"

"Get in, boy."

Billy scrabbled aboard the dray and settled his bony arse on the buckboard. "Where are we going?"

Jack snapped the reins. "You'll see."

They rolled through drifting fingers of mist, past buildings where candlelight was starting to appear in windows. Except for the distant barking of dogs, the only noise was the horse's hooves and the sound of their wheels, rumbling down the narrow street.

Billy glanced back at the wagon. "What's under the tarp, Mr. Burke?"

"Nothing."

"But there's somethin' there. I can see it."

"You want your ninepence, then shut up."

"All right." The boy was silent for about five seconds. "When do I get it?"

"After you help me move something."

"Like furniture?"

"Yeah." Jack spat onto the street. "Just like furniture."

They were almost to the Charles River now, rattling up North Allen Street. Daylight was gaining on them, but the fog still hung thick. As he neared his destination, it seemed to swirl ever closer, drifting in off the river to wrap them in its protective cloak. When at last they pulled to a stop, Jack could not see more than a few yards ahead of him, but he knew exactly where he was.

So did Billy. "Why are we at the hospital?"

"Wait here," Jack ordered the boy. He jumped off the dray, his boots landing hard on the stones.

"When do we move the furniture?"

"Gotta see if it's here first." Jack swung open the gate and walked into the hospital's rear courtyard. He needed to go only a few paces before he spotted what he'd been hoping to find: a coffin, with the lid newly nailed on. The name A. TATE had been scrawled on it. He lifted one end to test the weight, and confirmed that, yes, it was occupied and would soon be on its way. To potter's field, no doubt, judging by the rough pine.

He got to work prying up the lid. It did not take long, for there were only a few nails. No one cared if a pauper was properly secured in his coffin. He pulled off the lid, revealing the shrouded body within. Not so large, from the looks of it; even without Dim Billy, he could have dealt with this one.

He returned to the dray, where the boy was still waiting.

"Is it a chair? A table?" asked Billy.

"What're you babbling about?"

"The furniture."

Jack went around to the wagon and whisked off the tarp. "Help me move this."

Billy slithered off the buckboard and came around to the rear. "It's a log."

"You are so clever." Jack grabbed one end and dragged it from the wagon.

"Is it firewood?" asked Billy, grabbing the other end. "Don't it need to be split?"

"Just move it, eh?" They carried the log to the coffin and set it down. "Now help me lift this out," Jack ordered.

Billy took one look into the coffin and froze. "There's somebody in there."

"Come on, pick up that end."

"But it—it's someone *dead.*"

"You want your ninepence or not?"

Billy looked up at him, eyes enormous in the wan and skinny face. "I'm afraid o' dead people."

"They can't hurt you, idiot."

The boy backed away. "They come after you. The ghosts do."

"Ain't never seen a ghost."

The boy was still retreating, moving toward the gate.

"Billy. You get your arse back here."

Instead, the boy turned and fled from the courtyard, fading like a jerky marionette into the mist.

"Useless," grunted Jack. He took a breath, hauled up the shrouded body, and rolled it out of the coffin. It thudded onto the cobblestones.

Daylight was brightening fast. He had to work quickly, before anyone saw him. He heaved the log into the coffin, positioned the lid, and with a few swings of the hammer nailed it back into place. May you rest in peace, Mr. Log, he thought with a laugh. Then he dragged the corpse, still sewn into its shroud, across the courtyard to his wagon. There he paused, panting, to glance around at the street. He saw no one.

And no one sees me.

Moments later he was back on the dray, guiding his horse down North Allen Street. Glancing over his shoulder, he checked his tarp-covered cargo. He had not laid eyes on the corpse itself, but he didn't need to. Whether young or old, male or female, it was fresh, and that's all that mattered. This time, the fee needn't be shared with anyone, not even Dim Billy.

He'd just saved himself ninepence. That was worth a bit of extra effort.

Nine

ROSE AWAKENED to find Meggie sleeping beside her, and she heard the clucking and flapping of chickens, the rustle of straw. None of these sounds was familiar, and it took Rose a moment to remember where she was.

To remember that Aurnia was dead.

Grief seized her in its fist, squeezing so hard that for a moment she could not breathe. She stared up at the barn's rough-hewn beams, thinking: This is more pain than I can bear.

Something nearby beat a steady tattoo, and she turned to see a black dog staring at her, its wagging tail slapping against a bale of hay. It shook itself, sending straw and dust flying, then trotted over to lick her face, leaving a trail of slime on her cheek. Pushing it away, she sat up. The dog gave a bored whine and headed down the stairs. Peering over the edge of the hayloft, she saw it trot past a stabled horse, moving purposefully as though late for an appointment, and it disappeared through the open barn door. In the distance, a rooster crowed.

She looked around the loft and wondered where Billy had gone.

So this was where he sheltered. She saw hints of him here and there, amid the bales of hay and the rusting implements. A depression in the straw marked where he had slept last night. A chipped cup and saucer and trencher were set upon an overturned crate, like a place setting for a fine meal. She had to smile at his resourcefulness. Last night, Billy had disappeared for a short time and returned with a precious cup of milk, no doubt squeezed furtively from someone's cow or goat. Rose hadn't questioned his source as Meggie had sucked on the milk-soaked rag; she'd been grateful for anything with which to satisfy the baby's hunger.

But while the baby had been fed, Rose had eaten nothing since yesterday noon, and her stomach rumbled. She prowled through the hayloft, rooting in the straw until she found a hen's egg, still warm from that morning's laying. She cracked it open and tipped back her head. The raw egg slid down her throat, the yolk so slick and rich that her stomach instantly rebelled. She doubled over, nauseated, fighting to keep the egg down. It may be the only thing I eat today, she thought, and I will not waste it. At last her nausea eased, and as she raised her head, she spotted the little wooden box, tucked into a corner of the loft.

She lifted the hinged lid.

Inside were pretty pieces of glass, a seashell, and two whalebone buttons, treasures that Billy had collected as he roamed the streets of the West End. She'd noticed how his gaze was always fixed on the ground, his thin shoulders hunched over like an old man's, all to glean a penny here, a lost buckle there. Every day was a treasure hunt for Dim Billy, and a pretty button was enough to make him happy. For that he was a lucky boy, perhaps the luckiest in all of Boston, to be so easily pleased by a button. But you cannot eat buttons, and you cannot bury the dead and pay for it with worthless glass.

She shut the box and crossed to the window to peer out through smudged glass. In the yard below, chickens scratched in a garden that was little more than brown stalks and vines, withered in the cold.

Billy's treasure box suddenly reminded her of something she'd put in her pocket, something she'd completely forgotten until now. She pulled out the locket and chain and felt a sudden flash of grief at the sight of Aurnia's necklace. The locket was heart-shaped and the chain was feathery light, a delicate strand meant for a fine lady's neck. She remembered how it had gleamed around Aurnia's cream-white skin. How beautiful my sister was, she thought, and now she's merely food for worms.

This was gold. It would buy Aurnia a proper burial.

She heard voices and peeked out again through the window. A wagon filled with bales of hay had just rolled into the yard, and two men stood dickering over the price.

It was time to leave.

She scooped up the sleeping baby and made her way down the steps. Quietly, she slipped out the barn door.

By the time the two men finally agreed to the price of hay, Rose Connolly was already well away, shaking the straw from her skirt as she carried Meggie toward the West End.

A freezing mist clung to the ground of St. Augustine's cemetery, hiding the legs of the mourners who seemed to float, unattached to the earth, their torsos drifting only on fog. There are so many here today, thought Rose; but their sorrow was not for Aurnia. She watched the procession trail behind a small coffin that skimmed above the mist, and she could hear every sniffle, every sob, the sounds of heartbreak trapped and magnified, as though the air itself were weeping. The child's funeral moved past, black skirts and cloaks churning the mist into silvery whirlpools. No one glanced at Rose. Holding Meggie in her arms, she stood in a forlorn corner of the cemetery, beside the newly turned mound of earth. To them, she was but a ghost in the fog, her grief invisible to those blinded by their own.

"She's 'bout deep enough, miss."

Rose turned to look at the two gravediggers. The older one dragged a sleeve across his face, leaving streaks of mud on his cheek, where the skin was deeply seamed from years of exposure to sun and wind. Poor man, she thought, you're too old to still be wielding a shovel, to be hacking away at the frozen ground. But we all need to eat. And what would she be doing when she was his age, when she could no longer see well enough to thread her needle?

"Will there be no one else to see her laid to rest?" he asked.

"No one else," she said, and looked down at Aurnia's coffin. This was Rose's loss, hers alone, and she was too selfish to share it with anyone. She fought the sudden impulse to tear off the lid, to gaze once again on her sister's face. What if, by some miracle, she was not dead? What if Aurnia were to stir and open her eyes? Rose reached toward the coffin, then forced her hand back to her side. There are no miracles, she thought. And Aurnia is gone.

"Shall we finish, then?"

She swallowed her tears and gave a nod.

The old man turned to his partner, a blank-faced teenager who'd shoveled with lackadaisical effort, and who now stood slouched and indifferent. "Help me put her in."

Ropes creaked as they lowered the coffin, dislodging clots of dirt that thudded into the hole. I have paid for a grave all your own, darling, thought Rose. A private place of rest that you'll not need to share with some husband who paws you, some beggar who stinks. For once you'll sleep alone, a luxury that escaped you while you lived.

The coffin gave a jolt as it hit bottom. The boy had let his attention wander, and had played out the rope too quickly. Rose caught the look the old man gave the boy, a look that said, *I'll deal with you later*. The boy didn't even notice, and simply yanked his rope out of the hole. It came slithering up like a cobra, and the end slapped smartly against the pine box. Their task almost completed, the boy worked with more alacrity now as they filled the hole. Perhaps he was thinking of his lunch by a warm fire, and how all that kept him from it was this one grave. He had not seen the occupant of the coffin, nor did he seem to care. All that mattered was that this hole must be filled, and so he put his back into it, shovel after shovel full of soggy earth landing on the coffin.

At the other end of the cemetery, where the child was being laid to rest, a loud wail rose from the mourners, a woman's cry so ragged with pain that Rose turned and looked toward the other grave. Only then did she see the ghostly silhouette approaching them through the fog. The figure emerged from its veil of mist, and Rose recognized the face peering out from beneath the hood of the cape. It was Mary Robinson, the young nurse from the hospital. Mary paused and looked over her shoulder, as though sensing that someone was behind her, but Rose saw no one except the other mourners, who stood like a circle of statues around the child's grave.

"I didn't know where else to find you," said Mary. "I'm sorry for your sister. God rest her soul."

Rose wiped her eyes, smearing tears and mist across her cheek. "You were kind to her, Miss Robinson. Far kinder than . . ." She stopped, not wanting to invoke Nurse Poole's name. Not wanting to speak ill of the dead.

Mary moved closer. As Rose blinked away tears, she focused on the young nurse's tense face, her pinched eyes. Mary leaned in, and her voice dropped to a whisper, her words almost lost in the scrape of the gravediggers' shovels.

"There are people inquiring about the child."

Rose gave a weary sigh and looked down at her niece, who lay serene in her arms. Little Meggie had inherited Aurnia's sweet temperament, and she was content to lie quietly and study the world with her wide eyes. "I've given them my answer. She stays with her own people. With me."

"Rose, they're not from the infant asylum. I promised Miss Poole that I'd say nothing, but now I cannot remain silent. The night the baby was born, after you left the room, your sister told us . . ." Suddenly Mary fell still, her gaze riveted not on Rose, but on something in the distance.

"Miss Robinson?"

"Keep the child safe," Mary said. "Keep her hidden."

Rose turned to see what Mary was looking at, and when she saw Eben stride out of the fog, her throat went dry. Though her hands were shaking, she stood her ground, resolved not to be bullied. Not today, not here, beside her sister's grave. As he drew closer, she saw that he was carrying her satchel, the same bag she'd brought with her to Boston four months ago. Contemptuously, he threw it at her feet.

"I took the liberty of packing your belongings," he said. "Since you are no longer welcome at Mrs. O'Keefe's establishment."

She picked up the bag from the mud, her face flushing with outrage at the thought of Eben pawing through her clothes, her private possessions.

"And don't come begging for my charity," he added.

"Was that what you forced on me last night? Charity?"

Straightening, she met his gaze, and felt a thrill of satisfaction at the sight of his bruised lip. *Did I do that? Good for me.* Her cold retort clearly enraged him, and he took a step closer, then glanced at the two gravediggers still at work filling in the hole. He halted, his hand balled in a fist. Go ahead, she thought. Hit me, while I hold your daughter in my arms. Let the world see what kind of coward you are.

His lips peeled back, like an animal baring its teeth, and his words came out in a whisper, tight and dangerous. "You had no right to talk to the Night Watch. They came this morning, during breakfast. All the other lodgers are gossiping about it."

"I only told them the God's truth. What you did to me."

"As if anyone believes *you*. You know what I told Mr. Pratt? I told him what you really are. A little cock-tease. I told him how I took you in, fed you, housed you, just to please my wife. And this is how you repay my generosity!"

"Do you not even care that she's gone?" Rose looked down at the grave. "You didn't come here to say goodbye. 'Tis only to bully me, that's why you're here. While your own wife—"

"My own dear wife couldn't abide you, either."

Rose's gaze snapped up to his. "You're lying."

"Don't believe me?" He gave a snort. "You should have heard the things she whispered to me while you slept. What a burden you were, just a millstone she had to drag around, because she knew you'd starve without our charity."

"I worked for my keep! Every day, I did."

"As if I couldn't find a dozen other girls, cheaper girls, just as handy with a needle and thread? Go on, go out there, see what kind of position you land. See how long it takes before you're starving. You'll come back to me begging."

"For you?" It was Rose's turn to laugh, and she did, though hunger had clenched her stomach into a knot. She had hoped that Eben would awaken sober this morning, to feel at least a twinge of regret for what he'd done last night. That with Aurnia's death, he'd suddenly appreciate the treasure he'd lost, and would be a better man for his grief. But she'd been as foolishly trusting as Aurnia, to believe that he could ever rise above his petty pride. Last night, Rose had humiliated him, and in the light of day he stood stripped of all pretense. She saw no grief in his eyes, only wounded vanity, and now she took pleasure from slicing the wound even deeper.

"Yes, maybe I'll go hungry," she added. "But at least I look after my own. I see to my sister's burial. I'll raise her child. What kind of a man do you think people will call you when they hear you gave up your own daughter? That you didn't pay a penny to bury your own wife?"

His face flushed scarlet, and he glanced at the two diggers, who had finished their task and now stood listening, rapt with attention. Tight-lipped, he reached into his pocket and withdrew a handful of coins. "Here!" he snapped, and held them out to the diggers. "Take it!"

The older man glanced uneasily at Rose. "The lady here paid us already, sir."

"Goddamn it, take the bloody money!" Eben grabbed the man's dirt-stained hand and slapped the coins into his palm. Then he looked at Rose. "Consider my obligation fulfilled. And now you have something that belongs to *me*."

"You don't care a whit about Meggie. Why would you want her?"

"It's not the brat I want. It's the other things. Aurnia's things. I'm her husband, so by all rights her possessions come to me."

"There is nothing."

"The hospital told me they gave you her belongings last night."

"Is that all you want?" She removed the small bundle she'd tied around her waist and handed it to him. "It's yours, then."

He opened the bundle, and the soiled night frock and hair ribbon fell to the ground. "Where's the rest?"

"Her ring is there."

"This piece of tin?" He held up Aurnia's good-luck ring with the stones of colored glass. He snorted and tossed it at Rose's feet. "Worthless. You'll find one just like it on the finger of every cheap girl in Boston."

"She left her wedding ring at home. You know that."

"I'm talking about the necklace. A gold locket. Never told me how she got it, and all these months she refused to sell it, even though I could've used the money for the shop. For all that I've put up with, I deserve at least that much in return."

"You don't deserve one fine hair from her head."

"Where is it?"

"I pawned it. How do you think I paid for her burial?"

"It was worth far more than *this*," he retorted, pointing at the grave.

"It's gone, Eben. I paid for this grave, and you're not welcome here. You gave my sister no peace while she was alive. The least you can do is allow her to rest in peace now."

He glanced at the old gravedigger, who was glowering at him. Oh, Eben was quick to hit a woman when no one was looking, but now he had to struggle to keep his fists at his sides, his abusive tongue in check. All he said was, "You'll hear more about this later, Rose." Then he turned and walked away.

"Miss? Miss?"

Rose turned to the old digger, who met her gaze with a look of sympathy. "You already paid us. I expect you'll want this. It should keep you and the baby fed for a time."

She stared at the coins that he'd placed in her hand. And she thought: For a while, this will hold off our hunger. It will pay for a wet nurse.

The two laborers gathered up their tools and left Rose standing beside the fresh mound of Aurnia's grave. Once the dirt settles, she thought, I will buy you a stone marker. Perhaps I can save enough to engrave more than just your name, darling. A carving of an angel, or a few lines of a poem to tell the world how much emptier it is for having lost you.

She heard muffled sobs as the mourners from the other funeral now began to file out of the cemetery. She watched pallid faces swaddled in black wool float by in the mist. So many here to mourn the loss of a child. *Where are your mourners, Aurnia?*

Only then did she remember Mary Robinson. She glanced around, but did not see the nurse anywhere. The arrival of Eben, spoiling for a fight, must have driven her off. Yet another grudge Rose would always carry against him.

Drops of rain splashed her face. The other mourners, heads bent, filed from the cemetery toward waiting carriages and warm suppers. Only Rose lingered, clutching Meggie as rain muddied the earth.

"Sleep well, darling," she whispered.

She picked up her satchel and Aurnia's scattered belongings. Then she and Meggie left St. Augustine's and headed toward the slums of South Boston.

Ten

"MIDWIFERY IS the branch of medicine which treats of conception and its consequences. And today, you have heard some of those consequences. Many of them, alas, tragic . . ."

Even from the grand stairway outside the auditorium, Norris could hear the booming voice of Dr. Crouch, and he hastened up the steps, vexed that he had arrived so late for morning lectures. But last night he had once again spent in the gruff company of Wall-eyed Jack, an expedition that had taken them south to Quincy. The whole way, Jack had complained about his back, which was the only reason he had asked Norris to accompany him on this latest run. They had returned to Boston well after midnight, carting only one specimen in such poor shape that Dr. Sewall, upon peeling back the tarp, had grimaced at the smell. "This one has been in the ground for days," Sewall had complained. "Could you not use your noses? The stink alone should have told you!"

Norris could still smell that stink on his hair, his clothes. It did not ever leave you, but wormed its way like maggots under your skin, until every breath you inhaled was infused with it, and you could not tell living flesh from dead. He smelled it now as he climbed the stairs to the auditorium, like a walking corpse trailing its own scent of decay. He pulled open the door and quietly slipped into the lecture hall, where Dr. Crouch was now pacing the stage as he spoke.

". . . though a branch of medicine distinct from surgery and physic, the practice of midwifery requires knowledge of anatomy and physiology, pathology and . . ." Dr. Crouch paused, his gaze fixed on Norris, who had made it only a few paces down the aisle, in search of an empty seat. The sudden silence snagged the attention of everyone in the room more dramatically than any shout could have. The audience turned like a many-eyed beast and looked at Norris, who was pinned in place by all the stares.

"Mr. Marshall," said Crouch. "We're honored you've chosen to join us."

"I'm sorry, sir! I have no excuse."

"Indeed. Well, find a seat!"

Norris spotted an empty chair and quickly sat down, in the row just ahead of Wendell and his two friends.

On stage, Crouch cleared his throat and continued. "And so to conclude, gentlemen, I leave you with this thought: The physician is sometimes all that stands in the way of darkness. When we enter the gloomy chambers of sickness, we are there to do battle, to offer divine hope and courage to those pitiful souls whose very lives hang in the balance. So remember that sacred trust, which may soon be placed on your shoulders." Crouch planted his short legs on center stage, and his voice rang out like a call to war. "Be true to the calling! Be true to those who place their lives in your most worthy hands."

Crouch gazed up expectantly at his audience, which for a few seconds sat utterly silent. Then Edward Kingston rose to clap, loudly and conspicuously, a gesture that was not unnoticed by Crouch. Others quickly joined, until the whole hall echoed with applause.

"Well. I'd call that a Hamlet-worthy performance," said Wendell, his dry appraisal lost in the din of clapping hands. "When does he roll around on the floor and perform the death scene?"

"Hush, Wendell," cautioned Charles. "Do you want to get us all into trouble?"

Dr. Crouch left the stage and sat down in the front row with the other faculty members. Now Dr. Aldous Grenville, who was both dean of the medical college and Charles's uncle, stood to address the students. Though his hair was already silver, Dr. Grenville stood tall and unstooped, a striking figure who commanded the room with just one look.

"Thank you, Dr. Crouch, for a most illuminating and inspiring lecture on the art and science of midwifery. We move on to the final segment of today's program, an anatomical dissection presented by Dr. Erastus Sewall, our distinguished professor of surgery."

In the front row, portly Dr. Sewall rose heavily to his feet and strode onstage. There the two gentlemen heartily shook hands; Dr. Grenville once again sat down, granting Sewall the limelight.

"Before I proceed," said Sewall, "I wish to call on a volunteer. Perhaps a gentleman from among the first-year students would be bold enough to assist me as prosector?"

There was a silence as five rows of young men discreetly stared down at their own shoes.

"Come now, you must get your hands bloody if you're to understand the human machine. You've only just begun your medical studies, so you are strangers to the dissecting room. Today, I'll help you make the acquaintance of this marvelous mechanism, this intricate and noble fabric. If one of you will just be bold enough?"

"I will," said Edward, and he stood.

Professor Grenville said, "Mr. Edward Kingston has volunteered. Please join Dr. Sewall on the stage."

As Edward headed up the aisle, he shot a cocksure grin at his classmates. A look that said: *I'm no coward like the rest of you.*

"Where does he get his nerve?" Charles murmured.

"We will all get our turn up there," said Wendell.

"Look at how he drinks up the attention. I swear, I'd be trembling like a sinner."

Wheels rumbled across the wooden stage as a table was rolled out from the wings, propelled by an assistant. Dr. Sewall shed his coat and rolled up his sleeves as the assistant next brought out a small table with a tray of instruments. "Each one of you," he said, "will have a chance to wield the knife in the dissecting room. But even so, your exposure will be far too brief. With such a shortage of anatomical specimens, you must not let a single opportunity go to waste. Whenever a subject becomes available, I hope you will seize the chance to further your knowledge. Today, to our great good fortune, such an opportunity has presented itself." He paused to slip on an apron. "The art of dissection," he said as he tied it behind his waist, "is exactly that—an art. Today, I will show you how it should be done. Not like a knacker butchering a carcass, but like a sculptor, coaxing a work of art from a block of marble. That's what I intend to do today—not merely dissect a body, but reveal the beauty of every muscle and every organ, every nerve and blood vessel." He turned to the table where the body lay, still draped. "Let us reveal today's subject."

Norris felt anticipatory nausea as Dr. Sewall reached for the shroud. Already he had guessed who lay beneath it, and he dreaded the unveiling of the half-rotten corpse he and Wall-eyed Jack had unearthed last night. But when Sewall swept off the sheet, it was not the stinking man.

It was a female. And even from his seat in the auditorium, Norris recognized her.

Curly red hair cascaded over the edge of the table. Her head was turned slightly, so that she faced the audience with half-closed eyes and parted lips. The lecture hall had fallen so quiet that Norris could hear his own heartbeat pounding in his ears. *That corpse is Rose Connolly's sister. The sister she adored.* How in God's name had the girl's beloved sister ended up on the anatomist's table?

Dr. Sewall calmly picked up a knife from the tray and moved to the corpse's side. He seemed oblivious to the shocked silence that had fallen over the room, and when he regarded his subject, he might have been any tradesman, about to set to work. He looked at Edward, who stood frozen at the foot of the table. No doubt Edward, too, had recognized the body.

"I advise you to slip on an apron."

Edward did not seem to hear him.

"Mr. Kingston, unless you wish to soil that very fine coat you're wearing, I suggest you remove your jacket and put on an apron. Then come assist me."

Even arrogant Eddie, it appeared, had lost his nerve, and he swallowed hard as he donned the neck-to-ankle apron and rolled up his shirtsleeves.

Dr. Sewall made the first cut. It was a brutal slash, from breast-bone to pelvis. As the skin parted, the abdomen released its contents and loops of bowel spilled out, pouring forth from the open belly to hang in dripping streamers over the side of the table.

"The bucket," said Sewall. He looked up at Edward, who was staring down in horror at the gaping wound. "Will *somebody* position the bucket? Since my assistant here seems incapable of any purposeful movement whatsoever."

Uneasy laughter rippled through the audience at the spectacle of their overbearing classmate being so publicly yanked down a few notches. Flushing, Edward snatched up the wooden bucket from the instrument table and set it down on the floor, to catch the loops of dripping intestine as they slithered from the belly.

"Lying atop the bowel," said Dr. Sewall, "is a caul of tissue called the omentum. I have just sliced through it, releasing the intestines, which you now see cascading from the abdomen. In older gentle-men, especially those who have indulged too heartily in the pleasures of the table, this caul can be quite dense with fat. But in this young female subject, I find rather sparse deposits." He lifted the sheet of almost transparent omentum and held it up in bloodied hands for the audience to see. Then he leaned over the table and tossed the mass of tissue into the waiting bucket. It landed with a wet plop.

"Next, I shall clear away this bowel, which so thoroughly obstructs our view of the organs beneath. While any knacker who's butchered a cow or horse is well acquainted with the voluminous mass of intestine, new students attending their first dissection are frequently astonished when they encounter it for the first time. First I shall resect the small intestine, slicing it free at the level of the pyloric junction, where the stomach ends . . ."

He leaned in with his knife, and his hand came up holding one severed end of the bowel. He let it slither over the side of the table, and Edward caught it with his bare hand before it could splatter onto the floor. In disgust, he quickly dropped it into the bucket.

"Now I shall free it at the other end, where the small bowel becomes large bowel, at the ileocecal junction."

Again he reached in with his knife. He straightened, holding up the other severed end.

"To illustrate the marvels of the human digestive system, I should like my assistant to grasp that end of the small bowel and walk up the aisle, as far as he can go."

Edward hesitated, staring down in disgust at the bucket. Grimacing, he reached into the mass of entrails and came up holding the severed end.

"Go on, Mr. Kingston. Toward the back of the hall." Edward started up the center aisle, pulling his end of the bowel. Norris caught a foul whiff of offal and saw the student across the aisle clap his hand over his nose to mask the stench. And still Edward kept walking, dragging a coil of intestine behind him like a stinking rope until it finally lifted from the floor and stretched taut, dripping onto the floor.

"Behold the length," said Dr. Sewall. "We are looking at perhaps twenty feet of bowel. *Twenty feet*, gentlemen! And this is only the small intestine. I have left the large bowel in situ. Contained within the belly of every single one of you is this most marvelous of organs. Think of it as you sit there, digesting your breakfasts. No matter your station in life, rich or poor, old or young, within the cavity of your belly you are like every other man."

Or woman, thought Norris, his gaze not on the organ but on the gutted subject lying on the table. Even one so beautiful can be dissected down to a bucket of offal. Where was the soul in all this? Where was the woman who once inhabited that body?

"Mr. Kingston, you may come back to the stage, and the bowel can go back into the bucket. Next, we shall see what the heart and lungs look like, nestled within the chest." Dr. Sewall reached for an ugly-looking instrument and clamped its jaws around a rib. The sound of snapping bone echoed through the hall. He looked up at the audience. "You cannot get a good view of the thorax unless you look straight into the cavity. I believe it might be best if the first-year students rise from their seats and move closer for the rest of the dissection. Come, gather around the table."

Norris rose to his feet. He was closest to the aisle, so he was one of the first to reach the table. He stared down, not at the open thorax, but at the face of the woman whose innermost secrets were now being revealed to a room full of strangers. She was so lovely, he thought. Aurnia Tate had been in the full bloom of womanhood.

"If you'll gather 'round," said Dr. Sewall, "I should first like to point out an interesting finding in her pelvis. Based on the size of the uterus, which I can easily palpate right here, I would conclude that this subject has quite recently given birth. Despite the relative freshness of this corpse, you will note the particularly foul odor of the abdominal cavity, and the obvious inflammation of the peritoneum. Taking all these findings into account, I'm willing to offer a conjecture as to the likely cause of her death."

There was a loud thud in the aisle. One of the students said, alarmed: "Is he breathing? Check if he's breathing!"

Dr. Sewall called out: "What is the problem?"

"It's Dr. Grenville's nephew, sir!" said Wendell. "Charles has fainted!"

In the front row, Professor Grenville rose to his feet, looking stunned at the news. Quickly he made his way up the aisle toward Charles, pushing through the students crowded in the aisle.

"He's all right, sir," Wendell announced. "Charles is coming around now."

On stage, Dr. Sewall sighed. "A weak stomach is not a recommendation for someone who wishes to study medicine."

Grenville knelt at his nephew's side and patted Charles on the face. "Come come, boy. You've just gone a bit light-headed. It hasn't been an easy morning."

Groaning, Charles sat up and clutched his head. "I feel sick."

"I'll take him outside, sir," said Wendell. "He could probably use the fresh air."

"Thank you, Mr. Holmes," said Grenville. As he stood up, he himself looked none too steady.

We are all unnerved, even the most seasoned among us.

With Wendell's help, Charles rose shakily to his feet and was helped up the aisle. Norris heard one of the students snicker, "It would have to be Charlie, of course. Leave it to him to faint!"

But it could have happened to any one of us, thought Norris, looking around the auditorium at the ashen faces. What normal human being could watch this morning's butchery and not be appalled?

And it was not yet over.

On stage, Dr. Sewall once again picked up his knife and coolly eyed his audience. "Gentlemen. Shall we continue?"

Eleven

The present

JULIA DROVE NORTH, fleeing the heat of the Boston summer, and joined the weekend stream of cars headed north into Maine. By the time she reached the New Hampshire border, the temperature outside had fallen ten degrees. Half an hour later, as she crossed into Maine, the air was starting to feel chilly. Soon her views of forest and rocky coastline vanished behind a bank of fog, and from there northward the world turned gray, the road curving through a ghostly landscape of veiled trees and barely glimpsed farmhouses.

When she finally arrived at the beach town of Lincolnville that afternoon, the fog was so dense she could barely make out the massive outline of the Islesboro ferry docked at the pier. Henry Page had warned her that there'd be limited space aboard for vehicles, so she left her car parked in the terminal lot, grabbed her overnight bag, and walked onto the vessel.

If there was any view to be seen out the ferry window that day, she caught no glimpse of it during the crossing to Islesboro.

She walked off the boat into a disorientingly gray world. Henry Page's house was just a mile's walk from the island's terminal—"A nice stroll on a summer's day," he'd said. But in thick fog, a mile can seem like forever. She stayed well to the side of the road to avoid being hit by passing cars, and clambered off into the weeds whenever she heard an approaching vehicle. So this is summertime in Maine, she thought, shivering in her shorts and sandals. Though she could hear birds chirping, she couldn't see them. All she could see was the pavement beneath her feet and the weeds at the side of the road.

A mailbox suddenly appeared in front of her. It was thoroughly rusted, affixed to a crooked post. Staring closely, she could just make out the faded word on the side: STONEHURST.

Henry Page's house.

The one-lane dirt driveway climbed steadily through dense woods, where bushes and low branches reached out like claws to scrape at any passing vehicle. The farther she climbed, the more uneasy she felt about being stranded on this lonely road, on this fog-choked island. The house appeared so suddenly that she halted, startled, as if she'd just encountered a beast looming in the mist. It was made of stone and old wood that, over the years, had turned silvery in the salt air. Though she could not see the ocean, she knew it was nearby because she could hear waves slapping against rocks and seagulls crying as they wheeled overhead.

She climbed the worn granite steps to the porch and knocked. Mr. Page had told her he would be home, but no one came to the door. She was cold, she'd brought no coat, and she had nowhere to go except back to the ferry terminal. In frustration, she left her bag on the porch and walked around to the back of the house. Since Henry wasn't home, she might as well take a look at his view—if there was one to see today.

She followed a stone path to a back garden, overgrown with shrubs and scraggly grass. Though the grounds were clearly in need of a gardener's attention, she could tell this once must have been a showplace, judging by the elaborate stonework. She saw mossy steps leading downward into the mist, and low stone walls enclosing a series of terraced flower beds. Enticed by the sound of waves, she headed down the steps, past clumps of thyme and catmint. The sea had to be close now, and she expected at any second to catch a glimpse of the beach.

She stepped down, and her heel met empty air.

With a gasp, she scrabbled backward and her rear end landed hard on the stairs. For a moment she sat staring down through shifting curtains of fog to the rocks a good twenty feet below. Only now did she notice the eroded soil on either side of her, and the exposed roots of a tree that was barely clinging to the crumbling cliffside. Gazing down at the sea, she thought: I'd survive the drop, but it wouldn't take long to drown in that frigid water.

On unsteady legs she climbed back toward the house, fearful the whole way that the cliff would suddenly collapse, dragging her down with it. She was almost to the top when she saw the man waiting for her.

He stood with stooped shoulders, his gnarled hand gripping a cane. Henry Page had sounded old over the telephone, and this man looked ancient, his hair as white as the mist, his eyes squinting through wire-rimmed spectacles.

"The steps are unsafe," he said. "Every year, another one drops off the cliff. It's unstable soil."

"So I found out," she said, panting from her quick climb up the stairs.

"I'm Henry Page. You're Miss Hamill, I presume."

"I hope it's okay that I took a look around. Since you weren't home."

"I've been home the whole time."

"No one answered the door."

"You think I can just sprint down the stairs? I'm eighty-nine years old. Next time, try a little patience." He turned and crossed the stone terrace toward a set of French doors. "Come in. I already have a nice sauvignon blanc chilling. Although this cool weather might call for a red, not a white."

She followed him into the house. As she stepped through the French doors, she thought, This place looks as ancient as he is. It smelled of dust and old carpets.

And books. In that room facing the sea, thousands of old books were crammed in floor-to-ceiling shelves. An enormous stone fireplace took up one wall. Though the room was huge, with the fog pressing in against the sea windows, the space felt dark and claustrophobic. It did not help that there were a dozen boxes stacked up in the center of the room beside a massive oak dining table.

"These are a few of Hilda's boxes," he said.

"A few?"

"There are two dozen more down in the cellar, and I haven't touched those yet. Maybe you could carry them upstairs for me, since I can't quite manage with this cane. I'd ask my grandnephew to do it, but he's always so busy."

And I'm not?

He thumped over to the dining table, where the contents of one of the boxes were spread out across the battered tabletop. "As you can see, Hilda was a pack rat. Never threw away anything. When you live as long as she did, it means you end up with a lot of *stuff*. But this stuff, it turns out, is quite interesting. It's completely disorganized. The moving company I hired just threw things willy-nilly into boxes. These old newspapers here have dates anywhere from 1840 to 1910. No order to them whatsoever. I'll bet there are even older ones somewhere, but we'll have to open all the boxes to find them. It could take us weeks to go through them all."

Staring down at a January 10, 1840, issue of the *Boston Daily Advertiser*, Julia suddenly registered the fact he'd used the word *us*. She looked up. "I'm sorry, Mr. Page, but I wasn't planning to stay very long. Could you just show me what you've found concerning my house?"

"Oh, yes. Hilda's house." To her surprise, he walked away from her, his cane thudding across the wood floor. "Built in 1880," he yelled back as he headed into another room. "For an ancestor of mine named Margaret Tate Page."

Julia followed Henry into a kitchen that looked as if it had not been updated since the 1950s. The cabinets were streaked with grime, and the stove was splattered with old grease and what looked like dried spaghetti sauce. He rummaged around in the refrigerator and pulled out a bottle of white wine.

"The house was passed down through succeeding generations. Pack rats all of us, just like Hilda," he said, twisting a corkscrew into the bottle. "Which is why we're left with this treasure trove of documents. The house stayed in our family all these years." The cork popped out of the bottle and he looked at her. "Until you."

"The bones in my garden were probably buried before 1880," she said. "That's what the university anthropologist told me. The grave is older than the house."

"Could be, could be." He pulled down two wineglasses from the cabinet.

"What you've found in these boxes isn't going to tell us anything about the bones." *And I'm wasting my time here.*

"How can you say that? You haven't even looked at the papers yet." He filled the glasses and held one out to her.

"Isn't it a little early in the day to be drinking?" she asked.

"Early?" He snorted. "I'm eighty-nine years old and I have four hundred bottles of excellent wine in my cellar, all of which I intend to finish. I'm more worried that it's too *late* to start drinking. So please, join me. A bottle always tastes better when it's shared."

She took the glass.

"Now what were we talking about?" he asked.

"The woman's grave is older than the house."

"Oh." He picked up his own glass and shuffled back into the library. "It very well could be."

"So I don't see how what's in these boxes could tell me her identity."

He rifled through the papers on the dining table and plucked out one of them, which he set in front of her. "Here, Ms. Hamill. Here is the clue."

She looked down at the handwritten letter, dated March 20, 1888.

Dearest Margaret,

I thank you for your kind condolences, so sincerely offered, for the loss of my darling Amelia. This has been a most difficult winter for me, as every month seems to bring the passing of yet another old friend to illness and age. Now it is with deepest gloom that I must consider the rapidly evaporating years left to me.

I realize that this is perhaps my last chance to broach a difficult subject which I should have raised long ago. I have been reluctant to speak of this, as I know that your aunt felt it wisest to keep this from you . . ."

Julia looked up. "This was written in 1888. That's well after the bones were buried."

"Keep reading," he said. And she did, until the final paragraph.

For now, I enclose the news clipping, which I earlier mentioned. If you have no desire to learn more, please tell me, and I will never again mention this. But if indeed the subject of your parents holds any interest for you, then at my next opportunity, I will once again pick up my pen. And you will learn the story, the true story, of your aunt and the West End Reaper.

With fondest regards,
O.W.H.

"Do you realize who O.W.H. is?" asked Henry. His eyes, magnified by the lenses of his spectacles, gleamed with excitement.

"You told me over the phone it was Oliver Wendell Holmes."

"And you *do* know who he was?"

"He was a judge, wasn't he? A Supreme Court justice."

Henry gave a sigh of exasperation. "No, that's Oliver Wendell Holmes *Junior*, the son! This letter is from Wendell *Senior*. You must have heard of *him*."

Julia frowned. "He was a writer, wasn't he?"

"That's *all* you know about him?"

"I'm sorry. I'm not exactly a history teacher."

"You're a teacher? Of what?"

"The third grade."

"Even a third-grade teacher should know that Oliver Wendell Holmes Senior was more than just a literary figure. Yes, he was a poet and a novelist and a biographer. He was also a lecturer, a philosopher, and one of the most influential voices in Boston. And he was one more thing. In the scheme of his contributions to mankind, it was the most important thing of all."

"What was that?"

"He was a physician. One of the finest of his age."

She looked at the letter with more interest. "So this is historically significant."

"And the Margaret whom he addresses in the letter—that's my great-great-grandmother, Dr. Margaret Tate Page, born in 1830. She was one of the first women physicians in Boston. That's *her* house you now own. In 1880, when her house was built, she would have been fifty years old."

"Who is this aunt he speaks of in the letter?"

"I have no idea. I know nothing at all about her."

"Are there other letters from Holmes?"

"I'm hoping we'll find them here." He glanced at the dozen boxes stacked beside the dining table. "I've only searched these six so far. Nothing's organized, nothing's in order. But here is the history of your house, Ms. Hamill. *This* is what's left of the people who lived there."

"He said that he enclosed a clipping. Did you find it?"

Henry reached for a scrap of newspaper. "I believe this is what he referred to."

The clipping was so brown with age that she had trouble reading the tiny print in the gray light of the window. Only when Henry turned on a lamp was she able to make out the words.

It was dated November 28, 1830.

WEST END MURDER DESCRIBED AS "SHOCKING AND GROTESQUE"

At 10 PM Wednesday, officers of the Night Watch were called to Massachusetts General Hospital after the body of Miss Agnes Poole, a nurse, was discovered dead in a large puddle of blood on the back steps of the hospital. Her injuries, according to Officer Pratt of the Watch, left no doubt that this was an attack of the most brutal nature, most likely inflicted with a large cutting instrument such as a butcher knife. The lone witness remains unidentified to this reporter, out of concern for her safety, but Mr. Pratt confirms that it is a young woman, who described the assailant as "cloaked in black like the Grim Reaper, with the wings of a bird of prey."

"This murder took place in Boston," said Julia.

"A mere half-day carriage ride from your house in Weston. And the murder victim was a woman."

"I see no connection to my house."

"Oliver Wendell Holmes may be the connection. He writes to Margaret, who's living in your house. He makes this puzzling reference to her aunt, and to a killer known as the West End Reaper. Somehow, Holmes became involved in this murder case—a case he felt compelled to tell Margaret about over fifty years later. Why? What was this mysterious secret she was never supposed to know?"

The distant bellow of a ship's horn made Julia look up. "I wish I didn't have to catch the ferry. I'd really love to learn the answer."

"Then don't leave. Why not spend the night? I saw your overnight bag by the front door."

"I didn't want to leave it in my car, so I brought it over with me. I was planning to check into a motel in Lincolnville."

"But you can see all the work we have to do here! I have a perfectly nice guest room upstairs, with quite a spectacular view."

She glanced at the window, at fog that had grown even thicker, and wondered what view he was talking about.

"But perhaps it's not really worth your trouble. It seems I'm the only one who cares about history anymore. I just thought you might feel the same way, since you *touched* her bones." He sighed. "Oh, well. What does it matter? Someday, we'll all be just like her. Dead and forgotten." He turned. "The last ferry leaves at four thirty. You'd better head back to the landing now, if you want to catch it."

She didn't move. She was still thinking about what he'd said. About forgotten women.

"Mr. Page?" she said.

He looked back, a bent little gnome of a man clutching his knobby cane.

"I think I will spend the night."

For a man his age, Henry could certainly hold his drink. By the time they'd finished dinner, they were well into a second bottle of wine, and Julia was having trouble focusing. Night had fallen, and in the glow of lamplight everything in the room had blurred to a warm haze. They had eaten their meal at the same table where the papers were spread out, and alongside the remains of roast chicken was a stack of old letters and newspapers she had yet to examine. She could not possibly read them tonight, not the way her head was spinning.

Henry didn't appear to be slowing down at all. He refilled his glass and sipped as he reached for another document, one of an endless collection of handwritten correspondence addressed to Margaret Tate Page. There were letters from beloved children and grandchildren and medical colleagues from around the world. How could Henry still focus on the faded ink after all those glasses of wine? Eighty-nine years old sounded ancient, yet Henry was out-drinking her, and certainly outlasting her through this evening's reading marathon.

He glanced at her over the rim of his glass. "You've given up already?"

"I'm exhausted. And a little tipsy, I think."

"It's only ten o'clock."

"I don't have your stamina." She watched as he brought the letter right up to his spectacles, squinting to read the faded writing. She said, "Tell me about your cousin Hilda."

"She was a schoolteacher, like you." He flipped over the letter. Added, absently: "Never got around to having any children of her own."

"Neither did I."

"Don't you like children?"

"I love them."

"Hilda didn't."

Julia sank back in the chair, looking at the stack of boxes, the only legacy that Hilda Chamblett had left behind. "So that's why she was living alone. She didn't have anyone."

Henry glanced up. "Why do you think I live alone? Because I want to, that's why! I want to stay in my own house, not some nursing home." He reached for his glass. "Hilda was like that, too."

Stubborn? Irascible?

"She died where she wanted to," he said. "At home, in her garden."

"I just find it sad that she was lying there for days before anyone found her."

"No doubt, so will I. My grandnephew will probably find my old carcass sitting right here in this chair."

"That's a horrible thought, Henry."

"It's a consequence of liking one's privacy. You live alone, so you must know what I mean."

She stared at her glass. "It isn't my choice," she said. "My husband left me."

"Why? You seem like a pleasant enough young woman."

Pleasant enough. Right, that would bring the men running. His remark was so unintentionally insulting that she laughed. But somewhere in the middle of that laugh, the tears started. She rocked forward and dropped her head in her hands, struggling to get her emotions under control. Why was this happening now, why here, in front of this man she scarcely knew? For months after Richard left, she hadn't cried at all, and had impressed everyone with her stoicism. Now she could not seem to hold back the tears, and she fought them so hard her body was shuddering. Henry didn't say a word and made no attempt to comfort her. He simply studied her, the way he'd studied those old newspapers, as if this outburst was something new and curious.

She wiped her face and abruptly stood. "I'll clean up," she said. "And then I think I'll go to bed." She swept up the dinner plates and turned toward the kitchen.

"Julia," he said. "What's his name? Your husband."

"Richard. And he's my ex-husband."

"Do you still love him?"

"No," she said softly.

"Then why the hell are you crying over him?"

Leave it to Henry to so logically cut straight to the heart of the matter. "Because I'm an idiot," she said.

Somewhere in the house, a phone was ringing.

Julia heard Henry shuffle past her bedroom door, his cane thunking as he walked. Whoever was calling knew that he required extra time to reach the phone, because it rang more than a dozen times before he finally picked it up. Faintly she heard his answering "Hello?" Then, a few seconds later, "Yes, she's here right now. We've been going through the boxes. To be honest, I haven't decided yet."

Decided what? Who was he talking to?

She strained to make out his next words, but his voice had

dropped, and all she could hear was an indistinct murmur. After a moment his voice fell silent, and she heard only the sea outside her window, and the creaks and groans of the old house.

The next morning, by the light of day, the call did not seem at all disconcerting.

She rolled out of bed, pulled on jeans and a fresh T-shirt, and went to the window. She saw no view today, either. If anything, the fog looked even thicker, pressed so densely against the glass that she thought, if she poked her hand outside, it would sink into something that felt like gray cotton candy. I drove all the way up to Maine, she thought, and I never even saw the sea.

There was a sharp rap on her door, and she turned, startled.

"Julia!" Henry called. "Are you awake yet?"

"I'm just getting up."

"You must come downstairs at once."

The urgency in his voice made her immediately cross the room and open the door.

He was standing in the hall, his face alight with excitement. "I've found another letter."

Twelve

1830

A HAZE OF CIGAR SMOKE hung like a filmy curtain over the dissection room, the welcome odor of tobacco masking the stench of the cadavers. On the table where Norris worked, a corpse lay with its chest split open, and the resected heart and lungs rested in a foul-smelling mound in the bucket. Even the frigid room could not slow the inevitable process of decomposition, which had already been well under way by the time the corpses had arrived from the state of New York. Two days ago, Norris had watched the delivery of the fourteen barrels, sloshing with brine.

"New York is where we have to get them now, I've heard," Wendell commented as their four-student team hacked their way into the abdomen, bare hands diving into the ice-cold mass of intestines.

"There aren't enough paupers dying here in Boston," said Edward. "We coddle them and they stay too damn healthy. Then when they do die, you can't get at them. In New York, they just scoop the bodies out of potter's field, no questions asked."

"That can't be true," said Charles.

"They keep two different burial pits. Pit two is for the discards, the corpses no one's likely to claim." Edward looked down at their cadaver, whose grizzled face bore the seams and scars of many hard years. The left arm, once broken, had healed crooked. "I'd say this one was definitely from pit two. Some old Paddy, don't you think?"

Their instructor, Dr. Sewall, paced through the dissecting room, past tables of cadavers where young men worked four to a corpse. "I want you to complete the removal of all the internal organs today," he instructed. "They spoil quickly. Leave them too long, and even those of you who believe you possess strong stomachs will soon find the stench unbearable. Smoke all the cigars you wish, drown yourselves in whiskey, but I guarantee that a whiff of intestine left to decompose for a week will bring low even the hardiest among you."

And the weakest among us is already in trouble, thought Norris as he glanced across the table at Charles, whose pale face was wreathed in smoke while he frantically puffed on his cigar.

"You have seen the organs in situ, and witnessed for yourself some of the hidden gears of this miraculous machinery," said Sewall. "In this room, gentlemen, we illuminate the mystery of life. As you take apart God's masterpiece, examine the workmanship, observe the parts in their proper places. Witness how each is vital to the whole." Sewall paused at Norris's table and examined the organs lying in the bucket, lifting them out with bare hands. "Which one of you resected the heart and lungs?" he asked.

"I did, sir," Norris said.

"Fine job. Finest I've seen in the room." Sewall looked at him. "You've done this before, I take it."

"On the farm, sir."

"Sheep?"

"And pigs."

"I can tell you've wielded a knife." Sewall looked at Charles. "Your hands are still clean, Mr. Lackaway."

"I—I thought I'd give the others a chance to start."

"Start? They are already finished with the thorax and are into the abdomen." He looked down at the corpse and grimaced. "By the smell of this one, it's going bad fast. It'll rot before you even pick up your knife, Mr. Lackaway. What are you waiting for? Get your hands dirty."

"Yes, sir."

As Dr. Sewall walked out of the room, Charles reluctantly reached for the knife. Staring down at their prematurely rotting Paddy, he hesitated, his blade poised over the bowel. As he gathered his nerve, a chunk of lung suddenly flew across the table and smacked him in the chest. He gave a yelp and jumped back, frantically brushing away the bloody mass.

Edward laughed. "You heard Dr. Sewall. Get those hands dirty!"

"For pity's sake, Edward!"

"You should see your face, Charlie. You'd think I'd thrown a scorpion at you."

Now that Dr. Sewall was out of the room, the students turned boisterous. A flask of whiskey began making its rounds. The team at the next table propped up their corpse and shoved a lit cigar in its mouth. Smoke curled past sightless eyes.

"This is disgusting," said Charles. "I can't do this." He set down the blade. "I never *wanted* to be a doctor!"

"When do you plan to tell your uncle?" said Edward.

Fresh laughter exploded at the other end of the room, where a student's hat had found its way onto a dead woman's head. But Charles's gaze remained on Paddy, whose deformed left arm and crooked spine were mute testimony to a life of pain.

"Come on, Charlie," encouraged Wendell, and he held out a knife to him. "It's not so bad once you get started. Let's not allow this poor Paddy to go to waste. He has so much to teach us."

"You would say that, Wendell. You love this sort of thing."

"We've already peeled away the omentum. You can resect the small bowel."

As Charles stared at the offered knife, someone jeered from across the room: "Charlie! Don't faint on us again!"

Flushing a bright red, Charles took the knife. Grim-faced, he began to cut. But this was no skillful resection; these were savage slashes, his blade mangling the bowel, releasing a stench so awful that Norris lurched backward, lifting his arm to his face to stifle the smell.

"Stop," said Wendell. He grabbed Charles's arm, but his friend kept hacking away. "You're making a mess of it!"

"You told me to cut! You told me to get my hands bloody! That's what my uncle keeps telling me, that a doctor is worthless unless he's willing to gets his hands bloody!"

"We're not your uncle," said Wendell. "We're your friends. Now *stop.*"

Charles threw down the knife. Its thud was lost in the high-spirited bedlam of young men let loose upon a task so gruesome, the only sane response was perverse frivolity.

Norris picked up the knife and asked, quietly: "Are you all right, Charles?"

"I'm fine." Charles released a deep breath. "I'm perfectly fine."

A student stationed at the door suddenly hissed out a warning: "Sewall's coming back!"

Instantly the room fell quiet. Hats came off corpses. Cadavers resumed their positions of dignified repose. When Dr. Sewall walked back into the room, he saw only diligent students and serious faces. He crossed straight to Norris's table and came to a halt, staring at the slashed intestines.

"What the devil is *this* mess?" Appalled, he looked at the four students. "Who is responsible for this butchery?"

Charles appeared to be on the verge of tears. For Charles, every day seemed to bring some fresh humiliation, some new chance to reveal his incompetence. Under Sewall's gaze, he now seemed dangerously close to shattering.

Edward said, too eagerly: "Mr. Lackaway was trying to resect the small bowel, sir, and—"

"It's my fault," Norris cut in.

Sewall looked at him in disbelief. "Mr. Marshall?"

"It was—it was a bit of horseplay. Charles and I—well, it got out of hand, and we sincerely apologize. Don't we, Charles?"

Sewall regarded Norris for a moment. "In light of your obvious skill as a dissector, this poor conduct is doubly disappointing. Do not let it happen again."

"It won't, sir."

"I'm told that Dr. Grenville wishes to see you, Mr. Marshall. He waits in his office."

"Now? On what matter?"

"I suggest you find out. Well, go." Sewall turned to the class. "As for the rest of you, there will be no more tomfoolery. Proceed, gentlemen!"

Norris wiped his hands on his apron and said to his companions, "I'll have to leave you three to finish old Paddy."

"What's this about you and Dr. Grenville?" asked Wendell.

"I have no idea," said Norris.

"Professor Grenville?"

The dean of the medical college looked up from his desk. Backlit by the gloomy daylight through the window behind him, his silhouette resembled a lion's head, with its mane of wiry gray hair. As Norris paused on the threshold, he felt Aldous Grenville studying him, and he wondered what blunder on his part could have precipitated this summons. During his long walk down the hallway, he had searched his memory for some incident that might have called his name to Dr. Grenville's attention. Surely there'd been something, since Norris could think of no reason why the man would even notice, among the several dozen new students, a mere farmer's son from Belmont.

"Do come in, Mr. Marshall. And please close the door."

Uneasy, Norris took a seat. Grenville lit a lamp and the flame caught, casting its warm glow across the gleaming desk, the cherry bookshelves. The silhouette transformed to an arresting face with bushy side-whiskers. Though his hair was as thick as a young man's, it had gone silver, lending distinguished authority to his already striking features. He sank back into his chair, and his dark eyes were two strange orbs, reflecting the lamplight.

"You were there, at the hospital," said Grenville. "The night Agnes Poole died."

Norris was taken aback by the abrupt introduction of this grim subject, and he could only nod. The murder had been six days ago, and since then there had been wild gossip in town about who—or what—could have killed her. The *Daily Advertiser* had described a winged demon. Whispers about papists had been inevitable, no doubt launched from the lips of Watchman Pratt. But there had been other rumors as well. A preacher in Salem had spoken of evil afoot, of foul creatures and devil-worshiping foreigners who could only be combated by the righteous hand of God. Last night, the outrageous tales had inspired a drunken mob to chase a hapless Italian man down Hanover Street, forcing him to seek refuge in a tavern.

"You were the first to find the witness. The Irish girl," said Grenville.

"Yes."

"Have you seen her since that night?"

"No, sir."

"You are aware that the Night Watch is looking for her?"

"Mr. Pratt told me. I know nothing about Miss Connolly."

"Mr. Pratt led me to believe otherwise."

So this was why he'd been called here. The Night Watch wanted Grenville to press him for information.

"The girl hasn't been seen at her lodging house since that night," said Grenville.

"Surely she has family in Boston."

"Only her sister's husband, a tailor named Mr. Tate. He told the Night Watch that she was unstable, and prone to outrageous claims. She'd even accused *him* of base acts against her."

Norris remembered how Rose Connolly had dared to question the opinion of the eminent Dr. Crouch, an astonishingly bold act by a girl who should have known her place. But unstable? No, what Norris had seen on the ward that afternoon was a girl who'd merely stood her ground, a girl protecting her dying sister.

"I saw nothing unsound about her," he said.

"She made some rather startling claims. About that creature in the cape."

"She called it a *figure*, sir. She never said that it was in any way supernatural. It was the *Daily Advertiser* that called it the West End Reaper. She may have been frightened, but she was not hysterical."

"You can't tell Mr. Pratt where she might be?"

"Why does he think I can?"

"He suggested that you might be better acquainted with her . . . people."

"I see." Norris felt his face tighten. *So they think that a farm boy in a suit is still just a farm boy.* "May I ask why it's suddenly so urgent that he find her?"

"She's a witness, and she's only seventeen years old. There's her safety to consider. And the safety of her sister's child."

"I hardly imagine that Mr. Pratt cares one whit about their welfare. Is there another reason he seeks her?"

Grenville paused. After a moment, he admitted, "There is a matter, which Mr. Pratt would prefer not to see in the press."

"Which matter?"

"Concerning an item of jewelry. A locket that was briefly in the possession of Miss Connolly, before it found its way to a pawnshop."

"What's the significance of this locket?"

"It did not belong to her. By all rights, it should have gone to her sister's husband."

"You are saying that Miss Connolly is a thief?"

"I'm not saying it. Mr. Pratt is."

Norris thought about the girl and her fierce loyalty toward her sister. "I cannot imagine her to be such a criminal."

"How did she strike you?"

"A clever girl. And forthright. But not a thief."

Grenville nodded. "I'll pass along that opinion to Mr. Pratt."

Norris, believing the interview to be over, started to rise, but Grenville said, "A moment more, Mr. Marshall. Unless you have another engagement?"

"No, sir." Norris settled back into the chair. Sat, uncomfortably, as the other man quietly regarded him.

"You are satisfied thus far with your course of study?" asked Grenville.

"Yes, sir. Quite."

"And with Dr. Crouch?"

"He's an excellent preceptor. I'm grateful he took me on. I've learned a great deal about midwifery at his side."

"Although I understand you have strong opinions of your own on the subject."

Suddenly Norris was uneasy. Had Dr. Crouch complained about him? Was he now to face the consequences? "I did not mean to question his methods," he said. "I only wished to contribute—"

"Shouldn't methods be questioned if they do not work?"

"I should not have challenged him. I certainly don't have Dr. Crouch's experience."

"No. You have a farmer's experience." Norris flushed, and Grenville added, "You think I have just insulted you."

"I don't presume to know your intentions."

"I meant no insult. I've known many a clever farm boy. And more than a few idiot gentlemen. What I meant by my comment regarding farmers is that you've had practical experience. You've observed the process of gestation and birth."

"But as Dr. Crouch quite plainly pointed out to me, a cow cannot be compared to a human being."

"Of course not. Cows are far more companionable. Your father must agree, or he would not hide himself away on that farm."

Norris paused, startled. "You are acquainted with my father?"

"No, but I know of him. He must be proud of you, pursuing such a demanding course of study."

"No, sir. He's unhappy with my choice."

"How can that be?"

"He had thought to raise a farmer. He considers books a waste of time. I would not even be here, at the medical college, were it not for the generosity of Dr. Hallowell."

"Dr. Hallowell in Belmont? The gentleman who wrote your letter of recommendation?"

"Yes, sir. Truly, there's no kinder man. He and his wife always made me feel welcome in their home. He personally tutored me in physics and encouraged me to borrow books from his own library. Every month, it seemed, there'd be new ones, and he gave me complete access. Novels. Greek and Roman history. Volumes by Dryden and Pope and Spenser. It's an extraordinary collection."

Grenville smiled. "And you made good use of it."

"Books were my salvation," said Norris, and was suddenly embarrassed that he'd used a word so revealing. But salvation was precisely what books had meant to him during the bleak nights on the farm, nights when he and his father had little to say to each other. When they did speak, it was about whether the hay was still too wet, or how close the cows were to calving. They did not speak of what tormented them both.

And they never would.

"It's a pity that your father did not encourage you," said Grenville. "Yet you've come so far with such little advantage."

"I've found . . . employment here, in the city." Disgusting though his work with Jack Burke might be. "It's enough to pay for tuition."

"Your father contributes nothing?"

"He has little to send."

"I hope he was more generous with Sophia. She deserved better."

Norris was startled by the mention of that name. "You know my mother."

"While my wife Abigail was still alive, she and Sophia were the dearest of friends. But that was years ago, before you were born." He paused. "It was a surprise to us both when Sophia suddenly married."

And the biggest surprise of all, thought Norris, must have been her choice of a husband, a farmer with little education. Though Isaac Marshall was a handsome man, he had no interest in the music and books that Sophia so treasured, no interest in anything but his crops and his livestock. Norris said, hesitantly, "You do know that my mother is no longer living in Belmont?"

"I'd heard she was in Paris. Is she still there?"

"As far as I know."

"You don't know?"

"She hasn't corresponded. Life on the farm was not easy for her, I think. And she . . ." Norris stopped, and the memory of his mother's departure was like a fist suddenly closing around his chest. She'd left on a Saturday, a day he scarcely remembered, because he'd been so ill. And weeks later, he was still weak and wobbly on his feet when he'd come down to the kitchen to find his father, Isaac, standing at the window, staring out at the mist of summer. His father had turned to face him, his expression as distant as a stranger's.

"Your mother just wrote. She won't be coming back," was all Isaac had said before walking out of the house and heading straight to the barn to do the milking. Why would any woman choose to stay with a husband whose only passions were the ache of hard work and the sight of a well-plowed field? It was Isaac she had fled, Isaac who had driven Sophia away.

But as time went by without other letters, Norris had come to accept a truth that no eleven-year-old boy should have to face: that his mother had also fled from him, abandoning her son to a father who lavished more affection on his cows than on his own flesh and blood.

Norris took a breath, and as he exhaled, he imagined his pain being released as well. But it was still there, the old ache for just one glimpse of the woman who had given him life. And then broken his heart. So anxious was he to end this conversation that he said, abruptly: "I should return to the dissection room. Is that all you wished to see me about, sir?"

"There is one more thing. It's about my nephew."

"Charles?"

"He speaks highly of you. Even looks up to you. He was quite young when his father died of a fever, and I'm afraid that Charles inherited his father's delicate constitution. My sister thoroughly coddled him when he was a boy, so he's grown up on the sensitive side. It makes anatomical study all the more upsetting for him."

Norris thought of what he'd just witnessed in the anatomy lab: Charles, white-faced and trembling, as he took up the knife, as he slashed away in blind frustration.

"He is finding the studies difficult, and he receives little encouragement from his friend Mr. Kingston. Only ridicule."

"Wendell Holmes is a good and supportive friend."

"Yes, but you are perhaps the most skilled dissector in your class. That's what Dr. Sewall tells me. So I'd appreciate it, should you see that Charles needs any extra guidance . . ."

"I'd be happy to look out for him, sir."

"And you won't let Charles know we spoke of this?"

"You can trust me."

Both men stood. For a moment, Grenville studied him, silently taking his measure. "And so I shall."

Thirteen

EVEN A DISINTERESTED OBSERVER would be able to tell, with merely a glance, that the four young men who stepped into the Hurricane that night were not of equal standing. If a man could be judged by the quality of his topcoat, that alone would have set Norris apart from his three classmates; certainly it set him apart from the illustrious Dr. Chester Crouch, who had invited his four students to join him for an evening round of drinks. Crouch led the way across the crowded tavern to a table near the fireplace. There he shrugged off his heavy greatcoat with the fur collar and handed it to the girl who had scurried over the instant she'd spotted the group step through the door. The tavern maid was not the only female who'd taken note of their entrance. A trio of young ladies—shopgirls perhaps, or adventurous country visitors—were eyeing the young men, and one of them blushed at a glance from Edward, who merely shrugged at their attentions, so accustomed was he to looks from the ladies.

By the light of the roaring fire, Norris couldn't help admiring Edward's stylish neck stock tied *à la Sentimentale*, and the green topcoat with the silver buttons and velvet collar. The filth of the dissection room had not stopped Norris's three fellow students from wearing their fine shirts and Marseilles waistcoats while they'd cut into old Paddy. He himself would never risk a disastrous stain on such expensive muslin. His own shirt was old and frayed and not worth the price of Kingston's cravat alone. He looked down at his hands, where dried blood was still caked beneath his fingernails. *I shall go home with the stink of that old corpse clinging to my clothes,* he thought.

Dr. Crouch called out: "A round of brandy and water for my excellent students here. And a plate of oysters!"

"Yes, Doctor," the tavern girl said, and with a sly glance at Edward, she hurried past crowded tables to fetch the drinks. Though equally fashionable, Wendell was too short, and Charles too pale and timid, to attract the same admiring looks. And Norris was the one with the worn coat and rotting shoes. The one not worth a second glance.

The Hurricane was not a tavern that Norris frequented. Though he spotted here and there a shapeless coat or the faded uniform of a half-pay officer, he saw a crowd that was largely high-collared and well shod, and he spotted more than a few of his fellow medical students eagerly scooping up oysters with hands that only hours ago had wallowed in the blood of cadavers.

"The first dissection is merely an introduction," said Crouch, raising his voice to be heard in that noisy room. "You cannot begin to understand the machine in all its brilliance until you've seen the variability between young and old, male and female." He leaned toward his four students and spoke more quietly. "Dr. Sewall was hoping to secure a fresh shipment next week. He's offered as much as thirty dollars apiece, but there's a problem with supply."

"Surely people are still dying," said Edward.

"Yet we're faced with scarcity. In past years, we could rely on suppliers in New York and Pennsylvania. But everywhere now, we face competition. The College of Physicians and Surgeons in New York has enrolled two hundred students this year. The University of Pennsylvania four hundred. It's a race to acquire the same merchandise that every other school is scrambling for, and it gets worse every year."

"There's no such problem in France," said Wendell.

Crouch gave a sigh of envy. "In France, they understand what is vital to the common good. The medical school in Paris has full access to the charity hospitals. Their students have all the bodies they could possibly use for study. Now, *there's* the place to learn medicine."

The serving girl returned with their drinks and a platter of steaming oysters, which she laid on the table. "Dr. Crouch," she said. "There's a gentleman wishes to speak to you. Says it's his wife's time, and she's in distress."

Crouch glanced around the tavern. "Which gentleman?"

"He waits outside, with a carriage."

Sighing, Crouch stood up. "It appears I shall have to leave you."

"Shall we accompany you?" asked Wendell.

"No, no. Don't let the oysters go to waste. I'll see you all in the morning, on the ward."

As Dr. Crouch walked out the door, his four students wasted no time attacking the platter.

"He's right, you know," said Wendell, plucking up a succulent oyster. "Paris is the place to study, and he's not the only one to say it. We're at a disadvantage. Dr. Jackson has encouraged James to complete his studies there, and Johnny Warren will soon be headed to Paris as well."

Edward gave a dismissive snort. "If our education is so inferior, why are *you* still here?"

"My father thinks studying in Paris is an unnecessary extravagance."

Merely an extravagance for him, thought Norris. For me, an impossibility.

"Have you no wish to go?" said Wendell. "To learn at the feet of

Louis and Chomel? To study fresh cadavers, not these half-pickled specimens practically rotting off the bone? The French understand the value of science." He tossed the empty oyster shell onto the platter. "*That* is the place to learn medicine."

"When I go to Paris," Edward said with a laugh, "it won't be to study. Unless the subject is female anatomy. And one can study that anywhere."

"Although not as thoroughly as in Paris," said Wendell, grinning as he wiped hot juices from his chin. "If tales of the enthusiasm of French women are to be believed."

"With a large enough purse, one can buy enthusiasm anywhere."

"Which gives even short men like me hope." Wendell raised his cup. "Ah, I feel a poem coming on. An ode to French ladies."

"Please, no," groaned Edward. "No verse tonight!"

Norris was the only one who did not laugh at that. This talk of Paris, of women who could be bought, reopened the deepest wound of his childhood. *My mother chose Paris over me.* And who was the man who'd lured her there? Though his father refused to speak of it, Norris had been forced to come to that inevitable conclusion. Surely a man was involved. Sophia had been barely thirty, a bright and lively beauty trapped on a farm in quiet Belmont. On which of her trips to Boston had she met him? What promises had he offered, what rewards to compensate for the abandonment of her son?

"You're awfully quiet tonight," said Wendell. "Is it about that meeting with Dr. Grenville?"

"No, I told you it was nothing. Just about Rose Connolly."

"Oh. That Irish girl," said Edward, and he grimaced. "I have a feeling Mr. Pratt has more evidence against her than we're hearing. And it's not just about some fancy bauble she's stolen. Girls who steal are capable of worse."

"I don't know how you can say that about her," said Norris. "You don't even know her."

"We were all on the ward that day. She revealed a complete lack of respect for Dr. Crouch."

"It doesn't make her a thief."

"It makes her an ungrateful little brat. Which is just as bad." Edward tossed an empty shell onto the platter. "Mark my words, gentlemen. We'll be hearing more about Miss Rose Connolly."

Norris drank too much that night. He could feel the effects as he walked unsteadily home along the river, his belly filled with oysters, his face flushed from the brandy. It had been a glorious meal, the finest he'd enjoyed since arriving in Boston. So many oysters, more than he ever thought he could consume! But the glow from the alcohol could not ward off the bone-chilling wind that blew in from the Charles River. He thought of his three classmates, bound for their own far superior lodgings, and pictured the cheery fires and the snug rooms that awaited them.

An uneven cobblestone caught his shoe and he stumbled forward, barely catching himself before he fell. Dazed by drink, he stood swaying in the wind, and gazed across the river. To the north, at the far end of Prison Point Bridge, was the faint glow of the state prison. To the west, across the water, he saw the lights of the jail on Lechmere Point. Now, *this* was an uplifting view, to see prisons in every direction, a reminder of how far one could fall. From a gentleman to a mere tradesman, he thought, is just a matter of a wrong turn at business, a poor hand at cards. Forfeit the fine house and carriage, and suddenly one is merely a barber or a wheelwright. Take another tumble, incur another bad debt, and one wears a pauper's rags and sells matches on the street or sweeps dust for a penny. Yet another tumble and there one will be, shivering in a cell on Lechmere Point or staring through prison bars in Charlestown.

From there, one can tumble only one step lower, and that is into the grave.

Oh, yes, this was a grim view, but it was also what fed his ambition. He was driven not by the lure of endless platters of oysters or a taste for fine calfskin shoes or velvet collars. No, it was this view in the other direction, over the precipice, to where one might fall.

I must study, he thought. There's still time tonight, and I'm not so drunk that I can't read just one more chapter in Wistar's, cram a few more facts into my head.

But when he climbed the narrow stairs to his freezing attic room, he was too exhausted to even open the cover of the textbook, which sat on the desk by the window. To save on candlelight, he stumbled around in the dark. Better not to waste the light and wake up early, when his brain was fresh. When he could read by daylight. He undressed in the faint glow of the window, staring out across the hospital common as he untied his cravat, unbuttoned his waistcoat. In the distance, beyond the black swath of the common, lights flickered in hospital windows. He imagined the shadowy wards, echoing with coughs, and the long rows of beds where patients now slept. So many years of study lay before him, yet he had never doubted that he was meant to be here. That this moment, in this cold attic, was part of the journey he'd begun years ago as a boy, when he'd first watched his father slice open a slaughtered pig. When he'd beheld its heart still quivering in the chest. He had pressed his hand to his own chest, and felt his own beating heart, and had thought: We are alike. Pig and cow and man, the machine is the same. If I can only understand what drives the furnace, what keeps the wheels turning, I will know how to keep that machine working. I will know how to cheat Death.

He slipped off his suspenders, stepped out of his trousers, and draped them over the chair. Shivering, he climbed under the blanket. With a full stomach, and his head still swimming from brandy, he fell asleep almost instantly.

And almost instantly was awakened by a knocking on the door.

"Mr. Marshall? Mr. Marshall, are you there?"

Norris rolled out of bed and stumbled in a daze across the attic. Opening the door, he saw the elderly hospital groundsman, his face lit eerily by a flickering lantern.

"They need you, up at the hospital," said the old man.

"What's happened?"

"A carriage has turned over near the Canal Bridge. We've got injured comin' in, and we can't find Nurse Robinson. They've sent for other doctors, but with you being so close, I thought I should fetch you, too. Better a medical student than nothing."

"Yes, of course," said Norris, ignoring the unintended slight. "I'll be right there."

He dressed in the dark, fumbling for trousers and boots and waistcoat. He did not bother with a topcoat. If the scene were bloody, he would have to shed it anyway to keep it clean. He pulled on an overcoat against the chill and made his way down the dark steps, into the night. The wind blew from the west, thick with the stink of the river. He cut directly across the common, and his trouser legs were soon soaked from the wet grass. Already, his heart was pounding in anticipation. An overturned carriage, he thought. Multiple injuries. Would he know what to do? He didn't quail from the sight of blood; he'd seen his share of it in the slaughtering shed on the farm. What he feared was his own ignorance. He was so focused on the crisis ahead that at first he did not understand what he was hearing. But a few paces later he heard it again, and stopped.

It was a woman's moan, and it came from the riverbank.

A sound of distress, or merely a whore servicing a client? On other nights he had spied such couplings along the river, in the shadow of the bridge, had heard the whimpers and grunts of furtive ruttings. This was no time to spy on whores; the hospital waited for him.

Then the sound came again, and he stopped. *That was no carnal moan.*

He ran to the riverwalk and called out: "Hello? Who's there?" Staring down at the river's edge, he saw something dark lying close to where the water lapped. *A body?*

He scrambled over the rocks, and his shoes sank into black mud. It sucked at his soles, the cold seeping into cracked and rotting leather. As he slogged toward the water, his heart suddenly pounded faster, his breaths accelerating. It *was* a body. In the darkness, he could just make out the shape of a woman. She was lying on her back, her skirts submerged to the waist in the water. Hands numb with cold and panic, he grabbed her beneath the arms and dragged her up the bank until she was well free of the river. By then he was gasping from exertion, his own trousers soaked and dripping. He crouched down beside her and felt her chest for a heartbeat, a breath, any sign of life.

Warm liquid bathed his hand. Its unexpected heat was so startling that at first he did not register what his own skin was telling him. Then he stared down and saw the oily gleam of blood on his palm.

Behind him, a pebble clattered on rocks. He turned, and a chill lifted every hair on the back of his neck.

The creature stood on the bank above him. Its black cape fluttered like giant wings in the wind. Beneath the hood, a death's-head stared, white as bone. Hollow eyes looked straight at him, as if marking him as the next soul to be harvested, the next to feel the slash of its scythe.

So frozen in fear was Norris that he could not have fled, even if the creature had swooped at him, even if the blade had, in that instant, come hissing through the air. He could only watch, just as the monster watched him.

Then, suddenly, it was gone. And Norris saw only a view of the night sky and the moon, winking through a filigree of clouds.

On the riverwalk, lamplight appeared. "Hallo?" the hospital groundsman shouted. "Who's down there?"

His throat shut down by panic, Norris could produce only a choked: "Here." Then, louder: "Help. I need help!"

The groundsman came down the muddy bank, lantern swaying. Holding up the light, he stared down at the dead body. At the face of Mary Robinson. Then his gaze lifted to Norris, and the look on the old man's face was unmistakable.

It was fear.

Fourteen

NORRIS STARED DOWN at his hands, where the coat of dried blood was now cracked and flaking off his skin. He'd been called to assist in a crisis; instead, he had added more blood, more confusion to the chaos. Through the closed door, he could hear a man shrieking in pain, and he wondered what horrors the surgeon's knife was now performing upon that unfortunate soul.

No worse a horror than was inflicted upon poor Mary Robinson.

Only as he'd carried her into the building, into the light, had he seen the full horror of her injuries. He'd brought her into the hall, dripping a trail of blood, and a shocked nurse had mutely pointed him toward the surgery room. But as he'd laid Mary on the table, he already knew that she'd passed beyond the help of any surgeon.

"How well did you know Mary Robinson, Mr. Marshall?"

Norris looked up from his blood-encrusted hands and focused on Mr. Pratt from the Night Watch. Behind Pratt stood Constable Lyons and Dr. Aldous Grenville, both of whom had elected to remain silent during the interrogation. They hung back in the shadows, beyond the circle of light cast by the lamp.

"She was a nurse. I've seen her, of course."

"But did you know her? Did you have any relationship with her outside your work at the hospital?"

"No."

"None at all?"

"I'm engaged in the study of medicine, Mr. Pratt. I have little time outside of that."

"You live within sight of the hospital. Your lodgings are right at the edge of these grounds, and hers are but a short walk from this very building. You could have encountered Miss Robinson just by stepping out your door."

"That hardly counts as a relationship." Norris looked down at his hands again. *This is the most intimate I will ever be with poor Mary,* he thought. *With her blood clinging to my skin.*

Mr. Pratt turned to Dr. Grenville. "You have examined the body, sir?"

"I have. I should like Dr. Sewall to examine it as well."

"But can you render an opinion?"

Norris said, softly: "It's the same killer. The same pattern. Surely you know that already, Mr. Pratt?" He looked up. "Two incisions. One cut straight across the abdomen. Then a twist of the blade and a slash straight up, toward the sternum. In the shape of a cross."

"But this time, Mr. Marshall," interjected Constable Lyons, "the killer has taken it a step farther."

Norris focused on the senior officer of the Night Watch. Though he had never before met Constable Lyons, he knew of the man's reputation. Unlike bombastic Mr. Pratt, Constable Lyons was softspoken, and perhaps easily overlooked. For the past hour, he had allowed his subordinate Pratt complete control of the investigation. Now Lyons moved into the light, and Norris saw a compact gentleman of about fifty, with a trim beard and spectacles.

"Her tongue is missing," said Lyons.

Watchman Pratt turned to Grenville. "The killer sliced it out?"

Grenville nodded. "It would not be a difficult excision. All it re-quires is a sharp knife."

"Why would he do such a grotesque thing? Was it punishment? A message?"

"For that answer, you'd have to ask the killer."

Norris didn't like the way Pratt immediately turned to look at him. "And you say you saw him, Mr. Marshall."

"I saw *something*."

"A creature with a cape? With a face like a skull's?"

"He was exactly as Rose Connolly described him. She told you the truth."

"Yet the hospital groundsman saw no such monster. He told me he saw only you, bending over the body. And no one else."

"It was standing there for only an instant. By the time the groundsman came upon me, the creature was gone."

Pratt studied him for a moment. "Why do you think the tongue was taken?"

"I don't know."

"It's a monstrous thing to do. But if one were a student of anatomy, it might make sense to collect a body part. For scientific reasons, of course."

"Mr. Pratt," cut in Grenville, "you have no grounds on which to suspect Mr. Marshall."

"A young man who happened to be in the proximity of both murders?"

"He's a medical student. He *would* be found near this hospital."

Pratt looked at Norris. "You grew up on a farm, did you not? Have you any experience slaughtering animals?"

"These questions have gone far enough," said Constable Lyons. "Mr. Marshall, you're free to go."

"Sir," Pratt protested, indignant that his authority had just been usurped. "I don't believe we've pursued this far enough at all."

"Mr. Marshall isn't a suspect, and he shouldn't be treated as such." Lyons looked at Norris. "You may go."

Norris stood and crossed to the door. There he paused and looked back. "I know you didn't believe Rose Connolly," he said. "But now I've seen the creature, too."

Pratt gave a snort. "The Grim Reaper?"

"He's real, Mr. Pratt. Whether you believe me or not, *something* is out there. Something that chilled my very soul. And I hope to God I never see it again."

Again, someone was pounding on his door. What a nightmare I've had, thought Norris as he opened his eyes and saw daylight shining through his window. This is what comes from eating too many oysters, drinking too much brandy. It brings on dreams of monsters.

"Norris? Norris, wake up!" called Wendell.

Rounds with Dr. Crouch. I'm late.

Norris threw off his blanket and sat up. Only then did he see his greatcoat, draped over the chair, the fabric stained with broad smears of blood. He looked down at the shoes, which he'd left next to his bed, and saw mud-encrusted leather. And yet more blood. Even the shirt he was now wearing had splatters of brick red on the cuffs, the sleeves. It had not been a nightmare. He had fallen asleep with Mary Robinson's blood on his clothes.

Wendell pounded on the door. "Norris, we must talk!"

Norris stumbled across the room and opened the door to find Wendell standing in the dim stairway.

"You look awful," said Wendell.

Norris crossed back to the bed and sat down, groaning. "It was an awful night."

"So I've heard."

Wendell stepped inside and shut the door. As he looked around at the wretched little garret, he did not say a thing, nor did he need to; his opinion was plain on his face as he took in the rotting beams and the sagging floor and the straw-filled mattress set atop the bed frame of weathered planks. A mouse darted from the shadows, claws skittering across the floor, and it disappeared beneath the desk where a stained copy of Wistar's *Anatomy* lay open. It was so cold on this late-November morning that a fan of ice had formed inside the window.

"I imagine you're wondering why I didn't turn up at rounds," said Norris. He felt painfully exposed, sitting only in his shirt, and when he looked down, he saw his bare thighs stippled with goose bumps.

"We know why you didn't turn up. It's all they're talking about at the hospital. What happened to Mary Robinson."

"Then you know that I'm the one who found her."

"That's one of the versions, anyway."

Norris looked up. "There's another?"

"There are all sorts of rumors flying. Hideous rumors, I'm sorry to say."

Norris stared down again at his bare knees. "Would you hand me my trousers, please? It's bloody freezing in here."

Wendell tossed him the pants, then turned and looked out the window. As Norris dressed, he noticed bloodstains on the cuff of his trousers. Everywhere he looked, he saw Mary Robinson's blood on his clothes.

"What are they saying about me?" he asked.

Wendell turned to face him. "What a coincidence it is that you came so soon upon both death scenes."

"I wasn't the one who found Agnes Poole's body."

"But you were there."

"So were you."

"I'm not accusing you."

"Then what are you doing here? Come to take a peek at where the Reaper lives?" Norris rose to his feet, pulling on his suspenders. "It makes for good gossip, I imagine. Delicious tidbits to tell your Harvard chums over Madeira."

"You don't really think that about me, do you?"

"I know what you think of *me*."

Wendell crossed toward him. He was far shorter, and he stared up at Norris like an angry little terrier. "You've had a chip on your shoulder since the day you arrived. The poor farmer's boy, always on the outs. No one wants to be your friend because your coat isn't good enough, or you don't have enough spare change in your pocket. You really think that's my opinion of you? That you're not worthy of my friendship?"

"I know my proper place in your circle."

"Don't presume to read my mind. Charles and I made every attempt to include you, to make you feel welcome. Yet you hold us at arm's length, as though you've already decided any friendship is destined to fail."

"We're classmates, Wendell. Nothing more. We share a preceptor and we share old Paddy. Perhaps we share a round of drinks now and then. But take a look around this room. You can see we have little else in common."

"I have more in common with you than I'll ever have with Edward Kingston."

Norris laughed. "Oh, yes. Just look at our matching satin waistcoats. Name one thing we have in common, other than poor old Paddy on the table."

Wendell turned to the desk, where Wistar's lay open. "You've been studying, for one thing."

"You didn't answer my question."

"That *was* my answer. You sit here in this freezing attic, burning your candles down to the last puddle of tallow, and you're *studying*. Why? Just so you'll someday be able to wear a top hat? Somehow, I don't think so." He turned to Norris. "I think you study for the same reason I do. Because you believe in science."

"Now you're presuming to read *my* mind."

"That day on the ward, with Dr. Crouch. There was a woman who had been laboring for far too long. He advocated bleeding her. Do you remember?"

"What of it?"

"You challenged him. You said you'd experimented on cows. That bleeding them had shown no benefit."

"And for that I was soundly ridiculed."

"You must've known you would be. Yet you said it anyway."

"Because it was true. It's what the cows taught me."

"And you're not too proud to take your lessons from cows."

"I'm a farmer. Where else should I take my lessons?"

"And I'm a minister's son. Do you think the lessons I heard from my father's pulpit were nearly as useful? A farmer knows more about birth and death than you'll ever learn while sitting in a church pew."

With a snort, Norris turned and reached for his topcoat, the one item of clothing that had been spared from Mary Robinson's blood, only because he had left it behind last night. "You have some odd notions about the nobility of farmers."

"I recognize a man of science when I see one. And I've seen your generosity as well."

"My generosity?"

"In the anatomy room, when Charles made such a bloody mess of old Paddy. We both know Charlie's just one slip away from being booted out of school. But you stepped forward and covered for him when Edward and I didn't."

"That was hardly generosity. I just couldn't stand the thought of seeing a grown man cry."

"Norris, you're not like most of the others in our class. You have the *calling*. Do you think Charlie Lackaway cares about anatomy, about materia medica? He's here only because his uncle expects it of him. Because his late father was a doctor, and his grandfather, too, and he hasn't the spine to resist his family. And Edward, he doesn't even bother to hide his disinterest. Half the students are here to please their parents, and most of the others just want to learn a trade, something that will earn them a comfortable living."

"And why are *you* here? Because *you* have the calling?"

"I admit, medicine was not my first choice. But one can hardly make a living as a poet. Though I have been published in the *Daily Advertiser*."

Norris had to suppress a laugh. Now, *there* was a useless profession, reserved for lucky men with means, men who could afford to waste precious hours scribbling verse. He said, diplomatically, "I'm afraid I'm not familiar with your work."

Wendell gave a sigh. "Then you can see why I did not pursue poetry as a career. And I was most unsuited to the study of law as well."

"So medicine is merely a third choice. That hardly sounds like a calling."

"But it has *become* my calling. I know it's what I'm meant to do."

Norris reached for his greatcoat and paused for a heartbeat, his gaze on the bloodstains. He pulled it on anyway. A glimpse outside, at the frost on the grass, told him that today he would need every layer of warmth he could recruit from his meager wardrobe. "If you'll excuse me, I need to salvage what I can of this day. I need to explain my absence to Dr. Crouch. Is he still at the hospital?"

"Norris, if you go to the hospital, I must warn you what to expect."

Norris turned to face him. "What?"

"There's talk, you see, among the patients and staff. People are wondering about you. They're afraid."

"They think I killed her?"

"The trustees have been speaking with Mr. Pratt."

"They aren't listening to his rubbish?"

"They have no choice but to listen. They're responsible for enforcing order in the hospital. They can discipline any doctor on the staff. Certainly they can banish a lowly medical student from the wards."

"Then how would I learn? How would I pursue my studies?"

"Dr. Crouch is trying to reason with them. And Dr. Grenville has argued against the ban as well. But there are others . . ."

"Others?"

"Rumors, among the patients' families. And on the streets as well."

"What are they saying?"

"The fact that her tongue was removed has convinced some that the killer is a medical student."

"Or someone who's butchered animals," said Norris. "And I am both."

"I just came to tell you how things stood. That people are . . . well, afraid of you."

"And why aren't *you* afraid of me? Why do *you* assume I'm innocent?"

"I don't assume anything."

Norris gave a bitter laugh. "Oh, *there's* a loyal friend."

"Damn it, this is *exactly* what a friend would do! He'd tell you the truth. That your future's in jeopardy." Wendell turned toward the door. There he paused and looked at Norris. "You have more bull-headed pride than any son of wealth I've ever met, and you use it to paint the whole world black. I don't need a friend like you. I don't even *want* a friend like you." He yanked open the door.

"Wendell."

"You'd be wise to speak to Dr. Crouch. And give him credit for defending you. Because he, at least, deserves it."

"Wendell, I'm sorry," said Norris. And he sighed. "I'm not accustomed to assuming the best of people."

"So you assume the worst?"

"I'm seldom disappointed."

"Then you need a better circle of acquaintances."

At that, Norris laughed. He sat down on the bed and rubbed his face. "I daresay you're right."

Wendell closed the door and came toward him. "What are you going to do?"

"Against rumors? What can I do? The more I insist I'm innocent, the more guilty I look."

"You have to do something. This is your future."

And it hung by a thread. All it took was a few doubts, a few whispers, and the hospital trustees would ban him permanently from the wards. How easily a reputation is soiled, thought Norris. Suspicion would cling to him like a bloodstained cloak, frightening away all prospects, all opportunities, until the only path left to him was back to his father's farm. To a home shared with a cold and joyless man.

"Until this killer is caught," said Wendell, "everyone's eyes will be on you."

Norris looked down at his stained greatcoat, and with a chill, he remembered the creature standing above the riverbank, staring down at him. *I did not imagine him.*

Rose Connolly saw him, too.

Fifteen

ANOTHER WEEK of this bitter cold, thought Wall-eyed Jack, and the soil will be too frozen to dig. Soon they'd be storing the corpses in vaults above the ground, awaiting the spring thaw. There'd be heavy locks to get past, groundskeepers to bribe, a whole new set of complications to match the change in the weather. For Jack, it wasn't the blooming of apple blossoms or the autumn tumble of leaves that marked the cycling of the seasons; no, it was the quality of the dirt. In April, there was mud to contend with, so thick and greedy it would suck the boots right off your feet. In August, the clods were dry and crumbled easily to warm dust in his fist, a good time to dig, except that every scoop of the shovel would stir up an angry cloud of mosquitoes. In January, the shovel would ring like a bell if you hacked at the frozen ground, and the impact, pounding through the handle, would make your hands ache. Even a tended fire set upon the grave could take days to thaw the soil. Few corpses were buried in January.

But at the end of autumn, there were still riches to harvest.

So he guided his dray through the thickening dusk, the wooden wheels crackling over a thin crust of frozen mud. At this hour, on this lonely road, he met no one. Across a cornfield littered with brown and broken stalks, he saw a glimmer of candlelight in a farmhouse window, but no movement, and he heard no sounds save for the clop of the horse's hooves and the snapping of ice beneath the wagon wheels. This was farther than he liked to journey on such a bitter night, but he'd been left few choices. Grave watchers were now stationed at the Old Granary burying grounds, and at Copp's Hill on the North Side. Even the lonely cemetery at Roxbury Crossing was now patrolled. Every month, it seemed, he was forced farther and farther afield. There'd been a time when he'd needed to travel no farther than the Central Burying Ground on the Common. There, on a moonless night, with a team of fast diggers, he had his choice of paupers and papists and old soldiers. Whether rich or poor, a corpse was a corpse, and all brought the same coin. The anatomists did not care whether the flesh they cut was well fed or consumptive.

But the medical students had since spoiled that source, as well as most of the other nearby burying grounds, with their careless digging, their sloppy attempts at concealment. They showed up at cemeteries fueled with drink and bravado, and they left behind ruined graves and trampled earth, the evidence of desecration so blatant that even the paupers soon guarded their dead. Those damn students had ruined it for the professionals. Once, he could make a good living. But tonight, instead of a quick snatch, Jack was forced to drive on this endless back road, dreading the labors ahead. And all alone, too; with so few pickings these days, he was loath to pay a partner. No, tonight, he'd have to do it all by himself. He only hoped that any fresh grave he found was the work of diggers too lazy to bury their charge the full six feet.

There'd be no such shoddy grave for his body.

Wall-eyed Jack knew exactly how he'd be buried. He'd planned it well. Ten feet down, with an iron cage around him, and a watcher hired to guard him for thirty days. Long enough for his flesh to spoil. He had seen the work of the anatomists' knives. He'd been paid to dispose of the remains after they'd finished their hacking and sawing, and he had no desire to be reduced to a heap of severed limbs. No doctor would ever touch his body, he thought; already he was saving for his own burial, and he kept his treasure stashed in a box beneath the bedroom floor. Fanny knew what sort of grave he wanted, and he'd leave her enough to see it was done right, done proper.

If you had enough money, you could buy anything. Even protection from a man like Jack.

The low wall of the cemetery was ahead. He pulled his horse to a halt and paused in the road, scanning the shadows. The moon had fallen behind the horizon, and only stars lit the graveyard. He reached back for his shovel and lantern, and jumped off the dray. His boots crunched onto frost-heaved dirt. His legs were stiff from the long ride, and he felt clumsy as he scrambled over the stone wall, the lantern and shovel clanging together.

It did not take long for him to locate a fresh grave. The lantern light revealed a mound of turned soil not yet crusted over by ice. He glanced at the headstones on adjoining graves, to confirm which way the body would be oriented. Then he sank his shovel in the soil where the head would be. After only a few scoops of dirt, he was short of breath. He had to pause, wheezing in the cold, regretting that he had not brought along that young Norris Marshall. But damned if he'd relinquish even a dollar to another man when he could do the job himself.

Once again he sank the shovel into the dirt and was about to lift the next scoop when a shout made him freeze.

"There he is! Get him!"

Three lanterns were bobbing toward him, closing in so fast that he had no time to extinguish his light. In panic, he abandoned the lamp right there and fled, carrying only the shovel. Darkness hid his path, and every gravestone was an obstacle waiting to trip him like bony hands, preventing his escape. The cemetery itself seemed to be taking its revenge on him for all his past outrages. He tripped and fell to his knees, onto ice that cracked like glass.

"Over there!" came a shout.

A gun fired, and Jack felt the bullet hiss past his cheek. He lurched to his feet and scrambled over the stone wall, abandoning the shovel wherever it had fallen. As he climbed into the dray, another bullet whistled by so close he felt it flick his hair.

"He's getting away!"

One crack of the whip and the horse took off, the dray rattling wildly behind it. Jack heard one last gunshot, and then his pursuers fell behind, their lights fading into the darkness.

By the time he finally pulled the horse to a stop, it was wheezing, and he knew that if he did not let it rest he would lose it, too, as he had his shovel and his lantern. And then where would he be, a tradesman without his tools?

A trade he was getting too old for.

Tonight was a complete loss. And what of tomorrow, and the night after? He thought of the cash box under the bedroom floor, and the money he had saved. Not enough, it was never enough. There was the future to think of, his and Fanny's. If they could hold on to the tavern, they would not starve. But that was a bleak old age, if the best you could look forward to was *at least we will not starve*.

Even that was not assured. A man can always starve. A chimney fire, a stray hot cinder from the hearth, and the Black Spar, the establishment that Fanny's father had left them, would be gone. Then it would be up to Jack to keep them fed, a burden he was less and less able to bear as the years went by. It was not just that his knees were bad and his back ached; it was the business itself. New medical schools were springing up everywhere, and students needed corpses. Demand was up, bringing new snatchers into the trade. And they were younger, quicker, and more daring.

They had strong backs.

A week ago, Jack had shown up at Dr. Sewall's with a sadly deteriorated specimen—the best he could find that night. He'd seen six barrels in the courtyard, each stamped with the label: PICKLES.

"Those were just delivered," Sewall had told him as he counted out the money. "In good condition, too."

"This is only fifteen dollars," Jack had complained, looking at the money Sewall handed him.

"Your specimen's already rotting, Mr. Burke."

"I expect twenty."

"I paid twenty apiece for the ones in the barrels," Sewall said. "They're in much better shape, and I can get them six at a time. All the way up from New York."

To hell with New York, thought Jack as he huddled, shivering, in the dray. Where do I find a source in Boston? Not enough people were dying. What they needed was a good plague, something to clean out the slums in Southie and Charlestown. No one would miss that rabble. For once, let the Irish be good for something. Let them make him rich. To get rich, Jack Burke would sell his soul.

Maybe he already had.

By the time he got back to the Black Spar, his limbs were stiff, and he could barely climb out of the wagon. He stabled the horse, stamped the frozen clods from his boots, and walked wearily into the tavern, wanting nothing more than a seat by the fire and a glass of brandy. But as soon as he sank into a chair, he felt Fanny eyeing him from behind the counter. He ignored her, ignored everyone, and stared into the flames, waiting for the feeling to return to his numb toes. The establishment was almost empty; the cold had kept away their few regulars, and tonight only the most wretched of wanderers had been swept in from the streets. One man stood at the bar, digging desperately in filthy pockets for filthy coins. Nothing could dull the sting of a night this cold like a few precious ounces of rum. At a corner, another man had laid down his head, and his snores were loud enough to rattle the empty glasses that littered his table.

"You're back early."

Jack looked up at Fanny, who stood over him, her gaze narrow with questions.

"Not a good night" was all he said. He drained his glass.

"You think I've had a good night here?"

"Least you've spent it by the fire."

"With this lot?" She snorted. "Not worth the trouble of unlocking the door."

"Another flip!" the man at the bar yelled.

"Show me your coins first," shot back Fanny.

"I have 'em. They're somewhere in these pockets."

"Haven't come up with 'em yet."

"Have a little pity, missus. It's a cold night."

"And you'll be out in it straightaway if you can't pay for another drink." She looked back at Jack. "You came back empty-handed, didn't you?"

He shrugged. "They had watchers."

"You didn't try some other place?"

"Couldn't. Had to leave behind the shovel. And the lamp."

"You couldn't even bring home your own tools?"

He slammed down his glass. "That's *enough*!"

She leaned in closer. Said, softly: "There are easier ways to make money, Jack. You know that. Let me put out the word, and you'll have all the work you need."

"And get hanged for it?" He shook his head. "I'll stick to my own profession, thank you."

"You come home empty-handed more often than not these days."

"The picking's aren't good."

"That's all I hear you say."

"Because they aren't. They just get worse."

"You think my trade is doing any better?" She jerked her head toward the nearly deserted room. "They've all moved on to the Mermaid. Or the Plough and Star, or to Coogan's. Another year like this and we won't be able to keep it."

"Missus?" the man at the bar called. "I know I have the money. Just one more, and I promise I'll pay you next time."

Fanny wheeled around at him in fury. "Your promise is worthless! You can't pay, you can't stay. Get out." She stomped toward him and grabbed him by the jacket. "Go on, get out!" she roared.

"Surely you can spare one drink."

"Not one bloody drop!" She hauled the man across the room, yanked open the door, and shoved him out into the cold. She slammed the door, then turned, panting and red-faced. When Fanny was angry, it was a terrifying sight to behold, and even Jack shrank into his chair, quailing at what might happen next. Her gaze landed on the lone customer still remaining, the man who had fallen asleep at the corner table.

"You, too! It's time to leave!"

The man did not stir.

Being ignored was the final affront, one that made Fanny's face flush purple and the muscles bulge in her stout arms. "We're closed! Go!" She crossed to the man and gave him a hard cuff on the shoulder. But instead of waking, he rolled sideways and toppled off his chair, onto the floor.

For a moment, Fanny just stared down in disgust at his gaping mouth, his lolling tongue. A frown creased her forehead and she leaned in, shoving her face so close that Jack thought she was going to kiss the man.

"He ain't breathing, Jack," she said.

"What?"

She looked up. "You give him a look."

Jack hauled himself out of the chair and groaned as he knelt beside the man.

"You seen enough corpses," she said. "You oughta be able to tell."

Jack looked into the man's open eyes. Drool glistened on purple lips. When had he stopped snoring? When had the corner table fallen silent? Death had crept in so furtively they hadn't even noticed its entrance.

He looked up at Fanny. "What's his name?"

"I dunno."

"You know who he is?"

"Just some blow-in from the wharves. Walked in alone."

Jack straightened, his back aching. He looked at Fanny. "You strip off his clothes. I'll go harness the horse."

He didn't need to explain a thing to her; she met his gaze with a nod, a canny glint in her eye.

"We'll earn our twenty dollars after all," he said.

Sixteen

"RESURRECTIONIST," said Henry, "is an old word, no longer used. Most people today have no idea that it refers to a grave robber or a body snatcher."

"And Norris Marshall was one of them," said Julia.

"Only by necessity. It was clearly not his trade."

They sat at the dining table, the pages of the newly discovered letter from Oliver Wendell Holmes spread out beside their coffee cups and breakfast muffins. Although it was well past midmorning, the fog still hung thick outside the sea windows, and Henry had turned on all the lamps to brighten the murky room.

"Fresh corpses were valuable commodities in those days. So valuable, in fact, that there was a booming trade in them. All to supply the new medical schools that were popping up around the country." Henry shuffled over to one of his bookcases. From the yellowing volumes on the shelves, he pulled down a book and brought it back to the dining table where he and Julia had been reading over breakfast. "You must understand what it was like to be an American medical student in 1830. There were no real standards, no official certification for medical schools. Some were decent, others little more than moneymaking schemes to suck up tuition fees."

"And the college that Dr. Holmes and Norris Marshall attended?"

"Boston Medical College was one of the better ones. But even their students had to scramble for cadavers. A wealthy student could pay a resurrectionist to obtain a corpse for study. But if you were poor, like Mr. Marshall, you had to go out and dig up a body yourself. It appears this was also the way he paid for his tuition."

Julia shuddered. "Now, there's a work-study program I wouldn't want any part of."

"But it was a way for a poor man to become a doctor. Not an easy way, by any means. To get into medical school you didn't need a college degree, but you did need to be familiar with Latin and physics. Norris Marshall must have taught himself those subjects—no mean feat for a farmer's son without ready access to a library."

"He had to be incredibly bright."

"And determined. But the rewards were obvious. Becoming a doctor was one of the few ways to advance in society. Physicians were respected. Although while in training, medical students were viewed with disgust, even fear."

"Why?"

"Because they were thought of as vultures, preying on the bodies of the dead. Digging them up, cutting them open. To be sure, the students often brought condemnation on themselves by their antics, by all the practical jokes they played with body parts. Waving severed arms out the window, for example."

"They did that?"

"Remember, these are young men, only in their early twenties. And men that age aren't known for their superior judgment." He pushed the book toward her. "It's all in here."

"You've already read up on it?"

"Oh, I know a great deal about the subject. My father and grand-father were doctors, and I've heard these stories since I was a child. Almost every generation, in fact, has produced a doctor in our family. The medical gene skipped me, I'm afraid, but the tradition continues with my grandnephew. When I was growing up, my grandfather told me a story about a student who smuggled a woman's corpse out of anatomy lab. He put it in his roommate's bed, as a practical joke. They thought it was quite hilarious."

"That's sick."

"Most of the public would've agreed with you. Which explains why there were anatomy riots, when outraged mobs attacked schools. It happened in Philadelphia and Baltimore and New York. Any medical school, in any city, could find itself burned to the ground. Public horror and suspicion ran so deep that all it took was a single incident to touch off a riot."

"It seems to me their suspicions were well founded."

"But where would we be today if doctors couldn't dissect corpses? If you believe in medical science, then you must also accept the necessity of anatomical study."

In the distance, the ferry's horn bellowed. Julia looked at her watch and stood. "I need to get going, Henry. If I'm to catch the next boat."

"When you come back, you can help me bring up the boxes from the cellar."

"Is that an invitation?"

He thumped his cane on the floor in exasperation. "I thought it was understood!"

She looked at the stack of unopened boxes and thought of the treasures inside them, still unexplored, the letters still to be read. She had no idea if the identity of the skeleton in her garden might lie inside those boxes. What she did know was that the story of Norris Marshall and the West End Reaper had already lured her into its spell, and she was hungry to know more.

"You are coming back, aren't you?" said Henry.

"Let me check my calendar."

It was close to dinnertime when she finally arrived home in Weston. Here at least, the sun was shining, and she looked forward to lighting up the barbecue and sipping a glass of wine in the back garden. But when she pulled into her driveway and saw the silver BMW that was already parked there, her stomach clenched so tightly that just the thought of wine made her nauseated. What was Richard doing here?

She got out of her car and glanced around, but didn't see him. Only when she stepped out the kitchen door into the backyard did she spot him standing halfway down the slope, surveying the property.

"Richard?"

Her ex-husband turned as she walked into the yard to join him. It had been five months since she'd last seen him, and he looked fit and trim and more deeply tanned. It hurt to see just how good divorce had been to him. Or maybe it was all the country-clubbing he'd been doing lately with Tiffani-with-an-*i*.

"I tried calling, but you never pick up," he said. "I thought maybe you were avoiding my calls."

"I went up to Maine for the weekend."

He didn't bother to ask why; as usual, nothing she did really interested him. Instead, he gestured at her overgrown yard. "Nice piece of land. You could do a lot with this. There's even room for a pool."

"I can't afford a swimming pool."

"A deck, then. Clear out all that scrubby stuff down by the stream."

"Richard, why are you here?"

"I was in the neighborhood. Thought I'd drop by to take a look at your new place."

"Well, this is it."

"The house looks like it needs a lot of work."

"I'm fixing it up little by little."

"Who's helping you?"

"No one." Her chin tilted up on a note of pride. "I tiled the bathroom floor myself."

Again, he didn't even seem to register what she'd said. It was their usual one-way conversation. They both spoke, but she was the only one who really listened. Only now was she aware of it.

"Look, I've had a long drive and I'm tired," she said, turning toward the house. "I'm not really in the mood for company."

"Why have you been talking about me behind my back?" he asked.

She halted and looked at him. "What?"

"Frankly, I'm surprised, Julia. You never struck me as the bitter type. But I guess divorce brings out a person's real character."

For the first time, she heard the ugly note of anger in his voice. How had she missed it earlier? Even his posture should have been a clue, with his legs planted apart and his fists balled in his pockets.

"I don't have any idea what you're talking about," she said.

"Telling people that I was emotionally abusive to you? That I screwed around all during our marriage?"

"I never said that to anyone! Even if it might be true."

"What kind of shit are you talking about?"

"You *were* running around, weren't you? Did she know you were married when you started sleeping with her?"

"You so much as *whisper* that to anyone—"

"You mean, the truth? Our divorce wasn't even final yet, and you two were already picking out your new china. Everyone knows it." She paused as it suddenly occurred to her what this was all about. *Maybe not everyone does know.*

"Our marriage was over long before the divorce."

"Is that the version you're telling everyone? Because it's certainly news to me."

"You want the brutal truth about what went wrong? All the ways you held me back from what I *could* have been?"

She sighed. "No, Richard, I don't want to hear it all. I really don't care anymore."

"Then why the hell are you trying to screw up my wedding? Why are you spreading rumors about me?"

"Who's hearing these rumors? Your girlfriend? Or is it her daddy? Are you afraid he'll find out the truth about his new son-in-law?"

"Just promise me you'll stop it."

"I never said a word to anyone. I didn't even know about your wedding until Vicky told me."

He stared at her. Said, suddenly: "Vicky. That *bitch*."

"Go home," she said, and walked away.

"You get Vicky on the phone right now. You tell her to shut up."

"It's her mouth. I can't control it."

"Get your *fucking sister* on the phone!" he shouted.

A dog's noisy barks made her suddenly stop. Turning, she saw Tom standing at the edge of her garden, holding on to the leash as his dog, McCoy, leaped and strained to get free.

"Is everything okay, Julia?" Tom called out.

"Everything's fine," she said.

Tom moved closer, practically dragged up the slope by the insistent McCoy. He came within a few paces of them. "Are you sure?" he said.

"Look," snapped Richard, "we're having a private discussion."

Tom's gaze remained on Julia. "It wasn't so private."

"It's okay, Tom," said Julia. "Richard was just leaving."

Tom paused a moment longer, as though to confirm that the situation was under control. Then he turned and headed back toward the streamside path, pulling the dog behind him.

"Who the hell is that?" said Richard.

"He lives down the road."

An ugly smile crossed Richard's lips. "Is he the reason you bought this place?"

"Get out of my garden," she said, and walked toward the house.

As she stepped inside, she heard her phone ringing, but she

didn't run to answer it. Her attention was still focused on Richard. She watched through the window as he finally walked out of her backyard.

The answering machine kicked in. "Julia, I've just found something. When you get home, call me and I'll—"

She picked up the phone. "Henry?"

"Oh. You're there."

"I just got home."

A pause. "What's wrong?"

For a man who lacked even basic social skills, Henry had an uncanny ability to sniff out her moods. She heard a car engine start and carried the phone to the living room window, where she saw Richard's BMW pull away. "Nothing's wrong," she said. *Not now.*

"It was in box number six," he said.

"What was?"

"The last will and testament of Dr. Margaret Tate Page. It's dated 1890, when she would have been sixty. In it, she leaves her possessions to various grandchildren. One of them is a granddaughter named Aurnia."

"*Aurnia?*"

"An unusual name, no? I think this confirms without a doubt that Margaret Tate Page is our baby Meggie, grown up."

"Then the aunt whom Holmes mentioned in his first letter . . ."

"Is Rose Connolly."

Julia went back into her kitchen and looked out at the garden, at the same plot of land that another woman, long dead, had once gazed upon. *Who was buried in my garden all those years?*

Was it Rose?

Seventeen

1830

THE LIGHT THROUGH the grimy window had faded to little more than dull pewter. There were never enough candles in the workroom, and Rose could scarcely see her stitches as her needle plunged in and out of white gauze. Already she had completed the underslip of pale pink satin, and on her worktable were the silk roses and ribbons yet to be added to the shoulders and the waist. It was a fine gown meant for a ball, and as Rose worked, she imagined how the skirt would rustle when its wearer stepped onto the dance floor, how the satin ribbons would gleam by candlelight at the supper table. There would be wine punch in crystal cups, and creamed oysters and ginger cakes, and you could eat your fill and no one would leave hungry. Though she would never know such an evening, this gown would, and with every stitch she added some small part of herself, a trace of Rose Connolly that would linger among these folds of satin and gauze to swirl in the ballroom.

The light through the window was barely a gleam now, and she struggled to see the thread. Someday, she would look like the other women sewing in this room, their eyes fixed in perpetual squints, their fingers callused and scarred from repeated needle pricks. Even when they stood at the end of the day, their backs remained stooped, as though they were incapable of ever again standing tall.

The needle lanced Rose's finger and she gasped, dropping the gauze on the worktable. She brought her throbbing finger to her mouth and tasted blood, but it was not the pain that vexed her; rather, she was worried that she had stained the white gauze. Holding up the fabric to catch every feeble ray of light, she could just make out, in the fold of the seam, a dark fleck so tiny that it would certainly not be noticed by anyone else. Both my stitches and my blood, she thought, I leave on this gown.

"That will be enough for today, ladies," the foreman announced.

Rose folded the pieces she had worked on, set them on the table for the next day's labors, and joined the line of women waiting to collect their pay for the week. As they all pulled on cloaks and shawls for the cold walk home, Rose saw a few goodbye waves, a halfhearted nod in her direction. They did not yet know her well, nor did they know how long she would remain among them. Too many other girls had come and gone, and too many other efforts at friendship had gone to waste. So the women watched and waited, sensing perhaps that Rose was not one who would last.

"You, girl! Rose, isn't it? I need a word with you."

Heart sinking, Rose turned to face the foreman. What criticism would Mr. Smibart have of her today? For surely there *would* be criticism, delivered in that annoyingly nasal voice that made the other seamstresses giggle behind his back.

"Yes, Mr. Smibart?" she asked.

"It has happened again," he said. "And it cannot be tolerated."

"I'm sorry, but I don't know what I've done wrong. If my work's unsatisfactory—"

"Your work is perfectly adequate."

Coming from Mr. Smibart, *perfectly adequate* was a compliment, and she allowed herself a quiet sigh of relief that, for the moment, her employment here was not in jeopardy.

"It's the other matter," he said. "I cannot have outsiders disturbing me, inquiring about matters that you should deal with on your own time. Tell your friends you are here to *work*."

Now she understood. "I'm sorry, sir. Last week, I told Billy not to come here, and I thought he understood. But he has a child's mind, and he doesn't understand. I'll explain it to him again."

"It wasn't the boy this time. It was a man."

Rose went very still. "Which man?" she asked quietly.

"You think I have time to ask the name of every fellow who comes sniffing after my girls? Some beady-eyed fellow, asking all sorts of questions about you."

"What sort of questions?"

"Where you live, who your friends are. As if I'm your private secretary! This is a business, Miss Connolly, and I will not tolerate such interruptions."

"I'm sorry," she murmured.

"You keep saying that, yet the problem remains. No more visitors."

"Yes, sir," she said meekly and turned to leave.

"I expect you to deal with him. Whoever he is."

Whoever he is.

She shivered as she fought the piercing wind that whipped her skirts and numbed her face. On this cold evening, not even the dogs were about, and she walked alone, the last of the women to leave the building. It must be that horrid Mr. Pratt from the Night Watch asking about me, she thought. So far she'd managed to avoid him, but Billy had told her the man was inquiring about her around town, and all because she had dared to pawn Aurnia's locket. How had such a valuable piece of jewelry ended up in Rose's hands when it should have gone to the dead woman's husband?

The fuss is all Eben's doing, thought Rose. I accused him of attacking me so he retaliates by accusing me of being a thief. And of course, the Night Watch believes Eben, because all Irish are thieves.

She moved deeper into the warren of tenements, shoes cracking through ice into stinking puddles, the streets funneling into narrow alleys, as though South Boston itself were closing in around her. At last, she reached the door with the low arch and the stoop where the refuse from various suppers, bones gnawed clean, bread black with mold, lay awaiting the attentions of some starving dog desperate enough to eat a putrid meal.

Rose knocked on the door.

It was opened by a child with filthy cheeks, his blond hair hanging like a ragged curtain over his eyes. He could not be much older than four, and he stood mutely staring at the visitor.

A woman's voice yelled: "Fer God's sake, Conn, the cold's gettin' in! Shut the door!"

The silent boy scuttled off into some dark corner as Rose stepped in, closing the door against the wind. It took a moment for her eyes to adjust to the dimness of the low-ceilinged room, but little by little she began to make out the shapes. The chair by the hearth, where the fire had burned down to mere coals. The table with its stacked bowls. And all around her, the moving shapes of little heads. So many children. Rose counted eight at least, but surely there were others that she could not see, curled up sleeping in the shadowy corners.

"You brought your payment for the week?"

Rose focused on the enormous woman seated in the chair. Now that her eyes had adjusted, Rose could see Hepzibah's face, with its bulging double chin. Does she never leave that chair? Rose wondered. No matter what time of day or night Rose visited this grim address, she'd always found Hepzibah sitting like a fat queen in her throne, her little charges crawling about her feet like grimy supplicants.

"I've brought the money," said Rose, and she placed half her week's pay in Hepzibah's waiting hand.

"I just fed 'er. A greedy girl, that one, 'bout emptied me breast with just a few sucks. Drinks more than any babe I've nursed. I should charge you more for her."

Rose knelt to lift her niece from the basket and thought: *My sweet baby, how happy I am to see you!* Little Meggie stared up at her, and Rose was sure that her tiny lips curled into a smile of recognition. *Oh yes, you know me, don't you? You know I'm the one who loves you.*

There were no other chairs in the room, so Rose sat down on the filthy floor, among toddlers waiting for mothers to return from work and rescue them from Hepzibah's indifferent supervision. *If only I could afford better for you, dear Meggie,* she thought as she coaxed coos from her niece. *If only I could take you home to a snug, clean room where I could set your cradle by my bed.* But the room on Fishery Alley where Rose slept, a room she shared with twelve other lodgers, was even more grim, infested with rats and foul with disease. Meggie must never be exposed to such a place. Far better that she stay here with Hepzibah, whose fat breasts never ran dry. Here at least she'd be warm and fed. As long as Rose could keep the money coming.

It was only with the greatest reluctance that she finally laid Meggie back in the basket and stood to leave. Night had fallen, and Rose was both exhausted and hungry. It would do Meggie no good if her sole support fell ill and could not work.

"I'll be back tomorrow," said Rose.

"And same again next week," Hepzibah answered. Meaning the money, of course. For her, it was all about the money.

"You'll have it. Just keep her safe." Rose looked back with longing at the baby and said softly: "She's all that's left to me."

She stepped out the door. The streets were dark now, and the only source of light was the glow of candles through grimy windows. She rounded the corner and her footsteps slowed, stopped.

In the alley ahead waited a familiar silhouette. Dim Billy waved and came toward her, his impossibly long arms swinging like vines.

But it was not Billy she focused on; it was the man standing behind him.

"Miss Connolly," said Norris Marshall. "I need to speak to you."

She shot an irritated look at Billy. "You brought him here?"

"He said he's your friend," said Billy.

"Do you believe *everything* you're told?"

"I *am* your friend," said Norris.

"I'm without friends in this city."

Billy whined, "What about me?"

"*Except* for you," she amended. "But now I know I can't be trustin' you."

"He's not with the Night Watch. You only warned me about *them*."

"You do know," said Norris, "that Mr. Pratt is searching for you? You know what he's saying about you?"

"He's been saying I'm a thief. Or worse."

"And Mr. Pratt is a buffoon."

That brought a grim smile to her lips. "An opinion we have in common, that."

"We have something else in common, Miss Connolly."

"I can't imagine what that might be."

"I've seen, it too," he said quietly. "The Reaper."

She stared at him. "When?"

"Last night. It was standing over the body of Mary Robinson."

"Nurse Robinson?" She fell a step back, the news so shocking it felt like a physical blow. "*Mary* is dead?"

"You didn't know?"

Billy said, eagerly: "I was going to tell you, Miss Rose! I heard it this morning, up on the West End. She was cut, just like Nurse Poole!"

"The news is all over town," said Norris. "I wanted to speak to you before you hear some twisted version of what happened."

Wind whistled through the alley, and the cold pierced like nails through her cloak. She turned her face from the blast, and her hair whipped free of its scarf, lashing numb cheeks.

"Is there someplace warm where we can talk?" he asked. "Someplace private?"

She did not know if she could trust this man. On the first day they had met, at her sister's bedside, he had been courteous to her, the only man in that circle of students who had met her gaze with any real regard. She knew nothing about him, only that his coat was of inferior quality, and his cuffs were frayed. Gazing up the alley, she considered where to go. At this hour, the taverns and coffeehouses would be noisy and crowded, and there'd be too many ears, too many eyes.

"Come with me," she said.

A few streets away, she turned up a shadowy passage and stepped through a doorway. Inside, the air stank of boiled cabbage. In the hallway, a lone lamp burned in its sconce, the flame wildly shuddering as she swung the door shut against the wind.

"Our room's upstairs," said Billy, and he scampered up the steps ahead of them.

Norris looked at Rose. "He lives with you?"

"I couldn't leave him sleeping in a cold stable," she said. She paused to light a candle at the sconce, then, shielding the flame with her hand, she started up the stairs. Norris followed her up the dozen creaking steps to the dim and stinking room that housed the thirteen lodgers. In the glow of her candle, the sagging curtains that hung between straw mattresses looked like a regiment of ghosts. One of the lodgers was resting in a dark corner, and though he lay hidden in the shadows, they could hear the man's ceaseless hacking.

"Is he all right?" asked Norris.

"He coughs day and night."

Ducking his head beneath the low rafters, Norris picked his way across the mattress-strewn floor and knelt beside the sick lodger.

"Old Clary's too weak to work," said Billy. "So he stays in bed all day."

Norris made no comment, but he surely understood the significance of the blood-flecked bedclothes. Clary's pale face was so wasted by consumption that his bones seemed to gleam through his skin. All you had to do was look into his sunken eyes, hear the rattle of phlegm in his lungs, and you'd know that nothing could be done.

Without a word, Norris rose back to his feet.

Rose could see his expression as he looked around the room, taking in the bundles of clothes, the piles of straw that served as beds. The shadows were alive with skittering things, and Rose lifted her foot to crush something black as it darted past, feeling it crunch beneath her shoe. Yes, Mr. Marshall, she thought, this is where I live, in this infested room with a stinking waste bucket, sleeping on a floor that's so packed at night with lodgers, you must be careful which way you turn or you will find an elbow shoved in your eye or a dirty foot snagged in your hair.

"Over here's my bed!" declared Billy, and he plopped down on a pile of straw. "If we shut the curtain, we'll make a pretty room all to ourselves. You can sit there, sir. Old Polly won't notice that anyone's been using her bed."

Norris did not look at all eager to settle onto the bundle of rags and straw. As Rose slid the sheet across to give them privacy from the dying man in the corner, Norris stared down at Polly's bed, as though wondering how many vermin he might pick up by sitting there.

"Wait!" Billy leaped up to fetch the water bucket, which he brought sloshing back to their corner. "Now you can put the candle down."

"He's afraid of fire," said Rose as she carefully set the candle on the floor. And well Billy should be, in a room strewn with rags and straw. Only when she settled onto her own bed did Norris resignedly sit down as well. Curtained off in their own corner of the room, the three of them formed a circle around the flickering light, which cast spindly shadows on the hanging sheet.

"Now tell me," she said. "Tell me what happened to Mary."

He stared at the light. "I'm the one who found her," he said. "Last night, on the riverbank. I was walking across the hospital common when I heard her moans. She'd been cut, Miss Connolly, the same way Agnes Poole was cut. The same pattern, slashed into her abdomen."

"In the shape of a cross?"

"Yes."

"Does Mr. Pratt still blame papists?"

"I can't imagine that he does now."

She gave a bitter laugh. "Then you have your head in the sand, Mr. Marshall. There's no charge so outrageous that it can't be flung at the Irish."

"In the case of Mary Robinson, it's not the Irish on whom suspicion falls."

"Who would Mr. Pratt's unlucky suspect be this time?"

"I am."

In the silence that followed, she stared at the shadows playing on Norris's face. Billy had curled up like a tired cat beside his water bucket and now lay dozing, each breath rustling the straw. The consumptive man in the corner kept up his ceaseless coughing, his moist rattles a reminder that death was never far away.

"So you see," he said, "I know what it's like to be unfairly accused. I know what you've gone through."

"*You* know, do you? Yet it's myself who's looked at with suspicion every day of my life. *You* have no idea."

"Miss Connolly, last night I saw the same creature you did, but no believes me. No one else saw it. Worst of all, the hospital groundsman saw *me* bending over her body. I'm looked at with suspicion by the nurses, the other students. The hospital trustees may banish me from the wards. All I've ever wanted was to be a doctor. Now everything I've worked for is threatened, because so many doubt my word. Just as they doubted yours." He leaned closer, and the candle's glow painted his face with gaunt and spectral shadows. "You've seen it, too, that thing with the cape. I need to know if you remember the same things I do."

"I told you that night what I saw. But I don't think you believed me then."

"I admit, at the time your story seemed like . . ."

"A lie?"

"I would never make such an accusation against you. Yes, I thought your description far-fetched. But you were overwrought and clearly terrified." He added, quietly: "Last night, so was I. What I saw chilled me to the bone."

She looked at the candle flame. And whispered: "It had wings."

"A cape, perhaps. Or a dark cloak."

"And its face glowed white." She met Norris's gaze, and the light on his features brought back the memory with startling clarity. "White as a skull. Is that what you saw?"

"I don't know. The moon was on the water. Reflections can play tricks on the eye."

Her lips tightened. "I'm telling you what I saw. And in return, you offer explanations. 'It was just the *moon's reflection*'!"

"I'm a man of science, Miss Connolly. I can't help but seek logical explanations."

"And where is the logic in killing two women?"

"There may be none. Only evil."

She swallowed and said softly: "I'm afraid he knows my face."

Billy groaned and rolled over, his face slack and innocent in sleep. Looking at him, she thought: Billy understands nothing of evil. He sees a smile and does not understand that darkness may lie beneath it.

Footsteps thumped up the stairs, and Rose stiffened as she heard a woman's giggles, a man's laugh. One of the female lodgers had lured a client upstairs. Rose understood the necessity of it, knew that a few minutes with your legs spread could mean the difference between supper and a growling belly. But the noises the couple made, on the other side of that thin curtain, brought a mortified flush to Rose's cheeks. She could not bring herself to look at Norris. She stared down at her hands, knotted in her lap, as the couple groaned and grunted, as straw rustled beneath rocking bodies. And through it all, the sick man in the far corner kept coughing, drowning in bloody phlegm.

"And this is why you hide?" he asked.

Reluctantly, she looked at him, and found his gaze unflinching, as though he was determined to ignore the rutting and the dying that was happening only a few feet away. As if the filthy sheet had curtained them off into a separate world, where she was the sole focus of his attention.

"I hide to avoid trouble, Mr. Marshall. From everyone."

"Including the Night Watch? They're saying you pawned an item of jewelry that wasn't yours."

"My sister gave it to me."

"Mr. Pratt says you stole it. That you stripped it from her body while she lay dying."

She gave a snort. "My brother-in-law's doing. Eben wants his revenge, so he spreads rumors about me. Even if it was true, even if I *did* take it, I didn't owe it to him. How else was I supposed to pay for Aurnia's burial?"

"Her burial? But she . . . " He paused.

"What about Aurnia?" she asked.

"Nothing. It's just . . . an unusual name, that's all. A lovely name."

She gave a sad smile. "It was our grandmother's name. It means 'golden lady.' And my sister was truly a golden lady. Until she married."

Beyond the curtain, the grunts accelerated, accompanied by the forceful *slap-slap* of two bodies colliding. Rose could no longer look Norris in the eye. She stared down instead at her shoes, planted on the straw-littered floor. An insect crawled out from the straw where Norris was seated, and she wondered if he noticed it. She fought the urge to crush it with her shoe.

"Aurnia deserved better," Rose said softly. "But in the end, the only one standing at her grave was me. And Mary Robinson."

"Nurse Robinson was there?"

"She was kind to my sister, kind to everyone. Unlike Miss Poole. Oh, I had no love for *that* one, I'll admit, but Mary was different." She shook her head sadly.

The couple behind the curtain finished their rutting, and their grunts gave way to sighs of exhaustion. Rose had ceased paying attention to them; instead she was thinking of the last time she had seen Mary Robinson, at St. Augustine's cemetery. She remembered the woman's darting glances and jittery hands. And how she had suddenly vanished without saying goodbye.

Billy stirred and sat up, scratching his head and scattering pieces of dirty straw from his hair. He looked at Norris. "Are you sleeping here with us, then?" he asked.

Rose flushed. "No, Billy. He's not."

"I can move my bed to make room for you," said Billy. Then added, with a territorial note, "But I'm the only one gets to sleep next to Miss Rose. She promised."

"I wouldn't dream of taking your place, Billy," said Norris. He stood and brushed straw from his trousers. "I'm sorry to take up your time, Miss Connolly. Thank you for speaking to me." He pulled aside the curtain and started down the stairs.

"Mr. Marshall?" Rose scrambled to her feet and followed him. Already he was at the foot of the stairs, his hand on the door. "I must ask that you not inquire at my place of work again," she said.

He frowned up at her. "I'm sorry?"

"You threaten my livelihood if you do."

"I've never been to your place of employment."

"A man was there today, asking where I lived."

"I don't even know where you work." He opened the door, letting in a blast of wind that tugged at his coat and rippled the hem of Rose's skirt. "Whoever inquired about you, it wasn't me."

On this cold night, Dr. Nathaniel Berry is not thinking about death.

He's thinking instead about finding some willing quim, and why wouldn't he? He is a young man and he works long hours as the house physician at the hospital. He has no time to court women in the manner expected of a gentleman, no time for polite chitchat at soirées and musicales, no free afternoons for companionable walks on Colonnade Row. His life this year is all about serving the patients of Massachusetts General, twenty-four hours a day, and seldom is he allowed an evening away from the hospital grounds.

But tonight, to his surprise, he was offered a rare night of freedom.

When a young man must suppress too long his natural urges, those very urges are what drive him when at last he's let loose. And so when Dr. Berry leaves his hospital quarters, he heads directly toward the disreputable neighborhood of the North Slope, to the Sentry Hill Tavern, where grizzled seamen rub shoulders with freed slaves, where any young lady who walks through the door can be safely assumed to be in search of more than a glass of brandy.

Dr. Berry is not long inside the tavern.

After no more time than it takes to drink two rum flips, he comes walking back out again, with the chosen object of his lust laughing giddily at his side. He could not have chosen a more obvious whore than this disheveled tart with her tangled black hair, but she will serve his purposes just fine, so he leads her toward the river, where such assignations regularly take place. She goes along willingly, if a bit unsteadily, her drunken laughter echoing back along the narrow street. But as she catches sight of the water straight ahead, she suddenly halts, feet planted like a balky donkey's.

"What?" Dr. Berry asks, impatient to get beneath her skirts.

"It's the river. That girl was killed down there."

Of course Dr. Berry already knows this. After all, he knew and worked with Mary Robinson. But any sorrow he may feel over her death is secondary to the urgency of his current need. "Don't worry," he assures the whore. "I'll protect you. Come on."

"You ain't him, are you? The West End Reaper?"

"Of course not! I'm a doctor."

"They're sayin' *he* could be a doctor. That's why he's killin' nurses."

By now, Dr. Berry is getting desperate for relief. "Well, you're not a nurse, are you? Come along, and I'll make it worth your while." He tugs her a few feet farther, but once again she pulls to a stop.

"How do I know you won't slice me open like those poor ladies?"

"Look, the whole tavern just saw us leave together. If I were really the Reaper, do you think I'd take such a risk in public?"

Swayed by his unassailable logic, she allows him to lead her to the river. Now that he's so close to his goal, all he can think of is plunging deep into her. Mary Robinson does not even cross his mind as he practically drags the whore toward the water, and why should she? Dr. Berry feels no apprehension as he and the whore head toward the shadow of the bridge, where they cannot be seen.

But they can most certainly be heard.

The sounds rise from the darkness and drift up to the riverbank. The rustle of a skirt being yanked up, the heated breathing, the grunts of climax. In only a few minutes it is over, and the girl scurries back up the bank, a bit more disheveled perhaps, but a half eagle richer. She fails to notice the figure in the shadows as she hurries back to the tavern to troll for another client.

The oblivious girl just keeps walking, and does not even glance back toward the bridge where Dr. Berry lingers, fastening his trousers. She doesn't see what glides down the bank to meet him.

By the time Dr. Berry's final gasp of agony rises from the river, the whore is already back in the tavern, laughing in the lap of a sailor.

Eighteen

"You wished to speak to me, Dr. Grenville?" said Norris.

Dr. Grenville gazed across his desk, and his face, backlit by the morning sun, gave away nothing. The blow is about to fall, thought Norris. For days he'd been tormented by the rumors, by innuendo. He'd heard whispers in the halls, had caught the glances of his fellow students. As he stood facing Grenville, he prepared to hear the inevitable. Better to know the answer now, he thought, than to suffer through days or weeks of whispers before the final blow.

"You have seen the latest article in the *Daily Advertiser*?" asked Grenville. "About the West End murders?"

"Yes, sir." Why delay it any longer, he thought. Better to get it over with. He said, "I wish to know the truth, sir. Am I or am I not to be expelled from this college?"

"That's why you think I've called you here?"

"It is a reasonable assumption. Considering . . ."

"The rumors? Ah, yes, they are flying thick and furious. I've heard from the families of a number of our students. They're all concerned about the reputation of this college. Without our reputation, we are nothing."

Norris said nothing, but dread had settled like a stone in his stomach.

"The parents of those students are also worried about the well-being of their sons."

"And they think I am a threat."

"You can understand why, can't you?"

Norris looked him straight in the eye. "All they have to convict me is circumstance."

"Circumstance is a powerful voice."

"A misleading voice. It drowns out the truth. This medical college prides itself on its scientific method. Isn't that method all about seeking answers based on facts, not hearsay?"

Grenville leaned back in his chair, but his gaze remained fixed on Norris. Displayed in the office was evidence of how highly Grenville valued the study of science. On his desk, a grotesquely deformed human skull sat beside a normal one. In a corner hung a dwarf's skeleton, and on the shelves of the bookcase were specimens preserved in jars of whiskey: a severed hand with six fingers. A nose half eroded by tumor. A newborn with a single Cyclops eye. All these were silent testament to his fascination with anatomical oddities.

"I'm not the only one who's seen the killer," said Norris. "Rose Connolly has seen him, too."

"A monster with black wings and a skull's face?"

"There is *something* evil at work on the West End."

"Attributed by the Night Watch to the work of a butcher."

"And that's the real charge against me, isn't it? That I'm the son of a farmer. If I were Edward Kingston or your own nephew Charles, or the son of any prominent gentleman, would I still be a suspect? Would there be any doubt of my innocence?"

After a silence, Grenville said: "Your point is well taken."

"Yet it changes nothing." Norris turned to leave. "Good day, Dr. Grenville. I see I have no future here."

"Why would you *not* have a future here? Have I dismissed you from this school?"

Norris's hand was already on the doorknob. He turned back. "You said my presence was a problem."

"It is indeed a problem, but it's one that I'll deal with. I'm fully aware that you face a number of disadvantages. Unlike so many of your classmates, you did not come straight from Harvard, or indeed from any college. You're self-taught, yet both doctors Sewall and Crouch are impressed by your skills."

For a moment Norris could not speak. "I—I don't know how to thank you."

"Don't thank me yet. Things may still change."

"You won't regret this!" Again, Norris reached for the door.

"Mr. Marshall, there's one more thing."

"Sir?"

"When was the last time you saw Dr. Berry?"

"Dr. Berry?" This was a completely unexpected question, and Norris paused, perplexed. "It was yesterday evening. As he was leaving the hospital."

Grenville turned his troubled gaze to the window. "That was the last time I saw him, too," he murmured.

"Though there has been much speculation as to its etiology," said Dr. Chester Crouch, "the cause of puerperal fever remains open to debate. This is a most evil disease, which steals the lives of women just as they achieve their heart's desire, the gift of motherhood . . ." He stopped and stared.

So did everyone else, as Norris walked into the auditorium. Yes, the infamous Reaper had arrived. Did he terrify them? Were they all worried that he'd sit next to them, and his evil would rub off?

"Do find a seat, Mr. Marshall!" said Crouch.

"I'm trying to, sir."

"Over here!" Wendell stood. "We've saved a seat for you, Norris."

Acutely aware that he was being stared at, Norris squeezed his way up the row, past young men who seemed to flinch as he brushed past. He settled into the empty chair between Wendell and Charles. "Thank you both," he whispered.

"We were afraid you might not be coming at all," said Charles. "You should have heard the rumors this morning. They were saying—"

"Are you gentlemen *quite* finished with your conversation?" Crouch demanded, and Charles flushed. "Now. *If* you will allow me to continue." Crouch cleared his throat and began once again to pace the stage. "We are, at this moment, experiencing an epidemic in our lying-in ward, and I fear there are more cases to come. So we shall devote this morning's program to the subject of puerperal fever, otherwise known as childbed fever. It strikes a woman in the bloom of her youth, at precisely the time when she has the most to live for. Though her child might be safely delivered, and even thriving, the new mother still faces danger. It may manifest during labor, or the symptoms may develop hours, even days after the delivery. First, she feels a chill, sometimes so violent that her shaking will rattle the bed. This is followed inevitably by a fever that causes the skin to flush, the heart to race. But the true torment is the pain. It begins in the pelvic area and progresses to excruciating tenderness as the abdomen swells. Just to touch it, even a mere stroke of the skin, can induce screams of agony. There is often a bloody discharge, too, of a most foul and malodorous nature. The clothes, the bedsheets, indeed, even the entire sickroom may reek of the stench. You cannot imagine the mortifying distress of a gentlewoman, accustomed to the most scrupulous hygiene, who now finds the mere whiff of her body so repellent. But the worst is yet to come."

Crouch paused, and the audience was utterly silent, their attention riveted.

"The pulse grows more rapid," Crouch continued. "A fog clouds the mentation so that the patient sometimes does not know the day or the hour, or she mumbles incoherently. Often there is intractable vomiting, of indescribably foul matter. Respirations become labored. The pulse grows irregular. At which point, there is little left to offer except morphine and wine. Because death inevitably follows." He stopped and looked around the room. "In the months to come, you yourselves will see it, touch it, smell it. Some claim it's a contagion like smallpox. But if this is so, why does it not spread to the women in attendance, or to women who are not pregnant? Others say it is a miasma, an epidemic state of the air. Indeed, what other explanation might there be to account for the thousands of women dead of this illness in France? In Hungary? In England?

"Here, too, we are seeing many more of them. At our latest meeting of the Boston Society for Medical Improvement, my colleagues cited alarming numbers. One doctor has lost five patients in quick succession. And I have lost seven, in this month alone."

Wendell leaned forward, frowning. "My God," he murmured. "It truly is an epidemic."

"It has become such a terrifying prospect that many expectant mothers, in their ignorance, choose not to come to the hospital. But the hospital is where they can expect far superior conditions than in the filthy tenements, where no doctor attends them."

Abruptly Wendell stood. "A question, sir. If I may?"

Crouch glanced up. "Yes, Mr. Holmes?"

"Is there also such an epidemic in the tenements? Among the Irish in South Boston?"

"Not yet."

"But so many of them live in filth. Their diet is inadequate, their conditions in every way appalling. Under those conditions, shouldn't there be many such deaths?"

"The poor have a different constitution. They're made of sturdier stock."

"I've heard that women who suddenly give birth in the street or in the fields seldom come down with the fever. Is that also because of a stronger constitution?"

"That is my theory. I'll speak more of this in the weeks to come." He paused. "But now we move on to Dr. Sewall's anatomical presentation. His specimen today is, I regret to say, one of my own patients, a young woman who perished from the very illness I have just described. I now call on Dr. Sewall to demonstrate the anatomical findings."

As Dr. Crouch sat down, Dr. Sewall climbed to the stage, his massive girth creaking heavily on the steps.

"What you have just heard," said Sewall, "is the classic description of childbed fever. Now you shall see the pathology of this disease." He paused and gazed around the auditorium at the rows of students. "Mr. Lackaway! Will you come down here and assist me?"

"Sir?"

"You have yet to volunteer for any anatomical demonstration. Here is your chance."

"I don't think I'm the best choice—"

Edward, who was sitting behind Charles, said: "Oh, go *on*, Charlie." He gave him a clap on the shoulder. "I promise, someone will catch you this time when you faint."

"I'm waiting, Mr. Lackaway," said Sewall.

Swallowing hard, Charles stood and reluctantly made his way down to the stage.

Sewall's assistant rolled out the cadaver from the wing and removed the drape. Charles recoiled, staring at the young woman. Black hair cascaded from the table, and one arm, white and slim, dangled over the side.

"This should be amusing," said Edward, leaning forward to murmur in Wendell's ear. "How long do you think before he keels over? Shall we wager?"

"That isn't funny, Edward."

"Not yet it isn't."

On stage, Sewall uncovered his tray of instruments. He chose a knife and handed it to Charles, who looked at it as if he'd never seen a blade before. "This will not be a complete autopsy. We'll focus only on the pathology of this particular disease. You've been working on a cadaver all week, so by now you should be comfortable with dissection."

Edward murmured, "I give him ten seconds before he hits the ground."

"Hush," said Wendell.

Charles approached the body. Even from where he sat, Norris could see Charles's hand shaking.

"The abdomen," said Sewall. "Make your cut."

Charles pressed the knife to the skin. The whole audience seemed to hold their breath as he hesitated. Grimacing, he made a slice down the belly, but his cut was so shallow the skin did not even part.

"You'll have to be bolder than that, " said Sewall.

"I—I'm afraid I'll damage something important."

"You haven't even penetrated to the subcutaneous fat. Cut deeper."

Charles paused, gathering up his nerve. Again he sliced. Again it was too shallow, a stuttering incision that left large gaps of the abdominal wall intact.

"You'll have her shredded by the time you finally get into the cavity," said Sewall.

"I don't want to cut through the bowel."

"Look, you've already penetrated here, above the umbilicus. Poke a finger through and control your incision."

Though the room was not warm, Charles raised his sleeve to his forehead and wiped away sweat. Then, using one hand to stretch the belly wall taut, he sliced a third time. Pink loops slithered out, dripping bloody fluid onto the stage. He kept cutting, and his knife opened an ever-widening gap through which bowel spilled free. The putrid smell that rose from the cavity made him turn away, his face pale with nausea.

"Watch it. You've nicked the bowel!" barked Sewall.

Charles flinched, and his knife fell from his hand and thudded to the stage. "I've cut myself," he whimpered. "My finger."

Sewall gave an exasperated sigh. "Oh, go on, then. Sit down. I'll finish the demonstration myself."

Flushing with humiliation, Charles slunk off the stage and returned to his seat beside Norris.

"You all right, Charlie?" whispered Wendell.

"I was a disaster."

From behind, a hand clapped him on the shoulder. "Look on the bright side," said Edward. "At least this time, you didn't faint."

"Mr. Kingston!" boomed Dr. Sewall from the stage. "Would you care to share your comments with the rest of the class?"

"No, sir."

"Then kindly pay attention. This young woman nobly offered up her body for the benefit of future generations. The least you can do is pay her the respect of your silence." Dr. Sewall refocused on the cadaver, whose abdomen now gaped open. "You see, revealed here, the peritoneal membrane, and its appearance is quite abnormal. It is dull. In a healthy young soldier, killed quickly in combat, the membranes are bright and glistening. But in cases of childbed fever, the peritoneum lacks luster and there are pockets of pale and creamy fluid, foul smelling enough to turn the stomachs of even the most seasoned anatomist. I have seen bellies where the organs are drowning in this muck, and the intestines have numerous patches of hemorrhage. We cannot explain the reason for these changes. Indeed, as you've heard from Dr. Crouch, the theories for the cause of childbed fever are legion. Is it related to erysipelas or typhus? Is it an accident or merely providence, as Dr. Meigs in Philadelphia believes? I am no more than an anatomist. I can only show you what I have laid bare with my knife. By offering up her mortal remains for study, this subject has bestowed the gift of knowledge to every one of you."

Hardly a gift, thought Norris. Dr. Sewall always sang the praises of the unfortunate subjects who crossed his table. He pronounced them noble and generous, as though they had willingly offered themselves to be publicly hacked open and disemboweled. But this woman was no volunteer; she was a charity case, her body unclaimed by either family or friends. Sewall's praise was an unasked-for honor that almost certainly would have horrified her.

Dr. Sewall had split open the chest, and now he lifted out a lung for the audience to inspect. Only days ago, such a mutilation of the torso had shocked this group of medical students. Now these same men sat silent and unperturbed. No one looked away; no one lowered his head. They'd been introduced to the sights of the anatomy lab. They knew its smells, that unique mingling of decay and carbolic acid, and each had held the dissecting knife in his own hands. Glancing at his classmates, Norris saw a range of expressions from boredom to fierce concentration. Only a few weeks of medical study had stiffened their spines and steadied their stomachs so they could watch without disgust as Sewall excavated the heart and remaining lung from the chest. We've surrendered our sense of horror, thought Norris. It was the first step, a necessary step in their training.

There would be worse to come.

Nineteen

EARLY IN THE EVENING, Wall-eyed Jack had already singled him out. The sailor sat alone at a table, talking to no one, his gaze fixed only on the rum that Fanny set before him. Three drinks was all he had money for. He downed the last drink, and as Fanny waited, he rummaged through his pockets for more coins, but came up empty-handed. Jack could see Fanny's lips tighten, her eyes narrow. She had no patience for freeloaders. As far as she was concerned, if a man took up space at a table and enjoyed the feeble warmth of her hearth, he had better be able to afford to keep the rum flowing. Either you paid for another round, or you moved on. Even though the Black Spar was better than half empty tonight, Fanny allowed no exceptions. She didn't distinguish between the long-term patrons and the blow-ins; if they had no cash, they got no drinks, and out into the cold with them. That was the problem, thought Jack, watching Fanny's face turn ugly. That was why the Black Spar was a failing enterprise. Walk a ways down the street, into that new tavern, the Mermaid, and you'd find a laughing young barmaid and a generous fire that would put to shame the stingy flames in Fanny's hearth.

You'd also find a crowd, many of them Fanny's old regulars who'd fled the Black Spar. And no wonder; given a choice between a cheery barmaid and Fanny's scowl, any man in his right mind would head for the Mermaid. Already, he knew what she'd do next. First, she'd demand that the hapless sailor buy another round. And when he could not, she'd start in with her harangue. *You think that table's free? You think I can afford to let you sit here all night, taking a paying customer's place?* As if a line of paying customers stood waiting for the table. *I have the rent to pay and the tradesmen's bills. They don't work for free, and neither do I.* He could see her jaw tighten, her stout arms flexing for battle.

Before she could speak, Jack caught her gaze. He gave her a warning shake of his head. *Leave that one alone, Fanny.*

She stared at Jack for a moment. Then, with a nod of comprehension, she went behind the bar and poured a glass of rum. She came back to the sailor's table and set the glass before him.

The drink did not last long. A few gulps and it was all down his throat.

Fanny set another drink before him. She did it silently, calling no attention to the man's bottomless glass. This was not a crowd that was likely to notice anyway. In the Spar, a wise man kept to himself and minded his own drink. No one counted the number of times Fanny whisked away an empty glass and replaced it with a full one. No one cared that the man began to slump forward, his head resting on his arms.

One by one, as their pockets emptied, the customers staggered out into the cold, until there was only one man left, the snoring sea-man at the corner table.

Fanny crossed to the door, barred it shut, and turned to look at Jack.

"How much did you give him?" he asked.

"Enough to drown a horse."

The seaman gave a great rattling snore.

"He's still plenty alive," Jack said.

"Well, I can't very well pour it down his throat."

They stared down at the sleeping man, watching drool spill from his lips in a long, slimy strand. Above the frayed coat collar, his neck was grimy with coal dust. A fat louse, swollen with blood, crawled through a tangled net of blond hair.

Jack gave the shoulder a nudge; the man snored on, unaware.

Fanny snorted. "You can't expect them all to keel over nice and easy."

"He's a young one. Healthy looking." *Too healthy.*

"I just poured him a fortune's worth of free liquor. I'll never get it back."

Jack gave a harder shove. Slowly, the man tumbled out of the chair and thumped onto the floor. Jack stared at him for a moment, then bent down and rolled him onto his back. Damn it all. He was still breathing.

"I want my rum money out of this," insisted Fanny.

"Then *you* do it."

"I'm not strong enough."

Jack looked at her arms, thick and muscular from hefting trays and barrels. Oh, she was strong enough to strangle a man, all right. She just didn't want the responsibility.

"Go ahead, then," she insisted.

"I can't leave any marks on his neck. It'll raise questions."

"All they want's a body. They don't care where it comes from."

"But a man who's obviously been murdered—"

"Coward."

"I'm just telling you, it has to look natural."

"Then we'll make it look natural." Fanny stared down at the man for a moment, her eyes narrowed. Oh, you never wanted a woman like Fanny to look at you that way. Jack wasn't afraid of many things, but he knew Fanny well enough to know that when she set her mind against you, you were doomed. "Wait here," she said.

As if he was going anywhere.

He listened to her footsteps thumping up the stairs to their bedroom. A moment later she returned, carrying a threadbare cushion and a filthy rag. He understood at once what she had in mind, but even when she handed him the benign-looking instruments of death, he didn't move. He had dug up corpses with flesh falling off their bones. He had fished them out of the river, pried them out of coffins, shoved them into pickling barrels. But actually *making* a corpse was always a different matter. A hanging matter.

Still. Twenty dollars was twenty dollars, and who would miss this man?

He lowered himself onto creaking knees beside the drunken seaman and balled up the rag. The jaw had fallen slack, the tongue lolling to one side. He shoved the rag into the gaping mouth, and the man jerked his head and sucked in through his nostrils a whimpering breath. Jack lowered the cushion and pressed it over the mouth and nose. All at once the man came awake and clawed at the pillow, trying to tear it away, to breathe.

"Hold his arms! Hold his arms!" yelled Jack.

"I'm trying, damn it!"

The man bucked and twisted, boots pounding against the floor.

"I'm losing my grip! He won't lie still!"

"Then *sit* on him."

"*You* sit on him!"

Fanny pulled up her skirts and planted her hefty bottom on the squirming man's hips. As he bucked and twisted, she rode him like a whore, her face red and sweating.

"He's still fighting," said Jack.

"Don't let up the pillow. Press harder!"

Sheer terror had given the victim supernatural strength, and he clawed at Jack's arms, leaving bloody tracks with his nails. How long did it take a man to die, for pity's sake? Why couldn't he just surrender and save them all the trouble? A fingernail scraped across Jack's hand. With a roar of pain, Jack pressed down with all his weight, yet still the man fought him. *Damn you, die!*

Jack scrambled on top of the chest and sat on the ribs. Now they were both riding him, Fanny and Jack, she planted on his hips, Jack on his chest. Both of them were heavy, and their combined weight at last immobilized him. Only his feet were moving now, the heels of his boots battering the floor in a panicked tattoo. He was still clawing at Jack, but more feebly as the strength drained from his arms. Now the feet slowed their tempo, the boots flopping against the floor. Jack felt the chest give one last shudder beneath him, and then the arms went slack and slid away.

It was another moment before Jack dared to lift the pillow. He stared down at the mottled face, the skin imprinted by the pressure of coarse fabric. He pulled the rag, now soaked with saliva, from the man's mouth and tossed it aside. It landed with a wet thump.

"Well, that's done," said Fanny. She rose, panting, her hair in disarray.

"We need to strip him."

They worked together, peeling away the coat and shirt, the boots and trousers, all of it too worn and filthy to keep. No sense running the risk of being caught with a dead man's possessions. Still, Fanny searched the pockets and gave a grunt of outrage when she came up with a handful of coins.

"Look! He had money after all! Took all my free drinks and didn't say a word!" She turned and flung the man's clothes into the fireplace. "If he wasn't already dead, I'd—"

There was a knock on the door, and they both froze. Looked at each other.

"Don't answer it," whispered Jack.

Another knock, louder and more insistent. "I want a drink!" a slurred voice called out. "Open up!"

Fanny yelled through the door: "We're closed for the night!"

"How can you be closed?"

"I'm tellin' you we are. Go someplace else!"

They heard the man give the door one last angry thump of his fist, and then his curses faded away as he headed up the street, no doubt toward the Mermaid.

"Let's get 'im in the wagon," said Jack. He grabbed the naked man under the arms, startled by the unfamiliar heat of a newly dead corpse. The cold night would remedy that quick enough. Already, the lice were abandoning their host, swarming from the scalp and weaving their way through tangled hair. As he and Fanny hauled the body through the back room, Jack saw ravenous black dots leaping onto his arms, and he resisted the impulse to drop the corpse right then and there and slap away the insects.

Outside, in the stable yard, they swung the body into the dray and left it there, uncovered in the cold, as Jack harnessed the horse. Wouldn't do to deliver too warm a corpse. Though it probably wouldn't make a difference, as Dr. Sewall had never been one to ask questions.

Nor did he ask them this time. After Jack dropped the body onto Sewall's table, he stood by nervously as the anatomist peeled back the tarp. For a moment Sewall said nothing, though he must have registered the extraordinary freshness of this specimen. Holding a lamp close, he inspected the skin, tested the joints, peered into the mouth. No bruises, Jack thought. No wounds. Just some poor unfortunate sot he'd found collapsed dead on the street. That was the story. Then he noticed, with a flash of alarm, the louse crawling across the chest. Lice did not cling long to the dead, yet this body was still infested with them. *Does he see it? Does he know?*

Dr. Sewall set down the lamp and left the room. It seemed to Jack that he was gone a long time—far too long. Then Sewall returned, holding a bag of coins.

"Thirty dollars," he said. "Can you bring me more like this?"

Thirty? This was better than Jack had expected. He took the bag with a smile.

"As many as you can find," said Sewall. "I've got buyers."

"Then I'll find more."

"What happened to your hands?" Sewall was looking at the angry claw marks the dead man had left on Jack's flesh. At once Jack pulled his hands back, into the folds of his coat. "Drowned a cat. He didn't much appreciate it."

The bag of coins made a pleasant jingle in Jack's pocket as he steered the now empty dray over the cobblestones. What was a few scratches on the hand when you could walk away with thirty dollars? It was more than any other specimen had brought him. Visions of sacks bulging with coins shimmered in his head all the way home. The only problem was the clientele of the Black Spar; there simply weren't enough of them, and if he kept this up, there'd soon be none at all. It was that damn Fanny's fault, driving them away with her foul temper and stingy drinks. That had to be remedied at once. They'd start by showing a bit more generosity. No more watering down the rum, and maybe a bit of free food.

No, the food was a bad idea. It would only take longer to get them drunk. Better just to let the rum flow. What he had to do now was convince Fanny, which was no easy feat. But wave this sack of coins in front of her greedy face, and she'd see the light.

He rounded the corner into the narrow alley that led to his stable yard gate. Suddenly he yanked on the reins, drawing the horse to a stop.

A black-caped figure stood before him, silhouetted against the ice-slick gleam of cobblestones.

Jack squinted to make out a face. The features were shadowed by the hood, and as the figure approached, all he could see was the pale gleam of teeth.

"You've been busy tonight, Mr. Burke."

"I don't know what you mean."

"The fresher they are, the more they fetch."

Jack felt the blood freeze in his veins. *We were watched.* He sat still, heart thumping, his hands clutching the reins. *It only takes this one witness, and I'll swing from the gallows.*

"Your wife has let it be known that you seek easier ways to make a living."

Fanny? What the hell had she gotten him into now? Jack could almost imagine he saw the creature smile, and he shuddered. "What do you want?"

"A small service, Mr. Burke. I want you to find someone."

"Who?"

"A girl. Her name is Rose Connolly."

Twenty

In the lodging house on Fishery Alley, the nights were never silent.

A new lodger had joined them in that tightly packed room, an older woman recently widowed who could no longer afford her room on Summer Street, a private room with a real bed. Fishery Alley was where you landed when your luck crumbled beneath your feet, when your husband died or the factory closed or you were too old and ugly to turn a trick. This new lodger was doubly cursed, both widowed and sick as well, her body racked by wet coughs. Along with the consumptive man dying in the corner, theirs was a duet of coughs, accompanied by the nightly snores and sniffles and rustles. So many people were crammed together in the room that to empty your bladder meant tiptoeing across bodies to the pee bucket, and if by accident you trod on a stray arm or smashed someone's finger beneath your foot, your reward would be a howl and an angry slap on the ankle. And the next night, there'd be no sleep for you, because your own fingers would likely pay the penalty.

Rose lay awake, listening to the crackling of straw beneath restless bodies. She badly needed to urinate, but she was cozy beneath her blanket, and did not want to leave it. She tried to sleep, hoping that perhaps the urge would go away, but Billy suddenly whimpered and his limbs jerked out, as though to catch himself as he fell. She allowed his nightmare to play out; to wake him now would only burn its imprint into his memory. Somewhere in the darkness, she heard whispers and then the rustle of clothes and muffled panting as two bodies rocked together. We're no better than animals in a barnyard, she thought, reduced to scratching and farting and copulating in public. Even the new lodger, who had walked in with her head held high, was inexorably surrendering her pride, every day shedding another layer of dignity, until she, too, was peeing in the bucket like everyone else, hefting up her skirts in plain view to squat in the corner. Was she an image of Rose's future? Cold and sick and sleeping on filthy straw? Oh, but Rose was still young and sturdy, with hands eager to work. She could not see herself in that old woman, coughing in the dark.

Yet already Rose was just like her, sleeping shoulder-to-shoulder with strangers.

Billy gave another whimper and rolled toward her, his breath hot and foul on her face. She turned away to escape it and bumped up against old Polly, who gave her an irritated kick. Rose rolled resignedly onto her back and tried to ignore her ever-fuller bladder. She thought hungrily of baby Meggie. Thank God you are not sleeping here in this filthy room, breathing in this foul air. I'll see you grow up healthy, girl, even if my eyes go blind from threading needles, even if my fingers fall off from stitching day and night, sewing gowns for ladies who never need to worry about where their babies will get their milk. She thought of the gown she had completed yesterday, made of white gauze over an underslip of pale pink satin. By now it would have been delivered to the young lady who had ordered it. Miss Lydia Russell, the daughter of the distinguished Dr. Russell. Rose had worked feverishly to complete it on time, since

she'd been told that Miss Lydia needed it for the medical college reception tomorrow night, at the home of the dean, Dr. Aldous
Grenville. Billy had seen the house, and had described to Rose how
grand it was. He'd heard that the butcher had delivered haunches of
pork and a large basket of freshly slaughtered geese, and that all day
tomorrow Dr. Grenville's ovens would be roasting, baking. Rose
imagined the reception table, with its platters of tender meats and
cakes and succulent oysters. She imagined the laughter and the candlelight, the doctors in their fine topcoats. She imagined the ribbon-
bedecked ladies taking their turns at the piano, each vying to
display her skills to the young men assembled there. Would Miss
Lydia Russell sit at the piano? Would the skirt that Rose had sewn
for her drape nicely across the bench? Would it flatter its wearer's
figure and catch the eye of a certain favored gentleman?

Would Norris Marshall be there?

She felt a sudden twinge of jealousy that he might admire the
young lady who wore the gown Rose had labored over. She remembered his visit to this lodging house, and how his face had registered
dismay as he'd gazed at the louse-infested straw, at the dirty bundles
of clothes. She knew that he was a man of only modest means, but
he was beyond her reach. Even a farmer's son, if he carried a medical
bag, could one day be welcomed into the best parlors in Boston.

The only way Rose would ever set foot in those parlors was with
a mop in her hand.

She was jealous of the lady who would one day wed him. *She*
wanted to be the one to comfort him, the one he smiled at every
morning. But *I never will be*, she thought. *When he looks at me, he
sees only a seamstress or a kitchen girl. Never a wife.*

Once again Billy turned over, this time bumping right up against
her. She tried to push him away, but it was like trying to roll a limp
sack of flour. Resigned, she sat up. Her full bladder could no longer
be ignored. The piss bucket was on the far end of the room, and she
dreaded stumbling her way through the dark, across all those sleep-

ing bodies. Better to take the stairs, which were much closer, and go outside to pee.

She pulled on her shoes and cloak, crawled across Billy's sleeping body, and made her way down the stairs. Outside, the slap of cold wind made her suck in a startled breath. She wasted no time taking care of her needs. Glancing up and down Fishery Alley, she saw no one, and squatted right there on the cobblestones. With a sigh of relief, she stepped back into the lodging house and was about to climb the stairs when she heard the landlord call out:

"Who's there? Who's come in?"

Peeking through his doorway, she caught sight of Mr. Porteous, sitting with his feet propped up on a stool. He was half blind and always short of breath, and it was only with the help of his slovenly daughter that he managed to keep up the establishment. Not that there was much to do except collect the rent, dole out fresh straw once a month, and in the morning serve a bit of porridge, more often than not infested with mealworms. Otherwise, Porteous ignored the lodgers, and they ignored him.

"It's me," said Rose.

"Come in here, girl."

"I'm on my way upstairs."

Porteous's daughter appeared in the doorway. "There's a gentleman here to see you. Says he knows you."

Norris Marshall has come back was her first reaction. But when she stepped into the room and saw the visitor standing by the fireplace, bitter disappointment silenced any greeting from her lips.

"Hello, Rose," said Eben. "I've had a hard time tracking you down."

She owed her brother-in-law no pleasantries. Bluntly she asked, "What are you doing here?"

"I've come to make amends."

"The person you should make amends to is no longer here to forgive you."

"You have every right to reject my apologies. I'm ashamed of how I behaved, and every night I lie awake thinking of all the ways I could have been a better husband to your sister. I did not deserve her."

"No, you did not."

He came toward her, arms outstretched, but she did not trust his eyes; she never had. "This is the only way I know how to make it up to Aurnia," he said. "By being a good brother to you, a good father to my daughter. By taking care of you both. Go, fetch the baby, Rose. Let's go home."

Old Porteous and his daughter both watched with rapt expressions. They spent most of their lives confined to this gloomy front room, and this was probably the best entertainment they'd been treated to in weeks.

"Your old bed is waiting for you," said Eben. "And a crib, for the baby."

"I'm paid up here for the month," said Rose.

"*Here?*" Eben gave a laugh. "You can't possibly prefer *this* place!"

"Now then, Mr. Tate," cut in Porteous, suddenly realizing he'd just been insulted.

"How are your accommodations here, Rose?" asked Eben. "Have you your own room, with a fine feather bed?"

"I give them fresh straw, sir," said Porteous's daughter. "Every month."

"Oh! Fresh straw! Now *there's* something to commend this establishment."

The woman looked uneasily at her father. It had managed to penetrate even her thick skull that Eben's comments were not complimentary.

Eben took a breath, and when he spoke again, his voice was calmer. Reasonable. "Rose, please consider what I'm offering. If you're not happy, you can always return here."

She thought of the room upstairs, where fourteen lodgers lay wedged together, where the air smelled of piss and unwashed bodies, and your neighbor's breath reeked of rotting teeth. The boarding-house where Eben lived was not grand, but it was clean, and she would not be sleeping on straw.

And he was her family. He was all she had left.

"Go up and fetch her. Let's go."

"She's not here."

He frowned. "Then where is she?"

"She stays with a wet nurse. But my bag is upstairs." She turned toward the steps.

"Unless it has something of value, leave it! Let's not waste time."

She thought of the fetid room upstairs, and suddenly had no desire to return to it. Not now, not ever. Still, she was sorry to leave without telling Billy.

She looked at Porteous. "Please tell Billy to bring my bag 'round tomorrow. I'll pay him for it."

"The idiot boy? Does he know where to go?" asked Porteous.

"The tailor shop. He knows where it is."

Eben took her arm. "The night gets colder by the hour."

Outside, snowflakes had begun to swirl down from the darkness, fine, stinging flakes that settled treacherously onto cobblestones already slick with ice.

"Which way to this wet nurse?" Eben asked.

" 'Tis a few streets over." She pointed. "Not far."

Eben picked up the pace, urging her far too quickly on such precarious ground, and she had to cling to his arm as her shoes slipped and skated. Why such haste, she wondered, when a warm room assuredly waited for them? Why, after that impassioned appeal for her forgiveness, had he suddenly fallen silent? He'd called Meggie *the baby*, she thought. What kind of father doesn't even know his own daughter's name? As they drew closer to Hepzibah's door, she grew more and more uneasy. She'd never trusted Eben before; why should she trust him now?

She did not stop at Hepzibah's building, but walked straight past it and turned down another street. Kept leading Eben away from Meggie as she considered why he had really come for her tonight. His grasp offered no warmth, no reassurance, only the cold grip of control.

"Where is this place?" he demanded.

"A distance, still."

"You said it was close by."

"It's so late, Eben! Must we fetch her now? We'll wake the household."

"She's my daughter. She belongs with *me*."

"And how will you feed her?"

"It's all arranged."

"What do you mean, *all arranged?*"

He gave her a hard shake. "Just take me to her!"

Rose had no intention of doing so. Not now, not until she knew what he really wanted. Instead, she continued to lead him away, leaving Meggie far behind them.

Abruptly Eben jerked her to a stop. "What game are you playing with me, Rose? We've gone twice past this very street!"

" 'Tis dark, and these alleys confuse me. If we could wait until morning—"

"Don't lie to me!"

She yanked away from him. "A few weeks ago, you cared nothing about your daughter. Now suddenly you can't wait to get your hands on her. Well, I won't give her up now, not to you. And there's nothing you can do to make me."

"Maybe nothing I can do," he says. "But there's someone else who might convince you."

"Who?"

In answer, he grabbed her arm and pulled her up the street. With Rose stumbling behind him, he headed toward the harbor. "Stop struggling! I'm not going to hurt you."

"Where are we going?"

"To a man who could change your life. If you're nice to him." He led her to a building she did not know and knocked on the door.

It opened, and a middle-aged gentleman with gold-rimmed spectacles peered out at them over a flickering lamp. "I was about to give up and leave, Mr. Tate," he said.

Eben gave Rose a shove, forcing her ahead of him over the threshold. She heard the bolt slide home behind her.

"Where is the child?" the man asked.

"She won't tell me. I thought you could convince her."

"So this is Rose Connolly," the man said, and she heard London in his voice. An Englishman. He set down the lamp and looked her over with a thoroughness that alarmed her, though he himself was not a particularly alarming sort of man. He was shorter than Eben, and his thick side-whiskers were mostly gray. His topcoat was fashionably cut and well fitted, of fine fabric. Though not physically intimidating, his gaze was coolly formidable and penetrating.

"So much fuss over this mere girl."

"She's cleverer than she looks," said Eben.

"Let's hope so." The man started down a hallway. "This way, Mr. Tate. We'll see what she can tell us."

Eben took her arm, his firm grip leaving no doubt that she would go where he directed her. They followed the man into a room where she saw roughly made furniture and a floor scarred by gouges. The shelves were lined with tattered ledgers, the pages yellowed from disuse. In the hearth were only cold ashes. The room did not match the man, whose tailored coat and air of prosperity were better suited to one of the fine homes on Beacon Hill.

Eben pushed her into a chair. It took only one dark look from him to get his message across: *You will sit there. You will not move.*

The older man set the lamp down on a desk, stirring up a puff of dust. "You've been in hiding, Miss Connolly," he said. "Why?"

"What makes you think I've been hiding?"

"Why else would you call yourself Rose Morrison? That is, I believe, the false name you gave to Mr. Smibart when he hired you as a seamstress."

She shot a glare at Eben. "I didn't wish to encounter my brother-in-law again."

"That's why you changed your name? It had nothing to do with this?" The Englishman reached into his pocket and pulled out something that gleamed in the lamplight. It was Aurnia's necklace. "I believe you pawned this several weeks ago. Something that did not belong to you."

She stared at him in silence.

"So you *did* steal it."

She could not let that charge go unanswered. "Aurnia gave it to me!"

"And you so blithely rid yourself of it?"

"She deserved a decent burial. I had no other way to pay for it."

The Englishman glanced at Eben. "You didn't tell me that. She had a good reason to pawn it."

"It still wasn't hers," said Eben.

"And it sounds like it wasn't yours, either, Mr. Tate." The man looked at Rose. "Did your sister ever tell you where she got this necklace?"

"I used to think it was Eben. But he's too cheap."

The Englishman ignored Eben's glower and kept his focus on Rose. "So she never told you where she got it?" he asked.

"Why does it matter?" she shot back.

"This is a valuable piece of jewelry, Miss Connolly. Only someone of means could have afforded it."

"Now you'll claim Aurnia stole it. You're with the Night Watch, aren't you?"

"No."

"Who are you?"

Eben gave her a hard slap on the shoulder. "Show some respect!"

"For a man who won't even tell me his name?"

For her impudence, Eben raised his hand to deliver another blow, but the Englishman cut in: "There's no need for violence, Mr. Tate!"

"But you see what kind of girl she is! That's what I've had to put up with."

The Englishman moved toward Rose, his gaze boring into her face. "I'm not with the local authorities, if that's any reassurance."

"Then why do you ask me these questions?"

"I work for a client who shall remain nameless. I'm charged with the gathering of information. Information that, I'm afraid, only you can provide."

She gave a disbelieving laugh. "I'm a seamstress, sir. Ask me about buttons or bows, and I'll have an answer for you. Other than that, I don't see how I can help."

"But you can help me. You're the only one." He moved in so close she could smell sweet tobacco on his breath. "Where is your sister's child? Where is the baby?"

"He doesn't deserve her." She glanced at Eben. "What sort of father signs away the rights to his own daughter?"

"Just tell me where she is."

"She's safe and she's fed. That's all he needs to know. Instead o' paying a pretty penny for a fancy lawyer, he could've bought his girl milk and a warm crib."

"Is that what you think? That I'm in Mr. Tate's employ?"

"Aren't you?"

The Englishman gave a startled laugh. "Heavens, no!" he said, and she saw the angry flush of Eben's face. "I work for someone else, Miss Connolly. Someone who wants very much to know where the child is." He brought his face even closer, and she drew away, her back pressing into the chair. "Where is the baby?"

Rose sat silent, suddenly thinking of that day in St. Augustine's cemetery, when Aurnia's grave had yawned at her feet. Mary Robinson had appeared like a ghost from the mist, her face pale and taut, her gaze ceaselessly scanning the graveyard. *There are people inquiring about the child. Keep her hidden. Keep her safe.*

"Miss Connolly?"

She felt her own pulse throbbing in her neck as his gaze bore even deeper. She remained silent.

To her relief, he straightened and wandered to the other end of the room, where he casually ran a finger across a bookshelf and looked at the dust he'd picked up. "Mr. Tate tells me you're a clever girl. Is that true?"

"I wouldn't know, sir."

"I think you're entirely too modest." He turned and looked at her. "What a shame that a girl with your intelligence is forced to live so close to the edge. Your shoes look as if they're falling apart. And that cloak—when was it last washed? Surely, you deserve better."

"So do many others."

"Ah, but *you* are the one being offered an opportunity here."

"Opportunity?"

"A thousand dollars. If you bring me the child."

She was stunned. That much money could buy a room in a fine lodging house with hot meals every night. New clothes and a warm coat, not this cloak with its tattered hem. All the tempting luxuries she could only dream about.

All I have to do is surrender Meggie.

"I can't help you," she said.

Eben's blow came so quickly that the other man had no time to intervene. The impact made Rose's head snap sideways and she cringed in the chair, her cheek throbbing.

"That was not necessary, Mr. Tate!"

"You see how she is, though?"

"You can get more cooperation with a carrot than with a stick."

"Well, she just turned down the carrot."

Rose lifted her head and stared at Eben with undisguised hatred. No matter what they offered her, be it a thousand or ten thousand dollars, she would never give away her own flesh and blood.

The Englishman now stood before her, eyeing her face, where a bruise was surely starting to form. She didn't fear a blow from him;

this man, she guessed, was far more accustomed to using words and cash as his tools of persuasion, and left the violence to other men.

"Let's try again," he said to Rose.

"Or you'll have him hit me again?"

"I do apologize for that." He looked at Eben. "Leave the room."

"But I know her better than anyone! I can tell you when she's—"

"*Leave the room.*"

Eben shot Rose a poisonous look, then walked out, slamming the door behind him.

The man reached for a chair and dragged it over to Rose's. "Now, Miss Connolly," he said, sitting down to face her. "You know it's only a matter of time until we find her. Save us all the trouble and you'll be well rewarded."

"Why is she so important to you?"

"Not to me. To my client."

"Who *is* this client?"

"Someone who cares about the child's welfare. Who wants her to stay alive and healthy."

"Are you saying Meggie's in danger?"

"Our concern is that *you* may be. And if something happens to you, we'll never find the child."

"Now you're threatening me?" She forced a laugh, displaying a recklessness she did not really feel. "You've given up on the carrot, and you're back to the stick."

"You mistake my meaning." He leaned forward, his face deadly serious. "Both Agnes Poole and Mary Robinson are dead. You do know that?"

She swallowed. "Yes."

"You were a witness the night Agnes Poole died. You saw the killer. And he certainly knows that."

"Everyone knows who the killer is," she said. "I heard it yesterday, on the streets. Dr. Berry has fled town."

"Yes, that's what the newspapers have reported. Dr. Nathaniel Berry lived in the West End. He knew the two victims. He tried to kill a third—a prostitute, who claims she had to flee for her life. Now Dr. Berry's gone missing, so of course he must be the Reaper."

"Isn't he?"

"Do you believe everything you hear on the street?"

"But if he isn't the killer . . ."

"Then the West End Reaper may still be in Boston, and he could very well know your identity. After what happened to Mary Robinson, I'd be looking over my shoulder if I were you. We were able to find you, and so could anyone else. Which is why I'm so concerned about your niece's welfare. You're the only one who knows the baby's whereabouts. If anything happened to you. . ." He paused. "A thousand dollars, Miss Connolly. It would help you leave Boston. Help you find a comfortable new home. Give us the child, and the money's yours."

She said nothing. Mary Robinson's last words to her kept echoing in her head: *Keep her hidden. Keep her safe.*

Weary of her silence, the man finally stood. "Should you change your mind, you can find me here." He placed a calling card in her hand, and she stared down at the printed name.

Mr. Gareth Wilson
5 Park Street, Boston

"You'd do well to consider my offer," he said. "And to consider, too, the welfare of the child. In the meantime, Miss Connolly, do be careful. You never know what monster might be searching for you." He walked out, leaving her alone in that cold and dusty room, her gaze still fixed on the card.

"Are you insane, Rose?"

She looked up at the sound of Eben's voice, and saw him standing in the doorway.

"That's more money than you'll ever see! How dare you refuse it?"

Staring into his eyes, she suddenly understood why he cared. Why he was involved. "He promised you money, too, didn't he?" she said. "How much?"

"Enough to make it worth it."

"Worth giving up your child?"

"Haven't you figured it out? She's not *my* child."

"Aurnia would never—"

"Aurnia *did*. I thought it was mine, and that's the only reason I married her. But time tells the truth, Rose. It told me what kind of woman I really married."

She shook her head, still not willing to believe it.

"Whoever the father is," said Eben, "he wants that child. And he has enough to pay whatever it takes."

Money enough for a lawyer, she thought. Money enough to buy his mistress a fine necklace. Maybe even enough to buy silence. For what fine gentleman wants it known that he's fathered a child with a poor seamstress only a year out of Ireland?

"Take the money," said Eben.

She stood. "I'd starve before I give her up."

He followed her out of the room, to the front door. "You don't have much choice! How're you going to feed yourself? Keep a roof over your head?"

As she stepped outside, he yelled: "This time they were gentle with you, but next time you won't be so lucky!"

To her relief, Eben didn't follow her. The night had grown even colder, and she shivered as she retraced her steps to Fishery Alley. The streets were deserted, and invisible fingers of wind swept the snow in swirling furrows before her feet. Suddenly she halted and looked back. Had she just heard footsteps? She peered into the stinging mist, but saw no one behind her. *Don't go near Meggie, not tonight. They may be watching you.* Quickening her pace, she continued toward Fishery Alley, eager to escape the wind. What a fool she'd been to let Eben lure her from the relative comfort, poor though it was, of her lodging house. Poor Dim Billy was a better man, a truer friend, than Eben would ever be.

She made her way into the maze of South Boston. The cold had swept all sensible people off the streets, and as she passed a tavern, she heard the voices of men who'd gathered inside to escape the cold. Through the steamed windows she saw their silhouettes against the firelight. She did not linger, but walked on, hoping that old Porteous and his daughter had not already barred the door. Even her poor pile of straw, her patch of floor among the unwashed bodies, seemed a luxury this night, and she should not have so easily surrendered it. The sounds of the tavern faded behind her and she heard only the whistle of the wind through the narrow passage and the rush of her own breath. Fishery Alley was just around the next corner, and like a horse who has sighted its stable and knows that shelter lies ahead, she quickened her pace and almost skidded across the stones. She caught herself against a wall, and was just straightening when she heard the sound.

It was the rattle of a man clearing his throat.

Slowly, she approached the corner and peered around the building, into Fishery Alley. At first, all she saw were shadows and the dim glow of candlelight through a window. Then a man's silhouette emerged from the shelter of a doorway. He paced the alley, clapping his shoulders to stay warm. Clearing his throat again, he spat on the stones, then returned to the doorway and vanished back into shadow.

Silently she backed away from the corner. Perhaps the man's had too much to drink, she thought. Perhaps he'll soon be on his way home.

Or perhaps he's watching for me.

She waited, her heart thumping, as the minutes went by, as the wind flapped at her skirt. Again she heard him cough and spit, then there was a pounding on a door, and she heard Porteous's voice: "I told you, she's not likely to come back tonight."

"When she does, you send me word. No delay."

"I told you I would."

"You'll get your fee then. Only then."

"I'd better," said Porteous, and the door slammed shut.

Rose quickly ducked between buildings and watched from the shadows as the man emerged from Fishery Alley and walked right past her. She could not make out his face, but she could see his hulking silhouette and heard him wheeze in the cold. She waited long enough for him to be well away; only then did she emerge from her hiding place.

I do not have even a pitiful pile of straw to return to.

She stood shivering in the road, staring in desolation at the darkness into which the man had just vanished. She turned and walked in the opposite direction.

Twenty-one

The present

THE JOURNEY WAS familiar to Julia now, the same road north, the same ferry ride, even the same dense fog hiding her view of the crossing to Islesboro. This time, though, she was prepared for the damp weather, and was dressed in a sweater and jeans as she dragged her small roll-aboard suitcase up the dirt driveway to Stonehurst. When the weathered house suddenly loomed into view through the mist, she had the strange impression that it was welcoming her home, a surprising thing to feel considering her last visit with the irascible Henry. But there had been warm moments between them, too. A moment when, tipsy on wine, she'd looked across at his scowl, his weathered face, and thought: As cranky as Henry can be, there's an integrity to this man, an honesty that runs so deep, I know I can believe every word that comes out of his mouth.

She hauled her suitcase up the steps to the porch and knocked on the door. This time, she resolved to be patient and wait until he appeared. After a few moments, when he did not answer, she tried the front door and found it unlocked. Poking her head inside, she called out: "Henry?" She brought her suitcase into the house and yelled up the stairs: "Henry, I'm here!"

She heard no answer.

She walked into the library, where the sea windows admitted the gloomy light of another fog-bound afternoon. She saw papers scattered across the table, and her first thought was: *Henry, you've really made a mess of things now.* Then she spotted the cane lying on the floor, and the two skinny legs that poked out from behind the stack of boxes.

"Henry!"

He was lying on his side, his trousers soaked in urine. Frantic, she rolled him onto his back and bent close, to see if he was breathing.

He opened his eyes. And whispered: "I knew you'd come."

"I think he may have had an arrhythmia," said Dr. Jarvis. "I find no signs of a stroke or heart attack, and his EKG looks normal at the moment."

"At the moment?" asked Julia.

"That's the problem with arrhythmias. They can come and go without warning. Which is why I want to keep him on a monitored unit for the next twenty-four hours, so we can watch what his heart does." Jarvis looked across the room at the closed curtain, which hid their view of Henry's hospital bed, and he dropped his voice. "But we're going to have a hard time convincing him to stay that long. That's where you come in, Ms. Hamill."

"Me? I'm just his houseguest. You need to talk to his family."

"I've already called them. His grandnephew's driving up from Massachusetts, but he won't get here till midnight at the earliest. Until then, maybe you can talk Henry into staying in that bed."

"Where else is he going to go? The ferry's stopped running."

"Ha, you think that'd stop Henry? He'd just call some friend with a boat to bring him home."

"You sound like you know him pretty well."

"The whole medical staff knows Henry Page. I'm the only doctor he hasn't fired yet." Jarvis sighed and closed the hospital chart. "And I may be about to lose that exclusive status."

Julia watched Dr. Jarvis walk away and thought: When did I sign up for *this*? But *this* was the burden she'd taken on when she'd found Henry lying on his library floor. She was the one who'd called the ambulance, who'd accompanied him during the ferry ride to the mainland. For the past four hours, she'd sat in Penobscot Bay Medical Center, waiting for the doctors and nurses to finish their evaluation. Now it was nine PM, she was starving, and she had no place to sleep except the waiting room couch.

Through the closed curtain came Henry's complaining voice: "Dr. Jarvis told you I didn't have a heart attack. So why am I still here?"

"Mr. Page, don't you dare disconnect that monitor."

"Where is she? Where's my young lady?"

"She's probably left by now."

Julia took a deep breath and crossed to his bed. "I'm still here, Henry," she said, and stepped through the curtain.

"Take me home now, Julia."

"You know I can't."

"Why not? What's to stop you?"

"The ferry, for one thing. It stopped running at five."

"Call my friend Bart in Lincolnville. He has a boat with radar. He can get us across in the fog."

"No, I'm not going to. I refuse."

"You *refuse*?"

"Yes. And you can't make me."

He stared at her for a moment. "Well," he huffed, "someone's grown a spine."

"Your grandnephew's on his way. He'll be here later tonight."

"Maybe he'll do what I want."

"If he gives a damn about you, he'll say no."

"And what's *your* reason for saying no?"

She looked him straight in the eye. "Because a corpse can't help me go through those boxes," she said and turned to leave.

"Julia?"

She sighed. "Yes, Henry?"

"You'll like my grandnephew."

Through the closed curtain, Julia heard a doctor and nurse conferring, and she sat up, rubbing the sleep from her eyes. She had dozed off in the chair by Henry's bed, and the paperback novel she'd been reading had fallen on the floor. She picked up the book and glanced at Henry. He, at least, was sleeping comfortably.

"This is his most recent EKG?" a man asked.

"Yes. Dr. Jarvis said they've all been normal."

"You've seen no arrhythmias on the monitor?"

"Not so far."

The sound of shuffling paper. "His blood work looks good. Oops, I take that back. His liver enzymes are up a little. He must be into that wine cellar again."

"Do you need anything else, Dr. Page?"

"Other than a double shot of scotch?"

The nurse laughed. "At least *I* get to go off duty now. Good luck with him. You'll need it."

The curtain parted and Dr. Page stepped in. Julia stood to greet him, and her gaze fixed on a startlingly familiar face. "Tom," she murmured.

"Hi, Julia. I hear he's been giving you a hard time. On behalf of our whole family, I apologize."

"But you—" She paused. "*You're* his grandnephew?"

"Yeah. Didn't he tell you I lived in your neighborhood?"

"No. He never mentioned it."

Tom glanced in surprise at Henry, who was still sound asleep. "Well, that's bizarre. I told him that you and I had met. That's why he called you."

She motioned to him to follow her away from the bed. They stepped through the curtain and crossed to the nurses' station. "Henry called me because of Hilda's papers. He thought I'd be interested in the history of my house."

"Right. I told him that you wanted to know more about the bones in your garden. Henry's sort of our family historian, so I thought he might be able to help you." Tom glanced toward Henry's bed. "Well, he *is* eighty-nine. He might forget things."

"He's sharp as a tack."

"Are you talking about his mind or his tongue?"

At that she laughed. "Both. That's why it was such a shock for me when I found him on the floor. He seems so indestructible."

"I'm glad you were there. Thank you for everything you did." He touched her shoulder, and she flushed at the warmth of his hand. "He's not the easiest person to deal with, which is probably why he never got married." Tom looked down at the hospital chart. "He looks good on paper."

"I'd forgotten. Henry told me his grandnephew was a doctor."

"Yes, but not his. I specialize in infectious disease. Dr. Jarvis said there might be a little trouble with the old ticker."

"He wants to go home. He asked me to call some guy named Bart about a boat ride."

"You're kidding." Tom looked up. "Bart's still alive?"

"What are we going to do with him?"

"We?" He closed the chart. "How did Henry manage to rope you into this?"

She sighed. "I feel responsible, in a way. I'm the reason he's digging through those boxes and getting himself all worked up. Maybe it's too much for him, and that's why he collapsed."

"You can't make Henry do anything he doesn't want to do. When I spoke to him last week, he sounded more excited than I've heard him in years. Usually he's crotchety and depressed. Now he's just crotchety."

From behind the curtain came Henry's voice. "I heard that."

Tom grimaced and set down the chart. He crossed to Henry's bed and opened the curtain. "You're awake."

"Took you long enough to get here. Now let's go home."

"Whoa! What's the rush?"

"Julia and I have work to do. Twenty more boxes at least! Where is she?"

She joined Tom at the curtain. "It's too late to go home now. Why don't you go back to sleep?"

"Only if you promise you'll take me home tomorrow."

She looked at Tom. "What do you think?"

"That's up to Dr. Jarvis," he said. "But if he clears it, I'll help you get him home in the morning. And I'll hang around for a few days, just to make sure everything's okay."

"Oh, good!" said Henry, clearly delighted. "You'll be staying!"

Tom smiled in surprise at his granduncle. "Why Henry, it's so nice to be appreciated."

"*You* can bring up all the boxes from the cellar."

It was late the next afternoon when they brought Henry home on the ferry. Though Dr. Jarvis had ordered him to go straight to bed, of course Henry did no such thing. Instead, he stationed himself at the top of the cellar steps, shouting orders as Tom carried boxes up the stairs. By the time Henry finally retired to his bedroom that night, it was Tom who was exhausted.

With a sigh, Tom sank into an armchair by the fireplace and said: "He may be eighty-nine, but he can still make me jump through hoops. And if I dare ignore him, he's got that lethal-looking cane."

Julia looked up from the box of papers she'd been sorting through. "Has he always been this way?"

"As long as I can remember. Which is why he lives alone. No one else in the family wants to deal with him."

"Then why are you here?"

"Because I'm the one he keeps calling. He never had any children. By default, I guess I'm it." Tom looked at her hopefully. "Want to adopt a used uncle?"

"Not even if he comes with four hundred bottles of vintage wine."

"Oh. So he's introduced you to his wine cellar."

"We made a good dent in it last week. But the next time a man gets me drunk, I'd like him to be on the other side of seventy." She turned her attention to the documents they'd pulled out of box number fifteen that afternoon. It was a sheaf of old newspapers, most of them dating to the late 1800s and not relevant to the story of Norris Marshall. If pack rat behavior was genetic, then Hilda Chamblett had inherited it from her great-great-grandmother Margaret Page, who, it seemed, could not throw away anything, either. Here were old editions of *The Boston Post* and the *Evening Transcript* and recipe clippings so brittle that they crumbled at a touch. There were also letters, dozens of them, addressed to Margaret. Julia was sucked into reading every single one, intrigued by this glimpse into the life of a woman who, more than a hundred years ago, had lived in her house, had walked the same floors, climbed the same stairs. Dr. Margaret Tate Page had lived a long and eventful life, judging by the letters she'd collected through the years. And such letters! They came from eminent physicians around the world, and from adoring grandchildren traveling in Europe, describing the meals served, the dresses worn, the gossip shared. What a shame no one today has time to write such letters, Julia thought as she devoured the tale of a grandchild's flirtation. A hundred years after I am dead, what will anyone know about me?

"Anything interesting?" asked Tom. She was startled to find him standing right behind her, looking over her shoulder.

"This should all be interesting to you," she said, trying to focus on the letter and not on his hand, which was now resting on the back of her chair. "Since it's about your family."

He went around the table and sat down across from her. "Are you really here because of that old skeleton?"

"You think there's another reason?"

"This must be taking a lot of time away from your own life. Digging through all these boxes, reading all these letters."

"You don't know what my life's like right now," she said, staring down at the documents. "This has been a welcome distraction."

"You're talking about your divorce, aren't you?" When she looked up at him, he said: "Henry told me about it."

"Then Henry told you entirely too much."

"I'm amazed how much he learned about you in just one weekend."

"He got me drunk. I talked."

"That man I saw you with last week, in your garden. Was that was your ex-husband?"

She nodded. "Richard."

"If I may say so, it didn't sound like a friendly conversation."

She slumped back in her chair. "I'm not sure divorced couples *can* be friendly."

"It should be possible."

"Are you talking from personal experience?"

"I've never been married. But I'd like to think that two people who once loved each other would always have that bond between them. No matter what goes wrong."

"Oh, it sounds good, doesn't it? Eternal love."

"You don't believe in it."

"Maybe I did seven years ago, when I got married. Now I think Henry has the right idea. Stay single and collect wine instead. Or get a dog."

"Or plant a garden?"

She set down the letter she'd been reading and looked at him. "Yes. Plant a garden. It's better to watch something growing, not dying."

Tom leaned back in his chair. "You know, I get the strangest feeling when I look at you."

"What do you mean?"

"I feel like we've met somewhere before."

"We did. In my garden."

"No, before that. I swear, I remember meeting you."

She stared at the reflected firelight dancing in his eyes. *A man as attractive as you? Oh, I would have remembered.*

He looked at the stack of documents. "Well, I suppose I should give you a hand here, and stop distracting you." He pulled a few pages off the top. "You said we're looking for any reference to Rose Connolly?"

"Dig in. She's part of your family, Tom."

"You think those were her bones in your garden?"

"I just know that her name keeps popping up in those letters from Oliver Wendell Holmes. For a poor Irish girl, she left quite an impression on him."

He sat back to read. Outside, the wind had risen, and waves were breaking on the rocks. In the fireplace, a downdraft made the flames shudder.

Tom's chair gave a sudden creak as he rocked forward. "Julia?"

"Yes?"

"Did Oliver Wendell Holmes sign his letters with just his initials?"

She stared at the page that he'd slid across to her. "Oh, my God," she said. "We have to tell Henry."

Twenty-two

1830

TONIGHT, it did not seem to matter that he was a farmer's son.

Norris handed his hat and greatcoat to the parlor maid and felt a twinge of self-consciousness about the missing button on his waistcoat. But the girl gave him the same curtsy, the same deferential dip of the head that she'd given to the well-dressed couple ahead of him. And just as warm a welcome awaited him when he stepped forward to be greeted by Dr. Grenville.

"Mr. Marshall, we're delighted you could join us this evening," said Grenville. "May I present you to my sister, Eliza Lackaway."

That the woman was Charles's mother was immediately apparent. She had his blue eyes and pale skin, flawless as alabaster even in middle age. But her gaze was far more direct than her son's.

"You're the young man my Charles speaks so highly of," she said.

"I wouldn't know why, Mrs. Lackaway," Norris answered modestly.

"He said you're the most skilled dissector in his class. He said your work stands out for its neatness, and that no one else had teased out the facial nerves with such clarity."

It was an inappropriate topic for genteel company, and Norris glanced at Dr. Grenville for guidance.

Grenville merely smiled. "Eliza's late husband was a physician. Our father was a physician. And now she has the great misfortune of putting up with me, so she's quite accustomed to the most grotesque conversations around our supper table."

"I find it all quite fascinating," said Eliza. "When we were growing up, our father often invited us into the dissecting room. If I were a man, I, too, would have pursued the study of medicine."

"And you would have been splendid, dear," said Grenville, patting his sister's arm.

"So would any number of women, if we had only the opportunity."

Dr. Grenville gave a resigned sigh. "A topic that you will no doubt raise again and again tonight."

"Don't you think it's a tragic waste, Mr. Marshall? To ignore the talents and abilities of half the human race?"

"Please, Eliza, let the poor boy at least have a glass of sherry before you start into your pet subject."

Norris said, "I don't mind addressing the question, Dr. Grenville." He looked Eliza in the eye and saw fierce intelligence there. "I was raised on a farm, Mrs. Lackaway, so my experience is with livestock. I hope you don't find the comparison demeaning. But I have never observed a stallion to be cleverer than a mare, or a ram cleverer than a ewe. And if the welfare of offspring is threatened, it's the female of the species who's far more formidable. Even dangerous."

Dr. Grenville laughed. "Spoken like a Philadelphia lawyer!"

Eliza gave an approving nod. "I shall remember that answer. In fact, I shall borrow it the next time I'm drawn into debate on the issue. Where is this farm you grew up on, Mr. Marshall?"

"In Belmont, ma'am."

"Your mother must be proud of having raised such a forward-thinking son. I certainly would be."

The mention of his mother was an unwelcome stab to an old wound, but Norris managed to maintain his smile. "I'm sure she is."

"Eliza, you remember Sophia, don't you?" said Grenville. "Abigail's dear friend."

"Of course. She used to visit us often in Weston."

"Mr. Marshall is her son."

Eliza's gaze swung back to Norris with sudden intensity, and she seemed to recognize something in his face. "You're Sophia's boy."

"Yes, ma'am."

"Why, your mother hasn't visited us in years, not since poor Abigail died. I do hope she is well?"

"She's very well, Mrs. Lackaway," he said, but even he could hear the lack of conviction in his own voice.

Grenville gave him a clap on the back. "Go enjoy yourself. Most of your classmates are already here and well into the champagne."

Norris walked into the ballroom and paused, dazzled by what he saw. Young ladies glided by in butterfly-bright gowns. A massive chandelier glittered overhead, and everywhere, crystal sparkled. Against the wall was a long table with a lavish display of food. So many oysters, so many cakes! He'd never set foot in a room so grand, with its finely inlaid floor and carved pillars. Standing there in his tired evening coat and cracked shoes, he felt he'd wandered into someone else's fantasy, certainly not his own, for he had never even imagined an evening like this.

"Finally you're here! I was wondering if you would come at all." Wendell held two glasses of champagne. He handed one to Norris. "Is it as excruciating as you feared? Have you been snubbed, insulted, or otherwise abused yet?"

"After all that's happened, I didn't know how I'd be received."

"The latest issue of the *Gazette* should put you safely in the clear. Did you read the latest? Dr. Berry was spotted in Providence."

Indeed, if one was to believe the rumors flying around town, the fugitive Dr. Nathaniel Berry was hiding in a dozen places at once, from Philadelphia to Savannah.

"I still can't believe he could be the one," said Norris. "I never saw it in him."

"Isn't that often the case? Murderers rarely have horns and fangs. They look like everyone else."

"I saw only a fine physician."

"That prostitute claims otherwise. According to the *Gazette*, the girl's said to be so traumatized, they're calling for donations on her behalf. Even I have to agree with the ridiculous Mr. Pratt on this one. Dr. Berry must be the Reaper. And if it's not Dr. Berry, I'm afraid there's only one alternative suspect." Wendell eyed him over his champagne glass. "That would be you."

Uneasy under Wendell's gaze, Norris turned to survey the room. How many people were, at that moment, whispering about him? Despite Dr. Berry's disappearance, doubts about Norris surely lingered.

"Why the face?" said Wendell. "Are you trying to look guilty?"

"I wonder how many here still think that I am."

"Grenville wouldn't have invited you if he had any doubts."

Norris shrugged. "The invitation went out to all the students."

"You know why, don't you? Look around."

"At what?"

"All these young ladies searching for husbands. Not to mention all their desperate mamas. You can see there aren't enough medical students to go around."

At this, Norris laughed. "You must be in heaven."

"If this were really heaven, there wouldn't be so many girls who are taller than me." He noticed that Norris's gaze was not on the girls, but on the buffet table. "I think that at the moment, ladies are not your first priority."

"That juicy-looking ham over there definitely is."

"Then shall we make its acquaintance?"

Near the oysters, they met up with Charles and Edward. "There's more news about Dr. Berry," said Edward. "He was spotted in Lexington yesterday evening. The Night Watch is searching there now."

"Three days ago, he was in Philadelphia," said Charles. "Two days ago in Portland."

"And now he's in Lexington?" Wendell snorted. "The man really *does* have wings."

"That is how some *have* described him," said Edward, glancing at Norris.

"I never said he had wings," said Norris.

"But that girl did. That silly Bridget." Edward handed off his plate of empty oyster shells to a maid and now considered the wide array of choices to sample next. There were puddings in the shape of a fan and fresh cod dressed in salad.

"Try some of our cook's splendid honey cakes," suggested Charles. "They've always been my favorite."

"Aren't you eating?"

Charles took out a kerchief and dabbed his brow. His face was a bright pink, as if he'd been dancing, but the musicians had not yet started to play. "I'm afraid I have no appetite tonight. It was freezing in here just a while ago. Mother had them build up the fire, and now I think they've quite overdone it."

"It feels perfectly comfortable to me." Edward turned and beamed at a slender brunette in a pink gown as she glided past. "Excuse me, gentlemen. I think my appetite has moved on to other things. Wendell, you know that girl, don't you? Won't you introduce me?"

As Edward and Wendell drifted away in pursuit of the brunette, Norris frowned at Charles. "Are you unwell? You look feverish."

"I don't really feel up to being here tonight. But Mother insisted."

"I'm quite impressed by your mother."

Charles sighed. "Yes, she has that effect on everyone. I hope you didn't have to suffer through her *women should be doctors* speech."

"A bit of it."

"We have to hear it all the time, poor Uncle most of all. He says there'd be riots if he ever dared admit a woman to the college."

The musicians were now tuning their instruments, and already couples were pairing up or searching out likely dance partners.

"I think it's time for me to retire," said Charles, and once again dabbed his brow. "I'm really not feeling well at all."

"What's wrong with your hand?"

Charles looked down at the bandage. "Oh. It's that cut from the dissection. It's swollen up a bit."

"Has your uncle seen it?"

"If it gets any worse, I'll show it to him." Charles turned to leave, but his path was blocked by a pair of smiling young ladies. The taller one, dark-haired and wearing a gown of lime-green silk, said: "We're quite annoyed with you, Charles. When *will* you visit us again? Or are you snubbing us for a reason?"

Charles stood gawking at them. "I'm sorry, I haven't the foggi-est—"

"Oh, for pity's sake," the shorter girl said. "You promised to come this past March, remember? We were *so* disappointed when your uncle showed up in Providence without you."

"I had to study for exams."

"You could have come anyway. It was only for two weeks. We'd planned a party for you and you missed it."

"Next time, I promise!" said Charles, impatient to retreat. "If you'll excuse me, ladies, I'm afraid I have a touch of fever."

"Aren't you going to dance?"

"I'm feeling rather clumsy tonight." He looked desperately at Norris. "But let me introduce you to one of my most brilliant class-mates, Mr. Norris Marshall from Belmont. These are the Welliver sisters from Providence. Their father is Dr. Sherwood Welliver, one of my uncle's friends."

"One of his *dearest* friends," the taller girl amended. "We're visit-ing Boston for the month. I'm Gwendolyn. She's Kitty."

"So you're going to be a doctor, too?" said Kitty, her gaze beam-ing up at Norris. "All the gentlemen we meet these days seem to be doctors or about-to-be doctors."

The musicians had begun to play their first set. Norris caught a glimpse of the diminutive Wendell leading a far taller blonde across the floor.

"Do you dance, Mr. Marshall?"

He looked at Gwendolyn. And realized, suddenly, that Charles had managed to slip away and was at that moment making his escape, leaving him alone to face the Welliver sisters.

"Not well, I'm afraid," he admitted.

The girls both smiled at him, undeterred.

Kitty said, "We are *splendid* instructors."

The Welliver sisters were, indeed, fine instructors, patient through his missteps, his wrong turns, his brief befuddlement during the cotillion while other couples skillfully twirled around him. Wendell, dancing past, leaned in to offer him a whispered warning: "Take care around the sisters, Norrie. They'll consume alive any eligible bachelor!" But Norris was delighted just to be in their company. Tonight, he was a sought-after young man with prospects. He danced every dance, drank too much champagne, and ate too many cakes. And he allowed himself, just for this one night, to imagine a future of many such evenings.

He was one of the last guests to pull on his coat and leave the house. Snow was falling, fat luxurious flakes that tumbled down like soft blossoms. He stood outside on Beacon Street, his face lifted to the sky, and breathed in deeply, grateful for the fresh air after his exertions on the dance floor. Tonight, Dr. Aldous Grenville had made it clear to all of Boston that Norris Marshall had earned his approval. That he was worthy to step into the loftiest circles.

Norris laughed and caught a snowflake on his tongue. *The best is yet to come.*

"Mr. Marshall?" a voice whispered.

Startled, he turned and stared into the night. At first, all he saw was falling snow. Then a figure emerged from the curtain of white, the face framed by a tattered cloak. Ice encrusted her eyelashes.

"I was afraid I'd missed you," said Rose Connolly.

"What are you doing here, Miss Connolly?"

"I don't know who else to turn to. I've lost my job, and I have nowhere to go." She glanced over her shoulder, then back at him. "They're looking for me."

"The Night Watch has no interest in you now. You don't need to hide from them."

"It's not the Watch I'm afraid of."

"Then who?"

Her chin snapped up in alarm as Dr. Grenville's front door opened, spilling light from the house. "Thank you for a most enjoyable evening, Dr. Grenville!" said a departing guest.

Norris quickly turned and began to walk away, afraid that someone might see him speaking to this ragged girl. Rose followed him. Only when they were well down Beacon Street, almost to the river, did she fall into step beside him.

"Does someone threaten you?" he asked.

"They want to take her from me."

"Take whom?"

"My sister's child."

He looked at her, but her face was hidden by the hood of her cloak. All he saw, through the veil of falling snow, was a glimpse of alabaster cheek. "Who wants her?"

"I don't know who they are, but I know they're vicious, Mr. Marshall. I think they're the reason Mary Robinson is dead. And Miss Poole. Now I'm the only one still alive."

"You needn't worry. I've heard it on the best authority that Dr. Berry has fled Boston. They'll find him soon enough."

"But I don't believe Dr. Berry *is* the killer. I think he has fled for his life."

"Fled from whom? These mysterious people?"

"You don't believe a word I'm saying. Do you?"

"I don't understand what you're saying."

She turned to him. Beneath the shadow of her hood, her eyes gleamed from light reflected off the snow. "The day my sister was buried, Mary Robinson came to see me in the cemetery. She asked about the baby. She told me to keep her hidden, keep her safe."

"She was speaking of your sister's child?"

"Yes." Rose swallowed. "I never saw Mary again. The next I heard, she was dead. And *you* were the one who found her."

"What is the connection between these murders and your niece? I fail to see it."

"I think her very existence is a threat to someone. Living proof of a scandalous secret." She turned and scanned the dark street. "They're hunting us. They've driven me from my lodgings. I can't go to my job so I can't pay the wet nurse. I don't even dare go near her door, because they might see me there."

"They? These vicious people you speak of?"

"They want her. But I won't give her up, not for anything." She turned to him, her eyes burning in the darkness. "In their hands, Mr. Marshall, she may not survive."

The girl's gone mad. He stared into her eyes and wondered if this was what insanity looked like. He remembered his recent visit to her in that miserable lodging house, when he had thought Rose Connolly was a levelheaded survivor. Since then, something had changed, had driven her over the edge, into a delusional world filled with enemies.

"I'm sorry, Miss Connolly. I don't see how I can help you," he said, backing away. He turned and started walking again, in the direction of his lodgings, his shoes plowing two furrows through feathery snow.

"I came to you because I thought you were different. *Better.*"

"I'm only a student. What can I do?"

"You don't care, do you?"

"The West End murders have been solved. It's in all the newspapers."

"They want you to *believe* they've been solved."

"It's the Night Watch's responsibility, not mine."

"You certainly cared when *you* were the one they accused."

He walked on, hoping that she would tire of pursuing him. But she trailed after him like a troublesome dog as he headed north along the Charles River.

"It's all well and good now that you're off the hook, isn't it?" she said.

"I have no authority to delve any deeper into the matter."

"You yourself *saw* the creature. You found poor Mary's body."

He turned to face her. "And do you know how close I came to losing my position because of that? I'd be insane to raise any new questions about the murders. All it takes is a few whispers, and I could lose everything I've worked for. I'd be back on my father's farm!"

"Is it so terrible to be a farmer?"

"Yes! When my ambitions are so much higher!"

"And nothing must get in the way of your ambitions," she said bitterly.

He gazed in the direction of Dr. Grenville's house. He thought of the champagne he'd drunk, the elegantly dressed girls he'd danced with. Once, his ambitions had been far more modest. To earn the gratitude of his patients. To know the satisfaction of wrestling a sick child from the jaws of a mortal illness. But tonight, in Dr. Grenville's home, he'd glimpsed possibilities he'd never dreamed of, a world of comforts that could one day be his if he made no mistakes, allowed himself no missteps.

"I thought you would care," she said. "Now I find that what really matters to you are your grand friends in their grand houses."

Sighing, he looked at her. "It's not that I don't care. There's simply nothing I can do about it. I'm not a policeman. I have no business getting involved. I suggest you walk away from it as well, Miss Connolly." He turned.

"I can't walk away," she said. Her voice suddenly broke. "I don't know where else to go . . ."

He took a few steps and slowed. Stopped. Behind him, she was crying softly. Turning, he saw her slumped wearily against a gate, head bowed in defeat. This was a Rose Connolly he hadn't before seen, so different from the bold girl he'd met in the hospital ward.

"Have you no place to sleep?" he said, and saw her shake her head. He reached into his pocket. "If it's a matter of money, you can take what I have here."

Suddenly straightening, she glared at him. "I ask nothing for myself! This is for Meggie. It's *all* for Meggie." Angrily, she swept her hand across her face. "I came to you because I thought we had a bond, you and I. We've both seen the creature. We both know what it can do. You may not be afraid of it, but I am. It wants the baby. So it hunts me." She took a deep breath and hugged her cloak tighter, as though to ward off the eyes of the night. "I won't trouble you again," she said, and turned.

He watched her walk away, a small figure receding into the curtain of falling snow. My dream is to save lives, he thought, to battle heroically at countless sickbeds. Yet when a single friendless girl pleads for my help, I cannot be bothered.

The figure was almost lost now, in the swirl of white.

"Miss Connolly!" he called. "My room is a short walk from here. For tonight, if you need a place to sleep, it might serve you."

Twenty-three

THIS WAS A MISTAKE.

Norris lay in bed, considering what he would do with his guest come morning. In one moment of reckless charity, he had taken on a responsibility he did not need. It's only temporary, he promised himself; this arrangement could not continue. At least the girl had done her best to stay unobtrusive. She had slipped silently up the stairs behind him, alerting no one in the building to the fact that he'd smuggled in a female guest. She'd curled up like an exhausted kitten in the corner and almost immediately fallen asleep. He could not even hear her breathing. Only by looking across the room, seeing her shadowy form on the floor, did he even know she was there. He thought of the challenges in his own life—such minor ones when he considered what Rose Connolly must face every day on the streets.

But there's nothing I can do about it. The world is unjust, and I cannot change the world.

When he rose the next day, she was still sleeping. He thought of rousing her and sending her on her way, but he didn't have the heart. She slept as deeply as a child. By the light of day, her clothing looked even more ragged, the cloak obviously mended many times over, the hem of her skirt streaked with mud. On her finger glittered a ring set with stones of colored glass, a cheap version of the multicolored rings he saw on the hands of so many ladies, even his own mother. But this was a poor imitation, nothing but a tin ornament one would give a child. He found it oddly touching that Rose would so unabashedly wear such a trinket, as though proudly displaying her poverty right there on her finger. Poor though she was, her face was fine-boned and flawless, and her chestnut hair reflected the sun's gleam in coppery streaks. Were she resting on a pillow of fine lace instead of rags, she would rival any beauty from Beacon Hill. But in years to come, long before the bloom had left the cheek of a Beacon Hill girl, poverty would surely dim the glow of Rose Connolly's face.

The world is unjust. I cannot change it.

Though he could scarcely spare the money, he left a few coins beside her; it would feed her for a few days. She was still sleeping when he left the room.

Though he had never attended a service by the Reverend William Channing, he had heard of the man's reputation. Indeed, it was impossible not to know about Channing, whose reportedly spellbinding sermons attracted an ever-growing circle of devoted followers to the Unitarian church on Federal Street. Last night, at Dr. Grenville's reception, the Welliver sisters had loudly sung Channing's praises. "That's where you'll find anyone of consequence on a Sunday morning," Kitty Welliver had gushed. "We'll all be there tomorrow—Mr. Kingston and Mr. Lackaway and even Mr. Holmes, though he was raised a Calvinist. You shouldn't miss it, Mr. Marshall! His sermons are so impressive, so profound. Truly, he makes one *think*!"

While Norris doubted that a single profound thought ever

crossed Kitty Welliver's mind, he could not ignore her suggestion that he attend. Last night, he had glimpsed the circle in which he one day hoped to circulate, and that same circle would be seated that morning in the pews of the Federal Street church.

As soon as he stepped inside, he spotted familiar faces. Wendell and Edward sat near the front, and he started to make his way toward them, but a hand tapped his shoulder, and he suddenly found himself flanked on either side by the sisters Welliver.

"Oh, we hoped you'd come!" said Kitty. "Wouldn't you like to sit with us?"

"Yes, do!" said Gwendolyn. "We always sit upstairs."

So upstairs he went, forcibly marched by sheer feminine will, and found himself seated in the balcony, wedged between Kitty's skirts on the left and Gwendolyn's on the right. He soon discovered why the sisters preferred their isolated perch in the balcony: Here they were free to gossip straight through the Reverend Channing's sermon, which they clearly had little intention of listening to.

"Look, there's Elizabeth Peabody! She's looking quite severe today," said Kitty. "And what a horrid dress. So unflattering."

"You'd think the Reverend Channing would be tired of her company by now," Gwendolyn whispered back.

Kitty nudged Norris on the arm. "You have heard the rumors, haven't you? About Miss Peabody and the reverend? They're close." Kitty added, with sly emphasis, "*Very* close."

Norris peered over the balcony at the femme fatale at the center of the scandal, and saw a modestly dressed woman wearing unattractive spectacles and an expression of fierce concentration.

"There's Rachel. I didn't know she was back from Savannah," said Kitty.

"Where?"

"Sitting next to Charles Lackaway. You don't suppose the two of them . . ."

"I can't imagine. Don't you think Charles looks odd today? Such a sickly expression."

Kitty leaned forward. "He did claim he had a fever last night. Maybe he was telling the truth after all."

Gwendolyn giggled. "Or maybe Rachel is just *too* much to bear."

Norris tried to focus on the Reverend Channing's sermon, but it was impossible with these silly girls chattering away. Last night their high spirits had seemed charming, but today it merely irritated him that they talked only about who was sitting next to whom, which girl was dull, which girl was bookish. He thought, suddenly, of Rose Connolly, dressed in rags and curled up exhausted on his floor, and imagined the cruel things these girls might say about her. Would Rose waste any breath gossiping about another's girl's dress or a minister's flirtations? No, her concerns were elemental: how to fill her belly, where to shelter from the storm—the concerns of any base animal. Yet the Welliver sisters surely thought themselves far more civilized, because they had pretty dresses and the leisure to while away a Sunday morning in a church balcony.

He leaned against the railing, hoping that his look of concentration would be signal enough for Kitty and Gwendolyn to silence their chatter, but they just went on talking across his head. *Where did Lydia find that hideous hat? Do you see how Dickie Lawrence keeps staring at her? Oh, she told me something quite delicious this morning! The real reason Dickie's brother had to rush home from New York. It's all because of a young lady . . .* Good Lord, thought Norris, was there any scandal these girls did not know about? Any furtive glance they did not catch?

What would they say about Rose Connolly sleeping in his room?

By the time the Reverend Channing finally ended his sermon, Norris was desperate to escape the sisters, but they remained stubbornly seated, trapping him between them as the congregation began to file out.

"Oh, we can't leave yet," said Kitty, tugging him back down into his seat when he tried to rise. "You can see everything so much better from up here."

"See what?" he asked in exasperation.

"Rachel has practically draped herself over Charles."

"She's been pursuing him since June. Remember the picnic in Weston? At his uncle's country house? Charlie practically had to flee into the garden to escape her."

"Why are they still sitting? You'd think Charlie would have tried to get away by now."

"Maybe he doesn't want to escape, Gwen. Maybe she's truly snagged him. Do you think that's the real reason he didn't come visit us in March? She already had him in her clutches!"

"Oh. They're getting up now. See how she has her arm wrapped around his . . ." Kitty paused. "What on earth is *wrong* with him?"

Charles staggered from his seat into the aisle, and caught himself on the back of a bench. For a moment he swayed on his feet. Then his legs seemed to dissolve away beneath him, and slowly he sank to the floor.

The Welliver sisters gave a simultaneous gasp and jumped up. There was chaos below as parishioners crowded around the fallen Charles.

"Let me through!" called Wendell.

Kitty gave an exaggerated sob and pressed her hand to her mouth. "I do hope it's nothing serious."

By the time Norris had hurried downstairs and made his way through the crowd, Wendell and Edward were already kneeling beside their friend.

"I'm fine," Charles murmured. "Really I am."

"You don't look fine, Charlie," said Wendell. "We've sent for your uncle."

"There's no need to tell him about this."

"You're white as a sheet. Lie still."

Charles moaned. "Oh, God, I'll never live this down."

Norris suddenly focused on the bandage encasing Charles's left hand. The fingertips that protruded from the wrapping were red and swollen. He knelt and tugged at the bandage.

Charles gave a cry and tried to pull away. "Don't touch it!" he begged.

"Charlie," said Norris quietly. "I have to take a look. You know I do." Slowly, he removed the wrappings. When at last the blackened flesh beneath was revealed, he rocked back on his heels, horrified. He looked at Wendell, who said nothing, only shook his head.

"We need to get you home, Charlie," said Norris. "Your uncle will know what to do."

"It's been a few days since he nicked himself at the anatomy demonstration," said Wendell. "He knew his hand was getting worse. Why the blazes didn't he tell anyone? His uncle at least."

"And admit how clumsy and incompetent he is?" said Edward.

"He never even wanted to study medicine. Poor Charlie'd be perfectly happy spending his life right here, writing his little poems." Wendell stood at Dr. Grenville's parlor window, gazing out as a carriage and four rolled past. Only last night, this house had rung with laughter and music; now it was eerily silent except for the creak of footsteps upstairs, and the crackle of the fire in the parlor hearth. "He has no aptitude for medicine and we all know it. You'd think his uncle would accept it."

It was certainly obvious to everyone else, thought Norris. There'd been no student so unskilled with a knife, no one so ill prepared to tackle the grim realities of their chosen profession. The anatomy lab had been just a taste of what a physician faced. There would be far worse ordeals to come: the stench of typhus, the shrieks from the surgeon's table. Dissecting a corpse was nothing; the dead don't complain. The real horror was in living flesh.

They heard a knock at the front door. Mrs. Furbush, the housekeeper, scurried down the hall to greet the new visitor.

"Oh, Dr. Sewall! Thank heavens you've arrived! Mrs. Lackaway is frantic, and Dr. Grenville has already bled him twice, but it has not touched the fever, and he is anxious for your opinion."

"I'm not sure that my skills are yet needed."

"You may change your mind when you see his hand."

Norris glimpsed Dr. Sewall as he walked past the parlor doorway, carrying his instrument bag, and heard him climb the stairs to the second floor. Mrs. Furbush was about to follow him upstairs when Wendell called out to her.

"How is Charles?"

Mrs. Furbush looked at them through the doorway, and her only answer was a sad shake of the head.

Edward murmured, "This is starting to look quite bad."

From upstairs came the sound of men's voices, and Mrs. Lackaway's sobbing. We should leave, Norris thought. We're intruding on this family's grief. But his two companions made no move to depart, even as the afternoon wore on and the parlor maid brought them another pot of tea, another tray of cakes.

Wendell touched none of it. He sank into an armchair and stared with fierce concentration into the fire. "She had childbed fever," he said suddenly.

"What?" said Edward.

Wendell looked up. "The cadaver he dissected that day, when he cut himself. It was a woman, and Dr. Sewall said she died of childbed fever."

"So?"

"You saw his hand."

Edward shook his head. "A most gruesome case of erysipelas."

"That was gangrene, Eddie. Now he's febrile and his blood is poisoned, by something he must have acquired with one small nick of the knife. Is it only by chance, do you think, that the woman, too, died of a fulminating fever?"

Edward shrugged. "Many women die of it. There've been more this month than ever."

"And most of them were attended by Dr. Crouch," said Wendell quietly. Once again, he stared into the fire.

They heard heavy footsteps descend the stairs and Dr. Sewall appeared, his hulking frame taking up the entire doorway. He looked over the three young men gathered in the parlor, then said,

"You, Mr. Marshall! And Mr. Holmes, too. Both of you come up-stairs."

"Sir?" said Norris.

"I need you to hold down the patient."

"What about me?" said Edward.

"Do you really think you're ready for this, Mr. Kingston?"

"I—I believe so, sir."

"Then come along. We can certainly make use of you."

The three young men followed Sewall up the stairs, and with every step Norris's dread mounted, for he could guess what was about to happen. Sewall led them along the upstairs hallway, and Norris caught a fleeting glimpse of family portraits on the wall, a long gallery of distinguished men and handsome women. They stepped into Charles's room.

The sun was setting, and the last wintry light of afternoon glowed in the window. Around the bed, five lamps were burning. At their center lay a ghostly pale Charles, his left hand concealed beneath a drape. In a corner, his mother sat rigid with her hands balled tightly in her lap, her eyes aglow with panic. Dr. Grenville stood at his nephew's bedside, his head drooped in weary resignation. A row of surgical instruments gleamed on a table: knives and a saw and silk sutures and a tourniquet.

Charles gave a whimper. "Mother, please," he whispered. "Don't let them."

Eliza turned desperate eyes to her brother. "Is there no other way, Aldous? Tomorrow he might be better! If we could wait—"

"If he had shown us his hand earlier," said Grenville, "I might have been able to arrest the process. A bleeding, at the outset, might have drained the poison. But it's far too late now."

"He said it was just a small cut. Nothing of significance."

"I have seen the smallest cuts fester and turn to gangrene," said Dr. Sewall. "When that happens, there is no other choice."

"Mother, *please.*" Charles turned his panicked gaze to his class-mates. "Wendell, Norris—don't let them do this. Don't let them!"

Norris could offer no such promises; he knew what had to be done. He stared at the knife and bone saw laid out on the table and thought: Dear God, I don't want to watch this. But he stood firm, for he knew his assistance was vital.

"If you cut it off, Uncle," said Charles, "I'll *never* be a surgeon!"

"I want you to take another draught of morphine," said Grenville, lifting his nephew's head. "Go on, drink it."

"I'll never be what you wanted!"

"Drink it, Charles. All of it."

Charles settled back on the pillow and gave a soft sob. "That's all I ever wanted," he moaned. "That you be proud of me."

"I am proud of you, boy."

"How much have you given him?" asked Sewall.

"Four draughts now. I don't dare give him more."

"Then let's do it, Aldous."

"Mother?" pleaded Charles.

Eliza rose and tugged desperately at her brother's arm. "Could you not wait another day? Please, just another day!"

"Mrs. Lackaway," said Dr. Sewall, "another day will be too late." He lifted the drape that covered the patient's left arm, revealing Charles's grotesquely swollen hand. It was taut as a balloon, and the skin was greenish black. Even from where Norris stood, he could smell the rotting flesh.

"This has gone beyond simple erysipelas, madam," said Sewall. "This is wet gangrene. The tissue has necrosed, and in just the short time I have been here, it has swollen even larger, filling with poisonous gases. Already there is red streaking here, up the arm, toward the elbow, an indication that the poison is spreading. By tomorrow, it may well be up to the shoulder. And then nothing, not even amputation, will reverse it."

Eliza stood with her hand pressed to her mouth, her stricken gaze on Charles. "Then there is nothing else to be done? No other way?"

"I have attended too many cases like this. Men whose limbs were crushed in accidents or pierced by bullets. I've learned that once wet gangrene sets in, there is only a finite time in which to act. Too many times I've delayed, always to my regret. I've learned that it's better to amputate sooner than later." He paused, his voice softer, gentler. "The loss of a hand is not the loss of a soul. With luck, you will still have your son, madam."

"He is my only child," Eliza whispered through her tears. "I cannot lose him, or I swear I shall die."

"Neither of you will die."

"Do you promise it?"

"Fate is always in God's hands, madam. But I will do my best." He paused and glanced at Grenville. "Perhaps it would be best if Mrs. Lackaway stepped out of the room."

Grenville nodded. "Go, Eliza. Please."

She lingered for a moment, staring hungrily at her son, whose eyelids were drifting shut in a narcotic daze. "Let nothing go wrong, Aldous," she said to her brother. "If we lose him, there will be no one to comfort us in our old age. No one to take his place." Stifling a sob, she left the room.

Sewall turned to the three medical students. "Mr. Marshall, I suggest you remove your topcoat. There will be blood. Mr. Holmes, you will hold down the right arm. Mr. Kingston, the feet. Mr. Marshall and Dr. Grenville will take the left arm. Even four draughts of morphine will not be enough to mask this pain, and he will fight us. Complete immobilization of the patient is vital to my success. The only merciful way to do this is quickly, with no hesitation and no wasted effort. Do you understand, gentlemen?"

The students nodded.

Wordlessly, Norris removed his topcoat and placed it on a chair. He moved to Charles's left side.

"I'll try to preserve as much of the limb as possible," said Dr. Sewall as he tucked sheets beneath the arm to protect the floor and the mattress from blood. "But I'm afraid the infection has advanced too far for me to preserve the wrist. In any event, there are some surgical authorities—Dr. Larrey, for instance—who believe it's always advantageous to take off the forearm higher up, in its fleshy part. And that's what I plan to do." He tied on an apron and looked at Norris. "You will have a vital role in this, Mr. Marshall. Since you appear to me to be the strongest and the one with the steadiest nerves, I want you to take hold of the forearm, right above where I make my incision. Dr. Grenville will control the hand. As I work, he will be the one to pronate or supinate the forearm, which allows me access to all structures. First the skin is cut, then it's detached from the fascia. After I have divided the muscles, I will need you to apply the retractor, so that I can see the bones. Is all this clear?"

Norris could barely swallow, his throat was so dry. "Yes, sir," he murmured.

"You cannot quail from this. If you think this is beyond your ability, say it now."

"I can do it."

Sewall gave him a long, hard look. Then, satisfied, he reached for the tourniquet. His eyes betrayed no apprehension, no flicker of doubt about what he intended to do. There was no finer surgeon in Boston than Erastus Sewall, and his confidence revealed itself in the efficiency with which he wrapped the tourniquet around Charles's upper arm, above the elbow. He positioned the pad over the brachial artery and ruthlessly tied it tight, cutting off all circulation to the arm.

Charles stirred from his narcotic-induced sleep. "No," he moaned, "please."

"Gentlemen, take your positions."

Norris grasped the left arm and pinned the elbow to the edge of the mattress.

"You're supposed to be my friend." Charles focused his pitiful gaze on Norris, whose face was right above his. "Why are you doing this? Why do you let them hurt me?"

"Be strong, Charlie," said Norris. "It has to be done. We're trying to save your life."

"No. You're a traitor. You just want me out of your way!" Charles tried to pull free, and Norris tightened his grip, fingers digging into clammy skin. Charles was straining so hard, the muscles bulged in his arm, tendons taut as cords. "You want me dead!" screamed Charles.

"It's the morphine talking." Sewall calmly reached for his amputating knife. "It means nothing." He looked at Grenville. "Aldous?"

Dr. Grenville grasped his nephew's gangrenous hand. Though Charles was bucking and twisting now, he could not fight them all. Edward had pinned down the ankles and Wendell, the right shoulder. No amount of struggling, no piteous pleas, could stop the knife.

With the first slash of Sewall's blade, Charles shrieked. Blood splashed onto Norris's hands and dripped onto the sheets. Sewall worked so swiftly that in the few seconds Norris glanced away, repulsed, Sewall had finished his circling incision all the way around the forearm. When Norris forced himself to focus again on the wound, Sewall was already peeling the skin back from the fascia to form a flap. He worked with grim determination, heedless of the blood splattering across his apron, of the agonized shrieks, a sound so terrible it raised the hairs on the back of Norris's neck. The arm was now slippery with blood and Charles, fighting like a wild animal, almost wrenched free of Norris's grasp.

"Hold him, damn it!" roared Sewall.

Mortified, Norris tightened his grip. This was no time to be gentle. Deafened by Charles's screams, he hung on ruthlessly, his fingers digging in like claws.

Sewall put down his amputating knife and picked up a larger blade, to divide the muscles. With the brutal efficiency of a butcher, he made a few deep cuts and was down to bone.

Charles's screams choked into sobs. "Mother! Oh, God, I am dying!"

"Mr. Marshall!"

Norris stared down at the retractor that Sewall had just positioned in the wound.

"Take it!"

With his right hand, he kept his grip on Charles's arm. With his left, he tugged on the retractor, exposing the wound. There, beneath a scrim of blood and tissue strands, was the whiteness of bone. The radius, thought Norris, remembering the anatomical illustrations in Wistar's that he'd pored over so carefully. He remembered the mounted skeleton that he'd studied in anatomy lab. But those had been dry, brittle bones, so different from this living radius.

Dr. Sewall picked up the saw.

As Sewall cut through the radius and ulna, Norris felt the mutilation transmitted through the arm he was holding: the teeth of the saw rasping, the splintering.

And he heard Charles's screams.

In seconds, mercifully, it was over. The severed part came away in Grenville's hands, and only the stump remained. The worst of the butchery was finished; what came next was the more delicate task of tying off the vessels. Norris watched, awed by the skill with which Sewall teased free the radial and ulnar and interosseous arteries and ligated them all with silk sutures.

"I hope you've all been paying close attention, gentlemen," said Dr. Sewall as he proceeded to sew the skin flap closed. "Because one day, you will be called upon to perform such a task. And it may not be as simple an amputation as this one."

Norris looked down at Charles, whose eyes were now closed. His screams had faded to exhausted whimpers. "This hardly struck me as simple, sir," he said softly.

Sewall laughed. "This? This was only a forearm. Far worse is a shoulder, or a thigh. No mere tourniquet will suffice. Lose control of the subclavian artery or the femoral artery, and you will be stunned by how much blood can be lost, in mere seconds." He wielded the needle like an expert tailor, closing the fabric of human skin, leaving only a small gap open as a drainage hole. His suturing complete, he neatly bandaged the stump and looked at Grenville. "I've done what I could, Aldous."

Grenville gave a grateful nod. "I would not have trusted my nephew to anyone but you."

"Let's hope your trust was well placed." Sewall dropped his bloody tools into the basin of water. "Your nephew's life is now in God's hands."

"There may yet be complications," said Sewall.

A fire burned brightly in the parlor hearth, and Norris had gulped down several glasses of Dr. Grenville's excellent claret, but he could not seem to shake the chill that still lingered after what he had witnessed. He was once again wearing his topcoat, which he'd pulled on over his stained shirt. Looking down at his cuffs, peeking out from his jacket sleeves, he could see stray spatters of Charles's blood. Wendell and Edward, too, seemed to feel chilled, for they had pulled their chairs close to the hearth where Dr. Grenville was seated. Only Dr. Sewall seemed not to notice the cold. His face was flushed from so many glasses of claret, which had also served to slacken his posture and loosen his tongue. He sat facing the fire, his generous girth filling the chair, his stout legs splayed out before him.

"There are so many things that may yet go wrong," he said as he reached for the bottle and refilled his glass. "The days ahead are still dangerous." He set down the bottle and looked at Grenville. "She does know that, doesn't she?"

They all knew he spoke of Eliza. They could hear her voice upstairs, singing a lullaby to her sleeping son. Since Sewall had completed his terrible operation, she had not left Charles's room. Norris had no doubt she would be at his side for the rest of the night.

"She is not ignorant of the possibilities. My sister has been around physicians all her life. She knows what can happen."

Sewall took a sip and looked at the students. "I was only a bit older than you, gentlemen, when I was called on to perform my first amputation. You have had a gentle introduction. You've witnessed it under ideal conditions, in a comfortable room, well lit, with clean water and the proper tools at hand. The patient well prepared with generous doses of morphine. Nothing like the conditions I faced that day in North Point."

"North Point?" said Wendell. "You fought in the Battle of Baltimore?"

"Not *in* the battle. I'm certainly no soldier, and I wanted no part of that stupid, wretched war. But I was in Baltimore that summer, visiting my aunt and uncle. By then, I had completed my medical studies, but my skills as a surgeon were largely untested. When the British fleet arrived and began their bombardment of Fort McHenry, the Maryland Militia had urgent need of all available surgeons. I opposed the war from the beginning, but I could not ignore my duty to my countrymen." He took a deep swallow of claret and sighed. "The worst of the carnage was on an open field, near Bear Creek. Four hundred British troops had marched overland, hoping to reach Fort McHenry. But at Bouden's Farm, three hundred of ours stood waiting for them."

Sewall stared at the fire, as though seeing that field again, the British soldiers advancing, the Maryland Militia standing their ground. "It started with cannon fire, from both sides," he said. "Then, as they closed in, it advanced to musket fire. You're all so young; you probably have not seen the damage a lead ball can inflict on a human body. It does not pierce the flesh so much as crush it." He took another sip. "When it was over, the militia had two dozen dead and nearly a hundred wounded. The British suffered twice that many losses.

"That afternoon, I performed my first amputation. It was a clumsy one, and I have not forgiven myself for my mistakes. I made too many that day. I can't remember how many amputations I did on that field. The memory tends to exaggerate, so I doubt it was as many as I imagine. Certainly I did not approach the numbers that Baron Larrey claims he performed on Napoleon's soldiers in the Battle of Borodino. Two hundred amputations in a single day, or so he wrote." Sewall shrugged. "At North Point, I did perhaps only a dozen, but at the end of the day I was quite proud of myself, because most of my subjects were still alive." He drank down his claret and reached for the bottle yet again. "I didn't realize how little that meant."

"But you saved them," said Edward.

Sewall snorted. "For a day or two. Until the fevers started." He looked hard at Edward. "You know what pyemia is, don't you?"

"Yes, sir. It's blood poisoning."

"Literally, 'pus in the blood.' That was the worst fever of all, when wounds started to ooze a copious yellow discharge. Some surgeons believe that pus is a good sign—that it means the body is healing itself. But I believe quite the opposite. That it is, in fact, a signal to begin building the coffin. If not pyemia, there were other horrors. Gangrene. Erysipelas. Tetanus." He looked around the room, at the three students. "Have any of you witnessed a tetanic spasm?"

The three students shook their heads.

"It begins with a locked jaw, with the mouth clamped into a grotesque grin. It progresses to paroxysmal flexion of the arms and extension of the legs. The muscles of the abdomen become rigid as a board. Sudden spasms make the torso bow backward with such violence that it can snap bones. And through it all, the subject is awake and suffering the most heartbreaking agonies." He set down his empty glass. "Amputation, gentlemen, is only the first horror. Others may well follow." He looked at the students. "Your friend Charles faces dangers ahead. All I've done was remove the offending limb. What happens next depends on his constitution, his will to live. And on providence."

Upstairs, Eliza had ceased singing her lullaby, but they could hear the creak of floorboards as she paced Charles's bedroom. Back and forth, back and forth. If a mother's love alone could save a child, there would be no medicine more powerful than what Eliza now dispensed with every agitated step, every anxious sigh. *Did my own mother hover with such devotion over my sickbed?* Norris had only one vague memory, of waking up in a feverish daze to see a lone candle flickering by his bed, and Sophia bent over him, stroking his hair. Murmuring: "My one true love."

Did you mean it? Then why did you leave me that day?

There was a knock on the front door. They heard the parlor maid scurry down the hall to answer it, but Dr. Grenville made no attempt to rise. Exhaustion had pinned him to his chair, and he sat unmoving, listening to the conversation at the front door:

"May I speak to Dr. Grenville?"

"I'm sorry, sir," the parlor maid answered. "We have had a crisis in the household today, and the doctor is not up to seeing visitors. If you would leave your card, perhaps he will—"

"Tell him that Mr. Pratt of the Night Watch is here."

Grenville, still slumped in his chair, wearily shook his head at the unwelcome intrusion.

"I'm sure he'll be happy to speak to you another time," the maid said.

"This will only take a minute. He will want to hear this news." Already they could hear Pratt's heavy boots stomping into the house.

"Mr. Pratt, sir!" said the maid. "Please, if you could just wait while I ask the doctor—"

Pratt appeared in the parlor doorway, and his gaze swept across the men gathered in the room.

"Dr. Grenville," the maid said helplessly. "I did tell him you were not taking visitors!"

"That's all right, Sarah," said Grenville as he rose to his feet. "Clearly Mr. Pratt feels the matter is urgent enough to warrant this intrusion."

"I do, sir," said Pratt. His eyes narrowed as he focused on Norris. "So here you are, Mr. Marshall. I've been looking for you."

"He's been here all afternoon," said Grenville. "My nephew has taken seriously ill, and Mr. Marshall was kind enough to offer his assistance."

"I wondered why you were not at your lodgings," said Pratt, his gaze still fixed on Norris, who felt sudden panic. Had Rose Connolly been discovered in his room? Was that why Pratt was staring at him?

"That's the reason for this interruption?" asked Grenville, barely able to conceal his scorn. "Merely to confirm the whereabouts of Mr. Marshall?"

"No, Doctor," said Pratt, turning his gaze to Grenville.

"Then why?"

"You have not heard the news, then."

"I've been occupied all day with my nephew. I've not even left the house."

"This afternoon," said Pratt, "two young boys playing under the West Boston Bridge noticed what looked like a bundle of rags lying in the mud. When they took a closer look, they saw it was not rags, but the body of a man."

"The West Boston Bridge?" said Dr. Sewall, straightening in his chair at this disturbing news.

"Yes, Dr. Sewall," said Pratt. "I invite you to examine the body yourself. You'll have no choice but to draw the same conclusions I have, based on the injuries. In fact, it seems pretty clear to me and to Dr. Crouch that—"

"Crouch has already seen it?" asked Grenville.

"Dr. Crouch was on the wards when the body was carried into the hospital. A fortunate circumstance, actually, because he also examined Agnes Poole. He saw, at once, the similarities in the injuries. The peculiar pattern of the cuts." Pratt looked at Norris. "You would know what I'm talking about, Mr. Marshall."

Norris stared at him. "The shape of a cross?" he asked softly.

"Yes. Despite the . . . damage, the pattern is apparent."

"What damage?" asked Sewall.

"Rats, sir. Perhaps other animals as well. It's clear that the body has been lying there for some time. It's logical to assume that his death coincided with the date of his disappearance."

It was as if the temperature in the room had suddenly plunged. Though no one said a word, Norris could see stunned realization on all the faces.

"Then you have found him," Grenville finally said.

Pratt nodded. "The body is Dr. Nathaniel Berry's. He did not flee, as we all believed. He was murdered."

Twenty-four

The present

JULIA LOOKED UP from Wendell Holmes's letter. "Was Wendell Holmes right, Tom? Did that case of childbed fever have anything to do with Charles's blood poisoning?"

Tom stood at the window, staring out at the sea. The fog had started to lift that morning, and although the sky was still gray, they could finally see the water. Gulls skimmed past a background of silvery clouds. "Yes," he said quietly. "It was almost certainly related. What he described in his letter barely begins to touch on the horrors of childbed fever." He sat down at the dining table, across from Julia and Henry, and the light through the window behind him cast his face in gloomy shadow. "In Holmes's era," said Tom, "it was so common that during epidemics, one of every four new mothers died of it. They died so quickly, hospitals had to cram them two to a coffin. In one maternity ward in Budapest, laboring mothers had a view of the cemetery through the window, and a view of the autopsy room down the hall. No wonder women were terrified of childbirth. They knew that if they went into the hospital to have a baby, there was a good chance they would come out in a coffin. And you know the worst part of all? They were killed by their own doctors."

"You mean through incompetence?" said Julia.

"Through ignorance. In those days, they had no concept of germ theory. They wore no gloves, so doctors used their bare hands to examine women. They'd perform an autopsy on a corpse that was putrid with disease, then they'd go straight to the maternity ward, with filthy hands. They'd examine patient after patient, spreading infection right down the row of beds. Killing every woman they touched."

"It never occurred to any of them just to wash their hands?"

"There was one doctor in Vienna who suggested it. He was a Hungarian named Ignaz Semmelweis, who noticed that patients attended by medical students were far more likely to die of childbed fever than those attended by midwives. He knew that the students attended autopsies while the midwives didn't. So he concluded that some form of contagion was being spread from the autopsy room. He advised all his colleagues to wash their hands."

"It sounds like common sense."

"But he was ridiculed for it."

"They didn't follow his advice?"

"They hounded him out of his job. He ended up so depressed, he was committed to a mental institution. Where he cut his finger and suffered blood poisoning."

"Like Charles Lackaway."

Tom nodded. "Ironic, isn't it? That's what makes these letters so valuable. This is medical history, straight from the pen of one of the greatest doctors who ever lived." He looked across the table at Julia. "You do know, don't you? Why Holmes is such a hero in American medicine?"

Julia shook her head.

"Here in the United States, we hadn't heard of Semmelweis and his germ theory. Yet we were dealing with the same epidemics of childbed fever, the same appalling mortality rates. American doctors blamed it on bad air or poor circulation or even something as ridiculous as wounded modesty! Women were dying, and no one in America could figure out why." He looked down at the letter. "No one, that is, until Oliver Wendell Holmes."

Twenty-five

1830

SHELTERED IN A NOOK beneath a doorway, blocked from the worst of the wind, Rose gazed across the hospital common, her eyes fixed on Norris's attic window. She had been watching for hours, but now that darkness had fallen, she could no longer distinguish his building from among the rooflines silhouetted against the night sky. Why hadn't he come back? What if he did not return tonight? She hoped for a second night under Norris's roof, for a second chance to see him, to hear his voice. This morning, she'd awakened to find the coins he'd left for her, coins that would keep Meggie warm and fed for another week. In return for his generosity, she'd mended two of his threadbare shirts. Even if she hadn't owed him, she'd have been happy to mend those shirts, just for the pleasure of touching fabric that had brushed his back, fabric that had known the warmth of his skin.

She saw candlelight flicker to life in a window. His window.

She started across the hospital common. This time, he'll be anxious to listen to me, she thought. By now, he'd surely heard the latest news. She eased open the door to his building and peeked inside, then quietly slipped up the two flights of stairs to the attic. At his door she paused, her heart thumping hard. Because of her run up those steps? Or because she was about to see Norris again? She patted her hair, straightened her skirt, feeling foolish even as she did it, because all the effort was for a man who wouldn't give her a second glance. Why would he bother to look at Rose after dancing with all those fine ladies last night?

She'd glimpsed them as they'd left Dr. Grenville's house and stepped into their carriages, those lovely girls with their swishing silk gowns and velvet mantles and fur muffs. She'd watched how carelessly they allowed their hems to drag across the dirty snow, but of course *they* would not have to wash out the stains. *They* had not spent hours, as Rose had, bent over needle and thread, sewing in light so poor that her eyes would one day be pinched as permanently as if she had stitched puckers into her own skin. One season's round of parties and dances, and the poor old dress would be retired anyway, to make way for the newest styles, the latest shade of gauze. Lurking in the darkness outside Dr. Grenville's home, Rose had spotted the very gown that she herself had sewn, with the rose-colored silk. It adorned a round-cheeked young miss who had giggled all the way to her carriage. *Is that the kind of girl you prefer, Mr. Marshall? Because I cannot compete with that.*

She knocked. Stood with back straight and chin raised as she heard his footsteps approach the door. Suddenly he was standing before her, the light spilling from behind him into the gloomy staircase. "There you are! Where have you been?"

She paused, confused. "I thought I should stay away until you came home."

"You've been gone all day? No one has seen you here?"

His words stung her like a slap in the face. All day she'd been hungry to see him, and this was the greeting he gave her? *I'm the girl he wants no one to know about,* she thought. *The embarrassing secret.*

She said, "I only came back to tell you what I'm hearing on the street. Dr. Berry is dead. They found his body under the West Boston Bridge."

"I know. Mr. Pratt told me."

"Then you know as much as I do. Good night, Mr. Marshall." She turned.

"Where are you going?"

"I haven't had any supper." And would probably have none at all tonight.

"I've brought food for you. Won't you stay?"

She paused on the stairs, startled by the unexpected offer.

"Please," he said. "Come in. There's someone here who wishes to speak to you."

She still felt the sting of his earlier comment and sheer pride almost drove her to decline the invitation. But her stomach was rumbling, and she wanted to know who this *someone* might be. She stepped into the attic and focused on the little man standing near the window. He was no stranger; she remembered him from the hospital. Like Norris, Wendell Holmes was a medical student, but she was quick to spot the differences between the two. What she noticed first was the superior quality of Holmes's coat, which had been expertly tailored to his small shoulders, his narrow waist. He had eyes like a sparrow's, bright and alert, and while she studied him, she knew that he was studying her in kind and cannily taking her measure.

"This is my classmate," said Norris. "Mr. Oliver Wendell Holmes."

The little man nodded. "Miss Connolly."

"I remember you," she said. *Because you look like a wee elf.* But she did not think he would appreciate that observation. "I'm the one you wished to see, Mr. Holmes?"

"About the death of Dr. Berry. You've heard about it."

"I saw a crowd gathered near the bridge. They told me they'd found the doctor's body."

"This new development greatly confuses the picture," said Wendell. "By tomorrow, the newspapers will be stoking terror. *West End Reaper still at large!* The public will once again see monsters everywhere. It puts Mr. Marshall in a most uncomfortable position. Perhaps even a dangerous one."

"Dangerous?"

"When the public's frightened, it can turn irrational. It may try to mete out justice on its own."

She said to Norris: "Ah. So that's why you're suddenly willing to listen to me. Because now it affects *you*."

Norris gave an apologetic nod. "I'm sorry, Rose. I should have paid more attention to you last night."

"You were ashamed just to be seen with me."

"And now I'm ashamed of my behavior toward you. My only excuse is that I had much to consider."

"Oh, yes. Your *future*."

He sighed, a sound so defeated that she almost felt sorry for him. "I have no future. Not anymore."

"And how can I change that?"

"What matters now," said Wendell, "is that we learn the truth."

"The truth only matters to those who're unfairly accused," she said. "No one else cares."

"I care," Wendell insisted. "Mary Robinson and Dr. Berry would have cared. And the killer's future victims will most certainly care." He came toward her, his eyes so sharply focused on her that she felt he could see straight into her mind. "Tell us about your niece, Rose. The little girl whom everyone is searching for."

For a moment she said nothing, weighing how much she could trust Oliver Wendell Holmes. And decided that she had no choice *but* to trust him. She had reached her limit, and now she was nearly faint with hunger.

"I'll tell you," she said. "But first . . ." She looked at Norris. "You said you brought me food."

———

She ate as she told the story, pausing to rip into a chicken leg or stuff a chunk of bread into her mouth. This was not the way one of those fine ladies might eat, but then this meal didn't come with pretty china or silverware. Her last meal had been that morning, a shriveled scrap of smoked mackerel that the fishmonger had planned to toss to his cat but, out of pity, had handed to her instead. The few coins that Norris had left her that morning had not gone toward a meal for herself. Instead she'd pressed them into Billy's hand and asked him to deliver the money to Hepzibah.

For another week, at least, little Meggie would be fed.

And now, for the first time in days, she, too, could eat her fill. So she did, devouring both meat and cartilage, sucking the marrow, leaving a mound of broken chicken bones, gnawed clean.

"You truly have no idea who fathered your sister's child?" asked Wendell.

"Aurnia said nothing to me. Though she hinted . . ."

"Yes?"

Rose paused, setting down the bread as her throat closed tight from the memories. "She asked me to fetch the priest for last rites. It was so important to her, but I kept putting it off. I didn't want her to stop fighting. I wanted her to live."

"And she wanted to confess her sins."

"Shame kept her from telling me," Rose said softly.

"And the child's father remains a mystery."

"Except to Mr. Gareth Wilson."

"Ah yes, the mysterious lawyer. May I see the card he gave you?"

She wiped her greasy hand and reached in her pocket for Gareth Wilson's calling card, which she handed to Wendell.

"He lives on Park Street. An impressive address."

"A fine address doesn't make him a gentleman," she said.

"You don't trust him one whit, do you?"

"Look at the filthy company he keeps."

"You mean Mr. Tate?"

"He used Eben to find me. Which makes Mr. Wilson no better, no matter how fancy his address."

"Did he say anything at all about who his client might be?"

"No."

"Would your brother-in-law know?"

"Fool that he is, Eben wouldn't know a thing. And Mr. Wilson would be even more a fool to tell him."

"I doubt this Mr. Gareth Wilson is any sort of fool," said Wendell, looking at the address again. "Have you told any of this to the Night Watch?"

"No."

"Why not?"

"It's useless to speak to Mr. Pratt." Her tone of disdain left no doubt what she thought of the man.

Wendell smiled. "I'd have to agree."

"I think Dim Billy would make a better constable. Mr. Pratt wouldn't believe me, anyway."

"You're so sure of that?"

"No one believes the likes of me. We Irish need to be watched all the time, or we'll pick your pockets and steal your children. If you doctors didn't slit us open and poke around inside our chests, like in that book over there"—she pointed to the anatomy text on Norris's desk—"you'd probably think we didn't have hearts that look just like yours."

"Oh, I have no doubt you have a heart, Miss Connolly. And a generous one at that, to take on such a burden as your niece."

"Hardly a burden, sir. She's my own family." Her only family now.

"You're certain the child is safe?"

"As safe as I can make her."

"Where is she? May we see her?"

Rose hesitated. Though Wendell's gaze was unflinching, though he'd given her no reason to doubt him, still, this was Meggie's life at stake.

Norris said, "She seems to be at the center of it all. Please, Rose. We only want to be sure she's well protected. And healthy."

It was Norris's plea that convinced her. From their first meeting in the hospital, she had been drawn to him, had felt that, unlike the other gentlemen, he was someone she could turn to. Last night, by his charity, he had confirmed her faith in him.

She looked out the window. "It's dark enough. I never go there in daylight." She stood. "It should be safe now."

"I'll call a carriage," said Wendell.

"No carriage will make it down the alley where I'm taking you." She wrapped her cloak tight and turned to the door. "We walk."

In Hepzibah's world, shadows always reigned. Even when Rose had visited while the sun was shining, the light barely penetrated into the low-ceilinged room. In her zeal to keep warm, Hepzibah had nailed her shutters closed, turning her room into a dark little cave where the far corners remained eternally invisible. So the murky space Rose saw that night looked no different than always, with the fire reduced to glowing coals, and not even a single candle burning.

With a joyful laugh, Rose swept up Meggie from the basket and brought the little face up to hers, breathing in the familiar scents of her hair, her swaddling clothes. Meggie responded with a wet cough, and tiny fingers reached out to grasp a handful of Rose's hair. Mucus gleamed on her upper lip.

"Ah, my darling girl!" said Rose, hugging Meggie to her own empty breasts. Wishing that she could be the one to nourish her. The two gentlemen standing behind her remained strangely silent, watching as she fussed over the baby. She turned to Hepzibah. "Has she been ill?"

"Started coughing last night. You haven't been here in a few days."

"I sent money today. Billy brought it, didn't he?"

By the faint glow of the hearth, Hepzibah, with her fat neck, looked like an enormous toad planted in the chair. "Aye, the idiot boy brought it. I'll be needing more."

"More? But it was what you asked."

"She's keepin' me up now, that one. Coughing."

Norris said, "May we take a look at the baby? We'd like to confirm that she's healthy."

Hepzibah eyed him and gave a grunt. "Who might you gentlemen be, to care about some fatherless child?"

"We're medical students, madam. We care about all children."

"Ooh, fancy that!" Hepzibah laughed. "I can show you ten thousand of 'em, when you're done wi' this one."

Norris lit a candle at the hearth. "Bring the baby here, Rose. So I can get a better look at her."

Rose carried Meggie to him. The baby gazed up with trusting eyes as Norris peeled away the blanket and examined her chest, prodded her abdomen. Already he had the sure and confident hands of a doctor, Rose observed, and she imagined him as he would one day look, his hair streaked with gray, his gaze sober and wise. Oh, she hoped she would know him then! She hoped she could watch him gaze down at his own child. *Our own child.* Thoroughly he inspected Meggie, whose plump thighs were testimony to an adequate diet. But the baby was coughing, and strands of clear mucus trickled from her nostrils.

"She seems to have no fever," said Norris. "But there is congestion."

Hepzibah gave a dismissive grunt. "All the little ones have it. Not a child in South Boston who doesn't have snot under his nose."

"But she's so young."

"She eats more than enough. And for that as well, I'll need to be paid more."

Wendell reached into his pocket and withdrew a handful of

coins, which he placed in the wet nurse's hand. "There'll be more. But the child must stay well fed and healthy. Do you understand?"

Hepzibah stared at the money. And she said, with a new note of respect, "Oh, she will, sir. I'll be sure of it."

Rose stared at Wendell, stunned by his generosity. "I'll find a way to pay you, Mr. Holmes," she said, softly. "I swear to you."

"There's no need to talk of payment," said Wendell. "If you'll excuse us, Mr. Marshall and I need to speak alone." He looked at Norris, and the two men stepped outside, into the alley.

"Not just one, but *two* gentlemen paying your way, eh?" Hepzibah looked at Rose and gave a knowing cackle. "You must be quite a girl."

"This place is appalling!" said Wendell. "Even if she keeps the child well fed, *look* at the woman! She's grotesque. And this neighborhood—all these tenements—they're ridden with disease."

And they're filled with children, thought Norris, looking up the narrow alley at windows where candles flickered. Countless children, every bit as vulnerable as baby Meggie. They stood outside Hepzibah's door, shivering in a night that had fallen significantly colder in just the short time they'd been indoors. "She can't stay here," he agreed.

"The question is," said Wendell, "what's the alternative?"

"She belongs with Rose. That's where she'll be best cared for."

"Rose can't feed her. And if she's right about these murders, if she's truly being hunted, then she needs to stay as far away from the baby as she can get. She knows that."

"And it's breaking her heart. You can see it."

"Yet she's clear-eyed enough to realize it's necessary." Wendell glanced down the alley as a drunken man came tottering out of a doorway and staggered away in the other direction. "She's quite a resourceful girl. She *has* to be clever, just to keep body and soul together out on the streets. I have a feeling that, no matter the situation, Rose Connolly will find a way to survive. And keep her niece alive as well."

Norris remembered the wretched lodging house in which he'd visited her. He thought of the room crawling with insects, and the coughing man in the corner, and the floor covered with filthy straw. *Could I endure one night in such a place?*

"A remarkable girl," Wendell said.

"I've come to appreciate that."

"And quite a pretty one, too. Even under all those rags."

So I've noticed.

"What are you going to do with her, Norris?"

Wendell's question brought Norris up short. What *was* he going to do with her? This morning, he'd been resolved to send her on her way with a few coins and his best wishes. Now he realized he couldn't turn her out on the street, not when the whole world seemed poised to crush her. And the baby had become his concern as well. Who could not be charmed by such a serene and smiling child?

"No matter what you choose," said Wendell, "even if you send her away, your fates seem to be tied together."

"What do you mean?"

"The West End Reaper haunts you both. Rose believes she's stalked by him. The Night Watch believes you *are* him. Until he's caught, you and Rose won't be safe." Wendell turned and looked at Hepzibah's door. "Nor will the child."

Twenty-six

Now, THIS IS THE WAY to make a living, thought Jack Burke as he lumbered up Water Street, wearing his best coat and his clean boots. No mucking around in the dark and dodging bullets. No coming home with his clothes muddy and reeking of cadavers. With winter setting in and the ground frozen hard as rock, all the merchandise would be coming up from the south anyway, crammed into barrels labeled PICKLES or MADEIRA or WHISKEY. What a surprise would lie in store for any thief who hankered for a drink and secretly broke into one of those barrels. Poor thirsty man, to pry off the lid, his lips tingling with anticipation, only to find, instead of whiskey, a naked corpse preserved in brine.

A man might lose his taste for drink over that.

Too many of those barrels were coming up from Virginia and the Carolinas these days. Male or female, black or white, the merchandise found a ready market in all the medical schools, whose ravenous appetite for cadavers seemed only to grow every year. He could see how the business was going. He had seen the barrels in Dr. Sewall's yard and knew they didn't contain cucumber pickles. The competition had grown fierce, and Jack had a vision of endless trains, car after car loaded with just such barrels, bringing the southern dead, at twenty-five dollars apiece, to the dissection parlors of Boston and New York and Philadelphia. How could he compete with that?

Far easier to earn it the way he was doing today, walking in broad daylight, with clean boots, up Water Street. Not the finest neighborhood, but good enough for tradesmen, who were out in this clear, chill morning, their wagons filled with bricks or lumber or dry goods. It was a workingman's street, and the shop he arrived at should certainly cater to a workingman's taste and needs. But displayed behind the dusty glass was an evening coat that no workingman could possibly make use of. It was fashioned from brilliant crimson cloth and trimmed with gold lace, a coat that forced you to stop right there on the street and dream of a better life. A coat that said: *Even a man like you can look like a prince.* A useless thing for a tradesman, and the tailor certainly knew it, but he had chosen to display it anyway, as if to announce that he was destined for a better neighborhood.

A bell tinkled as Jack walked into the shop. Inside, far more commonplace items were displayed: cotton shirts and pantaloons and a dark cloth roundabout coat. Even a tailor with delusions of grandeur must cater to the practical needs of his clientele. While Jack stood breathing in the smell of wool and the acrid tang of dye, a dark-haired man with a neatly trimmed mustache emerged from the back room. The man looked Jack up and down, as if mentally taking his measure for a suit. He was smartly dressed, his jacket well fitted to his trim waist, and although he was not particularly tall, he had the ramrod posture of one who has an exaggerated impression of his own stature.

"Good morning, sir. May I be of service?" the tailor inquired.

"Are you Mr. Eben Tate?" asked Jack.

"Yes, I am."

Though Jack was wearing his good coat and a clean shirt, he had the distinct feeling that Mr. Tate had judged his clothes and found them wanting.

Eben said: "A good selection of reasonably priced woolen cloth has just come in from the Lowell mills. It would do quite nicely for a new greatcoat."

Jack looked down at his own coat and saw no reason why he would want a new one.

"Or perhaps you're in need of a topcoat or shirt? I can offer you some quite practical styles, something that would suit your profession. Which is . . . ?"

"I'm not in the market for anything," growled Jack, offended that with just one look, this stranger had pegged him as a customer in need of something *practical* and *reasonably priced*. "I'm here to ask you about a certain someone. Someone you know."

Eben's attention remained focused on Jack's barrel chest, as though he was estimating how many yards of cloth were required.

"I'm a tailor, Mr.—"

"Burke."

"Mr. Burke. If you're interested in a shirt or pantaloons, I can certainly help you. But I make it a point to avoid needless gossip, so I doubt I'm the one you want to speak to."

"It's about Rose Connolly. Do you know where I can find her?"

To Jack's surprise, Eben gave a laugh. "You, too, eh?"

"What?"

"Everyone seems to be interested in Rose."

Jack was confused. How many others had been hired to find her? How much competition did he have? "Well, where is she?" he asked.

"I don't know and I don't care."

"Wasn't she your wife's sister?"

"I still don't care. I'm embarrassed to admit she's any relation of mine. A piece of trash, that one, spreading lies about me. And a thief, too. That's what I told the Night Watch." He paused. "You're not with the Watch, are you?"

Jack avoided the question. "How can I find her?"

"What's she done now?"

"Just tell me where to find her."

"Last I knew, she was staying in some rathole down in Fishery Alley."

"She's not there anymore. Hasn't been there in days."

"Then I can't help you. Now, if you'll excuse me." Eben turned and vanished into the back room.

Jack remained where he was, frustrated by this impasse. And worried about the possibility that some other party might track down the girl before he did. Would he still be paid the finder's fee? Or would he have to be satisfied with what he'd already received? A generous sum, to be sure, but it wasn't enough.

It was never enough.

He stared at the doorway through which that prig of a tailor had retreated. "Mr. Tate?" he called.

"I've told you what I know!" came the answer, but not the man.

"There's money in it for you."

That was the magic word. In two heartbeats, Eben was out of the back room. "Money?"

How quickly two men can have a meeting of the minds. Their gazes met, and Jack thought: Here's a fellow who understands what's important.

"Twenty dollars," said Jack. "Find her for me."

"For twenty dollars, it's hardly worth my time. Anyway, I told you. I don't know where she is."

"Does she have any friends? Anyone who might know?"

"Just that half-wit."

"Who?"

"Skinny boy. Everyone knows him. Hangs around the West End, begging for pennies."

"You mean Dim Billy."

"That's the one. He was lodging with her over on Fishery Alley. Came around here looking for her. Brought her bag over, thinking she'd be with me."

"So Billy doesn't know where she is, either?"

"No. But he's got a nose on him." Eben laughed. "May be a half-wit, but he's good at finding things."

And I know where to find Billy, thought Jack as he turned to leave.

"Wait, Mr. Burke! You said there was money involved."

"For useful information. But it has to be useful."

"What if I found her myself?"

"You just let me know, and I'll see you get paid."

"Who's providing the fee? Who's paying *you?*"

Jack shook his head. "Believe me, Mr. Tate," he said. "You're better off not knowing."

BODY OF DR. BERRY FOUND

A most shocking turn of events has transpired in the search for the West End Reaper. On Sunday afternoon at one o'clock, two young boys playing along the Charles River discovered a man's body beneath the West Boston Bridge. Authorities have identified the corpse as none other than Dr. Nathaniel Berry, who vanished from his post as house physician earlier this month. A most appalling and clearly deliberate wound to his abdomen has been accepted as proof that this was not a suicide.

Dr. Berry was the subject of an extensive manhunt from Maine to Georgia, in connection with the recent slayings of two nurses at the hospital where he was employed. The sheer brutality of their deaths has evoked terror throughout the region, and the sudden disappearance of the doctor was interpreted by Constable Lyons of the Night Watch as a convincing indication of Dr. Berry's guilt in the matter. Dr. Berry's death now raises the disturbing likelihood that the West End Reaper remains at large.

This reporter can reveal on good authority that another suspect is currently under investigation, one who has been described as a young man in possession of both surgical and butchering skills. This gentleman, moreover, resides in the West End. Rumors that he is currently enrolled as a student at the Boston Medical College cannot be confirmed.

From gentleman to leper in the span of a single day, thought Norris, as he watched the front page of the *Daily Advertiser* flutter past him down the street. Was there anyone of consequence in Boston who had not read that damning article? Anyone who could not guess the identity of the "young man in possession of both surgical and butchering skills"? This morning, when he had walked into the auditorium for morning lectures, he'd noticed the startled glances and heard the sharp intakes of breath. No one had directly challenged his attendance. How could they, when he had not been formally charged with any crime? No, the *gentleman's* way of dealing with scandal was with whispers and innuendo, both of which he must now endure. Soon, his ordeal would end one way or another. After the Christmas holiday, Dr. Grenville and the school trustees would render their decision and Norris would know if he still had a place in the college

For now he was reduced to this: skulking on Park Street, spying on the one man who might know the Reaper's identity.

He and Rose had been watching the house all afternoon, and now the fading light took with it the day's last blush of color, leaving only dreary shades of gray. Across the street was Number Five, one of eight imposing row houses that faced the skeletal trees of the snow-blanketed Common. So far they had caught not even a glimpse of Mr. Gareth Wilson or of any visitors. Wendell's inquiries about the man had turned up little information, only that he'd recently returned from London, and that his Park Street home stood vacant for most of the year.

Who is your client, Mr. Wilson? Who paid you to track down a baby, to terrify a friendless girl?

The door to Number Five suddenly opened.

Rose whispered: "It's him. It's Gareth Wilson."

The man was warmly dressed in a black beaver hat and a voluminous greatcoat. He paused outside his front door to pull on black
gloves, then began to walk briskly up Park Street in the direction of
the State House.

Norris's gaze followed the man. "Let's see where he goes."

They allowed Wilson to reach the end of the block of row houses
before falling into step behind him. At the State House, Wilson
turned west and began to make his way up into the maze of the Beacon Hill neighborhood.

Norris and Rose followed him past stately brick homes and
winter-bare linden trees. It was quiet here, too quiet, and only an
occasional carriage rattled past. Their quarry gave no indication
that he realized he was being followed, and walked at a leisurely
pace, leaving behind the fine homes of Chestnut Street to wend his
way into more modest territory—not where a gentleman with an af-
fluent Park Street address would normally be wandering.

When Wilson abruptly turned into narrow Acorn Street, Norris
wondered if the man had suddenly realized he was being followed.
Why else would Wilson visit this tiny alley, occupied by mere
coachmen and retainers?

In the dim light of dusk, Wilson was almost invisible as he
walked down the shadowy passage. He stopped at a door and
knocked. A moment later the door opened, and they heard a man
say: "Mr. Wilson! It's a pleasure to see you back in Boston after all
these months."

"Have the others arrived?"

"Not everyone, but they'll be here. This dreadful business has
made us all quite anxious."

Wilson stepped into the house, and the door swung shut.

It was Rose who made the next move, walking boldly up the
alley as though she belonged there. Norris followed her to the doorway, and they stared up at the house. It was neither distinctive nor

grand, just one in a row of anonymous brick houses. Above the doorway was a massive lintel, and in the fading light, Norris could just make out the symbols carved in the granite.

"Someone else is coming," whispered Rose. Quickly she looped her arm in his, and they walked away, bodies pressed together like lovers, their backs turned to the man who had just entered the alley behind them. They heard a knock on the door.

The same voice that had greeted Gareth Wilson now said: "We wondered if you'd make it."

"I apologize for the state of my apparel, but I came straight from a patient's sickbed."

Norris came to a halt, too shocked to take another step. Slowly, he turned. Though he could not see the man's face through the shadows, he could make out a familiar silhouette, the broad shoulders filling out the generous greatcoat. Even after the man had stepped into the house, and the door swung shut, Norris stood rooted to the spot. *It cannot be.*

"Norris?" Rose tugged on his arm. "What is it?"

He stared up the alley at the doorway through which the new visitor had just entered. "I know that man," he said.

Dim Billy is an apt name for the boy who now shambles down the alley, his shoulders hunched forward, his neck extended like a stork's as he stares at the ground, as though in search of some treasure that he's lost. A penny perhaps, or a stray bit of tin, something that no one else would give a second glance to. But Billy Piggott is not like anyone else, or so Jack Burke said. A useless half-wit, Burke called the boy, a stray who wanders the streets always in search of a free meal, just like the equally stray black mutt who so often trots at the boy's heels. A half-wit the boy might be, but he is not entirely useless.

He is the key to finding Rose Connolly.

Until recently, Billy had lodged with Rose in a rathole on Fishery Alley. The boy must know where to find her.

And tonight, Dim Billy will almost certainly talk.

The boy suddenly stops and his head jerks up. Somehow he's sensed the presence of another in his alley, and his gaze seeks out a face. "Who's there?" he calls out. But his attention isn't focused on the shadow in the doorway; instead he looks at the far end of the alley, where a silhouette has just appeared, backlit by the glow of a streetlamp.

"Billy!" a man calls.

The boy stands still, facing the encroaching intruder. "What d'ya want with me?"

"I just want to talk to you."

"About what, Mr. Tate?"

"About Rose." Eben moves closer. "Where is she, boy?"

"I don't know."

"Come on, Billy. You do know."

"No I don't! And you can't make me tell you!"

"She's my own family. I only want to speak to her."

"You hit her. You're mean to her."

"Is that what she told you? And you believe her?"

"She only tells me the truth."

"That's what she'd have you believe." Eben's voice turns smooth, coaxing. "There's money in it for you if you help me find her. Even more if you help me find the baby."

"She says if I tell, they'll kill Meggie."

"So you do know where she is."

"She's just a baby, and babies can't fight back."

"Babies need milk, Billy. They need tender care. I can buy it for her."

Billy backs away. Idiot though he is, he can hear the insincerity in Eben Tate's voice. "I ain't talking to you."

"Where is Rose?" Eben advances. "Come *back here!*"

But the boy scrabbles away, quick as a crab. Eben makes a desperate lunge and stumbles in the dark. He goes sprawling facedown as Billy makes his escape, his footsteps receding into the darkness.

"Little bastard. Wait till I get my hands on you." Eben grunts as he rises to his knees. He is still on all fours when his gaze suddenly fixes on the shadowy doorway right beside where he has fallen. On the gleam of two leather shoes, planted almost in front of his nose.

"What? Who?" Eben scrambles to his feet as the figure emerges from the doorway, black cape sweeping across the icy stones.

"Good evening, sir."

Eben gives an embarrassed grunt and pulls himself up straight, swiftly reclaiming his dignity. "Well! This is not a place I'd expect to find—"

The thrust of the knife drives the blade so deep it strikes spine, and the handle transmits the impact against bone, a thrilling ache of ultimate power. Eben sucks in a breath as his body goes rigid, his eyes bulging in shock. He does not cry out; in fact, he makes no sound at all. The first stab is almost always met with the silence of the stunned.

The second slash is swift and efficient, releasing a gout of entrails. Eben collapses to his knees, hands pressed to the wound as though to hold back the waterfall of offal, but it spills from his belly and would have tripped him had he tried to flee. Had he been able to take even a single step.

Eben's is not the face the Reaper expected to stare down upon this night, but such are the vagaries of providence. Though it's not Billy's blood that funnels its way into the gutter and trickles between the cobblestones, there is a purpose yet for this harvest. Every death, like every life, has its use.

There is one more slice to make. Which part this time, which bit of flesh?

Ah, the obvious choice. By now, Eben's heart has ceased to beat. Only a little blood spills as the blade slits into the scalp and begins to peel away its prize.

Twenty-seven

"THESE ACCUSATIONS are extremely dangerous," said Dr. Grenville. "Before you take them any further, gentlemen, I advise you to consider the possible consequences."

"Norris and I both saw him come out of that building last night, on Acorn Street," said Wendell. "It *was* Dr. Sewall. And there were others at that house, others we recognized."

"And what of it? A gathering of gentlemen is hardly an extraordinary occurrence." Grenville gestured to the room in which they now sat. "We three are now having a meeting in my parlor. Is this to be taken as a suspicious gathering?"

"Consider who those men were," said Norris. "One was Mr. Gareth Wilson, recently returned from London. A most mysterious individual with few friends in town."

"You've been inquiring into Mr. Wilson's affairs, all because of what some silly girl told you? A girl I have yet to lay eyes on?"

"Rose Connolly strikes us both as a reliable witness," said Wendell.

"I can't judge the reliability of a girl I've never met. Neither can

I allow you to slander a man as respected as Dr. Sewall. Good God, I *know* his character!"

Wendell asked, quietly: "Do you, sir?"

Grenville rose from his chair and paced in agitation to the hearth. There he stood with his back turned to them, his gaze on the fire. Outside, Beacon Street had fallen silent in the deepness of night, and the only sounds were the crackling flames and the occasional creak of servants' footsteps. They heard such footsteps now, approaching the drawing room, and there was a soft knock on the door. A parlor maid appeared, carrying a tray of cakes.

"I'm sorry to interrupt, sir," she said. "But Mrs. Lackaway asked me to bring this in for the young gentlemen."

Grenville didn't even turn from the fire, just said, brusquely: "Leave it. And close the door behind you."

The girl set the tray on a side table and quickly withdrew.

Only when her footsteps had receded down the hall did Grenville finally say: "Dr. Sewall saved my nephew's life. I owe him for my sister's happiness, and I refuse to believe he's involved in any way with these murders." Grenville turned to Norris. "You, better than anyone, know what it's like to be a victim of rumors. Based on all the tales now circulating about you, you possess horns and cloven hooves. Do you think it's been easy for me to be your champion? To defend your place in our college? Yet I have done so because I refuse to be swayed by malicious gossip. I tell you now, it'll take far more than this to rouse my suspicions."

"Sir," said Wendell, "you haven't heard the names of the other men at that meeting."

Grenville turned to him. "And you spied on them as well?"

"We simply took note of who came and went from Acorn Street. There was also a gentleman who seemed familiar to me. I followed him to an address at Twelve Post Office Square."

"And?"

"It was Mr. William Lloyd Garrison. I recognized him, because I heard him speak this past summer, at the Park Street church."

"Mr. Garrison, the abolitionist? Do you feel it's a crime to advocate the freeing of slaves?"

"Not at all. I find his position a most noble one."

Grenville looked at Norris. "Do you?"

"I'm in complete sympathy with the abolitionists," said Norris. "But there are disturbing things being said about Mr. Garrison. A shopkeeper told us—"

"A shopkeeper? Now *that* is a reliable source indeed."

"He told us that Mr. Garrison is often seen out late at night, moving in a most furtive manner in the vicinity of Beacon Hill."

"I, too, am often out late at night, due to the needs of my patients. Some might call my movements furtive as well."

"But Mr. Garrison is no physician. What would draw him out at all hours of the night? Acorn Street in particular seems to attract visitors not from the neighborhood. There are reports of eerie chanting heard in the night, and last month, bloodstains were found on the cobblestones. All these things have deeply alarmed people in the neighborhood, but when they complained to the Night Watch, Constable Lyons resisted any investigation. Even odder, he issued orders that the Watch is to avoid Acorn Street entirely."

"Who told you this?"

"The shopkeeper."

"Consider your source, Mr. Marshall."

"We would be more skeptical," said Wendell, "except there was one more familiar face that emerged from the house. It was Constable Lyons himself."

For the first time, Dr. Grenville was stunned silent. He stared at the young men in disbelief.

"Whatever is going on in that house is being shielded at the highest levels," said Norris.

Grenville gave a sudden laugh. "Do you realize, Mr. Marshall, that Constable Lyons is the only reason you are not in custody? His dimwit associate, Mr. Pratt, was ready to arrest you, but Lyons stayed his hand. Even with all the rumors, the whispers against you, Lyons has been your ally."

"You know this to be fact?"

"He told me. He's under pressure from all sides—the public, the press, everyone is braying for an arrest, any arrest. He knows full well that Mr. Pratt covets his position, but Lyons won't be rushed. Not without evidence."

"I had no idea, sir," said Norris quietly.

"If you want to remain at liberty, I suggest you not antagonize your defenders."

"But Dr. Grenville," said Wendell, "there are so many unanswered questions. Why did they meet at such a modest address? Why would men of such diverse occupations come together late at night? Finally, the residence itself is interesting. Or, rather, one detail of that residence." Wendell looked at Norris, who removed a folded sheet of paper from his pocket.

"What is this?" asked Grenville.

"These symbols are carved on the granite lintel above the doorway," said Norris. He gave the sheet to Grenville. "I went back this morning, to examine it by daylight. You can see two pelicans facing each other. And between them, there's a cross."

"You'll find many a cross on buildings in this city."

"That's not just any cross," said Wendell. "This one has a rose at its center. This isn't a papist symbol. It's the cross of the Rosicrucians."

Abruptly Grenville crumpled the sheet. "Absurd. You're chasing phantoms."

"The Rosicrucians are real. A society so secret, no one knows the identity of its members. There are reports, here and in Washington, that their influence is growing. That they indulge in sacrifices. That among their victims are children, whose innocent blood is spilled in secret rituals. This child that Rose Connolly protects seems to be at the center of this mystery. We assumed the baby's sought by the man who fathered her. Now we witness these secret meetings on Acorn

Street. We hear reports of blood on the cobblestones. And we wonder if another motive entirely is at work here."

"Child sacrifice?" Grenville threw the drawing into the fire. "This is thin evidence indeed, Mr. Marshall. When I meet with the trustees after Christmas, I'll need more than this to defend you. How can I support your enrollment if my sole argument is an outlandish conspiracy theory, hatched by a girl I've never met? A girl who refuses to meet with me?"

"She trusts few people, sir. Even fewer since we spotted Constable Lyons on Acorn Street."

"Where is she? Who shelters her?"

Norris hesitated, embarrassed to reveal the scandalous fact that he, an unmarried man, allowed the girl to sleep only a few feet from his own bed.

He was grateful when Wendell interjected smoothly: "We have arranged for her lodgings, sir. I assure you, she's in a safe place."

"And the baby? If this child is in such danger, can you guarantee its safety?"

Norris and Wendell looked at each other. Little Meggie's welfare was, in fact, a matter that worried them both.

"She, too, remains hidden, sir," said Wendell.

"And her circumstances?"

"Far from ideal, I admit. She's fed and cared for, but in the most unclean surroundings."

"Then bring her here, gentlemen. I should like to see this mysterious child whom everyone seems so intent upon. I assure you she'll be safe, and in the healthiest of households."

Again, Norris and Wendell exchanged glances. Could there be any doubt that Meggie would be far better off here than in Hepzibah's filthy hovel?

But Norris said, "Rose would never forgive us if we made such a decision without her. She's the one who cares most about the child. She's the one who must choose."

"You cede a great deal of authority to a seventeen-year-old-girl."

"She may be only seventeen. But she deserves respect, sir. Against all the odds, she's survived, and she's kept her niece alive as well."

"You would stake a child's life on this girl's judgment?"

"Yes. I would."

"Then your *own* judgment is in question, Mr. Marshall. A mere girl *cannot* be trusted with such a grave responsibility!"

A knock on the door made them all turn. Eliza Lackaway, looking concerned, stepped into the room. "Is everything all right, Aldous?"

"Yes, yes." Grenville released a deep breath. "We're just having a spirited discussion."

"We could hear you upstairs, which is why I've come down. Charles is awake now and would dearly love to see his friends." She looked at Wendell and Norris. "He wanted to make sure you didn't leave without saying hello."

"We wouldn't dream of it," said Wendell. "We were hoping he'd be up to seeing visitors."

"He's desperate for visitors."

"Go." Grenville brusquely waved the young men out of the room. "Our conversation is at an end."

Eliza frowned at her brother's rude dismissal of their visitors, but she refrained from commenting on it as she led Norris and Wendell out of the parlor and up the stairs. Instead, she spoke of Charles.

"He wanted to come downstairs to see you," she said, "but I insisted he stay in bed, as he's not yet steady on his feet. This is still a delicate time in his recovery."

They reached the top of the stairs, and once again, Norris caught a fleeting glimpse of the Grenville family portraits hanging in the second-floor hallway, a gallery of both young and old, men and women. He recognized Charles among them, posed in a dapper suit, standing beside a desk. His left elbow was propped jauntily on a stack of books with his hand draped over the leather spines, a hand he no longer possessed.

"Here are your friends, darling," said Eliza.

They found Charles looking pale, but with a smile on his face. His left wrist stump was discreetly hidden beneath the sheets.

"I could hear my uncle's voice booming through the floor," said Charles. "It sounded like quite a lively discussion downstairs."

Wendell drew up a chair to sit beside the bed. "Had we known you were awake, we'd have come up sooner."

Charles tried to sit up, but his mother protested: "No, Charles. You need to rest."

"Mother, I've been resting here for days and I'm sick of it. I'll have to get up sooner or later." With a grimace, he leaned forward, and Eliza quickly propped pillows behind his back.

"So how are you, Charlie?" asked Wendell. "Is it still so very painful?"

"Only when the morphine wears off. But I try never to let *that* happen." Charles managed a tired smile. "Still, I am better. And look at the bright side. I'll never have to apologize for not learning the piano!"

Eliza sighed. "That's not funny, dear."

"Mother, would you mind if I had some time alone with my friends? It feels like an eternity since I saw them."

"I'll take that as a sign you're feeling better." Eliza stood. "Gentlemen, please don't exhaust him. I'll check on you in a bit, darling."

Charles waited until his mother had left the room, then he gave an exasperated sigh. "God, she smothers me!"

"Are you really feeling better?" asked Norris.

"My uncle says all the signs are good. I haven't had a fever since Tuesday. Dr. Sewall looked at it this morning and he's satisfied with the wound." He regarded his bandaged wrist and said, "He saved my life."

At the mention of Dr. Sewall's name, neither Wendell nor Norris said a word.

"So now," said Charles, brightening as he looked at his friends. "Tell me the latest. What news is there?"

"We miss you in class," said Norris.

"*Fainting Charlie?* No wonder you all miss me. I can always be counted on to make everyone else look brilliant by comparison."

"You'll have all this time to study, lying here in bed," said Wendell. "When you come back to class, you'll be the most brilliant of us all."

"You know I'm not coming back."

"Of course you are."

"Wendell," said Norris quietly. "It's kinder to be honest, don't you think?"

"Really, this will all work out for the better," Charles said. "I was never meant to be a doctor. Everyone knows it. I have neither the talent nor the interest. It's always been about my uncle's hopes, my uncle's expectations. I'm not like you. Lucky you, always knowing exactly what you wanted to be."

"And what do you want to be, Charlie?" asked Norris.

"Ask Wendell. He knows." Charles pointed to his boyhood friend. "We were both members of the Andover Literary Club. He's not the only one prone to bursts of poetic verse."

Norris gave a startled laugh. "You want to be a *poet?*"

"My uncle hasn't accepted it yet, but now he's going to have to. And why shouldn't I choose a literary life? Look at Johnny Greenleaf Whittier. He's already finding success with his poems. And that writer fellow from Salem, Mr. Hawthorne. He's but a few years older than I, and I'll lay odds that he'll soon make a name for himself. Why not pursue what I'm passionate about?" He looked at Wendell. "What did you call it once? The drive to write?"

"The intoxicating pleasure of authorship."

"Yes, that's it! The intoxicating pleasure!" Charles sighed. "Of course, there's hardly a living to be made at it."

"Somehow," said Wendell drily as he looked around the well-appointed bedroom, "I doubt you need to be concerned about that."

"The problem is that my uncle thinks poems and novels are merely frivolous diversions, with no real significance."

Wendell gave a sympathetic nod. "Something my own father would say."

"Aren't you ever tempted to ignore him? To choose the literary life anyway?"

"But I don't have a wealthy uncle. And I've rather taken to medicine, anyway. It suits me."

"Well, it's never suited me. Now my uncle will have to accept it." He looked down at his stump. "There's nothing so useless as a one-handed surgeon."

"Ah, but a one-handed poet! You'll cut a most romantic figure."

"What lady would want me?" Charles asked plaintively. "Now that I've lost my hand?"

Wendell reached out to grasp his friend's shoulder. "Charlie, listen to me. Any lady who's worth knowing, who's worth loving, won't give one whit about your missing hand."

The creak of a footstep announced Eliza's return to the room. "Gentlemen," she said, "I think it's time for him to rest."

"Mother, we're just catching up."

"Dr. Sewall said you're not to exert yourself."

"All I've exerted so far is my tongue."

Wendell stood. "We do need to be going anyway."

"Wait. You never told me why you came to see my uncle."

"Oh, nothing really. It's just about that West End business."

"You mean the Reaper?" Charles's attention perked up. "I heard they found Dr. Berry's body."

Eliza cut in: "Who told you that?"

"The maids were talking about it."

"They shouldn't have. I want nothing to upset you."

"I'm not upset. I *want* to hear the latest."

"Not tonight," said Eliza, curtly ending the conversation. "I'll see your friends out now."

She accompanied Wendell and Norris down the stairs to the front door. As the two men stepped out, she said: "While Charles welcomes your visits, I do hope that next time you'll keep the conversation on pleasant and uplifting subjects. Kitty and Gwen Welliver were here this afternoon, and they practically filled his room with laughter. The kind of happy chatter he needs to hear, especially around Christmas."

From the brainless Welliver sisters? Norris preferred to be comatose. But all he said was, "We'll remember that, Mrs. Lackaway. Good night."

Outside, he and Wendell paused on Beacon Street, their breath clouding in the cold, and watched a lone horse and rider clop past, the man hunched deep within his greatcoat.

"Dr. Grenville is right, you know," said Wendell. "The child would be much better off here, with him. We should have taken him up on the offer."

"It's not our decision. The choice is Rose's."

"You trust her judgment that completely?"

"Yes, I do." Norris stared up the street as the horse and rider faded into the darkness up Beacon Street. "I think she's the wisest girl I've ever met."

"You *are* besotted with her, aren't you?"

"I respect her. And yes, I'm fond of her—who wouldn't be? She has the most generous heart."

"The word is *besotted*, Norris. Bewitched. In love." Wendell gave a knowing sigh. "And clearly she's just as besotted with you."

Norris frowned. "What?"

"Haven't you seen the way she looks at you, the way she hangs on your every word? The way she's tidied up your room and mended your coat and done everything possible to please you? Do you need any more obvious clue that she's in love with you?"

"In love?"

"Open your eyes, man!" Wendell laughed and gave him a clap on the shoulder. "I must go home for the holiday. I take it you're going to Belmont?"

Norris was still stunned by what Wendell had just said. "Yes," he said, dazed. "My father expects me."

"What about Rose?"

What about Rose, indeed?

She was all Norris thought about after he and Wendell parted. As he walked back to his lodgings, he wondered if his friend could possibly be right. Rose in love with him? He'd been oblivious to it. *But I never looked for it, either.*

From the street below, he could see candlelight flickering in his attic window. She's still awake, he thought, and suddenly he could not wait to see her. He climbed the stairs, feeling more anxious with each step. By the time he opened the door, his heart was pounding as much from anticipation as from exertion.

Rose had fallen asleep at the desk, her head resting on her folded arms, Wistar's *Anatomy* lying open before her. Looking over her shoulder, he saw that she'd been looking at an illustration of the heart, and he thought: What an extraordinary girl. The candle had guttered down to a mere puddle of wax, so he lit another. As he gently closed the cover of Wistar's, Rose stirred awake.

"Oh," she murmured, lifting her head. "You're back."

He watched her stretch, her neck arching, her hair tumbling loose. Looking into her face, he saw no artifice, no guile, just a drowsy girl trying to shake off sleep. The shawl she'd draped around her shoulders was of coarse, dun-colored wool, and when she wiped her hand across her cheek, she left behind a cindery smudge. He thought of how different she was from the Welliver sisters with their silk gowns and pretty fringed scarves and fine Morocco leather boots. There was not a moment, keeping company with those sisters, when he'd felt he was actually seeing them for who they were, so skilled were they at the dishonest game of flirtation. Not like this girl, who openly yawned and rubbed her eyes as naturally as any child awakening from a nap.

She looked up at him. "Did you tell him? What did he say?"

"Dr. Grenville reserves judgment. He wants to hear the story from your own lips." He leaned in close and placed his hand on her shoulder. "Rose, he made a generous offer, one that both Wendell and I think is for the best. Dr. Grenville has offered to take in Meggie."

She went rigid. Instead of gratitude, what flashed in her eyes was panic. "Tell me you didn't agree!"

"It would be so much better for her. Safer and healthier."

"*You had no right!*" She shot to her feet. Staring into her eyes, Norris saw the primal fierceness of a girl prepared to sacrifice everything for someone she loved. A girl so loyal that she'd endure anything to see her niece survive. "You gave him *Meggie?*"

"Rose, I'd never betray your trust!"

"She's not yours to give!"

"Listen to me. *Listen.*" He took her face in his hands and forced her to meet his gaze. "I told him *you're* the only one who'll decide. I told him I'd do only what *you* want. I follow your orders, Rose, whatever your wishes. You're the one who knows best, and I just want you to be happy."

"You mean that?" she whispered.

"Yes. Truly."

They stared at each other for a moment. Suddenly her eyes went bright with tears and she pulled away. How small she is, he thought. How fragile. Yet this girl has carried the weight of the world, and its scorn as well. *She's quite a pretty girl,* Wendell had said. Looking down at her now, Norris saw a pure and honest beauty that glowed even through the smudges of ash, a beauty that the Welliver sisters could never match. They were merely two simpering princesses dressed in satin. This girl had so little to her name, yet she'd taken that half-wit Billy under her wing. She'd scraped together all she owned to buy her sister a decent burial and keep her niece fed.

This is a girl who'd stand by me. Even if I don't deserve it.

"Rose," he said, "it's time for us to speak of the future."

"The future?"

"What happens next to you and Meggie. I must be honest: My prospects at the college are dim. I don't know if I can afford to keep this room, much less keep us all fed."

"You want me to leave." She said it as a statement of fact, as if no other conclusion was possible. How easy she made it for him just to send her away. How generously she absolved him of all guilt.

"I want you to be safe," he said.

"I don't break, Norrie. I can live with the truth. Just tell me."

"Tomorrow, I go home to Belmont. My father expects me for the holiday. I can tell you it won't be a cheerful stay. He's not one for celebration, and I'll probably spend it doing chores around the farm."

"You needn't explain." She turned. "I'll be gone in the morning."

"Yes, you'll be gone. With me."

Suddenly she turned back to him, her eyes wide with delight. "Go to Belmont?"

"It's the safest place for you both. There'll be fresh milk for Meggie, and a bed of your own. No one will find you there."

"I can bring her?"

"Of course we'll bring her. I wouldn't dream of leaving her behind."

Sheer delight sent her flying into his arms. Small though she was, she almost knocked him backward. Laughing, he caught her and twirled her around in the tiny room, and felt her heart beating joyfully against his.

Suddenly Rose pulled away and he saw the doubt in her face. "But what will your father say about me?" she asked. "About Meggie?"

He couldn't lie to her, certainly not with her gazing so directly into his eyes. "I don't know," he said.

Twenty-eight

IT WAS PAST THREE when the farmer stopped his wagon at the side of the Belmont road to let them off. They still had two miles to walk, but the sky was blue and the ice-crusted snow glittered bright as glass in the afternoon sun. As they trudged down the road with Meggie in Rose's arms, Norris pointed out which fields belonged to which neighbor. He would introduce her to them all, and they'd all adore her. The run-down house over there belonged to old Ezra Hutchinson, whose wife had died of typhus two years ago, and the cows in the adjoining field belonged to widow Heppy Comfort, who had her eye on the now eligible Ezra. The neat house across the road belonged to Dr. and Mrs. Hallowell, the childless couple who had been so kind to him over the years, who'd welcomed him into their home as if he were their own son. Dr. Hallowell had opened his library to Norris and last year had written the glowing recommendation letter to the medical college. Rose took in all this information with a look of eager interest, even the trivial tidbits about Heppy's lame calf and Dr. Hallowell's eccentric collection of German hymnals. As they neared the Marshall farm, her questions came more quickly, more urgently, as though she was feverish to know every detail of his life before they arrived. When they crested the rise, and the farm appeared on the horizon, she stopped to stare, her hand shielding her eyes from the setting sun's glare.

"It's not much to look at," he admitted.

"But it is, Norrie. It's where you grew up."

"I couldn't wait to escape from it."

"I wouldn't mind living here at all." Meggie stirred awake in her arms and gave a contented gurgle. Rose smiled at her niece and said, "I could be happy on a farm."

He laughed. "That's what I like about you, Rose. I think you could be happy anywhere."

"It's not the *where* that counts."

"Before you say *it's the people you live with*, you need to meet my father."

"I'm afraid to. The way you talk about him."

"He's a bitter man. You just need to know that ahead of time."

"Because he lost your mother?"

"She abandoned him. She abandoned both of us. He's never forgiven her."

"Have you?" she asked, and looked at him, her cheeks flushed pink from the cold.

"It's getting late," he said.

They walked on, the sun sinking lower, bare trees casting their spindly shadows across the snow. They came to the old stone wall, glistening with ice, and heard the bellowing of cows in the barn. As they neared the farm, it seemed to Norris that the house was smaller and humbler than he remembered. Had the clapboards been so weathered when he'd left only two months ago? Had the porch always sagged, the fence always leaned so crookedly? The closer they got, the heavier the burden of duty seemed to weigh on his shoulders, and the more he dreaded the coming reunion. Now he regretted dragging Rose and the baby into this. Though he'd warned her

that his father could be unpleasant, she showed no signs of apprehension, walking quite cheerfully beside him, humming to Meggie.
How could any man, even his father, dislike this girl? Surely she and
the baby will charm him, he thought. Rose will win him over, the
way she's won me over, and we'll all laugh together at supper. Yes, it
could be a good visit after all, and Rose will be the charm. My lucky
Irish girl. He looked at her and his spirits lifted because she seemed
so pleased to be here with him, trudging alongside the crooked
fence, toward a farmhouse that seemed ever more grim and dilapidated.

They stepped through the sagging gate into a front yard littered
with a broken cart and a pile of logs still to be split into firewood.
The Welliver sisters would quail at the sight of this yard, and he
imagined them in their dainty shoes trying to pick their way
through the hog-churned mud. Rose did not hesitate but simply
hiked up her skirt and followed Norris across the yard. The old sow,
disturbed by these visitors, gave a snort and trotted away toward the
barn.

Before they reached the porch, the door opened and Norris's father stepped out. Isaac Marshall had not seen his son in two months,
yet he called out no words of welcome; he merely stood on his
porch, watching in silence as his visitors approached. He wore the
same homespun coat, the same drab trousers as always, but the
clothes seemed to hang looser on his frame, and the eyes that peered
out from beneath the battered hat were more deeply sunk in hol-
lowed sockets. He offered only the flicker of a smile as his son
climbed the steps.

"Welcome home," said Isaac, but made no move to embrace his
son.

"Father, may I introduce you to my friend Rose. And her niece,
Meggie."

Rose stepped forward, smiling, and the baby gave a coo, as though
in greeting. "'Tis good to meet you, Mr. Marshall," Rose said.

Isaac kept his arms stubbornly at his side, and his lips tightened. Norris saw Rose flush, and at that moment, he had never disliked his own father more.

"Rose is a very good friend," said Norris. "I wanted you to meet her."

"She'll be staying the night?"

"I was hoping she could stay longer. She and the baby are in need of lodgings for a while. She can use the room upstairs."

"Then the bed'll have to be made up."

"I can do it, Mr. Marshall," said Rose. "I'll not be a bother. And I work hard! There's nothing I can't do."

Isaac gave the baby a long look. Then, with a grudging nod, he turned to go into the house. "I'd best see that we have enough for supper."

"I'm sorry, Rose. I'm so sorry."

They sat together in the hayloft with Meggie sound asleep beside them and gazed down in the soft lantern light at the cows feeding below. The pigs, too, had wandered into the barn and were grunting as they competed for prime bedding space among the piles of straw. Tonight, Norris found more comfort here, amid the din of the animals, than in the company of that silent man in that silent house. Isaac had said little during their holiday supper of ham and boiled potatoes and turnips, had asked only a few questions about Norris's studies, and then had seemed indifferent to the answers. The farm alone interested him, and when he did speak, it was about the fence that needed mending, the poor quality of hay this autumn, the laziness of the latest hired hand. Rose had sat right across from Isaac, but she might as well have been invisible, for he'd scarcely looked at her except to pass the food.

And she had been wise enough to keep her silence.

"It's the way he's always been," said Norris, staring down at the pigs rooting through straw. "I shouldn't have expected anything different. I shouldn't have put you through that."

"I'm glad I came."

"It must have been an ordeal for you tonight."

"You're the one I feel sorry for." Her face caught the glow of the lantern, and in the gloom of the barn Norris did not see her patched dress or her worn shawl; he saw only that face, gazing so intently at him. "'Tis a sad house you grew up in," she said. "Not any sort of home for a child."

"It wasn't always this way. I don't want you to think I had such a grim boyhood. There were good days."

"When did it change? Was it after your mother left?"

"Nothing was the same after that."

"How could it be? It's a terrible thing, to be abandoned. Bad enough when the one you love passes on. But when they *choose* to leave you . . ." She stopped. Taking in a deep breath, she looked down at the pen below. "I've always liked the smell of a barn. All of it, the animals, the hay, the stink. It's a good, honest smell, that it is."

He stared at the shadows, where the pigs had finally ceased rooting and were now huddled together for the night, softly grunting. "Who left you, Rose?" he asked.

"No one."

"You talked about people leaving you."

"I'm the one who did it," she said, and swallowed. "I did the leaving. What a fool I was! After Aurnia left for America, I followed her. Because I couldn't wait to grow up. I couldn't wait to see the world." She gave a regretful sigh and said, with tears in her voice: "I think I broke my mother's heart."

He didn't need to ask; he knew, just by the mournful droop of her head, that her mother was no longer alive.

She sat up straight and said firmly, "I'll never abandon anyone again. Ever."

He reached out to take her hand, so familiar to him now. It felt as if they had always held hands, had always shared secrets in the gloom of this barn.

"I understand why your father is bitter," she said. "He has a right to be."

Long after Rose and Meggie had gone to bed, Norris and Isaac sat together at the kitchen table, a lamp burning between them. Though Norris had drunk only sparingly from the jug of apple brandy, his father had been drinking it all evening, more than Norris had ever seen him drink before. Isaac poured himself yet another glass, and his hand was unsteady as he recorked the jug.

"So what is she to you?" said Isaac, gazing bleary-eyed over the rim of his glass.

"I told you, she's a friend."

"A girl? What are you, a Nancy-boy? You can't find a regular friend, like other men?"

"What do you have against her? The fact she's a girl? The fact she's Irish?"

"Is she knocked up?"

Norris stared at his father in disbelief. *It's the brandy talking. He can't mean it.*

"Ha. You don't even know," said Isaac.

"You have no right to say such things about her. You don't even know her."

"How well do *you* know her?"

"I haven't touched her, if that's what you're asking."

"Doesn't mean she isn't knocked up already. And she comes with a baby, too! Take her on, and you take on another man's responsibility."

"I hoped she'd be welcomed here. I hoped you'd learn to accept her, or maybe even love her. She's a hardworking girl, with the most generous heart I know. She certainly deserves better than the reception you gave her."

"I'm only thinking of your welfare, boy. Your happiness. You want to raise a child that isn't even your own?"

Abruptly Norris stood. "Good night, Father." He turned to leave the room.

"I'm trying to spare you the pain I knew. They'll lie to you, Norris. They're full of deceit, and you won't find out till it's too late."

Norris stopped, and with sudden comprehension, he turned to look at him. "You're talking about Mother."

"I tried to make her happy." Isaac gulped down the brandy and set the glass down hard on the table. "I tried my best."

"Well, I never saw it."

"Children don't see anything, don't know anything. There's a lot you'll never know about your mother."

"Why did she leave you?"

"She left you, too."

Norris could think of no retort for that painful truth. *Yes, she did leave me. And I'll never understand it.* Suddenly exhausted, he returned to the table and sat down. Watched as his father refilled his glass with brandy.

"What don't I know about Mother?" asked Norris.

"Things I should've known myself. Things I should've wondered. Why a girl like her would ever marry a man like me. Oh, I'm not a fool. I've lived on a farm long enough to know how long it takes for a sow to—" He stopped and lowered his head. "I don't think she ever loved me."

"Did you love her?"

Isaac lifted his damp gaze to Norris's. "What difference did it make? It wasn't enough to keep her here. *You* weren't enough to keep her here."

Those words, both cruel and true, hung in the air between them like spent gunpowder. They sat silent, facing each other across the table.

"The day she left," said Isaac, "you were sick. You remember?"

"Yes."

"It was a summer fever. You were so hot, we were afraid we'd lose you. Dr. Hallowell went to Portsmouth that week, so we couldn't call on him. All night, your mother stayed up with you. And all the next day. And still your fever wouldn't break, and we both thought for certain we'd lose you. And what does she do? Do you remember her leaving?"

"She said she loved me. She said she'd be back."

"That's what she told me. That her son deserved the best, and she was going to see that you got it. She put on her best dress and walked out of the house. And she never came back. Not that night, or the night after. I was here all alone, with a sick boy, and I had no way of knowing where she'd gone. Mrs. Comfort came to watch you while I searched. Every place I could think of, every neighbor she might have visited. Ezra thought he saw her riding south, on the Brighton road. Someone else saw her on the road to Boston. I couldn't think of why she'd go to either of those places." He paused. "Then a boy turned up at the door one day, with Sophia's horse. And the letter."

"Why have you never shown me that letter?"

"You were too young. Only eleven."

"I was old enough to understand."

"It's long gone now. I burned it. But I can tell you what it said. I'm not good at reading, you know that. So I asked Mrs. Comfort to look at it, too, just to be sure I understood." Isaac swallowed and looked straight at the lamp. "She said she couldn't be married to me any longer. She'd met a man, and they were leaving for Paris. *Go on with your life.*"

"There must have been more."

"There was nothing more. Mrs. Comfort can tell you."

"She explained nothing? She gave no details, not even his name?"

"I tell you, that's all she wrote."

"Was there nothing about me? She must have said something!"

Isaac said, quietly: "That's why I never showed it to you, boy. I didn't want you to know."

That his own mother hadn't even mentioned his name. Norris could not meet his father's gaze. Instead, he stared down at the scarred table, the table where he and Isaac had shared so many silent meals, listening only to the howl of the wind, the scrape of their forks against the plates. "Why now?" he asked. "Why did you wait all these years to tell me?"

"Because of *her*." Isaac looked toward the upstairs bedroom, where Rose was sleeping. "She has her eye on you, boy, and you have your eye on her. You make a mistake now, and you'll live with it for the rest of your life."

"Why do you assume she's a mistake?"

"Some men can't see it, even when it's staring them in the face."

"Mother was your mistake?"

"And I was hers. I watched her grow up. For years, I'd see her in church, sitting there in her pretty hats, always friendly enough to me, but always beyond me, too. And then one day, it's as if she suddenly *sees* me. And decides I'm worth a second glance." He reached for the jug and refilled his glass. "Eleven years later, she's trapped on this stinking farm with a sick boy. Of course it's easier to run away. Leave this behind and take up a fancy life with a new man." He set down the jug, and his gaze lifted toward the bedroom where Rose was sleeping. "You can't take 'em at their word, that's all I'm telling you. The girl comes with a sweet enough face. But what does it hide?"

"You misjudge her."

"I misjudged your mother. I only want to save you from the same heartache."

"I love this girl. I plan to marry her."

Isaac laughed. "I married for love, and see what came of it!" He lifted his glass, but his hand paused in midair. He turned and looked toward the door.

Someone was knocking.

They exchanged startled looks. It was deep into the night, not an hour for a neighborly visit. Frowning, Isaac picked up the lamp and went to open the door. The wind gusted in and the lamp almost went out as Isaac stood in the doorway, staring at whoever now faced him from his porch.

"Mr. Marshall?" a man said. "Is your son here?"

At the sound of that voice, Norris rose at once in alarm.

"What do you want with him?" asked Isaac. He suddenly stumbled backward as two men forced their way past him, into the kitchen.

"There you are," said Mr. Pratt, spotting Norris.

"What is the meaning of this?" demanded Isaac.

Watchman Pratt nodded to his companion, who stepped behind Norris, as though to cut off his escape. "You're returning with us to Boston."

"How dare you push your way into my home!" said Isaac. "Who are you?"

"The Night Watch." Pratt's gaze remained on Norris. "The carriage is waiting, Mr. Marshall."

"You're arresting my son?"

"For reasons he should already have explained to you."

"I'm not going until you tell me the charges," said Norris.

The man behind him shoved Norris so hard that he stumbled against the table. The jug of apple brandy toppled to the floor and shattered.

"Stop it!" cried Isaac. "Why are you doing this?"

"The charges are murder," said Pratt. "The murders of Agnes Poole, Mary Robinson, Nathaniel Berry. And now, Mr. Eben Tate."

"Tate?" Norris stared at him. Rose's brother-in-law murdered as well? "I know nothing about his death! I certainly did not kill him!"

"We have all the proof we need. It's now my duty to return you to Boston, where you will face trial." Pratt nodded to the other Watchman. "Bring him."

Norris was forced forward, and had just reached the doorway when he heard Rose cry out: "Norris?"

He turned and saw her panicked gaze. "Go to Dr. Grenville! Tell him what's happened!" he managed to shout just before he was shoved out the door and into the night.

His escorts forced him into the carriage, and Pratt signaled the driver with two hard raps on the roof. They rolled away and headed down the Belmont road toward Boston.

"Even your Dr. Grenville can't protect you now," said Pratt. "Not against this evidence."

"What evidence?"

"You can't guess? A certain item in your room?"

Norris shook his head, perplexed. "I have no idea what you're talking about."

"The jar, Mr. Marshall. I'm amazed you'd keep such a thing."

The other Watchman, sitting across from them, stared at Norris and muttered: "You're a sick bastard."

"It's not every day one finds a human face sloshing about in a jar of whiskey," said Pratt. "And in case there's any doubt left at all, we found your mask, as well. Still splattered with blood. Played it close to the edge with us, didn't you? Describing the same mask that you yourself wore?"

The mask of the West End Reaper, planted in my room?

"I'd say it's the gallows for you," said Pratt.

The other Watchman gave a chuckle, as though he looked forward to a good hanging, just the sort of entertainment to enliven the dreary winter months. "And then your good doctor friends can have a go at you," he added. Even in the gloom of the carriage, Norris could see the man run his finger down his chest, a gesture that needed no interpretation. Other dead bodies traveled secret and circuitous routes to the anatomist's table. They were dug from graves under cover of night, by resurrectionists who risked arrest with every nocturnal foray into the cemetery. But the bodies of executed criminals went directly to the autopsy table with the full approval of the law. For their crimes, the condemned paid not only with their lives, but with their mortal remains as well. Every prisoner who stood on the gallows knew that execution was not the final indignity; the anatomist's knife would follow.

Norris thought of old Paddy, the cadaver whose chest he had split open, whose dripping heart he had held in his hands. Who would hold Norris's heart? Whose apron would be spattered with his blood as his organs splashed into the bucket?

Through the carriage window, he saw moonlit fields, the same farms along the Belmont road that he always passed on his journeys into Boston. This would be the last time he saw them, his last view of the countryside he'd spent his boyhood trying to escape. He'd been a fool to believe that he ever could, and this was his punishment.

The road took them east from Belmont, and the farms became villages as they rolled ever closer to Boston. Now he could see the Charles River, glittering beneath moonlight, and he remembered the night he had walked along the embankment and stared across those waters, toward the prison. That night he had counted himself lucky compared with the miserable souls behind bars. Now he came to join them, and his only escape would be the hangman.

The carriage wheels clattered onto the West Boston Bridge, and Norris knew that their journey was almost finished. Once over the bridge, it would be a short ride up Cambridge Street, then north toward the city jail. The West End Reaper, captured at last. Pratt's associate wore a smile of triumph, his teeth gleaming white in the darkness.

"Whoa! Whoa, there," their driver said, and the carriage came to a sudden stop.

"What's this now?" said Pratt, glancing out the window. They were still on the bridge. He called up to the driver, "Why have we stopped?"

"Got an obstruction here, Mr. Pratt."

Pratt threw open the door and climbed out. "Blast it all! Can't they get that horse out of the way?"

"They're trying, sir. But that nag's not getting up again."

"Then they should drag it off to the knacker. The beast is blocking the way for everyone."

Through the carriage window, Norris could see the bridge railing. Below flowed the Charles River. He thought of cold black water. There are worse graves, he thought.

"If this takes much longer, we should go 'round to the Canal Bridge."

"Look, there's the wagon now. They'll have the nag off in a minute."

Now. I will have no other chance.

Pratt was opening the carriage door to climb back in. As it swung open, Norris threw himself against it and tumbled out.

Knocked backward by the door, Pratt sprawled to the ground. He had no time to react; nor did his compatriot, who was now scrambling out of the carriage.

Norris caught a glimpse of his surroundings: the dead horse, lying where it had collapsed in front of its overloaded wagon. The line of carriages, backed up behind it on the bridge. And the Charles River, its moonlit surface hiding the turbid water beneath. He did not hesitate. This is all that's left to me, he thought, as he scrambled over the railing. Either I seize this chance or I give up any hope of life. *Here's to you, Rose!*

"Catch him! Don't let him jump!"

Norris was already falling. Through darkness, through time, toward a future as unknown to him as the waters toward which he plummeted. He knew only that the real struggle was about to begin, and in the instant before he hit the water, he braced himself like a warrior for battle.

The plunge into the cold river was a cruel slap of welcome to a new life. He sank over his head, into a blackness so thick he could not tell up from down, and he thrashed, disoriented. Then he caught the glimmer of moonlight above and struggled toward it, until his head broke the surface. As he took in a gasp of air, he heard voices shouting above.

"Where is he? Do you see him?"

"Call out the Watch! I want the riverbank searched!"

"Both sides?"

"Yes, you idiot! Both sides!"

Norris dove back into icy darkness and let the current carry him. He knew he could not fight his way upstream, so he yielded to the river and let it abet his escape. It bore him past Lechmere Point, past the West End, bringing him ever eastward, toward the harbor.

Toward the docks.

Twenty-nine

The present

JULIA STOOD at the ocean's edge and stared out to sea. The fog had finally dissipated, and she could see islands offshore and a lobster boat, cutting across water so calm it might be tarnished silver. She did not hear Tom's footsteps behind her, yet somehow she knew he was there, and could sense his approach long before he spoke.

"I'm all packed," he said. "I'll be catching the four thirty ferry. I'm sorry to have to leave you with him, but he seems to be stable. At least he hasn't had any arrhythmias in the past three days."

"We'll be fine, Tom," she said, her gaze still on the lobster boat.

"It's a lot to ask of you."

"I don't mind, really. I'd planned to spend the whole week anyway, and it's so beautiful here. Now that I can finally see the water."

"It is a nice spot, isn't it?" He came to stand beside her. "Too bad it's all going to slide into the sea one of these days. That house is on borrowed time."

"Can't you save it?"

"You can't fight the ocean. Some things are inevitable."

They were silent for a moment, watching as the boat growled to a stop and the lobsterman pulled up his traps.

"You've been awfully quiet all afternoon," he said.

"I can't stop thinking about Rose Connolly."

"What about her?"

"How strong she must've been, just to survive."

"When people need to, they usually find the strength."

"I never did. Even when I needed it most."

They walked along the ocean's edge, keeping away from the crumbling cliff.

"You're talking about your divorce?"

"When Richard asked me for it, I just assumed it was my fault that I couldn't keep him happy. That's what happens when day after day you're made to feel your job's not as important as his. That you're not as brilliant as his colleagues' wives."

"How many years did you put up with that?"

"Seven."

"Why didn't you leave?"

"Because I started to believe it." She shook her head. "Rose wouldn't have put up with it."

"That's a good mantra for you from now on. *What would Rose do?*"

"I've come to the conclusion that I'm no Rose Connolly."

They watched as the lobsterman tossed his trap back in the water.

"I have to leave for Hong Kong on Thursday," said Tom. "I'll be there for a month."

"Oh." She fell silent. So it would be a whole month before she saw him again.

"I love my work, but it means I'm not home half the time. Instead, I'm chasing epidemics, tending to other lives while forgetting I have one of my own."

"But you have so much to contribute."

"I'm forty-two and my housemate spends half the year at the dogsitter's." He stared at the water. "Anyway, I'm thinking of canceling this trip."

She felt her pulse suddenly quicken. "Why?"

"Partly because of Henry. He's eighty-nine, after all, and he won't be around forever."

Of course, she thought. It's all about Henry. "If he has problems, he can call me."

"That's a lot of responsibility. I wouldn't wish him on anyone."

"I've grown rather attached to him. He's a friend now, and I don't abandon my friends." She looked up as a seagull soared past. "It's strange how something like a bunch of old bones can bring two people together. People who have absolutely nothing in common."

"Well, he certainly likes you. He told me that if he was *just ten years younger* . . ."

She laughed. "When he first met me, I think he could barely tolerate me."

"Henry can barely tolerate anyone, but he ended up liking you."

"It's because of Rose. She's the one thing we have in common. We're both obsessed with her." She watched as the lobster boat motored away, leaving a white line etched on the bay's metallic gray surface. "I'm even having dreams about her."

"What sort of dreams?"

"It's as if I'm there, seeing what she saw. The carriages, the streets, the dresses. It's because I've spent way too much time reading all those letters. She's seeping into my subconscious. I can almost believe I was there, it's all starting to seem so . . . familiar."

"The way you seem familiar to me."

"I don't know why I should."

"Yet I keep having this feeling that I know you. That we've met."

"I can't think of any reason we would have."

"No." He sighed. "I can't, either." He looked at her. "So I guess there's no reason for me to cancel my trip. Is there?"

There was more to that question than either one of them was acknowledging. She met his gaze, and what she saw in his eyes scared her, because at that instant she saw both possibility and heartbreak. She was ready for neither.

Julia looked at the sea. "Henry and I will do fine."

That night, Julia once again dreamed of Rose Connolly. Except this time, Rose was not the girl with the patched clothes and the ash-smudged face, but a sedate young woman with upswept hair and wisdom in her eyes. She stood amid wildflowers as she gazed down a slope, toward a stream. It was the same gentle slope that would one day become Julia's garden, and on this summer day, tall grass rippled like water in the wind, and dandelion fluff swirled in the golden haze. Rose turned, and there was a grassy field, and a few tumbled-down stones marking the spot where another house had once stood, a house that was now gone, burned to the ground.

From over the crest a young girl came running, her skirts flying behind her, her smiling face flushed from the heat. She flew toward Rose, who swept her up in her arms and swung her around and around, laughing.

"Again! Again!" the girl cried as she was set back on her feet.

"No, your auntie's dizzy."

"Can we roll down the hill?"

"Look, Meggie." Rose gestured toward the stream. "Isn't this a lovely spot? What do you think?"

"There are fish in the water, and frogs."

"It's a perfect place, isn't it? Someday, you should build your house here. Right here on this spot."

"What about that old house up there?"

Rose gazed up at the charred stone foundation near the top of the crest. "It belonged to a great man," she said softly. "It burned down when you were just two years old. Maybe someday, when you're older, I'll tell you about him. About what he did for us." Rose inhaled deeply and gazed toward the stream. "Yes, this is a fine place to build a house. You must remember this spot." She reached for the girl's hand. "Come. Cook's expecting us back for lunch."

They walked, the aunt and her niece, their skirts rustling through tall grass as they strode together up the slope, until they went over the crest, and only Rose's auburn hair could be seen glinting above the swaying grass.

Julia woke up with tears in her eyes. *That was my garden. Rose and Meggie walked in my garden.*

She climbed out of bed and went to the window, where she saw the pink light of dawn. At last all the clouds were gone and today, for the first time, she saw sunshine over Penobscot Bay. I'm so glad I stayed long enough to see this sunrise, she thought.

She tried to be quiet and not wake Henry as she tiptoed down the stairs and into the kitchen to make coffee. She was about to turn on the faucet to fill the carafe when she heard the distinct sound of rustling paper in another room. She set down the carafe and peeked into the library.

Henry was slumped in a chair at the dining table, his head drooping, a blizzard of paper spread out before him.

Alarmed, she ran toward him, fearing the worst. But when she grasped his shoulder he straightened and looked at her. "I found it," he said.

Her gaze fell to the handwritten pages that lay on the table in front of him, and she saw the three familiar initials: O.W.H. "Another letter!"

"I think it may be the last one, Julia."

"But this is wonderful!" she said. Then she noticed how pale he was, and that his hands were shaking. "What's wrong?"

He handed her the letter. "Read it."

Thirty

1830

THE GRUESOME OBJECT had been steeping for two days in whiskey, and at first, Rose did not recognize what the jar contained. All she saw was a flap of raw meat submerged in a tea-colored brew. Mr. Pratt turned the jar and held it up to Rose's face, forcing her to take a closer look.

"Do you know who this is?" he asked.

She gazed into the jar, where the object preserved in that unsavory bath of liquor and old blood suddenly bobbed up against the glass, which magnified every feature. Rose recoiled in horror.

"It's a face you should recognize, Miss Connolly," said Pratt. "It was stripped from a body found two nights ago in a West End alley. A body carved with the sign of the cross. The body of your brother-in-law, Mr. Eben Tate." He set the jar down on Dr. Grenville's table.

Rose turned to Grenville, who looked equally shocked by the evidence in his parlor. "That jar was never in Norris's room!" she said. "He wouldn't have asked me to come here if he didn't believe in you, Dr. Grenville. Now you have to believe in *him*."

Pratt reacted with an unperturbed smile. "I think it's quite clear, Doctor, that your student Mr. Marshall deceived you. He *is* the West End Reaper. It's only a matter of time before he's apprehended."

"If he's not already drowned," said Grenville.

"Oh, we know he's still alive. This morning, we found footprints in the mud, coming out of the water near the docks. We will find him, and justice will be served. This jar is all the proof we need."

"All you have is a specimen pickled in whiskey."

"And a bloodstained mask. A white mask, just as certain witnesses"—he looked at Rose—"have described."

Rose said, "He's innocent! I'll testify—"

"Testify to what, Miss Connolly?" Pratt gave a dismissive snort.

"You planted that jar in his room."

Pratt advanced on her with a look of such fury that she flinched. "You little whore."

"Mr. Pratt!" said Grenville.

But Pratt's gaze remained on Rose. "You think your testimony will be worth anything? I know full well that you've been living with Norris Marshall. That he even took his strumpet home for Christmas to meet his dear old dad. Not only do you lie underneath him, now you're lying *for* him. Did he kill Eben Tate as a favor to you? Did he take care of your troublesome brother-in-law?" He placed the jar back in its cloth-lined evidence box. "Oh, yes, a jury will certainly believe *your* testimony!"

Rose said to Grenville: "The jar was not in his room. I swear to it."

"Who authorized the search of Mr. Marshall's room?" asked Grenville. "How did the Night Watch even think to look there?"

For the first time, Pratt appeared uneasy. "I only did my duty. When a report comes in—"

"What report?"

"A letter, advising the Night Watch that we might find certain items of interest in his room."

"A letter from whom?"

"I am not at liberty to say."

Grenville gave a comprehending laugh. "Anonymous!"

"We found the evidence, didn't we?"

"You would stake a man's life on that jar? On that mask?"

"And you, sir, should think twice before you stake your fine reputation on a killer. It should be obvious by now that you've sorely misjudged the young man, and so has everyone else." He lifted the evidence box and added, with a note of satisfaction, "Everyone but me." He gave a curt nod. "Good night, Doctor. I'll see myself out."

They listened to Pratt's footsteps as he walked down the hall, and then the front door closed behind him. A moment later, Dr. Grenville's sister, Eliza, swept into the parlor.

"Has that awful man finally left?" she asked.

"I'm afraid it looks quite grim for Norris." Grenville sighed and sank into a chair by the fire.

"Is there nothing you can do to help him?" asked Eliza.

"This has gone beyond even my influence."

"He counts on you, Dr. Grenville!" said Rose. "If both you and Mr. Holmes defend him, they'll be forced to listen."

"Wendell will testify in his defense?" asked Eliza.

"He's been in Norris's room. He knows that jar wasn't there. Or the mask, either." She looked at Grenville. "It's all my fault. It's all to do with me, with Meggie. The people who want her, they'd do anything."

"Including send an innocent man to the gallows?" said Eliza.

"That's the least of it." Rose approached Grenville, her hands outstretched in a plea for him to believe her. "The night Meggie was born, there were two nurses and a doctor in the room. Now they're all dead, because they knew my sister's secret. They learned the name of Meggie's father."

"A name you've never heard," said Grenville.

"I wasn't in the room. The baby was crying, so I carried her out. Later, Agnes Poole demanded I give her up, but I refused." Rose swallowed and said softly. "And I've been hunted ever since."

"So it's the child they want?" said Eliza. She looked at her brother. "She needs protection."

Grenville nodded. "Where is she, Miss Connolly?"

"Hidden, sir. In a safe place."

"They could find her," he said.

"I'm the only one who knows where she is." She looked him in the eye and said, evenly: "And no one can make me tell."

He met her gaze, taking her measure. "I don't doubt you for an instant. You've kept her safe from harm this long. You, better than anyone, know what's best." Abruptly he stood. "I must go out."

"Where are you going?" Eliza asked.

"There are people I need to consult in this matter."

"Will you be home for supper?"

"I don't know." He walked into the hallway and pulled on his greatcoat.

Rose followed him. "Dr. Grenville, what shall I do? How can I help?"

"Remain here." He looked at his sister. "Eliza, see to the girl's needs. While she's under our roof, she must not come to harm." He walked out, and an icy gust of wind blew in, stinging Rose's eyes. She blinked away sudden tears.

"You don't have anywhere to go, do you?"

Rose turned to Eliza. "No, ma'am."

"Mrs. Furbush can make a bed for you, in the kitchen." Eliza's gaze swept Rose's patched dress. "And a change of clothes, certainly."

"Thank you." Rose cleared her throat. "Thank you for everything."

"My brother's the one you need to thank," said Eliza. "I only hope this business does not ruin him."

It was the grandest house Rose had ever set foot in, certainly the grandest house she'd ever slept in. The kitchen was warm, the coals in the fireplace still aglow and throwing off heat. Her blanket was of heavy wool, not like the threadbare cloak with which she'd wrapped herself on so many cold nights, a sorry old rag that smelled of every lodging house, every filthy straw bed she'd ever slept in. The briskly efficient housekeeper, Mrs. Furbush, had insisted on tossing that cloak, along with the rest of Rose's worn clothing, into the fire. As for the girl herself, Mrs. Furbush had called for soap and a great deal of hot water, because Dr. Grenville insisted that a clean household was a healthy household. Now bathed and wearing a fresh gown, Rose lay in unaccustomed comfort in a cot near the fireplace. She knew that Meggie, too, was warm and safe tonight.

But what of Norris? Where did he sleep tonight? Was he cold and hungry? Why had she heard no news?

Though the supper hour had come and gone, Dr. Grenville had not returned. Rose had waited all evening with her ear cocked, but had heard neither his voice nor his footstep. "It's the nature of his profession, girl," Mrs. Furbush had said. "A doctor can't be expected to work regular hours. Patients are always bringing him out into the night, and there are times he doesn't come home till dawn."

Long after the rest of the household had retired, Dr. Grenville still had not returned. And Rose lay awake. The coals in the hearth had lost their glow and were fading to ash. Through the kitchen window, she could see a tree, silhouetted by moonlight, and could hear the branches sway in the wind.

And now she heard something else: footsteps creaking on the servants' stairway.

She lay still, listening as the creaks drew closer, as the footsteps moved into the kitchen. One of the maids, perhaps, here to restoke the fire. She could just make out the shadowy figure, slipping through the darkness. Then she heard a chair tip over, and a voice muttered: "*Blast* it all!"

A man.

Rose rolled out of bed and scrambled to the hearth, where she fumbled in the darkness to light a candle. As the flame flared to life, she saw the intruder was a young man in a nightshirt, his fair hair in a tangled swirl from sleep. He froze at the sight of her, clearly as startled to see her as she was to see him.

It's the young master, she thought. Dr. Grenville's nephew, whom she'd been told was recuperating upstairs in his bedroom. A bandage encased the stump of his left wrist, and he swayed, unsteady on his feet. She set down the candle and ran forward to catch him as he sagged sideways.

"I'm all right, I'm fine," he insisted.

"You should not be up, Mr. Lackaway." She righted the chair that he had just overturned in the darkness and gently lowered him into it. "I'll fetch your mother."

"No, don't. Please!"

That desperate entreaty made her stop.

"She'll only fuss at me," he said. "I'm tired of being fussed at. I'm tired of being trapped in my room, just because she's terrified I'll catch a fever." He looked up at her with pleading eyes. "Don't wake her. Just let me sit here for a while. Then I'll go back up to bed, I promise."

She sighed. "As you please. But you shouldn't be up all alone."

"I'm not alone." He managed a weak smile. "You're here."

She felt his gaze follow her as she crossed to the hearth to stir the coals back to life and add more wood. Flames leaped up, throwing their welcome warmth into the room.

"You're that girl all the maids are talking about," he said.

She turned to look at him. The rekindled fire cast new light on his face, and she saw finely etched features, a refined brow and lips that were almost girlish. Illness had sapped its color, but it was a handsome, sensitive face, more boy than man.

"You're Norris's friend," he said.

She nodded. "My name's Rose."

"Well, Rose. I'm his friend, too. And from what I hear, he needs every friend he can get."

The gravity of what Norris faced suddenly weighed so heavily on her shoulders that Rose sank into a chair at the table. "I'm so afraid for him," she whispered.

"My uncle knows people. People of influence."

"Even your uncle has his doubts now."

"But you don't?"

"Not a one."

"How can you be so sure of him?"

She looked Charles straight in the eye. "I know his heart."

"Truly?"

"You think I'm a moonstruck girl."

"It's just that one reads so many poems about devotion. But seldom do we actually encounter it."

"I wouldn't waste my devotion on a man I didn't believe in."

"Well, Rose, if ever I face the gallows, I'll count myself lucky to have a friend like you."

She shuddered at his mention of the gallows and turned to stare at the hearth, where flames were rapidly consuming the log.

"I'm sorry, I shouldn't have said that. They've given me so much morphine, I don't know what I'm saying anymore." He looked down at his bandaged stump. "I'm no good for anything these days. Can't even get around on my own two feet."

"It's late, Mr. Lackaway. You shouldn't be out of bed at all."

"I only came down for a nip of brandy." He gave her a hopeful look. "Would you fetch it for me? It's in that cupboard over there." He pointed across the kitchen, and she suspected that this was not the first time he'd made a nocturnal raid on the brandy bottle.

She poured him only a knuckle's worth, which he drank down in one gulp. Though he clearly expected more, she put the bottle back in the cupboard and said firmly: "I'll help you back to your room."

With her candle to light their way, she guided him up the steps to the second floor. She had not been upstairs before, and as she helped him down the hallway, her gaze was drawn to all the marvels revealed by candlelight. She saw richly patterned carpet and a gleaming hall table. On the wall was a gallery of portraits, distinguished men and women rendered with such life-like detail that she felt their eyes following her as she guided Charles to his room. By the time she helped him to his bed, he was starting to stumble, as though that small bit of brandy, on top of all the morphine, had tipped him into full intoxication. He flopped onto his mattress with a sigh.

"Thank you, Rose."

"Good night, sir."

"He's a lucky man, Norris is. To have a girl who loves him as much as you do. The sort of love that poets write about."

"I don't know anything about poetry, Mr. Lackaway."

"You don't have to." He closed his eyes and sighed. "You know the real thing."

She watched as his breaths deepened, as he sank into sleep. *Yes, I know the real thing. And now I could lose it.*

Carrying the candle, she left his room and stepped back into the hallway. There she suddenly halted, her gaze frozen on a face that stared back at her. In the gloom, with only the glow of the flame to illuminate the hall, the portrait seemed so startlingly real that she stood rooted before it, stunned by the unexpected familiarity of those features. She saw a man with a thick mane of hair and dark eyes that reflected a lively intelligence. He seemed eager to engage her in debate from his perch on the canvas. She stepped closer so that she might examine every shadow, every curve of that face. So entranced was she by the image, she did not hear the approaching footsteps until they were only a few feet away. The nearby creak made her whirl, so startled that she almost dropped the candle.

"Miss Connolly?" said Dr. Grenville, frowning at her. "May I ask why you are wandering about the house at this hour?"

She heard the note of suspicion in his voice and flushed. He assumes the worst, she thought; about the Irish, they always assume the worst. "It was Mr. Lackaway, sir."

"What about my nephew?"

"He came down to the kitchen. I didn't think he was steady on his feet, so I helped him back to his bed." She gestured toward Charles's door, which she had left open.

Dr. Grenville peered into the room at his nephew, who was sprawled uncovered on the bed and snoring loudly.

"I'm sorry, sir," she said. "I wouldn't have come upstairs if he didn't—"

"No, I'm the one who should apologize." He sighed. "It's been a most trying day, and I'm weary. Good night." He turned.

"Sir?" she said. "Is there news of Norris?"

He stopped. Reluctantly he turned to look at her. "I'm afraid to say there's little cause for optimism. The evidence is damning."

"The evidence is false."

"The court must determine that. But in court, innocence is determined by strangers who'll know nothing about him. What they know is what they've read in the newspaper or heard in the tavern. That Norris Marshall lives in proximity to all four murders. That he was found bending over the body of Mary Robinson. That the excised face of Eben Tate was discovered in his quarters. That he is a skillful anatomist as well as a butcher. Taken separately, these points might be defended against. But when presented in a court of law, his guilt will seem undeniable."

She stared at him in despair. "Is there no defense we can offer?"

"I'm afraid men have gone to the gallows for less."

In desperation she recklessly grasped his sleeve. "I cannot see him hanged!"

"Miss Connolly, not all hope is lost. There may be a way to save him." He took her hand and held it as he looked straight into her eyes. "But I will need your help."

Thirty-one

"BILLY. Over here, Billy!"

The boy looked around in confusion, searching the shadows for whoever had just whispered his name. A black dog capered at his feet. Suddenly it gave an excited bark and came trotting toward Norris, who was crouched behind a stack of barrels. The mutt, at least, thought no ill of him, and was wagging its tail, delighted to play a friendly game of hide-and-seek with a man it did not even know.

Dim Billy was more cautious. "Who is it, Spot?" he asked, as if fully expecting the dog to answer him.

Norris stepped out from behind the barrels. "It's me, Billy," he said, and saw the boy begin to back away. "I won't hurt you. You re-member me, don't you?"

The boy looked at his dog, who was now licking Norris's hand, clearly unconcerned. "You're Miss Rose's friend," he said.

"I need you to take her a message."

"The Night Watch says you're the Reaper."

"I'm not. I swear I'm not."

"They're searching for you, all up and down the river."

"Billy, if you're her friend, you'll do this for me."

The boy looked at his dog again. Spot had sat down at Norris's feet and was wagging its tail as it watched the conversation. While the boy might be a dimwit, he knew enough to trust a dog when it came to judging a man's intentions.

"I want you to go to Dr. Grenville's house," said Norris.

"The big one, on Beacon?"

"Yes. Find out if she's there. And give her this." Norris handed him a folded scrap of paper. "Put it into her hands. *Only* her hands."

"What's it say?"

"Just give it to her."

"Is it a love note?"

"Yes," Norris answered too quickly, impatient for the boy to be off.

"But I'm the one who loves her," Billy whined. "And I'm goin' to marry her." He threw the note down. "I ain't bringing her your love note."

Swallowing his frustration, Norris picked up the scrap of paper. "I want to tell her she's free to go on with her life." He placed the note back in Billy's hand. "Take it to her, so she knows. Please." He added. "She'll be angry with you if you don't."

That did it; Billy's biggest fear was of displeasing Rose. The boy stuffed the note into his pocket. "I'd do anything for her," he said.

"Don't tell anyone you saw me."

"I'm not a half-wit, y'know," Billy retorted. He walked off into the night, the dog trotting at his heels.

Norris did not linger, but quickly moved on, striding down the dark street in the direction of Beacon Hill. As well meaning as Billy might be, Norris did not trust him to keep a secret, and he had no intention of waiting for the Night Watch to come looking.

Assuming they believed he was still alive and still in Boston these three days later.

The clothes he'd stolen were ill fitting, the trousers too large, the shirt too tight, but the heavy cloak concealed all, and with a Quaker hat shoved down low over his brow, he walked purposefully down the street, neither skulking nor hesitating. I may not be a murderer, he thought. But now I'm most certainly a thief. Already he faced the gallows; the commission of a few more crimes scarcely mattered. Survival was all he cared about, and if it meant lifting a cloak from a tavern hook or snatching trousers and shirt from a drying line, then that's what a freezing man had to do. If he was going to be hanged anyway, he might as well be guilty of a real crime.

He turned a corner, into narrow Acorn Street. It was the same alley where Gareth Wilson and Dr. Sewall had met, in the home with the pelicans carved on the lintel. Norris chose a dark doorway in which to wait and huddled on the stoop, hidden in shadow. By now, Billy would have reached Grenville's home; by now, the note should be in Rose's hand, a note on which he'd written only one line:

Tonight, under the pelicans.

If it fell into the hands of the Night Watch, they'd have no idea what it meant. But Rose would know. Rose would come.

He settled down to wait.

The night deepened. One by one, lamps inside houses were extinguished and the windows on tiny Acorn Street fell dark. Occasionally, he heard the clip-clop of a horse and carriage passing by on much busier Cedar Street, but soon even that traffic faded to silence.

He hugged the cloak more tightly and watched his breath cloud in the darkness. He'd wait here all night, if he had to. If by dawn she had not come, then he'd return tomorrow night. He had enough faith in her to believe that once she knew he waited for her, nothing would keep her away.

His legs grew stiff, his fingers numb. The last of the windows on Acorn Street fell dark.

Then, emerging from around the corner, a figure appeared. A woman, framed from behind by lamplight. She paused in the middle of the alley, as though struggling to see into the darkness.

"Norrie?" she called softly.

At once he stepped from the doorway. "Rose," he said, and she ran toward him. He swept her into his embrace and felt like laughing as he swung her around, so happy to finally see her again. She felt weightless in his arms, lighter than air, and in that moment he knew they were forever bound to each other. The plunge into the Charles River had been both a death and a rebirth, and this was his new life, with this girl who had no fortune to offer him, no family name, nothing except love.

"I knew you'd come," he murmured. "I knew."

"You must listen to me."

"I can't stay in Boston. But I can't live without you."

"This is important, Norris. Listen!"

He fell still. It was not her command that caused him to freeze; it was the silhouette of a burly figure moving toward them, from the other end of Acorn Street.

The clatter of hooves behind Norris made him swing around, just as a carriage and two horses pulled to a stop, blocking his other escape route. The door swung open.

"Norris, you have to trust them," said Rose. "You have to trust *me*."

From the alley behind him came a familiar voice. "It's the only way, Mr. Marshall."

Startled, Norris turned to the broad-shouldered man who stood facing him. "Dr. Sewall?"

"I suggest you get into that carriage," said Sewall. "If you want to live."

"They're our friends," said Rose. She reached for his hand and tugged him toward the carriage. "Please, let's get in before anyone sees you."

He had no other choice. Whatever awaited him, Rose had willed it so, and he trusted her with his life. She led him to the carriage and tugged him in after her.

Dr. Sewall, who did not climb in, swung their door shut. "God-speed, Mr. Marshall," he said through the window. "I hope we'll meet again someday, under less trying circumstances."

The driver slapped the reins, and the carriage rolled away.

Only as Norris settled back for the ride did he focus on the man sitting in the carriage across from him and Rose. The glow of a street lamp illuminated the man's face, and Norris could only stare in astonishment.

"No, this is not an arrest," said Constable Lyons.

"Then what is it?" asked Norris.

"It is a favor, to an old friend."

They rode out of the city, across the West Boston Bridge, and through the village of Cambridge. It was the same route by which Norris had been transported as a prisoner only a few nights earlier, but this was a far different journey, one he traveled not with a sense of doom, but with hope. The entire way, Rose's small hand stayed entwined with his, a silent reassurance that all was according to plan, that he need not fear betrayal. How could he ever have suspected the worst of her? This lone girl, he thought, has stood by me faithfully and unflinchingly, and I do not deserve her.

The town of Cambridge gave way to dark countryside and empty fields. They drove north, toward Somerville and Medford, past villages of dark houses huddled together beneath the winter moon. It was not until the outskirts of Medford that the carriage finally turned into a cobblestoned yard and slowed to a stop.

"You'll rest here for a day," said Constable Lyons, swinging open the door and stepping out. "Tomorrow, you'll receive directions to the next safe house, in the north."

Norris climbed from the carriage and stared up at a stone farmhouse. Candlelight glowed in the windows, a flickering welcome to furtive travelers. "What is this place?" he asked.

Constable Lyons did not answer. He led the way to the door and knocked twice, paused, then knocked once more.

After a moment the door opened and an elderly woman wearing a lace night bonnet peered out, holding up a lamp to see her visitors' faces.

"We have a traveler," said Lyons.

The woman frowned at Norris and Rose. "These two are most unusual fugitives."

"These are most unusual circumstances. I bring them at the personal request of Dr. Grenville. Both Mr. Garrison and Dr. Sewall have agreed to it, and Mr. Wilson has given his assent as well."

The old woman finally nodded and moved aside to let the three visitors enter.

Norris stepped into an ancient kitchen, the ceiling blackened from the soot of countless cooking fires. Dominating one wall was an enormous stone hearth where the night's embers still glowed. Overhead hung sheaves of herbs, dried bunches of lavender and hyssop, wormwood and sage. Norris felt Rose tug his hand, and she pointed up at the carved emblem, mounted on the crossbeam. A pelican.

Constable Lyons saw what they were staring at, and he said: "That is an ancient symbol, Mr. Marshall, and one we revere. The pelican represents self-sacrifice for the greater good. It reminds us that as we give, so shall we receive."

The old woman added, "It's the seal of our sisterhood. The order of the Roses of Sharon."

Norris turned to look at her. "Who are you? What is this place?"

"We're members of the Rose Cross, Sir. And this is a way station for travelers. Travelers in need of sanctuary."

Norris thought of the modest town house on Acorn Street, with the pelicans carved into the lintel. He remembered that William Lloyd Garrison had been one of the gentlemen in the house that night. And he remembered, too, the whisperings of nearby shop-keepers, of strangers moving about in the neighborhood after dark, a neighborhood that Constable Lyons had decreed off limits to Night Watch patrols.

"They're abolitionists," said Rose. "This is a house of hiding."

"A way station," said Lyons. "One of many stops the Rosicru-cians have established between the south and Canada."

"You shelter slaves?"

"No man is a slave," said the old woman. "No man has the right to own another. We're all free."

"Now you understand, Mr. Marshall," said Constable Lyons, "why this house and the house on Acorn Street must never be spo-ken of. Dr. Grenville assured us that you are a supporter of the abo-litionist movement. If you are ever captured, you must not say a word about these outposts, for you'll endanger untold lives. People who have suffered miseries enough for ten lifetimes."

"I swear to you, I'll reveal nothing," said Norris.

"It's a dangerous business we're in," said Lyons. "Never more than now. We can't afford to have our network revealed, not when so many would root us out and destroy us if they could."

"You are all members of the order? Even Dr. Grenville?"

Lyons nodded. "Again, a secret not to be revealed."

"Why are you helping me? I'm not a fugitive slave. If you believe Mr. Pratt, I'm a monster."

Lyons gave a snort. "And Pratt is a toad. I would have him tossed out of the Night Watch if I could, but he has maneuvered his way into the public eye. Open up a newspaper these days, and all you'll read are the deeds of *heroic* Mr. Pratt, *brilliant* Mr. Pratt. In truth, the man is an imbecile. Your arrest was to be his crowning triumph."

"And this is why you help me? Merely to deny him that triumph?"

"That would hardly be worth the trouble I've gone to. No, we help you because Aldous Grenville is utterly convinced of your in-nocence. And to let you be hanged would be a grave injustice." Lyons looked at the old woman. "I leave him here with you now,

Mistress Goode. Tomorrow, Mr. Wilson will return with provisions for his journey. There was no time tonight to make such arrangements. In any event, it will be dawn soon, and it's best that Mr. Marshall waits till tomorrow nightfall to start his next leg." He turned to Rose. "Come, Miss Connolly. Shall we return to Boston?"

Rose looked stricken. "Can I not stay with him?" she asked, her eyes bright with tears.

"A lone traveler moves more quickly and safely. It's important that Mr. Marshall is unencumbered."

"But we part so suddenly!"

"There is no choice. Once he's safely away, he will send for you."

"I've only just found him again! Can't I stay with him, just tonight? You said Mr. Wilson will come tomorrow. I'll return to Boston with him then."

Norris grasped her hand more tightly and said, to Lyons: "I don't know when I'll see her again. Anything could happen. Please, allow us these last few hours together."

Lyons gave a sigh and nodded. "Mr. Wilson will be here before noon tomorrow. Be ready to leave then."

They lay in darkness, their bed illuminated only by the moonglow through the window, but it was enough light for Rose to see his face. To know that he was looking at her as well.

"You promise you'll send for me and Meggie?" she said.

"As soon as I've reached a safe place, I'll write to you. The letter will come from another name, but you'll know it's from me."

"If only I could go with you now."

"No, I want you to stay safe in Dr. Grenville's house, not suffer on some godforsaken road with me. And what a comfort to know that Meggie's cared for. Truly, you've found the best place possible."

"The one place I knew you'd tell me to hide her."

"My clever Rose! You know me so well."

He cupped her face, and she sighed at the warmth of his hands.

"The best is yet to come for us. You have to believe that, Rose. All these trials, all these miseries, will just make our future so much the sweeter." Gently he pressed his lips to hers, a kiss that should have made her heart soar. Instead it brought a sob to her throat, for she did not know when, if ever, they would meet again. She thought of the journey that lay ahead for him, of secret way stations and wintry roads, all leading toward what? She couldn't picture the future, and that's what frightened her. Always before, as a girl, she'd been able to imagine what was to come: her years working as a seamstress, the young man she would meet, the children she would bear. But now, when she looked ahead, she saw nothing, not a home with Norris, nor children, nor happiness. Why had the future suddenly vanished? Why could she not see beyond this night?

Is this the only time we will ever have?

"You'll wait for me, won't you?" he whispered.

"Always."

"I don't know what I can offer you except a life in hiding. Always looking over our shoulders, always watching for a bounty hunter. It's not what you deserve."

"Nor you."

"But you have a choice, Rose. I'm so afraid that one day you'll wake up and regret this. I'd almost rather we never see each other again."

Moonlight blurred through her tears. "You can't mean that."

"I do mean it, but only because you deserve to be happy. I want you to have a chance at a real life."

"Is that truly what you want?" she whispered. "That we live our lives apart?"

He said nothing.

"You must tell me now, Norrie. Because if you don't, I'll always be waiting for your letter. I'll wait until my hair is white and my grave is dug. And even then, I'll be waiting . . ." Her voice broke.

"Stop. Please stop." He wrapped his arms around her and pulled her against him, "If I were truly unselfish, I'd tell you to forget me.

I'd tell you to find your happiness elsewhere." He gave a sorrowful laugh. "But it seems I'm not so noble after all. I'm selfish and I'm jealous of any man who'll ever have you or love you. I want to be that man."

"Then be him." She reached up and clutched at his shirt. "Be him."

She could not see into the future; she could see only as far as these next few hours, and tonight might be all the future they'd ever have. With every heartbeat she could feel their time together slipping away, receding beyond the reach of anything but memory and tears.

And so she took what time they had left together and wasted none of it. With feverish hands she pulled at the hooks and laces of her gown, her breaths quick and frantic with the need for haste. So little time; dawn would be upon them. Never before had she made love to a man, but somehow she knew what to do. She knew what would please him, what would bind him to her for always.

Moonlight shone down, rich as cream, on her breasts, on his bare shoulders, on all the secret places, the sacred places, they had never shown each other. This is what a wife gives her husband, she thought, and though the shock of his entry stole her breath, she rejoiced in it because pain was how a woman marked the triumphs in her life, in lost virginity, in the birth of every child. *You are my husband now.*

Even before the night lifted, she heard the crowing of a rooster. Stirring awake, she thought: Insane old bird, fooled by the moon, announcing false dawn to a world still asleep. But it was no false dawn that soon glimmered in the window, and she opened her eyes to see that darkness had lifted to a cold and sullen gray. In despair, she watched the day brighten, the sky deepen to blue, and though she would hold back the morning if she could, already she felt Norris's breathing change, felt him surface from whatever dreams had kept him so soundly entwined around her.

He opened his eyes and smiled. "It's not the end of the world," he said, seeing her mournful face. "We'll live through this, too."

She blinked away tears. "And we'll be happy."

"Yes." He touched her face. "So very happy. You just have to believe."

"I don't believe in anything else. Only you."

Outside, a dog was barking. Norris rose and went to look out the window. She watched him standing there, his bare back framed in the morning light, and hungrily committed every curve, every muscle to memory. This will be all I have to comfort me until I hear from him again, she thought. The memory of this moment.

"Mr. Wilson is here to fetch you," said Norris.

"So soon?"

"We should go down to meet him." He came back to the bed. "I don't know when I'll have another chance to say this. So let me say it now." He knelt down on the floor beside her and took her hand in his. "I love you, Rose Connolly, and I want to spend my life with you. I want to marry you. If you'll have me."

She stared at him through tears. "I will, Norrie. Oh, I will."

He pressed her palm to his and smiled at Aurnia's trinket of a ring, which never left her finger. "And I promise that the next ring you wear," he said, "won't be a sad bit of tin and glass."

"I don't care about a ring. I only want you."

Laughing, he pulled her into his arms. "You'll be an easy wife to support!"

A loud knock made them both stiffen. The old woman's voice called through the door: "Mr. Wilson has arrived. He needs to return at once, to Boston, so the young lady had best come downstairs." The old woman's footsteps thumped back down the stairs.

Norris looked at Rose. "I promise you, this is the last time we'll ever part," he said. "But now, love, it's time."

Thirty-two

OLIVER WENDELL HOLMES sat in Edward Kingston's parlor, listening to Kitty Welliver on his left and to her sister, Gwendolyn, on his right, and decided that being imprisoned in Hell would be far more tolerable. Had he known that the Welliver sisters were visiting Edward today, he would have stayed away—at least ten days' ride away. But once one has set foot in the house of one's host, it is the height of rudeness to immediately flee from it, screaming. At any rate, by the time he considered that option, it was too late, for Kitty and Gwen had leaped up from the chairs where they had been so prettily perched, and each had snagged an arm by which they pulled Wendell into the parlor, like hungry spiders hauling in their next meal. Now I'm truly done for, he thought, as he balanced a cup of tea on his lap, his third this visit. He was trapped here for the rest of the afternoon, and it was a matter of waiting to see whose bladder reached its bursting point first, forcing its owner to end the visit.

The young ladies, alas, appeared to have bladders of iron, and they cheerfully sipped cup after cup of tea as they gossiped with Edward and his mother. Not wishing to encourage them, Wendell remained mostly silent, which bothered the girls hardly at all, since they scarcely paused long enough for him to get in a word anyway. If one sister did pause, say, to draw breath, the other cut right in with some fresh gossip or catty observation, a truly marathon stream of words limited only by the need to inhale.

"She said it was a truly horrid crossing and she almost died of it. But then I spoke to Mr. Carter, and he said it was nothing, just a small Atlantic storm. So you see, she's exaggerating again—"

"—as usual. She *always* exaggerates. Like the time she *insisted* that Mr. Mason was a world-famous architect. Then we found out he'd built one little opera house in Virginia, quite an unimpressive work, I'm told, and certainly not on the level of Mr. Bulfinch . . ."

Wendell suppressed a yawn and stared out the window as the sisters rambled on about people he could not have cared less about. *There's a poem in this somewhere*, he thought. *A poem about useless girls in pretty dresses. Dresses sewn by other girls. Invisible girls.*

". . . and he assured me that bounty hunters will catch up with him eventually," said Kitty. "Oh, I *knew* there was something unsavory about him. I could *sense* the evil."

"So could I!" said Gwen with a shudder. "That morning in church, sitting beside him—why, it gave me the chills."

Wendell's attention snapped back to the sisters. "Are you talking about Mr. Marshall?"

"Of course we are. It's all anyone's been talking about. But you've been in Cambridge the last few days, Mr. Holmes, so you've missed all the gossip."

"I heard quite enough of it in Cambridge, thank you."

"Is it not shocking?" said Kitty. "To think we dined and danced with a murderer? And *such* a murderer? To slice off someone's face! Cut out someone's tongue!"

I know two women's tongues I'd like to cut out.

"I've heard," said Gwen, her eyes bright with excitement, "that he has an accomplice. An Irish girl." She lowered her voice to say the scandalous word: "An *adventuress*."

"You have heard nonsense!" snapped Wendell.

Gwen stared at him, shocked by his blunt rebuttal.

"You silly girls have no idea what you're talking about. Either of you."

"Oh, dear," Edward's mother quickly interjected, "I do believe the teapot's empty. I think I should call for more." She picked up a bell and vigorously rang it.

"But we do know what we're talking about, Mr. Holmes," Kitty said. Her pride was now at stake, and that superseded any pretense at courtesy. "We have sources close to the Night Watch. *Intimately* associated with it."

"Someone's gossipy wife, I assume."

"Why, that is a most ungentlemanly phrase."

Mrs. Kingston again rang the servant's bell, this time desperately. "Where *is* that girl? We need fresh tea!"

"Wendell," said Edward, trying to smooth things over. "There's no need to take offense. It's only idle talk."

"*Only?* They are talking about Norris. You know as well as I do that he's incapable of committing such atrocities."

"Then why has he run away?" said Gwen. "Why did he leap from that bridge? Surely, that's the action of a guilty man."

"Or a frightened one."

"If he's innocent, he should stay and defend himself."

Wendell laughed. "Against the likes of you?"

"Really, Wendell," said Edward. "I think it's best if we just change the subject."

"Where *is* that girl?" said Mrs. Kingston, sweeping to her feet. She crossed to the door and called out: "Nellie, are you deaf? *Nellie!* We will have more tea at once!" She swung the door shut with a bang and thumped back to her chair. "I tell you, it's impossible to find decent help these days."

The Welliver sisters sat in resentful silence, neither one caring to look in Wendell's direction. He had crossed the boundary of gentlemanly behavior, and this was his punishment: to be ignored and unspoken to.

As if it matters to me, he thought, whether I am addressed by idiots. He set down his cup and saucer. "I do thank you for the tea, Mrs. Kingston," he said. "But I fear I must be going." He stood; so did Edward.

"Oh, but a fresh pot is coming!" She glanced toward the door. "If that scatterbrained girl will just do her job."

"You're quite right," Kitty said, purposefully ignoring Wendell's existence. "There is no decent help these days. Why, our mother had a dreadful time this past May, after our chambermaid left. She was only three months with us when she ran off and got married, with no advance notice. Simply abandoned us, leaving us high and dry."

"How irresponsible."

Wendell said, "Good afternoon, Mrs. Kingston. Miss Welliver, Miss Welliver."

His hostess nodded a farewell, but the two girls did not acknowledge him. They continued to chatter on as he and Edward started toward the door.

"And you know how difficult it is to find decent help these days in Providence. Aurnia was hardly a jewel, but at least she knew how to keep our wardrobe in order."

Wendell was just about to step out of the parlor when he suddenly stopped. Turning, he stared at Gwen, who prattled on.

"It took us a whole month to find someone suitable to replace her. By then it was already June, and time to pack up for our summer house in Weston."

"Her name was Aurnia?" said Wendell.

Gwen looked around, as though wondering who could possibly have spoken to her.

"Your chambermaid," he said. "Tell me about her."

Gwen coolly met his gaze. "Why on earth would this interest you, Mr. Holmes?"

"Was she young? Pretty?"

"She was about our age, wouldn't you say, Kitty? As for pretty—well, that depends on one's standards."

"And her hair—what color was it?"

"Why on earth . . ."

"*What color?*"

Gwen shrugged. "Red. Quite striking, really, though these flame-haired girls are all *so* prone to freckles."

"Do you know where she went? Where she is now?"

"Why should we? The silly girl didn't say a word to us."

Kitty said, "I think Mother might know. Only she won't tell us, because it's not the sort of thing one talks about in polite company."

Gwen looked accusingly at her sister. "Why didn't you share this with me before? I tell you *everything!*"

Edward said, "Wendell, you seem uncommonly concerned about a mere servant."

Wendell returned to his chair and sat down, facing the clearly flummoxed Welliver sisters. "I want you to tell me everything you can remember about this girl, starting with her full name. Was it Aurnia Connolly?"

Kitty and Gwen looked at each other in astonishment.

"Why, Mr. Holmes," said Kitty. "However did you know?"

"There's a gentleman here to see you," said Mrs. Furbush.

Rose looked up from the nightshirt that she had been mending. At her feet was the basket of garments that she had labored over that day, Mrs. Lackaway's skirt with the sagging hem, Dr. Grenville's trousers with the frayed pocket, and all the shirts and blouses and waistcoats needing buttons reattached and seams reinforced. Since returning to the household that morning, she had focused all her grief on a frenzy of mending and stitching, the one skill with which she could repay their kindness to her. All afternoon, she had sat hunched in this corner of the kitchen, sewing in silence, her misery so plainly written on her face that the other servants had respectfully allowed her her privacy. No one had disturbed her, nor even tried to speak to her. Until now.

"The gentleman's at the back door," said Mrs. Furbush.

Rose placed the nightshirt in her basket and stood. As she crossed the kitchen, she could feel the housekeeper watching her curiously, and when she reached the door, she understood why.

Wendell Holmes was standing in the servants' entrance, a strange place for a gentleman to come calling.

"Mr. Holmes," said Rose. "Why do you come the back way?"

"I need to speak to you."

"Do come inside. Dr. Grenville is at home."

"This is a private matter, for your ears only. May we speak outside?"

She glanced over her shoulder and saw the housekeeper watching them. Without a word, she stepped out, pulling the kitchen door shut behind her. She and Wendell moved into the side yard, where bare trees threw skeletal shadows in the cold light of sunset.

"Do you know where Norris is?" he asked. When she hesitated, he said, "This is urgent, Rose. If you know, you *must* tell me."

She shook her head. "I promised."

"Promised whom?"

"I cannot break my word. Even for you."

"Then you *do* know where he is?"

"He's safe, Mr. Holmes. He's in good hands."

He grasped her by the shoulders. "Was it Dr. Grenville? Is *he* the one who arranged the escape?"

She stared into Wendell's frantic eyes. "We can trust him, can't we?"

Wendell gave a groan. "Then it may already be too late for Norris."

"Why are you saying this? You're scaring me."

"Grenville will never let Norris live to stand trial. Too many secrets would come out, damaging secrets that will destroy this household." He glanced up, at the imposing home of Aldous Grenville.

"But Dr. Grenville has always defended Norris."

"And do you wonder why a man of such influence would stake his reputation defending a student with no name, no family connections?"

"Because Norris is innocent! And because—"

"He did it to keep him out of the courtroom. I think he wants Norris tried in the court of public opinion, and on the front page of newspapers. There, he's already been found guilty. All it takes is a bounty hunter to commit the execution. You do know there's a bounty on his head?"

She swallowed back tears. "Yes."

"It will all end quite conveniently. When the West End Reaper is tracked down and killed."

"Why would Dr. Grenville do this? Why would he turn against Norris?"

"There's no time to explain it now. Just tell me where Norris is, so I can warn him."

She stared at him, not knowing what to do. She'd never doubted Wendell Holmes before, but now, it seemed, she must doubt everyone, even those whom she had trusted most.

"At nightfall," she said, "he leaves Medford and travels north, on the Winchester road."

"His destination?"

"The town of Hudson. The mill house, on the river. There's a carved pelican on the gate."

He nodded. "With any luck, I'll catch up with him long before he reaches Hudson." He turned to leave, then halted and looked back at her. "Not a word to Grenville," he warned. "Above all, don't tell *anyone* where the child is. She must remain hidden."

She watched him run out of the side yard, and an instant later heard horse's hooves clatter away. Already, the sun was low in the sky, and within the hour Norris would set out along the Winchester road. What better time than after dark to spring an ambush on a lone traveler?

Hurry, Wendell. Be the one to reach him first.

A gust swept the side yard, twirling dead leaves and dust, and she squinted against the sting. Through narrowed eyelids, she caught a glimpse of something moving across the walkway. The wind died, and she stared at a dog that had wandered in through the Beacon Street gate. The dog sniffed at the bushes, pawed around in the ashes that had been sprinkled across the slippery walkway. Then it lifted a leg, relieved itself against a tree, and headed back toward the gate. As she watched it trot out of the yard, she suddenly realized that she had lived through this moment before. Or a moment very much like it.

But it had been at night. With that image came a gnawing sense of sadness, a remembrance of grief so terrible that she wanted to shove the memory away, back into the dark hole of forgotten pain. But she held on to the memory, stubbornly tugging on that fragile thread, until it led her back to the moment in time when she had stood at a window, holding her newborn niece and looking out into the night. She remembered a horse and phaeton arriving in the hospital courtyard. She remembered Agnes Poole stepping out from the shadows to speak to the phaeton's occupant.

And she remembered one more detail: the jittery horse, its hooves clattering nervously as a dog had trotted past. A large dog, silhouetted against the glossy cobblestones.

That was Billy's dog there that night. Was Billy there as well?

She ran out the gate and was about to set off down Beacon Street when she heard a voice that made her freeze.

"Miss Connolly?"

She turned to see Dr. Grenville standing at his front door.

"Mrs. Furbush said that Mr. Holmes was visiting. Where is he?"

"He—he left, sir."

"Without even speaking to me? That's most peculiar. Charles will be disappointed his friend left without saying a word to him."

"He stayed only a moment."

"Why did he come? And why on earth to the back door?"

She flushed under his gaze. "He only stopped to ask how I am faring, sir. He didn't wish to disturb you so close to mealtime."

Grenville studied her for a moment. She couldn't read his face, and she hoped that he could not read hers.

"When you see Mr. Holmes again," he said, "tell him that his visits are never a disturbance. Day or night."

"Yes, sir," she murmured.

"I believe Mrs. Furbush is looking for you." He went back into the house.

She glanced up Beacon Street. The dog had vanished.

Thirty-three

It was nearly midnight when the household at last fell silent.

Lying in her cot in the kitchen, Rose waited for the voices upstairs to fade, for the creak of footsteps to cease. Only then did she rise from the cot and pull on her cloak. She slipped out the back door and made her way along the side of the house, but just as she was about to emerge into the front yard, she heard a carriage rattle to a stop before the home, and she pulled back into the shadows.

Someone pounded on the front door. "Doctor! We need the doctor!"

A moment later the door opened and Dr. Grenville said, "What is it?"

"A fire, sir, over near Hancock's Wharf! Two buildings are gone, and we don't know how many injuries. Dr. Sewall asks for your assistance. My carriage stands waiting for you, sir, if you'll come now."

"Let me get my bag."

A moment later the front door slammed shut, and the carriage rolled away.

Rose emerged from her hiding place and slipped out the front gate, onto Beacon Street. Ahead, on the horizon, the night sky glowed an alarming red. A wagon careened past her, bound toward the burning wharf, and two young men ran by, anxious to join the spectacle. She did not follow them; instead she made her way up the quiet slope of Beacon Hill, toward the neighborhood known as the West End.

Twenty minutes later, she slipped into a stable yard and eased open the barn door. In the darkness, she heard the soft clucking of chickens and smelled horses and sweet hay.

"Billy?" she called softly.

The boy did not answer. But somewhere above, in the hayloft, a dog whined.

She made her way through the shadows to the narrow staircase and crept up the steps. Billy's spindly silhouette was framed in the window. He stood staring at the red glow to the east.

"Billy?" she whispered.

He turned to her. "Miss Rose, look! There's a fire!"

"I know." She climbed into the loft, and the dog trotted up to lick her hand.

"It's getting bigger. Do you think it could jump all the way here? Should I get a bucket of water?"

"Billy, I need to ask you something."

But he paid no attention to her; his gaze was fixed on the fire's glow. She touched his arm and felt him trembling.

"It's over on the wharves," she said. "It can't come this far."

"Yes it can. I saw a fire jump onto my da, all the way from the roof. If I'd had a bucket, I could've saved him. If only I'd had a bucket."

"Your father?"

"Burned him black, Miss Rose, like cooked meat. When you light a candle, you should always keep a bucket."

In the east, the glow brightened and a flame leaped up, clawing the sky like an orange pitchfork. The boy backed away from the window as though ready to flee.

"Billy, I need you to remember something. This is important."

He kept his gaze on the window, as though afraid to turn his back on the enemy.

"The night Meggie was born, a horse and phaeton came to the hospital to take her away. Nurse Poole said it was someone from the infant asylum, but she was lying. I think she sent word to Meggie's father. Meggie's *real* father."

He still wasn't paying attention.

"Billy, I saw your dog at the hospital that night, so I know you were there, too. You must have seen the phaeton in the courtyard." She grasped his arm. "Who came to get the baby?"

At last he looked at her, and by the glow through the window she saw his bewildered face. "I don't know. It was Nurse Poole wrote the note."

"What note?"

"The one she told me to give him."

"She told you to deliver a note?"

"Told me there'd be half a dollar if I was quick about it."

She stared at the lad—a lad who could not read. What better messenger than Dim Billy, who'd happily run any errand for a few coins and a pat on the back?

"Where did she send you with the note?" Rose asked.

His gaze was back on the flames. "It's growing. It's coming this way."

"Billy." She shook him hard. "Show me where you took the note."

He nodded, retreating from the window. "It's away from the fire. We'll be safer there."

He led the way down the steps and out of the barn. The dog followed them, tail wagging, as they headed up the north slope of Beacon Hill. Every so often, Billy stopped to look east, to see if the flames were following them.

"Are you sure you remember the house?" she asked.

"'Course I remember it. Nurse Poole said there'd be a half dollar in it for me, but there wasn't. Came all this way, and the gentleman wasn't even at home. But I wanted my half dollar, so I gave the note to the maid. And she shut the door in my face, just like that. Stupid girl! I never got my half dollar. I went back to Nurse Poole, and she didn't give me no half dollar either."

"Where are we going?"

"This way. You know."

"I don't know."

"Yes, you do."

They came down the hill onto Beacon Street. Again, he glanced east. The sky was an ugly orange, and smoke was blowing toward them, carrying the smell of catastrophe in the air. "Hurry," he said. "Fire can't cross the river." He began to trot up Beacon Street, moving steadily toward the Mill Dam.

"Billy, show me where you delivered the note. Take me *right* to the door!"

"Here it is." He pushed through a gate and stepped into a yard. The dog trotted in after him.

She halted on the street and stared up in shock at Dr. Grenville's house.

"I took it to the back door," he said. He headed around the corner of the house and vanished into shadows. "Here's where I brought it, Miss Rose!"

She remained frozen in place. *So this was the secret Aurnia told in the birthing room that night.*

She heard the dog growl.

"Billy?" she said. She followed him into the side yard. The shadows were so thick, she could not see him. For a moment she hesitated, her heart thudding as she peered into the darkness. She took a few steps forward then halted as the dog came creeping toward her, growling, the ruff of his neck standing up.

What was wrong with him? Why was he afraid of her?

She stopped dead in her tracks as a chill screamed up her spine. The dog was not growling at her, but at something *behind* her.

"Billy?" she said, and turned.

"I want no more blood spilled. And see that you keep my carriage clean. There's already a mess here, and I'll have to mop up this path before daylight."

"I'm not doing this alone. You want it done, ma'am, you'll take an equal part in it."

Through the hammering pain in her head, Rose heard their muffled voices, but she could not see them, could not see anything. She opened her eyes and confronted a darkness as black as the grave. Something pressed down upon her, so heavy that she could not move, could barely draw in a breath. The two voices continued arguing, near enough for her to hear every agitated whisper.

"What if I'm stopped on the road?" the man said. "What if someone spots me with this carriage? I have no reason to be driving it. But if you're with me—"

"I've paid you quite enough to take care of this."

"Not enough for me to risk the gallows." The man paused at the growl of Billy's dog. "Bloody mutt," he said, and the dog's yelp of pain faded to retreating whimpers.

Rose fought to take in a breath, and she inhaled the scent of dirty wool and an unwashed body, alarmingly familiar smells. She worked one arm free and groped at what was lying on top of her. She touched buttons and woolen fabric. Her hands moved past a frayed collar and suddenly touched skin. She felt a jaw, slack and lifeless, a chin with the first pitiful bristles of an immature beard. And then something slimy, something that coated her fingers with the rich smell of rust.

Billy.

She pinched his cheek, but he didn't move. Only then did she realize he was not breathing.

". . . either you come with me, or I won't do it. I won't risk my neck for this."

"You forget, Mr. Burke, what I know about you."

"Then I'd say we're even. After tonight."

"How dare you." The woman's voice had risen, and Rose suddenly recognized it. *Eliza Lackaway.*

There was a long pause. Then Burke gave a dismissive laugh. "Go on, go ahead and shoot me. I don't think you'd dare. Then you'll have three bodies to dispose of." He gave a snort and his footsteps moved away.

"All right," said Eliza. "I'll come with you."

Burke gave a grunt. "Climb in back with 'em. Anyone stops us, I'll let you talk us out of it."

Rose heard the carriage door open and felt the vehicle sag with the new weight. Eliza pulled the door shut. "Go, Mr. Burke."

But the carriage did not move. Burke said, softly: "We have a problem, Mrs. Lackaway. A witness."

"What?" Eliza suddenly took in a startled breath. "Charles," she whispered, and scrambled out of the carriage. "You shouldn't be out of bed! Go back into the house at once."

"Why are you doing this, Mother?" asked Charles.

"There's a fire on the docks, darling. We're bringing the carriage around, in case they need to transport the injured."

"That's not true. I saw you, Mother, from my window. I saw what you put in the carriage."

"Charles, you don't understand."

"Who are they?"

"They're not important."

"Then why did you kill them?"

There was a long silence.

Burke said, "He's a witness."

"He's my *son!*" Eliza took a deep breath, and when she spoke again she sounded calmer and in control. "Charles, I'm doing this for you. For your future."

"What does killing two people have to do with my future?"

"I will *not* tolerate another one of his bastards turning up! I cleaned up my brother's mess ten years ago, and now I'll do it again."

"What are you talking about?"

"It's your inheritance I'm protecting, Charles. It came from my father, and it belongs to you. I won't see one penny of it go to the brat of a *chambermaid*!"

There was a long silence. Then a stunned-sounding Charles said, "The baby is *Uncle's*?"

"That shocks you?" She laughed. "A saint my brother is not, yet every accolade goes to *him*. I was just the daughter, to be married off. *You* are my accomplishment, darling. I won't see your future destroyed." Eliza climbed back into the carriage. "Now go back to bed."

"And the child? You would kill a baby?"

"Only the girl knew where it was hidden. The secret died with her." Eliza pulled the carriage door shut. "Now let me finish this. Let's go, Mr. Burke."

"Which way?" asked Burke.

"Away from the fire. There'll be too many people there. Go west. It'll be quietest on Prison Point Bridge."

"Mother," said Charles, his voice breaking in despair. "If you do this, it's not in my name. *None* of this is in my name!"

"But you'll accept it. And one day, you *will* appreciate it."

The carriage rolled away. Trapped beneath Billy's body, Rose lay perfectly still, knowing that if she moved, if Eliza discovered she was still alive, it would take only a blow on the head to finish the job. Let them think she was dead. It might be her only hope of escape.

Through the rattle of the carriage wheels, she heard the voices of people on the street, the clatter of another vehicle racing past. The fire was pulling crowds east, toward the burning wharves. No one would notice this lone carriage moving leisurely west. She heard a dog's insistent barking—Billy's dog, running after his dead master.

She'd told him to go west. Toward the river.

Rose thought of a body she'd once seen fished out of the harbor. It had been in the summertime, and when the body had bobbed to the surface, a fisherman dragged it out and brought it back to the pier. Rose had joined the crowd that gathered to stare at the corpse, and what she'd seen that day bore little resemblance to anything human. Fish and crabs had nibbled away at the flesh, turning eyes to empty sockets, and the belly had bloated, the skin stretched taut as a drum.

That's what happens to a drowned body.

With every rumble of the carriage wheels, Rose was being carried closer to the bridge, closer to the final plummet. Now she heard the horse's hooves clopping against wood, and knew they had started across busy Canal Bridge, toward Lechmere Point. Their final destination was the far quieter Prison Point Bridge. There two bodies could be rolled into the water, and no one would witness it. Panic made Rose's heart pound like a wild animal trying to beat its way free. Already she felt as if she were drowning, her lungs desperate for air.

Rose could not swim.

Thirty-four

"AURNIA CONNOLLY," said Wendell, "was a chambermaid in the Welliver household in Providence. After only three months in their employ, she abruptly left that position. That was in May."

"May?" said Norris, comprehending the significance.

"By then she would have been aware of her condition. Soon thereafter, she married a tailor with whom she was already acquainted. Mr. Eben Tate."

Norris stared anxiously at the dark road ahead. He was at the reins of Wendell's two-man shay, and for the past two hours they had driven the horse hard. Now they were approaching the village of Cambridge, and Boston was just a bridge crossing away.

"Kitty and Gwen told me their chambermaid had flame-colored hair," said Wendell. "She was nineteen years old and said to be quite fetching."

"Fetching enough to catch the eye of a most distinguished house-guest?"

"Dr. Grenville visited the Wellivers back in March. That's what the sisters told me. He stayed there for two weeks, during which time they noticed he would often sit up quite late, reading in the parlor. After the rest of the household had retired for the night."

In March. The month that Aurnia's child would have been conceived.

Their fast-moving shay suddenly bounced hard over a rut in the road, and both men scrambled to hold on.

"Slow down, for God's sake!" said Wendell. "This isn't the place to break an axle. This close to Boston, someone might recognize you."

But Norris did not rein in the horse, even though the animal was already heaving hard, and it still had a long journey ahead of it tonight.

"This is madness for you to go back to the city," said Wendell. "You should be as far away as you can get."

"I won't leave Rose with him." Norris leaned forward as if by sheer will he could force their little shay to move more quickly. "I thought she would be safe there. I thought I was protecting her. Instead, I've delivered her straight to the killer's house."

The bridge was ahead. One short ride across the Charles River, and Norris would be back in the city that he'd fled only yesterday. But tonight, that city had changed. He slowed their exhausted horse to a walk and gazed across the water, at the orange glow in the night sky. Along the west bank of the Charles, a small but excited crowd had gathered to watch as distant flames lit up the horizon. Even this far from the blaze, the air was heavy with the smell of smoke.

A boy ran past their shay, and Wendell called out: "What's burning?"

"They say it's Hancock's Wharf! They're calling for volunteers to help fight it!"

Which means there'll be fewer eyes elsewhere in town, thought Norris. Fewer chances I'll be recognized. Nevertheless, he pulled up the collar of his greatcoat and lowered the brim of his hat as they started across the West Boston Bridge.

"I'll go to the door to fetch her," said Wendell. "You stay with the horse."

Norris stared ahead, his hands tightening around the reins. "Nothing must go wrong. Just get her out of that house."

Wendell grasped his friend's arm. "Before you know it, she'll be sitting right here beside you, and you'll be on your way together." He added ruefully: "With my horse."

"Somehow, I'll return him to you. I swear, Wendell."

"Well, Rose certainly believes in you. That should be good enough for me."

And I believe in her.

Their horse clopped off the bridge, onto Cambridge Street. The glow of the wharf fire was dead ahead, and the road seemed eerily empty, the air thicker with smoke and black motes of ash. Once he and Rose were out of this city, they'd head west to collect Meggie. By sunrise, they'd be well away from Boston.

He turned the horse south, toward Beacon Street. Even here the road was eerily empty, and the night even more ominous with the smell of smoke. The air itself seemed to close in around Norris like an ever-tightening noose. Grenville's house was now just ahead, and as they neared the front gate, the horse suddenly reared, startled by a moving shadow. Norris hauled on the reins as the shay lurched and tilted, and finally managed to regain control. Only then did he see what had panicked the animal.

Charles Lackaway, dressed only in his nightshirt, stood in the front yard, staring at Norris with dazed eyes. "You came back," he murmured.

Wendell jumped out of the shay. "Just let him take Rose and say nothing. Please, Charlie. Let her go with him."

"I can't."

"For God's sake, you were my *friend*. All he wants is to take Rose."

"I think . . ." Charles's voice broke into a sob. "I think she has killed her."

Norris scrambled out of the shay. Grabbing Charles by the collar of his nightshirt, he pinned him to the fence. "Where is Rose?"

"My mother—she and that man took her—"

"*Where?*"

"To Prison Point Bridge," Charles whispered. "I think it's too late."

In an instant Norris was back in the shay. He did not wait for Wendell; the horse could move faster with only one man in tow. He cracked the whip and the horse broke into a gallop.

"Wait!" Wendell called, running after him.

But Norris only swung the whip harder.

The carriage stopped.

Wedged into the floor of the carriage, trapped under the weight of Billy's body, Rose could no longer feel her own legs. They were numb and useless to her, dead limbs that might as well belong to Billy's corpse. She heard the door open, felt the carriage sway as Eliza stepped out onto the bridge.

"Wait," Burke cautioned. "There's someone coming."

Rose heard the steady clip-clop of a horse crossing the bridge. And what would the rider think as he passed the carriage parked at the side? Would he glance at the man and woman who stood at the railing, looking at the water? Did he think Eliza and Burke were lovers, meeting furtively on this lonely span? Billy's dog began to bark, and she could hear it scratching at the carriage, trying to reach its dead master. Would the passing horseman mark that odd detail? The dog barking and clawing at the carriage, the couple nonchalantly ignoring it as they stood with backs turned, facing the water?

She tried to shout for help, but she could not draw in a deep breath and her voice was muffled beneath the heavy oilcloth draped over her and Billy. And the dog, that noisy dog, kept barking and scratching, drowning out what meager cries she could produce. She heard the horse trot past, and then the sound of the hooves faded as the rider moved on, never realizing that his inattention had just condemned a woman to death.

The carriage door swung open.

"Damn it, I thought I heard something. One of them is still alive!" Eliza said.

The oilcloth flew off. The man grabbed Billy's body and rolled it out of the carriage. Rose sucked in a deep breath and screamed. Her cry was immediately cut off by a thick hand over her mouth.

"Hand me my knife," Burke said to Eliza. "I'll shut her up."

"No blood in the carriage! Just throw her in the water now, before someone else comes!"

"What if she can swim?"

His question was answered by the sudden rip of cloth as Eliza tore Rose's petticoat into strips. With brutal efficiency she tied Rose's ankles together. A wad of cloth was stuffed into Rose's mouth, then the man bound her wrists.

The dog's barking became frenzied. It circled the carriage now, howling, but it stayed just beyond the reach of their kicks.

"Throw her in," Eliza said. "Before that bloody dog draws any more—" She paused. "Someone else is coming."

"Where?"

"Do it *now*, before they see us!"

Rose gave a sob as the man hauled her out of the carriage. She squirmed in his arms, her hair whipping his face as she tried to thrash her way free. But his arms were too powerful, and it was too late for him to entertain any second thoughts about what he was going to do. As he carried her to the railing, Rose caught a glimpse of Billy, lying dead beside the carriage, his dog crouched beside him. She saw Eliza, her hair wild and windblown. And she caught a view of the sky, the stars muted by a haze of smoke.

Then she fell.

Thirty-five

NORRIS HEARD THE SPLASH, even from Lechmere Point. He could not see what had just fallen into the water, but he spotted the carriage stopped on the bridge ahead. And he heard a howling dog.

As he drew closer, he saw the boy's body sprawled beside the carriage's rear wheel. A black dog crouched beside it, teeth bared and growling as it held off the man and woman trying to get near the fallen man. *It's Billy's dog.*

"We couldn't stop the horse in time!" the woman called out. "It was a horrible accident! The boy ran straight in front of us and . . ." She stopped, staring in recognition as Norris climbed out of the shay. "Mr. Marshall?"

Norris yanked open the carriage door but did not see Rose inside. From the floor, he plucked up a torn strip of cloth. *From a woman's petticoat.*

He turned to Eliza, who stared at him, mute. "Where is Rose?" he asked. He looked at Wall-eyed Jack, who was already backing away, preparing to flee.

That splash. They'd thrown something into the water.

Norris ran to the railing and stared into the river. He saw rippling water, silvered by moonlight. And then a shudder, as something broke the surface, then sank again.

Rose.

He scrambled over the railing. Once before, he had plunged into the Charles River. That time, he had docilely surrendered his fate to the whims of providence. This time, he surrendered nothing. As he flung himself off the bridge, he stretched out his arms as though to seize this one last chance at happiness. He sliced into water so cold it made him suck in a startled gasp. He surfaced, coughing. Paused only long enough to heave in and out several deep breaths, washing his lungs with air.

Then he plunged, once again, underwater.

In the darkness, he flailed blindly at anything within reach, feeling for a limb, a bit of cloth, a fistful of hair. His hands met only empty water. Out of breath, he popped to the surface again. This time he heard a man's shouts from the bridge above.

"There's someone down there!"

"I see him. Call the Night Watch!"

Three quick breaths, then once again, Norris dove. In his panic, he did not even register the cold or the growing chorus of shouts above. With every passing second, Rose was slipping away from him. Arms churning, he clawed at the water, as frantic as a drowning man. She might be only inches from his grasp, but he could not see her.

I am losing you.

A desperate need for air drove him back to the surface for another breath. There were lights on the bridge above, and more voices. Feckless witnesses to his despair.

I would rather drown than leave you here.

One last time he dove. The glow of the lanterns above faintly penetrated the dark water in shifting ribbons of light. He saw the shadowy strokes of his own arms, saw clouds of sediment. And drifting just below, he saw something else. Something pale, billowing like sheets in the wind. He lunged toward it, and his hand closed around cloth.

Rose's limp body drifted toward him, her hair a swirl of black.

At once he kicked upward, pulling her with him. But when they broke the surface and he gasped in lungfuls of air, she was limp, as lifeless as a bundle of rags. *I am too late*. Sobbing, gasping, he hauled her toward the riverbank, kicking until his legs were so exhausted they would scarcely obey him. When at last his feet touched mud, he could not support his own weight. He half crawled, half stumbled out of the water, and dragged Rose up the bank, onto dry land.

Her wrists and ankles were bound; she was not breathing.

He rolled her onto her stomach. *Live, Rose! You have to live for me*. He placed his hands on her back and leaned in, squeezing her chest. Water gushed from her lungs and spilled out of her mouth. He pressed again and again, until her lungs were empty, but still she lay unresponsive.

Frantic, he tore the bindings from her wrists and turned her onto her back. Her face, smudged with grime, stared up at him. He pressed his hands against her chest and leaned in, trying to expel the last drops of water from her lungs. Again and again he pressed as his tears and river water dripped onto her face.

"Rose, come back to me! Please, darling. Come back."

Her first twitch was so faint, it might only have been his desperate imagination. Then, suddenly, she shuddered and coughed, a wet and racking cough that was the most beautiful sound he'd ever heard. Laughing and crying at once, he turned her onto her side and brushed sopping hair from her face. Though he could hear footsteps approaching, he did not look up. His gaze was only on Rose, and when she opened her eyes, his face was the first thing she saw.

"Am I dead?" she whispered.

"No." He wrapped his arms around her shivering body. "You're right here with me. Where you'll always be."

A pebble clattered across the ground, and the footsteps came to a standstill. Only then did Norris look up to see Eliza Lackaway, her cape billowing in the wind. *Like wings. Like the wings of a giant bird.* Her gun was pointed straight at him.

"They're watching," Norris said, glancing up at the people who stood on the bridge above. "They'll see you do it."

"They'll see me kill the West End Reaper." Eliza shouted toward the crowd: "Mr. Pratt! It's Norris Marshall!"

Voices on the bridge rose in excitement.

"Did you hear that?"

"It's the West End Reaper!"

Rose struggled to sit, clinging to Norris's arm. "But I know the truth," she said. "I know what you did. You can't kill us both."

Eliza's arm wavered. She had only one shot. Even as Mr. Pratt and two men from the Night Watch gingerly worked their way down the steep bank, she was still standing there, undecided, her gun swinging between Norris and Rose.

"Mother!"

Eliza went rigid. She looked up at the bridge, where her son was now standing beside Wendell.

"Mother, don't!" Charles pleaded.

"Your son told us," said Norris. "He knows what you did, Mrs. Lackaway. Wendell Holmes knows, too. You can kill me here, now, but the truth is already out. Whether I live or die, your future has already been decided."

Slowly, her arm dropped. "I have no future," she said softly. "Whether it ends here, or on the gallows, it's over. The only thing I can do now is to spare my son." She raised her gun, but this time it was not pointed at Norris; it was aimed at her own head.

Norris lunged toward her. Grabbing her wrist, he tried to wrench the gun free, but Eliza resisted, fighting with the viciousness of a wounded animal. Only when Norris twisted her arm did she finally release her grip. She stumbled back, howling. Norris stood pitilessly exposed on the riverbank with the gun in his hand. In the space of a heartbeat, he realized what was about to happen. He saw Watchman Pratt take aim. He heard Rose's anguished scream of "*No!*"

The impact of the bullet slammed the breath from his lungs. The gun dropped from his hand. He staggered and sprawled backward on the mud. A strange silence fell over the night. Norris stared up at the sky but heard no voices, no footsteps crowding in, not even the swish of the water against the bank. All was calm and peaceful. He saw stars above, winking brighter through the clearing haze. He felt no pain, no fear, only a sense of astonishment that all his struggles, all his dreams, should come down to this moment at the water's edge, with the stars shining down.

Then, as though from far away, he heard a sweet and familiar voice, and he saw Rose, her head framed by stars, as though she gazed down from the heavens.

"Is there nothing you can do?" she cried. "Please, Wendell, you must save him!"

Now he heard Wendell's voice as well, and heard cloth rip as his shirt was torn open. "Bring the lamp closer! I must see the wound!"

Light spilled down in a golden shower, and as the wound was revealed, Norris saw Wendell's expression, and read the truth in his eyes.

"Rose?" Norris whispered.

"I'm here. I'm right here." She took his hand and leaned close as she stroked back his hair. "You're going to be fine, darling. You're going to get well, and we'll be happy. We'll be *so* happy."

He sighed and closed his eyes. He could see Rose floating away from him, carried on the wind so swiftly that he had no hope of reaching her. "Wait for me," he whispered. He heard what sounded like a distant clap of thunder, a lonely blast of gunfire that echoed through the gathering darkness.

Wait for me.

Jack Burke yanked up the floorboard in his bedroom and frantically scooped out the money he had hidden there. His life's savings, close to two thousand dollars, clattered into the saddlebag.

"What're you doing, taking it all? Are you mad?" asked Fanny.

"I'm leaving."

"You can't take it all! That's mine, too!"

"You don't have a noose hangin' over *your* head." Suddenly his chin shot up and he froze.

Someone was pounding downstairs, on the door. "Mr. Burke! Mr. Jack Burke, this is the Night Watch. You will open this door at once!"

Fanny turned to go downstairs.

"No!" said Jack. "Don't let them in!"

She looked at him with narrowed eyes. "What'd you do, Jack? Why've they come for you?"

Downstairs, the voice yelled: "We'll break down the door if you don't let us in!"

"Jack?" said Fanny.

"She's the one did it!" said Jack. "She killed the boy, not me!"

"What boy?"

"Dim Billy."

"Then let *her* go to the gallows."

"She's dead. Picked up the gun and shot herself with the whole world watchin'." He rose to his feet and slung the heavy saddlebag over his shoulder. "I'm the one'll be blamed for it all. Everything *she* paid me to do." He headed for the stairs. Out the back way, he thought. Just saddle the horse and go. If he could get a few minutes' head start, he could lose them in the dark. By morning, he'd be well on his way.

The front door crashed open. Jack froze at the bottom of the stairs as three men burst in.

One of them stepped forward and said, "You're under arrest, Mr. Burke. For the murder of Billy Piggott, and the attempted murder of Rose Connolly."

"But I didn't—it wasn't me! It was Mrs. Lackaway!"

"Gentlemen, take him into custody."

Jack was hauled forward so roughly he stumbled to his knees, dropping the saddlebag on the floor. In an instant Fanny darted forward and snatched it up. She backed away, hugging the precious contents to her breasts. As the Night Watch yanked her husband back to his feet, she made no move to help him, said not a word in his defense. That was his last glimpse of her: Fanny greedily cradling his life's savings in her arms, her face calm and impassive as Jack was led out the tavern door.

Sitting in the carriage, Jack knew exactly how it would all turn out. Not just the trial, not just the gallows, but beyond. He knew where the bodies of executed prisoners invariably ended up. He thought of the money he'd so carefully saved for his precious lead coffin with the iron cage and the gravesitter, all to defeat the efforts of resurrectionists like himself. Long ago, he'd promised himself that no anatomist would ever cut open his belly, hack at his flesh.

Now he looked down at his own chest and gave a sob. Already, he could feel the knife begin to cut.

It was a house in mourning and a house shamed.

Wendell Holmes knew that he was intruding upon the private agonies of the Grenville home, but he made no move to depart, and no one asked him to. Indeed, Dr. Grenville did not even seem to notice that Wendell was in the parlor, sitting quietly in the corner. Wendell had been a part of this unfolding tragedy from the beginning, and it was only fitting that he should be present now, to witness the end of it. What he saw, in the wavering firelight, was a broken Aldous Grenville hunched deep in a chair, with his head bowed in grief. Constable Lyons sat facing him.

The housekeeper, Mrs. Furbush, timidly entered the parlor with a tray of brandy, which she set down upon the end table. "Sir," she said quietly, "I gave young Mr. Lackaway that draught of morphine you requested. He's asleep now."

Grenville said nothing, merely nodded.

Constable Lyons said to her: "And Miss Connolly?"

"She won't leave the young man's body, sir. I have tried to pull her away, but she stays by his coffin. I don't know what we'll do with her when they come to take him in the morning."

"Leave her be. The girl has every reason to grieve."

Mrs. Furbush withdrew, and Grenville said, softly: "As do we all."

Lyons poured a glass of brandy and put it into his friend's hand. "Aldous, you cannot blame yourself for what Eliza did."

"I do blame myself. I didn't *want* to know, but I should have suspected." Grenville sighed and drank down the brandy in one gulp. "I knew she would do anything for Charles. But to *kill* for him?"

"We don't know that she did it all herself. Jack Burke swears he's not the Reaper, but he may have been involved."

"Then she most certainly instigated it." Grenville stared down at his empty glass and said softly, "Eliza always wanted to be the one in control, ever since we were children."

"Yet how much control does a woman ever truly have, Aldous?"

Grenville's head drooped, and he said softly: "Poor Aurnia had the least of all. I have no excuse for what I did. Only that she was lovely, so lovely. And I'm nothing but a lonely old man."

"You tried to do the honorable thing. Take comfort in that. You engaged Mr. Wilson to find the child, and you were ready to provide for her."

"Honorable?" Grenville shook his head. "The *honorable* thing would have been to provide for Aurnia months ago, instead of handing her a pretty necklace and walking away." He looked up, torment in his eyes. "I swear to you, I didn't know she was carrying my child. Not until the day I saw her laid open on the dissection table. When Erastus pointed out that she'd recently given birth, that's when I realized I had a child."

"But you never told Eliza?"

"No one but Mr. Wilson. I fully intended to see to the child's welfare, but I knew Eliza would feel threatened. Her late husband was unlucky with his finances. She has been living here on my charity."

And this new child could claim it all, thought Wendell. He thought of all the slurs against the Irish that he'd heard from the lips of the Welliver sisters and Edward Kingston's mother; indeed, from almost every society matron in the best parlors of Boston. That her own darling son, who had no talent for earning a livelihood, would now have his future threatened by the spawn of a chambermaid would be the ultimate outrage for Eliza.

Yet it was an Irish girl who had, in the end, outwitted her. Rose Connolly had kept the child alive, and Wendell could imagine Eliza's mounting fury as the girl managed to elude her, day after day. He thought of the savage slashes on Agnes Poole's body, the torture of Mary Robinson, and he understood that the real target of Eliza's rage was Rose and every girl like her, every ragged foreigner who crowded the streets of Boston.

Lyons took Grenville's glass, refilled it, and handed it back to him. "I am sorry, Aldous, that I did not take control of the investigation sooner. By the time I stepped in, that idiot Pratt already had the public in a blood frenzy." Lyons shook his head. "I'm afraid young Mr. Marshall was the unfortunate victim of that hysteria."

"Pratt must be made to pay for that."

"Oh, he will pay. I'll see to it. By the time I'm finished, his reputation will be dirt. I won't rest until he's hounded out of Boston."

"Not that it matters now," said Grenville softly. "Norris is gone."

"Which offers us a possibility here. A way to limit the damage."

"What do you mean?"

"Mr. Marshall is beyond our help now, and beyond further harm. He cannot suffer any more than he already has. We could allow this scandal to simply die quietly."

"And not clear his name?"

"At the expense of your family's?"

Wendell had been silent up to this point. But now he was so appalled, he could not hold his tongue. "You'd let Norris go to his grave as the West End Reaper? When you know he's innocent?"

Constable Lyons looked at him. "There are other innocents to consider, Mr. Holmes. Young Charles, for example. It's painful enough for him that his mother chose to end her own life, and so publicly. Would you also force him to live with the stigma of having a murderess as a mother?"

"It's the truth, isn't it?"

"The public is not owed the truth."

"But we owe it to Norris. To his memory."

"He's not here to benefit from any such redemption. We'll lay no accusations at his feet. We'll simply remain silent, and allow the public to draw its own conclusions."

"Even if those conclusions are false?"

"Whom does it harm? No one who still breathes." Lyons sighed. "At any rate, there's still a trial to come. Mr. Jack Burke will almost certainly hang for the murder of Billy Piggott, at the very least. The truth may well be revealed then, and we can't suppress it. But we need not advertise it, either."

Wendell looked at Dr. Grenville, who had remained silent. "Sir, you would allow such an injustice against Norris? He deserved better."

Grenville said, softly: "I know."

"It's a false honor your family clings to, if it requires you to blacken the memory of an innocent man."

"There is Charles to think of."

"And that's all that matters to you?"

"He is my nephew!"

A voice suddenly cut in: "And what of your son, Dr. Grenville?"

Startled, Wendell turned to stare at Rose, now standing in the parlor doorway. Grief had drained her face of all color, and what he saw bore little resemblance to the vibrant young girl she once was. In her place he saw a stranger, no longer a girl but a stone-faced woman who stood straight and unyielding, her gaze fixed on Grenville.

"Surely you knew you fathered another child," she said. "He *was* your son."

Grenville gave an anguished groan and dropped his head in his hands.

"He never realized," she said. "But I saw it. And you must have, too, Doctor. The first time you laid eyes on him. How many women have you taken advantage of, sir? How many other children have you fathered out of wedlock, children you don't even know about? Children who are even now struggling just to stay alive?"

"There are no others."

"How could you know?"

"I *do* know!" He looked up. "What happened between Sophia and me was a long time ago, and it was something we both regretted. We betrayed my dear wife. Never again did I do so, not while Abigail lived."

"You turned your back on your own son."

"Sophia never told me the boy was mine! All those years he was growing up in Belmont, I didn't know. Until the day he arrived at the college, and I saw him. Then I realized . . ."

Wendell looked back and forth between Rose and Grenville. "You can't be speaking of *Norris?*"

Rose's gaze was still fixed on Grenville. "While you lived in this grand house, Doctor, while you rode in your fine carriage to your country home in Weston, he was tilling fields and slopping pigs."

"I tell you, I didn't know! Sophia never said a word to me."

"And if she had, would you have acknowledged him? I don't think so. And poor Sophia had no choice but to marry the first man who'd have her."

"I *would* have helped the boy. I *would* have seen to his needs."

"But you didn't. Everything he accomplished was by his efforts alone. Does it not make you proud, that you fathered such a remarkable son? That in his short life, he rose so far above his station?"

"I am proud," said Grenville softly. "If only Sophia had come to me years ago."

"She tried to."

"What do you mean?"

"Ask Charles. He heard what his mother said. Mrs. Lackaway told him she didn't want *another* one of your bastards suddenly showing up in the family. She said that ten years ago, she was forced to clean up your mess."

"Ten years ago?" said Wendell. "Isn't that when—"

"When Norris's mother vanished," said Rose. She drew in a shaky breath, the first hint of tears breaking her voice. "If only Norris had known! It would have meant everything to him, to know that his mother loved him. That she didn't abandon him, but was instead murdered."

"I have no words in my own defense, Miss Connolly," said Grenville. "I have a lifetime of sins to atone for, and I intend to." He looked straight at Rose. "Now it seems there is a little girl somewhere in need of a home. A girl whom I swear to you will be given every comfort, every advantage."

"I'll hold you to that promise," said Rose.

"Where is she? Will you take me to my daughter?"

Rose met his gaze. "When the time is right."

In the hearth, the fire had guttered out. The first light of dawn was brightening the sky.

Constable Lyons rose from his chair. "I leave you now, Aldous. As for Eliza, this is your family, and how much you choose to acknowledge is your decision. At the moment, the public's eyes are on Mr. Jack Burke. He is their current monster. But soon, I'm sure, there'll be another one to catch their attention. This much I know about the public: Their hunger for monsters is insatiable." He nodded farewell and left the house.

After a moment, Wendell, too, rose to depart. He had intruded upon the household far too long, and had spoken his mind too bluntly. So it was with a note of apology in his voice that he took his leave of Dr. Grenville, who did not stir but remained in his chair, staring at the ashes.

Rose followed Wendell into the foyer. "You have been a true friend," she said. "Thank you, for all that you've done."

They embraced, and there was no awkwardness despite the wide gulf of class that separated them. Norris Marshall had brought them together; now grief over his death would forever bind them. Wendell was about to step out the door when he paused and looked back at her.

"How did you know?" he said. "When Norris himself did not?"

"That Dr. Grenville is his father?"

"Yes."

She took his hand. "Come with me."

She led him up the stairs to the second floor. In the dim hallway she paused to light a lamp and carry it toward one of the portraits hanging on the wall. "Here," she said. "This is how I knew."

He stared at the painting of a dark-haired young man who stood beside a desk, his hand resting atop a human skull. His brown eyes gazed straight at Wendell, as though in direct challenge.

"It's a portrait of Aldous Grenville when he was nineteen years old," said Rose. "That's what Mrs. Furbush told me."

Wendell could not tear his gaze from the painting. "I did not see it until now."

"I saw it at once. And I had no doubt." Rose stared at the young man's portrait, and her lips curved into a sad smile. "You always recognize the one you love."

Thirty-six

Dr. Grenville's fine carriage took them west on the Belmont road, past farmhouses and wintry fields that were now familiar to Rose. It was a pitilessly beautiful afternoon, and the snow glittered beneath clear skies just as it had glittered when she had walked this road only two weeks ago. *You walked beside me then, Norrie. If I close my eyes, I can almost believe you are here with me now.*

"Is it much farther?" asked Grenville.

"Only a bit, sir." Rose opened her eyes and blinked at the empty glare of the sun. And the hard truth: *But I will never see you again. And I will miss you every day of my life.*

"This is where he grew up, isn't it?" said Grenville. "On this road."

She nodded. "Soon we'll come to Heppy Comfort's farm. She had a lame calf that she brought into the house. And then she grew so fond of it, she could never slaughter it. Next door to her there'll be Ezra Hutchinson's farm. His wife died of typhus."

"How do you know all this?"

"Norris told me." And she would never forget. As long as she lived, she would remember every word, every moment.

"The Marshall farm is on this road?"

"We're not going to Isaac Marshall's farm."

"Then where?"

She peered ahead at the tidy farmhouse that had just come into view. "I see the house now."

"Who lives there?"

A man who was kinder and more generous to Norris than his own father.

As the carriage came to a stop, the farmhouse door opened, and elderly Dr. Hallowell emerged on the porch. By the bleak expression on his face, Rose knew that he had already learned of Norris's death. He came forward to help her and Dr. Grenville from the carriage. As they climbed the steps, Rose was startled to see yet another man emerge from the house.

It was Isaac Marshall, looking infinitely older than he had only weeks before.

The three men who stood on the porch had been brought together by grief over one young man, and words did not come easily to any of them. In silence they regarded one another, the two men who had watched Norris grow up, and the one man who should have.

Rose slipped past them into the house, drawn by what the men's ears were not attuned to: a baby's soft cooing. She followed the sound into a room where gray-haired Mrs. Hallowell sat rocking Meggie.

"I've come back for her," said Rose.

"I knew you would." The woman looked up with hopeful eyes as she handed over the baby. "Please tell me we'll see her again! Tell me we can be part of her life."

"Oh, you will, ma'am," said Rose, smiling. "And so will everyone who loves her."

The three men all turned as Rose came out onto the porch, carrying the baby. At the instant Aldous Grenville gazed for the first time into his daughter's eyes, Meggie smiled up at him, as though in recognition.

"Her name is Margaret," said Rose.

"Margaret," he said softly. And he took the child into his arms.

Thirty-seven

The present

JULIA CARRIED her suitcase downstairs and left it by the front door. Then she went into the library, where Henry was sitting among the boxes, now ready to be transported to the Boston Athenaeum. Together, she and Henry had organized all the documents and resealed the boxes. The letters from Oliver Wendell Holmes, however, they had carefully set aside for safekeeping. Henry had laid them out on the table, and he sat reading them yet again, for at least the hundredth time.

"It pains me to give these up," he said. "Perhaps I should keep them."

"You already promised the Athenaeum you'd donate them."

"I could still change my mind."

"Henry, they need to be properly cared for. An archivist will know how to preserve them. And won't it be wonderful to share this story with the whole world?"

Henry slouched stubbornly in his chair, eyeing the papers like a miser who won't give up his fortune. "These mean too much to me. This is personal."

She went to the window and gazed at the sea. "I know what you mean," she said softly. "It's become personal for me, too."

"Are you still dreaming about her?"

"Every night. It's been weeks now."

"What was last night's dream?"

"It was more . . . impressions. Images."

"What images?"

"Bolts of cloth. Ribbons and bows. I'm holding a needle in my hand and sewing." She shook her head and laughed. "Henry, I don't even know how to sew."

"But Rose did."

"Yes, she did. Sometimes I think she's alive again, and speaking to me. By reading the letters, I've brought her soul back. And now I'm having her memories. I'm reliving her life."

"The dreams are that vivid?"

"Right down to the color of the thread. Which tells me I've spent entirely too much time thinking about her." *And what her life could have been.* She looked at her watch and turned to him. "I should probably head down to the ferry."

"I'm sorry you have to leave. When will you come back to see me?"

"You can always come down to see me."

"Maybe when Tom gets back? I'll visit you both on the same trip." He paused. "So tell me. What did you think of him?"

"Tom?"

"He's eligible, you know."

She smiled. "I know, Henry."

"He's also very picky. I've watched him go through a succession of girlfriends, and not a single one lasted. You could be the exception. But you have to let him know you're interested. He thinks you're not."

"Is that what he told you?"

"He's disappointed. But he's also a patient man."

"Well, I do like him."

"So what's the problem?"

"Maybe I like him too much. It scares me. I know how fast love can fall apart." Julia turned to the window again and looked at the sea. It was as calm and flat as a mirror. "One minute you're happy and in love, and everything is right with the world. You think nothing can go wrong. But then it does, the way it did for me and Richard. The way it did for Rose Connolly. And you end up suffering for it all the rest of your life. Rose had that one short taste of happiness with Norris, and then she had to live all those years with the memory of what she'd lost. I don't know if it's worth it, Henry. I don't know if I could stand it."

"I think you're taking the wrong lesson from Rose's life."

"What's the right lesson?"

"To grab it while you can! Love."

"And suffer the consequences."

Henry gave a snort. "You know all those dreams you've been having? There's a message there, Julia, but it's wasted on you. *She* would have taken the chance."

"I know that. But I'm not Rose Connolly." She sighed. "Goodbye, Henry."

She had never seen Henry look so dapper. As they sat together in the director's office of the Boston Athenaeum, Julia kept stealing glances at him, amazed that this was the same old Henry who liked to putter around his creaky Maine house in baggy pants and old flannel shirts. She'd expected him to be wearing that same wardrobe when she'd picked him up at his Boston hotel that morning. But the man she'd found waiting for her in the lobby was wearing a black three-piece suit and carrying an ebony cane with a brass tip. Not only had Henry shed his old clothes, he'd shed his perpetual scowl as well, and he was actually flirting with Mrs. Zaccardi, the Athenaeum's director.

And Mrs. Zaccardi, all of sixty years old, was obligingly flirting right back.

"It's not every day we receive a donation of such significance, Mr. Page," she said. "There's a long line of eager scholars who can't wait to get their hands on these letters. It's been quite some time since any new Holmes material has surfaced, so we're delighted you chose to donate it to us."

"Oh, I had to think about it long and hard," said Henry. "I considered other institutions. But the Athenaeum has, by far, the prettiest director."

Mrs. Zaccardi laughed. "And you, sir, need new glasses. I'll promise to wear my sexiest dress if you and Julia will join us tonight at the trustees' dinner. I know they'd love to meet you both."

"I wish we could," said Henry. "But my grandnephew is flying home from Hong Kong tonight. Julia and I plan to spend the evening with him."

"Then next month, perhaps." Mrs. Zaccardi stood up. "Once again, thank you. There are few native sons so deeply revered in Boston as Oliver Wendell Holmes. And the story he tells, in these letters . . ." She gave an embarrassed laugh. "It's so heartbreaking, it makes me choke up a little. There are so many stories we'll never get to hear, so many other voices lost to history. Thank you for giving us the tale of Rose Connolly."

As Henry and Julia walked out of the office, his cane made a smart *clack-clack*. At this early hour on a Thursday morning, the Athenaeum was nearly empty, and they were the only passengers in the elevator, the only visitors who strolled through the lobby, Henry's cane echoing against the floor. They passed a gallery room, and Henry stopped. He pointed to the sign outside the current exhibit: BOSTON AND THE TRANSCENDENTALISTS: PORTRAITS OF AN ERA.

"That would be Rose's era," he said.

"Do you want to take a look?"

"We have all day. Why not?"

They stepped into the gallery. They were alone in the room, and they could take as long as they wanted to examine each painting and lithograph. They studied an 1832 view of Boston Harbor from Pemberton Hill, and Julia wondered: Is this a view that Rose glimpsed when she was alive? Did she see that same pretty fence in the foreground, the same vista of rooftops? They moved on, to a lithograph of Colonnade Row, with its tableau of smartly dressed ladies and gentlemen standing beneath stately trees, and she wondered if Rose had passed beneath those very trees. They lingered before portraits of Theodore Parker and the Reverend William Channing, faces that Rose might have passed on the street or glimpsed in a window. *Here is your world, Rose, a world that has long since passed into history. Like you.*

They circled the gallery, and Henry came to an abrupt standstill. She bumped into him, and could feel his body had gone rigid.

"What?" she said. Then her gaze lifted to the oil painting he was staring at, and she, too, went instantly still. In a room full of strangers' portraits, this face did not belong; this face they both knew. The dark-haired young man gazing back at them from the painting stood beside a desk, with his hand laid upon a human skull. Though he had the heavy sideburns and topcoat and intricately tied cravat of his era, his face was startlingly familiar.

"My God," said Henry. "That's Tom!"

"But it was painted in 1792."

"Look at the eyes, the mouth. It's definitely our Tom."

Julia frowned at the label mounted beside the portrait. "The artist is Christian Gullager. It doesn't say who the subject is."

They heard footsteps in the lobby, and spotted one of the librarians walking past the gallery.

"Excuse me!" Henry called. "Do you know anything about this painting?"

The librarian came into the room and smiled at the portrait. "It's really quite nice, isn't it?" she said. "Gullager was one of the finest portrait painters of that era."

"Who's the man in the painting?"

"We believe he was a prominent Boston physician named Aldous Grenville. This would have been painted when he was around nineteen or twenty, I think. He died quite tragically in a fire, around 1832. In his country home in Weston."

Julia looked at Henry. "Norris's father."

The librarian frowned. "I've never heard he had a son. I only know about his nephew."

"You know about Charles?" asked Henry, surprised. "Was he notable?"

"Oh, yes. Charles Lackaway's work was very much in vogue in his time. But honestly, between you and me, his poems were quite awful. I think his popularity was mostly due to his romantic cachet as *the one-handed poet.*"

"So he did become a poet after all," said Julia.

"With quite a reputation. They say he lost his hand in a duel over a lady. The tale made him quite popular with the fair sex. He ended up dying in his fifties. Of syphilis." She gazed at the painting. "If this was his uncle, you can see that good looks certainly ran in the family."

As the librarian walked away, Julia remained transfixed by the portrait of Aldous Grenville, the man who had been Sophia Marshall's lover. I now know what happened to Norris's mother, thought Julia. On a summer's evening, when her son lay feverish, Sophia had left his bedside and had ridden to Aldous Grenville's country house in Weston. There she planned to tell him that he had a son who was now desperately ill.

But Aldous was not at home. It was his sister, Eliza, who heard Sophia's confession, who entertained her plea for help. Was Eliza thinking of her own son, Charles, when she chose her next action? Was it merely scandal she feared, or was it the appearance of another heir in the Grenville line, a bastard who'd take what her own son should inherit?

That was the day Sophia Marshall vanished.

Nearly two centuries would pass before Julia, digging in the weed-choked yard that was once part of Aldous Grenville's summer estate, would unearth the skull of Sophia Marshall. For nearly two centuries Sophia had lain hidden in her unmarked grave, lost to memory.

Until now. The dead might be gone forever, but the truth could be resurrected.

She stared at Grenville's portrait and thought: You never acknowledged Norris as your son. But at least you saw to the welfare of your daughter, Meggie. And through her, your blood has passed on, to all the generations since.

And now, in Tom, Aldous Grenville still lived.

Henry was too exhausted to come with her to the airport.

Julia drove alone through the night, thinking of the conversation she had had with Henry a few weeks ago:

"You've taken the wrong lesson from Rose Connolly's life."

"What's the right lesson?"

"To grab it while you can. Love!"

I don't know if I dare, she thought.

But Rose would. And Rose did.

An accident in Newton had cars backed up two miles on the turnpike. As she inched forward through traffic, she thought about Tom's phone calls over the past weeks. They'd talked about Henry's health, about the Holmes letters, about the donation to the Athenaeum. Safe topics, nothing that required her to bare any secrets.

"You have to let him know you're interested," Henry had told her. "He thinks you're not."

I am. But I'm afraid.

Trapped on the turnpike, she watched the minutes tick past. She thought of what Rose had risked for love. Had it been worth it? Did she ever regret it?

At Brookline, the turnpike suddenly opened up, but by then she knew she would be late. By the time she ran into Logan Airport's Terminal E, Tom's flight had landed, and she faced a crammed obstacle course of passengers and luggage.

She began to run, dodging children and carry-ons. When she reached the area where passengers were exiting customs, her heart was pounding hard. I've missed him, she thought as she plunged into the crowd, searching. She saw only strangers' faces, an endless throng of people she did not know, people who brushed past her without a second glance. People whose lives would never intersect with hers. Suddenly it seemed as if she'd always been searching for Tom, and had always just missed him. Had always let him slip away, unrecognized.

This time, I know your face.

"Julia?"

She whirled around to find him standing right behind her, looking rumpled and weary after his long flight. Without even stopping to think, she threw her arms around him, and he gave a laugh of surprise.

"What a welcome! I wasn't expecting this," he said.

"I'm so glad I found you!"

"So am I," he said softly.

"You were right. Oh, Tom, you were right!"

"About what?"

"You told me once that you recognized me. That we'd met before."

"Have we?"

She looked into a face that she'd seen just that afternoon gazing back at her from a portrait. A face that she'd always known, always loved. *Norrie's face.*

She smiled. "We have."

1888

And so, Margaret, you have now heard it all, and I am at peace that the tale will not die with me.

Though your aunt Rose never married or had children of her own, believe me, dear Margaret, you gave her enough joy for several lifetimes. Aldous Grenville lived only a brief time beyond these events, but he took such pleasure from the few years he had with you. I hope you will not hold it against him that he never publicly acknowledged you as his daughter. Remember instead how generously he provided for you and Rose, bequeathing to you his country estate in Weston, on which you have now built your home. How proud he would have been of your keen and inquisitive mind! How proud to know that his daughter was among the first to graduate from the new female medical college! What a startling world this has become, where women are allowed, at last, to achieve so much.

Now the future belongs to our grandchildren. You wrote that your grandson Samuel has already shown a remarkable aptitude for science.

You must be delighted, as you, better than anyone, know that there is no nobler profession than that of a healer. I dearly hope young Samuel will pursue that calling, and continue the tradition of his most talented forebearers. Those who save lives achieve a form of immortality of their own, in the generations they preserve, in the descendants who would not otherwise be born. To heal is to leave your stamp on the future.

And so, dear Margaret, I end this final letter with a blessing to your grandson. It is the highest blessing I could wish upon him, or upon anyone.

May he be a physician.

Yours faithfully,
O.W.H.

Author's Note

In March 1833, Oliver Wendell Holmes left Boston and sailed to France, where he would spend the next two years completing his medical studies. At the renowned École de Médicine in Paris, young Holmes had access to an unlimited number of anatomical specimens, and he studied under some of the finest medical and scientific minds in the world. He returned to Boston a far more accomplished physician than most of his American peers.

In 1843, at the Boston Society for Medical Improvement, he presented a paper titled "The Contagiousness of Puerperal Fever." It would prove to be his greatest contribution to American medicine. It introduced a new practice that now seems obvious, but which, in Holmes's day, was a radical new idea. Countless lives were saved, and miseries avoided, by his simple yet revolutionary suggestion: that physicians should simply *wash their hands*.